The Shadow of the Black Earl

A Leo Moran Murder Mystery

CHARLES E. MCGARRY

Polygon

First published in Great Britain in 2018 by Polygon, an imprint of Birlinn
Ltd, West Newington House, 10 Newington Road, Edinburgh EH9 1QS

www.polygonbooks.co.uk

1

ISBN 978 1 84697 423 6
eBook ISBN 978 1 78885 019 3

British Library Cataloguing-in-Publication Data
A catalogue record for this book is available
on request from the British Library.

Typeset by Biblichor Ltd, Edinburgh

Printed and bound in Great Britain by Clays Ltd, Elcograf S.p.A.

To my siblings Anne, Aileen, John, Michael and Clare

Disaster will come upon disaster,
And rumour will be upon rumour.
Then they will seek a vision from a prophet.

THE BOOK OF EZEKIEL 7:26

Funeral

THE funeral took place in Kentish Town, with the sun daring to challenge the turbid firmament. Leo and Stephanie watched the preliminaries from across the road. The church was a Neo-Gothic shard of light stone implanted at an intersection of tall Victorian terraces: mellowed tobacco brick contrasting with white-rendered ground floors, pediments and columns. A block westwards, the buildings were coated fully with lime and painted in lovely pastel shades: sky blue, mint green, seashell pink and wisteria. It was curious, mused Leo, how the capital seemed to retain these pleasant, leafy backstreets, as though as a necessary counterpoint to the hubbub at her soul. Lungs to oxygenise the burgeoning metropolis with just enough tranquillity to stop her tilting into insanity.

The pitch of a two-litre sports engine broke the quiet, the exhaust crackling and braying. It belonged to a 1937 two-seater Aston Martin, sleek and volcano red, which entered the street from Leo's right. The driver expertly parked to the side of the church, turned off the ignition, disembarked gracefully and popped off a pair of driving goggles. She was dressed in a fitted, chocolate-brown trouser suit, her hair obscured by a cloche hat, her arched eyebrows accentuating pretty West Indian features. She joined the throng that was beginning to gather at the churchyard gate.

Next chugged in a Rolls-Royce Phantom hearse, a mourner with a top hat and a walking cane marching purposefully ahead. As though providentially, the sun breached the cloud cover and pooled the part of the street reserved for this stately vehicle with golden light. Leo instinctively removed his trilby and clasped it in front of him, bowing his head slightly. Two more ancient cars – a dark-blue Phantom Mk I and a canary-yellow Austin Twenty – cruised in sedately and double parked. From these emerged a gaggle of people, including four eccentric-looking elderly ladies who waved their sticks and barked in bourgeois Dublin accents, irritated that they had not been deposited nearer to the church. This contingent wore colourful clothes and distinctly unfunereal feathery hats. They kept shouting at each other and adjusting their hearing aids until they were ushered inside. A concerned-looking priest, a bemused deacon and three smirking altar servers had materialised at the church entrance.

The irregularity of the proceedings and the cleric's unease escalated with the approach, from Leo's left, of some mode of carnival procession. It was heralded by its musical accompaniment, performed with gusto by an elderly Dixieland jazz troupe. The vanguard, just ahead of the band, comprised a dozen or so children in animal costumes, supervised by a stilt walker who wore huge, multi-coloured pantaloons and a wizard's hat. The little ones carried portraits of the deceased at different life stages, thus confirming that this jamboree was indeed connected to the impending rites. After the band came the main body of the parade, 'mourners' who smiled and pranced and danced as they progressed. These were people aged from their teens to their seventies, all of whom were dressed in outlandish garb. They could be divided approximately into three factions. First were the fairies and nymphs, then the harlequins, and, bringing up the rear, a sect wearing Regency-era garments, wigs and make-up. As the remains were withdrawn from the hearse, the ragtime of Jelly Roll Morton came to an abruptly reverent conclusion. Streamers and petals were cast onto the coffin, and Leo was struck by how unfazed the chief mourner and undertakers seemed by these incongruous events, practised as they were in the dying art of English restraint. Meanwhile, a nearby dog walker regarded the scene over his steel-rimmed spectacles with utter astonishment.

'What's next – a troop of elephants?' quipped Stephanie under her breath.

'A Spitfire fly-past?' proposed Leo.

'A motorcycle cavalcade of the local Women's Institute?'

'The Lord Mayor in his coach, accompanied by the Worshipful Company of Fishmongers?'

It was nice to have her with him, Leo considered, and kind of her to accompany him south from Glasgow for moral support. He was fed up always attending such affairs alone. However, Stephanie had herself met Gilbert Doyle, albeit just once, and had liked him immensely.

As for Leo, he had been heartily fond of the Irish bachelor and had enjoyed their fledgling friendship. News of his sudden death had been a cause of genuine sorrow, and unfortunately prior to this Leo had already succumbed to one of his depressions. He had fallen prey to isolation, lassitude and despondency. This was mostly because he was suffering delayed trauma from killing an evildoer in self-defence at Loch Dhonn in Argyll a year and a half ago. Left alone to his nightmares, Leo would relive the blade entering the man's throat, steel broaching skin and cartilage. The obscene frothing sound as the fiend's life force dissipated into the ether. Then the heavy silence of absence. The deceased had even started to visit him from through the veil. Leo had glimpsed his leering face in the mirrors of pub gantries, or, when he raised the drawing-room blinds in his eyrie apartment, seen him standing on the lovely pink granite bridge which spanned the River Kelvin, glaring up at him. Stephanie, and Leo's downstairs neighbour Rocco, had been stalwart in their concern for their friend, regularly knocking on his door and offering sustenance and solidarity, but Leo had largely rejected their kindly overtures.

'By the way, I wish you to know I have changed my mind about my final arrangements,' he murmured to Stephanie. This was a riff on a typically morbid recent theme of Leo's, whereby he would grandiosely inform Stephanie of his latest ideas for his send-off. 'I am considering a surface burial, as favoured by certain Native American tribes and the ancient Celts. I'm drawn to the notion of my remains being weighed down by a cairn of primeval rocks and my flesh rapidly breaking down as a source of protein for the flora and fauna – following all due and proper Christian rites, of course.'

'Well, put it in writing and email it to me,' replied Stephanie. Her disinterest was feigned – secretly she was highly amused by Leo's eccentric flights of whimsy.

From among the more orthodoxly attired attendees clustered by the churchyard gate, Leo picked out some familiar faces. Some of them had only recently been with the deceased, when he spent a happy holiday at the Greatorix country pile, Biggnarbriggs Hall. However, Leo's depression had caused him to forgo the invitation to join Gilbert *et alia* on the verdant estate for the bitter teats of Glasgow taverns. Looking smart in his Charterhouse uniform was Alexander, scion of the Greatorix family.

He stood in front of his widower father, the sixteenth baron and life peer, who was flanked by his brother Fordyce, Leo's best friend, and Evelyn, the youngest sibling. There were a few others from Kirkcudbrightshire: Jimmy Handley, who Leo had met on previous visits to the hall, and a couple who would be identified to him as Maxwell Blythman and his stunningly attractive wife Cynthia. Leo glumly and self-indulgently wondered how many would attend his funeral when it arrived. A couple of priests, his chess rivals old Arnstein and Frederick Norvell, and his friends Stephanie, Fordyce and Evelyn. His mother, if she outlived him (which given his general regimen was not unlikely), Rocco, and perhaps Mrs Godomski from flat 2F2, but she was in the grip of some agoraphobia which stretched back to the year of grace 1939.

From his left, a fellow mourner, a diminutive individual who Leo speculated resembled how Keith Moon would have looked had he survived to middle age, uttered, 'Ruddy good send-off for the old dear. Oh God, I'm going to miss him!' He then began weeping softly.

'My dear chap,' consoled Leo as he proffered a monogrammed linen handkerchief and patted the man gently on the back.

'Thanks, friend. Do you know, the sisters wanted to give him an open coffin, but they couldn't,' said Moonie in a rather camp, antiquated London accent drenched with glottal stops. He dabbed his eyes and cleared his throat. 'Apparently the poor old sod had such a look of terror locked on his face, as though he'd seen the Angel of Death. He had a dodgy ticker, you know. Must've felt it coming on. The heart attack, I mean. Realised he was a goner.'

'He was such a fine man,' stated Leo comfortingly, but Moonie's words had animated a peculiar sense of foreboding within his breast. He reflected how Gilbert had indeed been a fine man, one of those fellows of immense gregariousness typical to the Emerald Isle, who had lived by a relentless crusade to find humour in anything and everything as an antidote to life's oppressiveness. He had possessed no little talent as an actor and songster, and had been the life and soul of countless parties. Gilbert had trodden the boards in six continents and upon many a ship, and Fordyce had once told Leo that he had seemed an unlikely friend for his late father (they had met at an after-show party during the late baron's London days), who had been a reserved man. Nonetheless, the pair had hit it off, and Gilbert had spent numerous holidays at Biggnarbriggs

Hall, and become an avuncular figure to the Greatorix offspring. After the baron's death, Gilbert had continued to visit the hall, which is how Leo had come to make his acquaintance.

Inside the church it quickly became clammy, especially up in the mezzanine where Leo and Stephanie were. He envied the free-spirited performers their flimsy costumes. Sometimes it cost one dear not to let the side down; this was a funeral, and not so much as a single button on his shirt would be unfastened. Furthermore, he refused steadfastly to join the trend growing among the congregation to utilise as a hand fan the order of service, which featured a cover image of a smiling, bow-tied Gilbert, his grey eyes sparkling within his broad, handsome Celtic face (it was very possibly a snap from his Mediterranean cruise days).

However, such was the heat-induced torpor by which he found himself now being reduced, and under-stimulated as he was by the protracted, inaudible eulogies, that it took Leo a good deal of effort not to lose focus. He found his attention being drawn to the sanctuary lamp, again and again. Then he felt a sensation primordial yet familiar and he let go; he let himself slip into the vision, contained entirely within the halo of that small red flame.

Water flowing in near darkness, only a limited quantity of light glancing upon its surface. There is a sense of that water not as a force refreshing but of a source malignant. And there is a feeling of that black malignancy flowing this very summer, and on other summers and winters lang syne.

Leo came to, sweating and gasping for breath. He glanced around, glad that he hadn't obviously disturbed anyone, other than Stephanie, who was mouthing the words 'Are you okay?'

Leo nodded and then succumbed to the temptation to unfasten his top button. He inhaled deeply, recovered himself, and tried to tune into the priest's words.

The wake, which was held in the ramshackle old house in which Gilbert had lived with his sisters, soon threatened to get uproariously Irish. Leo escaped to the overgrown rear garden for a breather, musing upon his own Hibernian forebears' penchant for wildly celebratory send-offs in

Glasgow tenements. He had even heard tell of the deceased being propped up in his coffin the night before the funeral with his stiff dead fingers clasped around a whisky glass.

Leo smiled and took a swig of his Scotch and soda. Some instinct drew his gaze towards where the garden bordered a local park. And there, beneath the London planes on the other side of the railings, stood the most extraordinary-looking creature: a man of wan, porcine features, his blond hair barely concealing the lumpen contour of his cranium, cruel blue eyes set beneath the ugly fold of his brow. He was wearing a black jacket of formal cut, a waistcoat, a dark-green silk shirt with an intricate pattern and a high collar, and a bolo tie that incorporated a moonstone set in silver. His expression was fierce, and it was difficult to tell whether this was his facial default or an actual reflection of his inner nature.

Leo started as someone touched his arm. It was Stephanie.

'Are you all right?' she enquired. 'You look like you've seen a ghost.'

'Admirable, my dear. It's just that there's a peculiar fellow standing over there staring at me in the most insolent manner.'

However, when Leo looked back towards the park the man had gone.

'Earlier, inside the church, you seemed perturbed,' said Stephanie.

'I told you – I'm perfectly fine, old girl.'

'What's bothering you, Leo? You promised not to bottle things up. To tell me if things were going wrong.'

Leo sighed. 'I confess when I saw the man looking at me just then, some unnamed dread stirred within me. And during the funeral Mass I experienced a brief vision. Just water flowing in shadow, but it chilled me to the marrow. I sense something ill augurs. A summer of discontent.'

'A new case?'

'Very possibly. And I'm not sure I have the appetite for it. Or the strength.'

Day One

L EO drove his Mark VI 1956 Humber Hawk southwards as clouds
scudded across the azure. The car's two-tone paint job was still
glorious in turquoise and cream, and the familiar, pleasant odour of
the upholstery evoked happy childhood days from what seemed like
another lifetime.

At Ayr, he chose the longer route in order to reach a part of Galloway
as yet *terra incognita* to him. He came off the main road and took a
single tracker for a while, following an idyllic river – the Cree – through
a gorgeous, translucently sun-dappled tunnel of oak, ash and beech. The
countryside opened into wide farmland, a patchwork of colour stitched
together by hedges and punctuated by the odd broadleaved tree, gently
rising towards a delightful village church with a square tower in the
distance. Galloway was until recently entirely unknown to Leo, and he
had found it to be quite charming, a Scotland in miniature with its
timbered hills, rugged coastline, rivers and pleasant pastures.

The leaven of beauty made Leo's spirits rise as he chugged onwards,
communing upon an orange cream. What a difference a day makes, he
considered, recalling the miserable state in which he had woken the
previous morning, having resumed his recent drinking campaign upon
his return from Gilbert's funeral in London. The ferocious misery of the
hangover had swelled and swelled, and then, just when it threatened to
overwhelm him, the telephone had sounded from the hall. Leo had let the
device ring to answerphone and listened out, desperately hoping it was a
friendly voice and not a robot trying to suggest he had recently been
involved in a car accident; at that moment he could have been convinced
of anything.

It had been Fordyce.

'Greetings, old stick! I hope you have been in passable fettle since the
funeral. Parting company with those held in noble regard always plunges

one into a brown study, but at least it was a fittingly magnificent send-off. As it happens, I communicate on the subject of dear Gilbert. His will stipulated that his ashes be dispersed at Loch Quien, near to the Greatorix lands, where he spent many a tranquil hour. We would like you to be present at the ceremony. Furthermore, having discussed the idea with Evelyn, we are to commence a period of summer skylarks to honour our late friend. Feasting, games, pageantry – the kind of gaiety and frolics of which Gilbert would have approved. Anyway, Leo, I suggest you get down here at your earliest convenience and stay as long as you wish. I sense things have been a bit rough for you of late. You'd be better off among friends.'

Dear, sweet Fordyce, Leo had thought as he brought his seltzer remedy through to the cool, shaded solace of the drawing room, silent but for the soft, soothing rhythm of the Winterhalder & Hoffmeier pearl-dialled clock. A rain shower, unexpected and brief, had begun hissing outside, as though commissioned to further diffuse the tension. After taking a sip of his seltzer, he had reclined upon the *chaise longue* and closed his eyes. 'Be not solitary, be not idle,' had advised a fellow melancholic, Robert Burton, but when Leo recalled the parliament inside his head to an emergency debate and began examining the proposal, no overall majority was forthcoming. Therefore he had telephoned his mother, who with trademark gentle wisdom persuaded her son that a few weeks of fresh air, fishing and general futility was just the tonic he required. He just hoped that the brief vision he had experienced in the church in Kentish Town had not portended a forthcoming case, and was simply a random fragment of interference on the astral plane.

As he skirted the rear of Newton Stewart, the handsome burgh town which sat in the shadow of the granite massif of Cairnsmore of Fleet, Leo noted bunting spanning the road, to mark Galloway Pageant week. He swung north, taking the Queen's Way towards Kirkcudbrightshire. This pass through the forest park, linking Newton Stewart with the southern districts of the Glenkens, was imposing. The area was interlaced with watercourses and wooded thick with a mixture of species, especially coniferous ones. The light and landscape constantly evolved, and Leo's mood along with them. At one point a monoculture of myrtle-green fir trees spread to the brow of a law – a weird, artificial sheen to it. Then there was a section of gloomy forestry stubble and muir. Then a large expanse of water, light resting upon it. Then an enchanting stretch of natural deciduous woodland.

Leo's hands had been badly burned in a house fire a number of years ago. The left, which had sustained some fourth-degree injury, would have been a mere purple claw had it not been repaired to almost full functionality by a brilliant NHS surgeon, yet both remained unsightly, and sometimes when undertaking menial tasks he experienced a painful twinge. However, the ergonomics of steering and gear shifting gave him barely any discomfort. Yet Leo generally disliked driving, an activity which was always accompanied by a faint sense of anxiety. This had increased a level when he entered this lonely mountain road, and it rose another notch when he noted the Humber engine running a touch rough, the pistons stuttering somewhat. He decided to try to limp to Biggnarbriggs Hall and from there telephone the garage at St John's Town of Dalry where he had bought four-star on previous visits.

It was with a sense of relief that he reached New Galloway, familiar territory at last, and turned south down the highway. He passed a mountain of rhododendron on his left flowering pink, violet and red, and to his right a stand of Wellingtonia lorded over the road at the foot of Cairn Edward Hill, the lower ramparts of which were densely clothed by spruce, larch and birch. Loch Ken opened out within its ragged parameters, the sails of windsurfs and dinghies peppering its glittering surface. Beautiful firs now stood above the road, and Leo then drove though a sun-drenched wood, a playful sprinkling of rain delicately filtering into the lime and yellow world.

The Humber spluttered as it entered Balmakethe parish and traversed the final stretch towards the hall. The land was gently rolling, with well-tended golden fields to the east and low deciduous woodland to the west, above which were the heavily forested hills and high moors where sheep eked out an existence. Biggnarbriggs was the largest settlement in the parish, and it – along with the stately house a mile northwards, seat of the Greatorix family – took its name from the ancient stone bridge that spans Biggnar Burn on the village's main drag. The blackthorn hedgerows gave way to a screen of silver birch, and through this Leo soon glimpsed the sparkling water of Loch Grenoch, then Biggnar Burn, then a first, tantalising sight of the hall's venerable tower peering through its cloak of oak, maple and alder. Finches and spyugs flitted in front of the car and blades of sunlight flashed on the windscreen. A pair of romancing collared doves took flight as Leo slowed and indicated at the mouth of the grand drive. The Humber rolled over a quaint bridge that spanned the burn and up the shadowy avenue, ivy and rhododendron tangled in with the trees. The borders had been planted thick with wildflowers of all colours – Evelyn's handiwork, no doubt – like the background to a Klimt painting. The canopy opened to reveal the house in all its glory. Two lions passant guarded the gates, and upon one of the pillars was the enamelled family crest. Leo paused near the gatehouse, which incorporated a little arch leading into a rear courtyard where the old stables were located, and greeted Chas Shaw, who was strolling towards him. His dog, an unpredictable Staffordshire Bull Terrier Leo had come to dislike on his previous visits, growled. Chas called out 'Nero!' and silenced the creature.

'Howdy, Pilgrim. The old girl's no' sounding too healthy,' he said in his steady, monotone voice. Chas was in his mid-fifties, nearly six foot in height and of powerful build. He lived alone in the gatehouse, and was ghillie and foreman for the Greatorix land and an adjoining estate.

'Quite. I'm thankful I resisted the romantic inclination to come via the Raiders' Road, otherwise I don't think she'd have made it.'

Chas exhaled a stream of cigarette smoke. He wore a checked shirt, and favoured sideburns to compensate for his receding black hairline – its widow's peak lent him a rather vampiric air. His face was broad and quite handsome, but his eyes were beady, and Leo had previously wondered if there wasn't a hint of a sneer when he smiled. Furthermore, at times such as at this very juncture, he would simply stare – letting a silence play out when it was his turn to speak, as though to disconcert his interlocutor. Leo determined to sit it out, betraying not a jot of discomfort in this power play. Perhaps he was an arrogant man, Leo considered. A macho man, a womaniser.

'It's a rough old road that, right enough,' confirmed Chas at last, before requesting that Leo gun the engine, in order that he could feel over the exhaust pipe.

'Suction's no' right. Probably a burnt exhaust valve. If you keep driving with it, it could damage the engine. Do you want me and Brian to have a look at her later? We're cheaper than any garage.'

'That would be most kind. Will it require a new part?'

'We should be able to grind it down for you,' replied Chas, before rapping the roof of the vehicle twice in informal farewell and taking his leave.

Leo edged the Humber through the gates, the gravel popping and cracking beneath the tyres.

Biggnarbriggs Hall nestled beneath the foothills of the Southern Uplands and was brushed by the fringes of Galloway Forest Park. Scoulag Hill was to the immediate northwest, a modest protuberance with various higher peaks to its north and west. To the east were the diminutive rises of Meikle Cairn and Little Cairn, then further away higher blue ridges stretching northwards through the haze from the Solway Firth. The hall was positioned exactly at the border of two worlds: the soft, rolling meadows and tamed farmland, and the feral timbered hills. Leo imagined the grounds and lawns being hewn from the fecund forest, the soil's wanton impulse trammelled by the axe and the scythe.

He parked the Humber, disembarked, breathed deeply of the sweet air and regarded the hall, a grand Scottish Baronial manor. Leo had previously taken a keen interest in its history. Some of the original sixteenth-century building prevailed, notably the melancholy granite tower to the north. A wing had been added in the eighteenth century but most of that had been demolished and replaced after structural damage caused by a fire in 1870. The twelfth baron, Fordyce's great-great-grandfather, resolved to build a house worthy of the high gentry, and had enlisted a prominent Glasgow firm of architects. The new wings, two T-storeys with dormers protruding from the steep slate roofs, were in the Victorian Renaissance style, the walls rendered in pink and elaborated with polished sandstone pilasters and margins. The east-facing side was notable for its impressive *porte-cochère*, which housed the fine main door. Felicia light-pink rose climbed on the right-hand side of the wall, while thick English ivy almost completely clad the left. To the west of the house was a single-storey early-Victorian construction with a crawstepped gable, which the 1870s work had incorporated at its tip and was used as a parlour. The hall's south-facing elevation, with its five tripartite bays, was the grandest, and beautifully proportioned. French doors opened out from a drawing room onto a terrace with a splendid balustrade. From this, steps descended to the lawns below.

Fordyce, who had heard the Humber's complaining engine, bounded through the main door, dashed over to greet his friend and enveloped him in an unselfconscious bear hug. Fordyce had been concerned for Leo's wellbeing of late, and had an inkling that he had entered a shadowy realm. 'Let him get soused down here where at least we can look after him,' he had confided to his sister. Leo could feel Fordyce's pronounced midriff straining through his shirt; too much good country living, he supposed. He placed his hands on his pal's shoulders and gazed down at him, regarding his oversized head with its thinning blond hair, his kind grey eyes. A year and a half had passed since they had first met at Loch Dhonn, and they had become blood brothers.

Leo stated simply, 'It feels marvellous to be back at the hall.'

Evelyn and three Springer Spaniels were next to rush out, the dogs' excitement at a visitor quickly diminishing when they detected the presence of Nero nearby. Evelyn was wearing a summer dress with a wildly colourful botanical print. She was aged in her forties, a petite woman with small features and strawberry-blonde curls. Like Fordyce she was a sweet and caring person, something of a delicate creature who was gloriously unaware of her eccentricities. Leo kissed her on both cheeks.

'I've put you in the blue room, Leo. I know you liked it last time.'

'First class. Thank you, Evelyn.'

Brian McGhie materialised to carry the considerable quantity of luggage into the great hall. He was an industrious, subdued man who wore overalls and a default blank expression. A local in his late thirties, he was general factotum to the hall and the estate, and lived in a little house just to the rear of the hall with his wife Unity, the part-time housekeeper, and their two children. Brian was over six feet in height and had a slim, athletic build. He had straight, spiky dark-brown hair and small hazel eyes.

Leo, Fordyce and Evelyn followed Brian through the great hall, which was dressed with light that streamed in through the tall, south-facing windows, and up the grand staircase. As he climbed, Leo admired portraits of worthy Greatorixes ancient and living by artists as fabled as Allan Ramsay and William Ranken. He enquired if the baron would be returning tomorrow when the House of Lords rose for summer.

'Didn't Fordyce tell you?' replied Evelyn. 'He's in Romania with our nephew until mid-August. Charity commitments. The baron is sorry to miss the Galloway Pageant, to say nothing of the scattering of the ashes and our summer skylarks. I think Fordyce is glad to have you here, in his brother's absence.'

'I most certainly am,' confirmed Fordyce.

'We both are,' continued Evelyn. 'You give us some . . . spiritual comfort. Anyway, it's our first event this evening.'

'Dinner, followed by a secret surprise!' said Fordyce.

'Jimmy Handley of Scarrel House is coming over – you already know him,' said Evelyn. 'And a few other neighbours who'd met Gilbert. The Major, from Maidenhead House. Rachael Kidd, from Sannox House. And Maxwell and Cynthia Blythman of the Ridings.'

'Splendid. I'm always glad to meet new people.'

'You might recognise Cynthia from her work in television,' added Evelyn. 'She presented lifestyle and travel programmes. On Zest TV.'

'Dearest sis, I hardly think Leo spends his afternoons watching Zest TV!' teased Fordyce.

'I saw the Blythmans at Gilbert's funeral,' Leo reminded Evelyn, 'although I never got the chance to be introduced.'

Leo was installed in his room and left alone to unpack, having entrusted his car keys to Brian after he had explained about Chas's offer of a repair. He took a moment to enjoy the fine southerly view from his window of the great lawns and the gently undulating meadows beyond, which were bordered on both sides and to the mile-distant extremity by sun-embroidered trees. The landscape was crowned with the glory of summer. The rose garden was not far to the right, just before the tree line. Straight ahead, beyond the terrace, was a section of topiary dotted with stone statues of figures from antiquity and centred by a large fountain. There was a circular Leyland cypress maze and a summer-house, then an ornamental lake. Leo turned to gaze around the heavily furnished room with its comforting woody odour. The fireplace was resplendent amid Delft tiles depicting wandering minstrels. Two brass chambersticks and a filled Waterford decanter and tumblers perched upon the mantelpiece.

Having unpacked and consumed two large drams from the decanter, Leo took a bath and changed into his classic-cut dinner suit. He then set off for a preprandial stroll to stretch his legs. On the terrace, he noticed that the Midgeater had been switched on in anticipation of the evening's onslaught. A woodpigeon cooed softly from a bough. Leo walked towards the lake to ponder the intriguing folly that sat upon a tiny island, his feet crunching on the gravel path. A faint fragrance of the forest lushness carried on the breeze to relieve the dusty heat smell. He went by the fountain, with its recumbent Neptune and attendant nymphs, and circumvented the maze. The folly was a temple of Venus, and its mellowed stone looked agreeable in the softening light. It was set upon a disc of drystane and mortar, and the core was bullet-shaped and largely closed but for some high lancet apertures. The portico was two Doric columns supporting a pedimented lintel that contained a tympanum detailing the birth of Venus. The lake itself flowed gently; it was evidently an artificial lagoon, syphoned no doubt from where the Scoulag Burn tumbled through nearby woods. Two punts bobbed gently on the surface, tethered to a little pier, and a pair of perfect-white mute swans glided haughtily through the water.

Leo turned to enjoy the view of the hall and his attention was arrested by a figure pacing slowly on the terrace. It was a woman, her head bowed as though in deep reflection. She was slender, her straight chestnut hair falling to shoulder length, and she wore an elegant, sleeveless black maxi dress with a scooped neckline, which revealed tanned skin. Leo could discern that she carried a sadness to her. Suddenly she tensed, like a cat become aware of being watched, and glanced around, but she didn't seem to notice Leo. She then walked more purposefully towards the west wing, where she lingered at the hall's aviary. Leo was intrigued, and found himself trying to catch up with her. She was probably Rachael Kidd, who Evelyn had mentioned was to dine with them.

To the west, the estate was girdled by a beautiful, broad, sloping belt of mixed greenwood and shrubbery, and to the northwest this insinuated itself into the pines that embroidered Scoulag Hill. Brian had once told Leo that it was a constant war to keep the vegetation from encroaching on the trimmed lawns. The aviary, with its separate sections for parrots and finches, sat close to this jungle, and when Leo reached it the mystery woman had evidently taken her leave, so he strolled round to the rear of the mansion and entered the kitchen garden. This walled domain was Brian's pride and joy, and Leo reverently inspected the burgeoning bounty that kept the hall virtually self-sufficient for most of the year. As well as plantations, there were glasshouses and polytunnels incubating all manner of fruits and vegetables. The larger potato plot had been plundered and Leo hoped to relish this year's main crop of Ayrshires that very evening. He strolled into the adjoining Secret Garden (there was nothing secret about it; it was merely named so by Evelyn, her whimsy inspired by Frances Hodgson Burnett's book), where the walls wept with ivy. It was a world of birdbaths, wooden benches, shrubberies and melancholy little trees.

Leo exited via an old oak gate peeling green paint, and found himself standing on a grassy stretch between a fruit orchard and the rear of the house in which the McGhies resided. He could see Brian's souped-up Audi Quattro parked outside. An earthen path ran off to his right, where scrub fragmented the light, and broken-down hutches and a decrepit rowing boat on a trailer languished. The McGhie abode was a low cottage kept in sterling fettle by Brian. Its walls were finished with white harling, with the sills and trims painted periwinkle, and it had a trellised porch festooned with Unity's handicrafts. She was sitting on the greensward in the lee of the cottage, dressed in a white crocheted smock and sandals, and was apparently occupied by wickerwork. Her beautiful golden-haired children, a girl, aged six, and a four-year-old boy whom Leo had mistaken for a female the first time they had met due to his flowing locks, ran barefoot amongst the daisies and dandelions, chasing a homemade kite that streamed colourful ribbons.

Unity McGhie was an extremely pretty woman, an English rose with delicate features, faultless white teeth and dazzling pale-blue eyes. However, she always seemed either unaware of or uninterested in her beauty. Tonight she was wearing her light-blonde hair bunched upon the crown of her head; rogue strands tumbled enticingly onto her sun-browned shoulders. Leo had often considered that she and Brian made an odd couple, not insomuch as he was out of her league, but in that they seemed to have so little in common. He was a pragmatic, phlegmatic man, whereas she was quixotic and flighty to the point that it seemed as though some planetary influence was working upon her. Whenever Leo had seen them together there seemed to be no communion beyond their children and their mutual narrative. Their story had begun when she, taking a respite from her bohemian London existence, had holidayed in the area, and her 2CV had broken down on a back road.

Brian had happened by and repaired the vehicle, and asked her out for a drink in Castle Douglas that evening. Unity had accepted, and had perhaps subsequently fallen more in love with the Ken Valley and the notion of living the rural idyll than with Brian himself. Not long after they were wedded, his garage business went bust, and they had taken up their respective roles at Biggnarbriggs Hall.

Leo said hello to the kids and greeted Unity politely, then complimented this year's crops. She proffered a punnet brimming with strawberries, and he selected a portly specimen, savouring its sweet fragrance and gorgeous flesh.

'The earth bestows upon us her bounty, as long as we show her proper respect,' she said. 'And give proper thanks. Hence corn dollies for Lùnastal.' She smiled and raised the item she was constructing so that Leo could better view it. 'Just a few days to go!'

After they had first met, Leo, upon noticing Unity's use of words such as 'owd' (for 'old'), 'dunna' (for 'do not') and the archaic 'hark', had enquired as to her origins and discovered she was from rural Shropshire. Her parents and her sister, with whom she was in nightly telephone contact, still lived in their village.

'Are you in fact a pagan?' enquired Leo in a rather disapproving tone.

'I am . . . a Wiccan!'

Leo paused, then decided to steer the conversation into less controversial territory. 'The little ones are coming on; they're a credit to you both,' he said. 'And what a lovely, peaceful environment in which to raise them.'

'Peaceful apart from Nero. Although animals will be like that if you maltreat them, poor beast.'

'Evelyn says she loves having the children living on the estate.'

'Evelyn is *such* a dear,' remarked Unity, gazing dreamily at her offspring. 'Are you on duty tonight, for dinner?'

'Yes. All that yucky meat. The way it smells and . . . *glistens*. The Blythmans have arrived,' she said, rolling her eyes. 'I saw their fancy sports car. I'm just taking a quick break before the madness begins. Brian will be here soon to look after the children.'

Leo glanced at his watch. It was approaching seven o'clock, the time Fordyce had requested they meet for drinks, so he bade Unity farewell, but after a few paces she called out after him. 'Leo, do you remember the first time we met?'

He knew what was coming next. 'Why, of course,' he replied, forcing a smile as he turned to face her.

'Do you remember how I knew that Leo was your name, even before we'd been introduced?'

'Yes, indeed I do.'

'I believe I'm touched with the gift of *darna shealladh* . . . just like you.'

Of course, the woman could easily have heard his name from anyone prior to his arrival that first time he had visited the hall, Leo thought, as he gritted his teeth. His gift had been a cross to bear, and like the harrowed mental patient who is irked when they hear other people appropriate a mild form of their condition, he felt somehow affronted when folk laid such easy claim to second sight.

'Aye, we should meet up and polish each other's crystal balls some time,' he muttered to himself as he walked towards the hall.

Upon the gravel were now parked a well-preserved brown 1980s Audi 100, a jungle-green Mini Countryman and a Series 1 E-Type Roadster. Leo paused to admire the gorgeous silver lines of the Jag, before entering the hall. He wiped the dust from his dress shoes, glanced in a mirror and strode forth to join the party.

The drawing room was the centrepiece of Biggnarbriggs Hall, more ornate and formal than the parlour to the west of the house which was known as the rose salon. Sunshine poured in through the French doors. The walls were dressed in Pompeian red silk and hung with lavishly large artworks. Leo was greeted by Fordyce, who was wearing a brown-and-cream houndstooth dinner jacket with a chocolate collar and matching bow tie, and was busying himself preparing drinks by a lovely polished mahogany Edwardian cabinet.

'*Apéritif*, old stick?'

'Don't mind if I do. Vermouth and bitters, if you please.'

As Fordyce mixed Leo's drink, Evelyn and the guests who had arrived stepped in from the terrace. First was Jimmy Handley, who strode over to Leo and gripped his hand with a smile and a 'How are you, old boy?', then Maxwell and Cynthia Blythman, and then the mystery woman Leo had seen earlier.

Forevermore Leo would recall tenderly that moment in that gorgeous chamber when he saw her framed by the summer evening light. She gazed at him intently for an uncomfortably long time, and he fancied that the ticking of the grandfather clock had slowed to a virtual stop. She was a little taller than he had thought outside, with hazel eyes which sparkled with intelligence and wit. Her beauty was possessed unassumingly, in that Leo wasn't sure if her thoughtful, slender features only particularly appealed to him, and that if required to state an opinion other men would suggest that she was merely pretty enough in a girl-next-door sort of a way. Not that he would have cared less. What was objectively evident was that she wasn't arrestingly beautiful like Unity, or indeed glamorous and sexy like Cynthia, but to Leo she was infinitely preferable. She held a glass of dry sherry in her left hand, and Leo had to consciously disguise his relief when he saw it was ring-free. Not that this necessarily betokened singleness nowadays.

'My dears, let me do introductions,' said Evelyn, who looked an anachronism in her peach silk tea gown and pearls. 'Rachael Kidd, may I present Leo Moran.'

Leo strode forwards and took her hand, bowing magnificently to kiss it. '*Enchanté*,' he said, then feigned irony in order to join in the joke when he saw the amusement lighting on her face.

'Pleased to meet you,' she said softly.

Evelyn then introduced Maxwell, a surly fellow who looked as though he'd rather be somewhere else, and Cynthia, who Leo found to be instantly appalling.

'Pleased to make your acquaintance at last. I saw you both at Gilbert's funeral,' said Leo.

'We were in the Smoke for a few days anyway. I had a charity do to attend. So we thought we'd pop over and do the churchy thing,' said Cynthia.

'More champagne, Cynthia?' enquired Fordyce.

'Thank you, darling.'

She commandeered Leo for several minutes, Maxwell standing sulkily alongside them, all the time Leo wishing he was getting to know Rachael.

Cynthia Blythman, *née* Marchpane was in her early forties and originally from Dollar in Clackmannanshire. Tall and leggy, her tight-fitting, sleeveless red gown revealed that she had eradicated any womanly curves in the gymnasium. Her wedding band bore the largest diamond Leo had ever seen outside a museum. The life had been brutally tonged out of her hair, its natural light-brown affected by a metallic pearl hue. Her facial structure was exquisitely pronounced. Heavy make-up made her eye sockets seem cavernous, and she had full lips and a thin, rather angular nose. Cynthia's movements were feline, and her speech, laden with fashionable inflexions, exuded confidence; Leo wondered if she was the sort of woman who generally got what she wanted. She and Maxwell were childless; he eight years her senior, a wealthy local man who had made his fortune as a hedge fund manager and who nurtured pretensions of being a country laird. He wore chunky spectacles, and had florid skin and oily, shaggy hair which was greying at the temples. His overall lack of physical appeal made Leo wonder that he was not punching above his weight. Certainly he failed to detect any real warmth between the couple.

Fordyce tinkled a little bell, and the party fell silent to listen to him make a moving speech in honour of Gilbert, culminating in a toast in his memory. About halfway through, the final guest, who Leo deduced was the Major, marched in with military bluster, late but unapologetic, muttering something about 'the feasting always being good at the hall' as he helped himself to a large vodka and tonic.

He was a tall man of upright bearing in his mid-sixties, with ruddy cheeks, blond hair, broad, weathered features and vividly blue eyes. He seemed strong and fit for his age, and looked resplendent in his scarlet dress uniform. After the toast, Fordyce introduced him, and having provided Leo with his second crushing handshake of the evening (Jimmy's, too, had sent a twinge through Leo's damaged nerves; Maxwell's had been like gripping a dead haddock), the retired officer informed him that he was an old friend of the family. Fordyce explained that the Major lived at the nearby Maidenhead House, and that he helped the Greatorixes in the mutual management of their estates. For example, Chas Shaw was ghillie for both of them. The trio chatted for a while, Leo noticing how the Major moved his head almost robotically from side to side, and tended to fix his subject with an unwavering glare. He was something of a bore, with a stentorious voice that bore a hint of white South Africa. Leo found himself feeling relieved when the dinner gong sounded plangently.

The guests entered the dining room through a connecting door, and Leo took a moment to drink in its harmonious magnificence, which was amplified by the evening light. The tea-green walls were decorated with exuberant stucco rosettes and motifs, and the room's highlight was a colossal Baroque marble fireplace, the flanks classical shepherdesses feeding lambs, the upper parts intricately carved. Frans Snyders' epic *Stag Hunt in the Snow* hung above in a beautiful frame.

Leo was thrilled to discover that his place card seated him beside Rachael, which more than made up for having to endure the Major to his left. Cynthia, who was between Jimmy and Maxwell, directly faced him, and Fordyce and Evelyn were at either end of the table.

The Major rose to propose the loyal toast, which offended Leo's sensibilities. Therefore he utilised an old Jacobite trick whereby he subtly held a filled drinking glass under his goblet in order to signify his true allegiance to 'The King over the Water'.

Unity and Mrs Grove the cook, a cheerful plump woman with a Cumbrian accent, aided by Evelyn, attended to the serving. Meanwhile Fordyce played *sommelier*, floating around as he generously supplied an eminently drinkable Chablis followed by a 2000 Château La Fleur de Gay. The meal consisted of *feuilletés au fromage*, then raspberry sorbet, brown Windsor soup served from a splendid burnished silver tureen, poached trout, and an *entrée* of Strasbourg goose liver pâté in black summer truffles. This was followed by mutton cutlets with a mushroom puree (with which Leo was delighted to sample the kitchen garden's Ayrshires), then it was peaches in Chartreuse jelly with blancmange, followed by cheese, crystallised fruits and coffee. Mrs Grove had excelled herself, and Leo later gave her his heartfelt compliments.

At the meal's outset, Unity, who had been waiting by a magnificent mahogany sideboard, began serving the pastry *hors d'œuvres* once Mrs Grove had brought them through. As she did so, an unpleasant incident occurred. The linen napkins had all been carefully folded into a pleasing fan arrangement upon the little plates, and the guests had all dismantled these and placed them on their laps. Apart from Cynthia. She had left hers *in situ*, evidently in the belief that this was a task beneath her. Therefore, when Unity arrived at her place and saw the obstruction, she had to go back to the sideboard in order to deposit the serving tray there, return to Cynthia, unfold her napkin and place it on her lap, all the while smiling awkwardly as her tormentor looked on serenely. Leo felt sorry for Unity, and more than a touch annoyed at Cynthia.

During the meal, he found Rachael to be quietly seductive, an alluring pool of calm energy amid the loud spikiness of Cynthia's egotism. She was aged in her forties and had a small birthmark on her left cheek which elongated whenever she smiled, imbuing her with a sort of vulnerability. Leo subtly enquired as to her relationship status, but when he saw her expression alter (she had an appealing way of pursing her lips when she wished her rose-like mouth not to betray amusement) he wondered if he hadn't been quite so subtle after all. And, glory of glories, she was indeed a free agent. However, a familiar feeling of self-doubt soon replaced Leo's delight as his inner voice bombarded him with a dozen reasons why he was unworthy of her.

As their conversation unfolded, Leo happened to mention that he had noticed her earlier, strolling on the terrace. He wasn't sure if it was his imagination, but the remark seemed to take her off guard. It transpired that Rachael had been holidaying in the area for a number of years, and had eventually bought Sannox House, a villa on a nearby back road. She was spending more and more of her time down here, sometimes even commuting to Glasgow for work, although she still maintained an apartment in the city.

'What is it that you do?' enquired Leo.

'I'm a civil servant.'

'Oh, what specifically?'

'Criminal injuries.'

'What a coincidence – I expect you know Frederick Norvell. I play chess with him from time to time.'

'No, I'm afraid not,' said Elaine, stiffening a little.

'But you must, my dear,' said Leo, somewhat surprised. 'He's a Higher Executive Officer.'

'Oh, yes. I think I know who you mean,' she said quietly. 'But he's in a different section.'

Leo couldn't help but wonder if Rachael had been a touch evasive.

The pair's attention was naturally drawn back to the main intercourse of the table, which Cynthia was dominating. Maxwell maintained his brooding demeanour, as though irritated by his wife, while the other guests seemed content to let her chatter away; for some extraordinary reason Jimmy even seemed to find her fascinating. It irked Leo that Cynthia paid so much attention to Fordyce, and not, he suspected, because she particularly liked him, but because she particularly liked the fact that he was gay – a trophy friend. She was being cloyingly patronising and the suggestive tone of her enquiries was inappropriate for a private and genteel person such as Fordyce.

'We need to find you a nice boy, darling,' concluded Cynthia, before turning to Leo.

'Are you gay?'

'No.'

'Do you have a partner?'

'No, I do not have a wife.'

'Girlfriend?'

'No.'

Leo glanced at Rachael after he replied. Was it his imagination or did a reaction, a blush of intrigue, flash across her countenance?

'Why not?' asked Cynthia with unvarnished insolence.

'That is rather an intrusive question, but since you enquire, it's because I've been unwilling to settle,' replied Leo.

Cynthia then went on to regale the assembly with tales of the widespread travels she had undertaken in her role as a television presenter for a Freeview channel. She was one of those people who thought that such foreign experiences somehow on their own elevated her, and provided her with cause to condescend upon her associates as underdeveloped and unenlightened. As though everyone in dull old Blighty should feel fortunate that she had deigned to descend upon them like some exotic bird to regale them with yarns about sunnier, more fragrant climes which smelled of tamarisk, woodbine and wild liquorice.

'It's so lovely being looked after by your people, Fordyce,' she said as Unity placed a platter upon the table. 'We're a servant down since Angelica stomped off in a strop, and on Janice's nights off we have to fend for ourselves.'

'As a committed socialist I will never be quite comfortable with people waiting on me,' declared Leo, pouncing on the opportunity for revenge on Unity's behalf. 'Furthermore, I believe it is the mark of a man, or a woman, how they conduct themselves when dealing with serving staff, in that within that temporary bubble they possess all the transactional power, and are unveiled as either a gentle king or a cruel despot.'

For a moment the only sound was the soft chinking of silver against china as Leo, unfazed and triumphant, turned his attention to the pâté.

'So you're a Bolshie, eh?' scoffed the Major. 'You want to tear this place down, yet I notice you're still content to enjoy the luxury and conviviality of it, among persons of quality and rank.'

The blimpish military man seemed to enjoy playing the irascible reactionary.

'I am not a Bolshevik. I am an egalitarian, inasmuch as I'm one of the old-fashioned, democratic variety. I wish to tear nothing down; I simply want this for everyone.'

'Pah! As though there's enough to go around.'

'I'm not saying we should have . . . equality of outcome,' said Leo vaguely, by now bored with this turn in the conversation.

The Major tapped the side of his nose and said in a low voice, 'I detect a flicker of doubt in yer convictions, m'lad!'

'Nothing of the kind!' snapped Leo. In truth, the Major had touched a nerve. Leo's socialism had been rooted in workers' rights and state provision for the poor. Nowadays, he worried that the Left was populated by ideologues who wanted to annihilate the last underpinnings of Western civilisation.

'Ha – the man doth protest too abruptly! *Chin-chin*, old boy,' said the Major, clinking his glass off Leo's. 'We'll make a pragmatist out of you yet.'

At one point during the main course, Fordyce stood to light the candles with a taper and then replenished Leo's glass. As he was doing so, Leo happened to glance at Rachael and wondered if she was registering his rate of consumption, which was notably more prodigious than that of the other men, none of whom were exactly bridled in their intake themselves. He felt a surge of embarrassment.

'I'll take another mouthful, please, Fordyce,' trilled Cynthia. 'It really is a darling little number. Goes perfectly with the meat.'

'Cynthia's quite the wine expert,' Jimmy informed Leo.

'Oh, I'd hardly say expert, Jimmy,' she said with counterfeit modesty. 'I simply had to swot up for one of my progs. Perhaps you've seen *The Beauty and the Feast*?' she asked Leo.

'I'm afraid I seldom watch television,' he replied, recalling that earlier Cynthia had seemed annoyed to discover that he hadn't recognised her C-List phizog.

'She's seldom on these days,' muttered Maxwell.

Cynthia pretended not to hear. 'My number one rule is: Never, Ever New World,' she announced with a degree of hauteur.

'Actually, there are many excellent non-European wines, in my opinion,' said Leo.

'What would you have selected to accompany this mutton dish, Cynthia?' enquired Fordyce. 'You can be brutally truthful, and I promise I won't be offended. Did I make a good choice?'

'You made an *excellent* choice, darling,' she smarmed. 'However, were this *chez moi* . . . I must in all honesty admit that I would have selected a good Barolo.'

'Thus I am exposed as a Philistine!' declared Fordyce good-naturedly.

'A fair suggestion,' observed Leo drily. 'However, I would respectfully venture not, in fact, best suited to this sauce. Barolo would be a touch overpowering for its delicate flavours. I would suggest that Fordyce's wine is more tender, and not without its own complexities, and therefore a superior pairing. Alternatively, I would recommend a Cabernet Merlot from the better vineyards in Victoria, Australia. Or, mellower still, a nice Chilean Carménère. The Colchagua Valley has produced some superb vintages.' Cynthia flashed a look of pure hatred at Leo. 'Cheers,' he said, raising his replenished glass to her.

The meal careered messily to its conclusion as Maxwell, somewhat inebriated, finally took the floor, pontificating at length about his lineage being 'the appointed keepers of the King's castle of Threave', as all the while his wife rolled her eyes and passed disdainful remarks. By the time coffee was served, Cynthia's reproval had silenced her husband, and Fordyce described the planned after-dinner jollity. With some melodrama he related the legend of Biggnarbriggs Hall. The story went that an eighteenth-century ancestor had been brutally murdered and his restless spirit was said to have haunted the place ever since. Tonight, the gang were to resurrect a game which he, his older brother and Evelyn had invented during their childhood. The house's lights were to be switched off. Fordyce would play the part of the ghost while the others – in pairs – were to evade him. They were allowed to carry electric torches (Unity produced these from the sideboard on cue). Once a couple were caught, they were to retire to the drawing room, the only part of the house that would remain lit, and await the game's conclusion. Only the gun room, where the dogs were, was out of bounds. The last couple not to have been touched by Fordyce's dead hand would be the winners, and walk off with an excellent vintage Château Ducru-Beaucaillou apiece. Fordyce would alert them to the fact that they had won by sounding the gong at the foot of the grand staircase.

'How do we decide who pairs who, Fordyce?' enquired Leo.

'We shall draw lots, old stick.'

'Bags I be in charge,' said Cynthia. She collected the place cards and put them into a top hat Fordyce had provided. Evelyn rummaged in the sideboard for a blank card and a pen, wrote Unity's name on it – she was to make up the numbers – and dropped it inside the hat. Leo wondered if Cynthia wasn't piqued that the hired help had been permitted to join in.

'Right,' said Cynthia. 'First out is . . . little old me!' She withdrew another card. 'And I'm paired with . . . Jimmy!'

Leo noticed Cynthia and Jimmy exchange a meaningful glance, and he speculated inwardly if the lottery had been rigged. Maxwell appeared to be simmering with resentment. Evelyn was next out of the hat, and paired with Maxwell.

Meanwhile, Jimmy lit a cigarette with a tarnished silver lighter as though to savour a victory, his ten-pack testament to either penury or a delusion that he was quitting the habit. The fifty-eight-year-old's handsomeness was becoming compromised by his portliness and ruddy boozer's complexion. As a member of the Stewartry of Kirkcudbright petty gentry, Jimmy Handley had excelled at Merchiston Castle and then Edinburgh University, but his career as a tea grower, a trader in antiques, a movie producer (Gilbert had helped) and, finally, a broker had all ended in ignominy. He lived alone in Scarrel House a few miles to the east, surviving on dwindling funds, having long since sold off the family silver. He had been a close friend of Gilbert, and Fordyce and Evelyn's late parents, and Leo found him to be fine company. However, on previous occasions he had noticed that when Jimmy consumed too much alcohol his usually laidback good humour could descend into moroseness and pomposity, and he would sometimes express bitterness regarding his two ex-wives.

Leo's attention returned to the hat; he fervently hoped that he would be paired with Rachael. The Major was out next. Leo felt a flutter of nerves as Cynthia pulled out another card. Unity's name was on it, which left Leo with Rachael. He tried not to betray his elation.

The participants followed Fordyce out of the room, chatting excitedly. They approached the grand staircase and went up two flights to the attic level. There, Fordyce revealed a chamber which contained a gargantuan, ancient fuse box.

'Right, my dears – torches on!' he commanded. Leo struggled with the stiff switch on his because of his damaged hands, so Rachael did it for him, and then smiled at him kindly. Fordyce then pulled various oversized switches, but not the one that controlled the drawing-room lighting, plunging the rest of the house into shadow. 'Now, ladies and gentlemen, pray be so good as to follow me back downstairs.' Once at the foot of the staircase, Fordyce addressed them again. 'I will now retreat to the drawing room, where I will wait precisely fifteen minutes for you to conceal yourselves.' He shone his torch upwards at his face and assumed a Vincent Price accent: 'Then I shall come for you, my dears, and have my vengeance!'

Once Fordyce had disappeared, the players strategised urgently in their pairs. Cynthia and Jimmy were first off, rushing back up the stairs. The Major and Unity were next, creeping in the direction of the rose salon, with the former muttering some nonsense about showing audacity under fire; despite that room's proximity to Fordyce's starting point, he knew of a closet in which they could conceal themselves. Evelyn led a silent Maxwell upwards, explaining that they would install themselves behind a massive wardrobe in the lavender room.

Leo and Rachael looked at each other.

'So, my lady, are you afraid of ghosts?'

'I'd have to believe in them first.'

'Then I propose we demonstrate a bold approach and explore the lofts of this great edifice.'

Rachael smiled coquettishly, took him by a purple hand and led him upwards. And Leomaris Peregrine Moran felt his very spirit soar within him.

The attic windows were not covered, and although the moon was new, Leo and Rachael's exploration was aided by the summer gloaming. Many of the rooms, which were presumably once servants' quarters and smelled of old wood, stour and mothballs, were now storage areas filled with artworks sheathed in cloths, toys, obsolete furniture, bird cages and creepy headless mannequins. Rachael terrified herself by catching her own reflection in the speckled glass of a cheval mirror. Then there was a chilling moment when the torchlight illuminated a marionette with the twisted, wicked face of a witch. At one point, Rachael placed her hand on Leo's arm as in the corridor outside came the pad of footsteps and the unmistakeable report of Cynthia and Jimmy's voices.

'They're on our patch,' whispered Rachael.

'Then let us delve deeper, back in time.'

Leo now led Rachael, finding the corridor perpendicular to the one they had already traversed. He calculated that two floors below them was the library, which he knew was connected to the remnants of the sixteenth-century portion of the house. This corridor terminated at a door, and Leo tried the handle. It opened, and revealed a windowless, pitch-black chamber. The flooring and roofing were nineteenth-century, probably replaced after the 1870 fire. The walls were constructed from large granite slabs, and on the one facing them was another door, distinctive due to its archaic, arched design.

'I'll wager that leads to the tower. Come on, let's try it,' proposed Leo, already striding across the boards. He twisted the fossilised handle, an extravagant, S-shaped affair.

'It won't give,' he said. 'It must be locked or seized up.'

There was a brief hiatus in which a mutual sexual energy seemed to stir, and Leo wondered if now was the time to draw Rachael towards him, or if this ambience was all in his imagining. The trouble was he had simply grown out of the habit of trusting his instincts in such matters; it had been *so long*. The spell was broken by the sound of someone walking slowly towards them down the corridor from where they had entered. It was one person's footsteps, and therefore presumably Fordyce. Leo frantically flashed his torch around, but there was nowhere to hide. They killed their lights and listened as the door mechanism turned.

But no one came in.

The stood perfectly still for a minute or so, the dark silence pressing upon them. Then Rachael whispered, 'He must have gone away.'

They switched their torches back on and crossed the floor, then slowly opened the door. The corridor was empty.

'He must have crept off; perhaps he heard some of the others,' hissed Leo.

They walked on quietly, keeping their torches pointed downwards. When they reached the T-junction, Leo peered round the corner, shining his torch left and right.

'All clear,' he whispered. 'Let's deposit ourselves in one of the old servants' rooms.'

At that moment, Leo thought he heard a man's voice somewhere to his left make an exclamation; a bump to the head on a rafter or – could it be? – an orgasm. He thought of Jimmy up here somewhere with Cynthia. Therefore he led Rachael to the right, and they sneaked down the corridor until Leo chose a door, turned the handle and pushed. And as they regarded the ghoulish face of the figure standing before them, Leo started violently and uttered an oath while Rachael let out a gasp of sheer terror.

The figure reached out its right arm and grabbed Leo by the shoulder.

'Fordyce, you devil!' exclaimed Leo good-naturedly, once he had recovered himself.

'Sorry if I gave you a jolt, old stick; perhaps I went a little too far in the make-up department. Are you all right, Rachael?'

'Perfectly fine, thank you, Fordyce. You look amazing!'

While the guests had scrambled to their hiding places Fordyce had quickly powdered his skin white and applied prosthetic clay to make his face look misshapen and grotesque. The addition of some mascara and blood-red lipstick accentuated the ghastly effect. In his left hand he carried a hurricane lamp. 'Just something I threw together from the dressing-up trunk dear Gilbert kept here. He was a thespian, as you know.'

'Are we the first you've found?' asked Rachael.

'No, Evelyn and Maxwell are already waiting downstairs. Now, you two go down and join them, and I, meanwhile, shall get back to my haunting!'

Leo and Rachael entered a rather miserable atmosphere in the drawing room. Maxwell was slouched in one of the chamber's two blood-red Chesterfields and didn't join in when the others began chirpily analysing the game.

Leo went to the cabinet and poured sweet sherries for Evelyn and Rachael, and mixed a rusty nail for himself. 'What are you for, Maxwell?' he enquired.

'Bénédictine and Rémy Martin with ice. Use the XO, and plenty of it,' he commended rudely.

'Maxwell does so love his Bénédictine and brandy,' observed Evelyn conversationally, but he simply ignored her.

After a few minutes, they heard footsteps and Fordyce's familiar cough in the corridor outside, and a short while later the door opened and Unity appeared, looking somewhat harassed. The Major then came in, grinning inanely. 'Caught! Bloody caught like a hare in a gin!' he barked, before laughing manically. He poured himself a colossal dose of port wine and then plonked his derrière on the other Chesterfield, across from Maxwell.

'I'm just going to, er, pop to the loo,' mumbled Unity.

'Are you quite all right, dear?' asked Evelyn.

'I'm fine,' replied Unity, before departing.

'That makes Jimmy and Cynthia the winners,' stated Leo.

It took Fordyce several minutes of enthusiastic gong-bashing to rouse the victors from their hidey-hole, and when they finally arrived in the drawing room, to a ripple of applause, they seemed rather flustered and flushed – Jimmy in particular. Evelyn handed them their prize bottles of Bordeaux.

'I think we require some fresh air after all that excitement,' said Cynthia.

'Good idea,' agreed Jimmy as he removed his jacket and tossed it on a sofa.

Cynthia opened the French doors. It was dark outside, or at least as dark as it got at this time of year. While Evelyn peeled off Fordyce's disguise, Jimmy commandeered the drinks cabinet, mixing a Black Russian for Cynthia, a port and ginger for Fordyce, and a Dubonnet and soda for himself. This he gulped down thirstily, before pouring himself another, this time *sans* soda and instead over ice with a twist. Leo privately considered it uncouth to consume an *apéritif* at such a late hour.

'Purely medicinal,' said Jimmy when he became aware of Leo's gaze.

'Pray let us all be seated,' said Fordyce, who had armed himself with the one bauble in the room that Leo disliked: a varnished sheep's skull, the horns of which had been hollowed out to accommodate a snuff container and a little scoop on a chain. Fordyce passed the grotesque thing to Leo, who took a dose. Leo then handed it to Jimmy, noticing as he did so that one of the fellow's cufflinks was missing. Also, he was sweating profusely and kept dabbing his brow with a handkerchief.

'So,' said Fordyce, addressing Jimmy, 'I think we'd all be curious to know: where *were* you hiding?'

'Behind an enormous dollhouse in one of the attics.'

'I was in that room. I should have looked harder!' said Fordyce.

'I must tell you, Fordyce,' said Rachael, 'you almost caught myself and Leo earlier than you did.'

'Oh really, my dear – when?'

'You know the old attic, the one which is abreast with the tower?' said Leo. 'We were in there when you came down the corridor and turned the handle.'

'But I wasn't in that corridor, my dears,' said Fordyce.

'Very funny,' said Leo.

'I'm not joking, old stick.'

'Spooky!' Evelyn laughed.

'It must have been someone else,' said Fordyce.

Before Leo could interrogate his friend further, Unity appeared. 'Excuse me, Fordyce,' she said. 'The police are at the door.'

'What on earth can they want at this hour?' wondered Evelyn.

'Please, Unity, show them in,' said Fordyce. He rose (as did the ever-gentlemanly Leo) to introduce himself and Evelyn to a female plainclothes officer, one Detective Chief Inspector Dalton. She was accompanied by a young male constable by the name of McLellan, who had an open, friendly face. They declined Fordyce's invitation that they be seated. Unity made to leave, but Dalton requested that she remain.

'Forgive my visage, Chief Inspector,' added Fordyce sheepishly, referring to the remnants of his horror make-up. 'We were playing a party game.'

'I apologise for interrupting it, and for calling so late, sir. I'm here regarding a missing person. A fifteen-year-old female from the village called Lauren McDowall. Does anyone know to whom I am referring?'

'You mean the daughter of Anthea McDowall, the café owner?' enquired Fordyce.

'Yes, sir.'

As it happened, everyone in the room, even the relative outsiders Leo and Rachael, confirmed that they knew who Lauren was: the strikingly pretty girl who helped out at her mother's business when she wasn't attending high school in Castle Douglas.

'She was last seen at just after nine p.m. yesterday,' continued Dalton. 'She was walking over the meadows south of your lake in a westerly direction, and wearing a denim jacket and a yellow skirt.'

Dalton related a summary of events. Lauren lived with her mother in a house on the edge of Biggnarbriggs village. At approximately 8.50 p.m. the previous evening she said she was popping out to meet a friend – she didn't state who – and promised not to be late. By midnight, Mrs McDowall was concerned that Lauren had not yet returned, so she called her mobile phone only to hear it ringing abandoned in her bedroom. She wasn't overly concerned because her daughter sometimes stayed out too late, and therefore retired. This morning Lauren still wasn't home and her bed hadn't been slept in. Her mother had called a few numbers but drew a blank, and therefore contacted the police. They conducted initial inquiries, speaking with Lauren's known associates, but no one had seen her, and their initial search of the environs hadn't yielded any trace of where she might have gone. There were also no immediately obvious clues on her laptop or mobile, and the girl hadn't been admitted to any local hospitals. Although the disappearance had only occurred the previous evening, the fact that Lauren had left her phone and hadn't packed any personal belongings was a cause for concern.

'Has anyone seen Miss McDowall, or been aware of anything out of the ordinary or anyone acting suspiciously in the local area?' concluded Dalton.

A murmur of 'no's.

Dalton was aged about forty-five, a buxom woman of average height who was wearing an unflattering business suit. She was plain-featured, and her straight brown hair was pulled back incredibly tightly, as though it had been painted on. She had clever hazel eyes set within a full face. She spoke clearly in a low-pitched Glasgow accent. She exuded an underlying toughness and had an air about her that commanded authority.

'You're sure you didn't see anyone on the estate?' she asked, addressing just Fordyce and Evelyn.

'Myself and Fordyce sat in the rose salon until about a quarter to ten,' said Evelyn. 'I'm afraid we were too engrossed in our piquet to look out over the grounds. Then we tidied the supper things in the kitchen . . . it was Unity and Mrs Grove's night off. We retired not long after ten, as we had a big day today.'

'Who are Unity and Mrs Grove?'

Unity identified herself. 'I live in the cottage round the back with my husband Brian – he's the gardener and caretaker – and our two children. Brian was away on a fishing trip last night, and I was busy with the kids.'

'And Mrs Grove, our cook, is an older lady who comes up from the village most evenings,' explained Evelyn. 'I had Brian drive her home earlier tonight.'

'Who else lives on or frequents the estate?'

'There's Chas Shaw,' said Fordyce. 'He lives alone in the gatehouse. He's the estate foreman and ghillie for our land and the land by Maidenhead House, south of here.'

'I've already spoken to Mr Shaw.'

'We also have a cleaner, Claire Hannay,' said Evelyn. 'She lives in Biggnarbriggs village and only comes here during the day. Sometimes, but not recently, she's accompanied by a girl or two from the village when there's lots to do.'

'And, at times, Brian or Chas will hire casual labour when there's lots needing doing on the estate, but not during the last couple of weeks,' added Fordyce.

'Was anyone else in the vicinity last night?' asked Dalton.

'Normally I would be, but my manservant Lyle and I were in the Rose and Crown in Castle Douglas all evening,' said the Major. 'We dined in the restaurant, then repaired to the bar.'

'And who are you, sir?'

'Major Jock Lindsay Balfour-MacWhinnie, DSO. I live at Maidenhead House, and my estate backs onto the land below the lake.'

'Who else resides there, sir?'

'Just Lyle. I doubt we would have seen anything even if we had been home. Too many trees.'

Dalton ensured that she was made aware of everybody else's identity and place of residence. Leo mentioned that he had only arrived from Glasgow that very day. The DCI checked if any of the female guests intended to walk home alone tonight; none did. Indeed, everyone, apart from the Major who lived within walking distance, was staying over at the hall. Dalton then urged the assembly to telephone the national non-emergency number and ask to be connected to her should any pertinent information occur to them, or if they were to see or hear anything of note.

'We shall do better than that, Chief Inspector,' said Fordyce. 'We'll have a thorough look around the estate and the surrounding woodland tomorrow morning.'

'Thank you, sir. Actually, I was about to mention that we've organised a search party for eight a.m. There will be volunteers from the village too; the more the better.' There was a general murmur of support for this initiative. 'I hope you don't mind, sir, but I asked that they meet by the summerhouse on your land.'

'Of course,' replied Fordyce.

'Inspector,' interposed Leo, 'is there any suggestion the girl might have . . . done herself a mischief?'

'She has no history of mental illness, and her mother says she is quite a self-possessed young woman who is generally in good spirits, allowing for the usual teenage moodiness. Apparently she seemed fine when her mother last saw her.'

'But you never know with young people nowadays,' brooded Fordyce. 'Cyberbullying and so forth can make kids do drastic things.'

'We're keeping an open mind,' stated Dalton.

'Was her home life happy?' enquired Leo.

'I can't divulge private details, sir, but I don't believe there was any significant domestic strife that would have compelled her to run off, and, as I said, she doesn't seem to have packed any belongings. Tomorrow we'll continue with our house-to-house inquiries and contact any outstanding associates. We'll also issue a press release. So, I'll wish you goodnight.'

'Gosh, her poor mother,' said Evelyn, after the police had departed. Unity had gone with them; they would escort her home and speak with Brian.

'Brandies all round,' said Fordyce.

'I'm sure she'll turn up,' said the Major.

After Fordyce had furnished everyone with large cognacs, he said to Evelyn, 'Dearest sis, I propose we dispense with the remaining summer skylarks – with the exception of the ashes spreading ceremony and the dinner afterwards – until young Lauren is found safe.'

'Agreed,' said Evelyn. She then turned to Rachael. 'Are you all right, my dear? You look awfully pale.'

'I'm fine, thanks, Evelyn.'

They sipped their drinks in silence. Then Evelyn said, 'You know, it brings back memories of the dreadful business that occurred round here back in '79.'

'What happened?' asked Rachael.

'A girl, Hazel Bannatyne, down from Glasgow on summer holiday with her family, went missing quite suddenly. She'd been out walking by herself. She was never seen again, and her body was never found. It was as though she had vanished into thin air.'

'How terrible. Who could have been responsible for such a thing?' enquired Rachael.

'There was briefly a druidic cult in these parts, back in the late seventies,' said Fordyce. 'They were based at an old farmstead over on the other side of Scoulag Hill. However, they spent a lot of time around this Early Bronze Age stone circle, which is through the woods just north of here, beyond our orchard.'

'The standing stones are why those woods are known locally as the Enchanted Forest,' interjected Evelyn.

'This crowd held ceremonies at the stones,' continued Fordyce. 'What is beyond doubt is that they possessed an interest in sacrifice, because animals were slaughtered there. Father was incandescent. They had this charismatic leader who called himself Talorc. Big, tall chap. Long since dead.'

'Did the police suspect the cult had sacrificed this poor girl?' asked Leo.

'Yes, but there wasn't a single lead,' replied Fordyce. 'They moved on soon afterwards, such was the suspicion that fell on them. Some folk have since speculated that it might have been Robert Black, the serial killer, who took the Bannatyne girl.'

'Unlikely,' said Rachael. 'Black mostly targeted younger females.'

'What age was the lass who went missing in 1979?' asked Leo.

'Sixteen,' said Fordyce, before addressing Evelyn. 'Dearest sis, you're shaking! Take a nip of brandy.' Fordyce went to stand by his sister, and placed a comforting hand on her shoulder.

Evelyn took a sip, then said, 'Fordyce, I've just realised that it was around this time of year when poor Hazel went missing. In fact, I'm sure it's precisely the same date! I know because I recall it was the day of late Great Uncle Hugo's birthday, which was July twenty-fifth . . . yesterday.'

'My remarkable sister never forgets a date,' said Fordyce.

'I can still remember it. Hugo had just blown out his candles when that girl's poor father knocked on the door, asking if we had seen his daughter. Daddy went out with him, and I could hear the pair of them shouting her name. Just shouting and shouting, but they never found her.' Evelyn began weeping, and Rachael came over to sit beside her. 'Oh, Fordyce, tell me that awfulness isn't going to happen all over again!'

After retiring, Leo found that he couldn't sleep. Despite having consumed a good deal of alcohol he felt remarkably clear-headed due to the sobering news brought by DCI Dalton.

Leo remembered Lauren McDowall from a few occasions when he and Fordyce had dropped by the café after fishing at Loch Quien. On one such time Mrs McDowall, a single parent, had snapped at her daughter for spending too long chatting with some male customers. And Leo had noticed Lauren's lip curl slightly. He instinctively knew what had amused her: that her mother was jealous. Because some seedier men who came into the café over-tipped her and feigned interest in her life plans; but they were not simply intrigued or charmed by her in some platonic or avuncular way. For, with her impeccable skin, brilliant white teeth, perfectly proportioned features and gorgeous chestnut hair, Lauren McDowall was about to blossom into womanhood in a manner quite beguiling. And already she possessed an unfocused sense of the power that this beauty bestowed upon her.

Leo had dreaded that the vision he had experienced in the church in London related to an impending case, which now was surely revealed as that of this missing girl. He drifted off to sleep, unaware that he would have only minutes to wait for the next instalment, the climax to which would awaken him abruptly in a state of horror.

Night-time in a rural setting. A band of men bear lit torches. They are wearing black cloaks and heavily draped cowls which obscure their faces. Their quarry has kindly, handsome features and is aged approximately thirty. He sits astride a fine bay mare and is clad in a hunting coat with big golden buttons, an ivory satin waistcoat and a full cravat of rich lace. His shoes are of polished black leather with heavy gold buckles, and he is wearing knee breeches and stockings. He has long hair and wears a high-cocked black felt hat. The garb seems eighteenth-century. The horseman is outraged with the band, his breath coming out as steam, therefore it must be cold. A torch is thrust forth to startle the mare; it shows the cloth of the horseman's coat as plum-coloured, his hair fair. One of his antagonists has crept round to his rear and strikes him on the back with an evil-looking club. The horseman is not felled but is clearly in pain. The leader of the band is a tall, powerful individual wearing a tricorne hat and apparently no cowl, but he is facing away from Leo's perspective. He steps forwards, reaches up and hauls the victim from his horse, casting him to the ground. Then, horror: the band gather around the stricken man and raise their bludgeons in unison. Then bring them down in a rain of blows, striking him again and again.

Day Two

THE summerhouse was a wooden construction with a small veranda and a shingle roof. It was situated in the shadow of a few Scots pines, where the lawns sloped gently down to the ornamental lake. The searchers gathered there, more than two dozen of them, mostly men. The sun was barely over the treetops and casting ragged yellow pools, and the temperature already portended a scorcher. The fair meadows blurred slightly as the dew burned off them. All of the previous night's diners were present, along with Chas Shaw and the McGhies, whose children were playing by the maze. Brian quietly identified some of the rest of the party for Leo's benefit. Lyle, the Major's butler, was there, as was the landlord from the Green Man, Biggnarbriggs' only public house, and several of his regulars.

Leo longed to speak with Rachael, who was chatting with Evelyn, but decorum counselled that now was not an appropriate time to pursue a romantic interest. Instead he sidled up to Unity, who was standing alone, absent-mindedly fondling the pentagram amulet she was wearing.

'Unity, I hope you don't mind my asking, but last night, during the ghost game . . . did the Major behave in an improper fashion? It's just that you appeared a little harassed afterwards.'

'Really, it was nothing,' she replied. 'The old goat had just had one too many clarets. He has a roving eye, and occasionally a roving hand, but he's quite harmless.'

Leo next approached the phalanx of police personnel who were positioned immediately around the summerhouse. DCI Dalton was standing on the wooden steps, viewing an Ordinance Survey map of the local area.

Even when she was a junior police officer, let alone after she had become one of Scotland's youngest female detective chief inspectors, none of Diane Dalton's colleagues would have dared to address her by the unkind epithet 'Double D'. She had overheard it – and the misplaced speculation regarding her sexual orientation – on more than one occasion, but had determined to ignore it. Dealing with humanity at its most criminal meant she had few expectations of people anyway, and a perpetual lack of romantic love had trimmed her demands on life. Detective work and it alone was what imbued her with any purpose, or indeed any sense of meaning. Her private life made room for dutiful visits to her frail, proud parents, the inevitable tabby at her cottage near Lochmaben, Blu-ray box sets, two sessions of Transcendental Meditation per day and vigorous hikes across the Southern Uplands. The latter two activities helped to keep a stress-related condition, the cause of her request for a transfer away from Glasgow, at bay.

Dalton knew she was demanding of her juniors and that her toughness kept friendships at arm's length, but it also made potential enemies think twice. Nonetheless, she maintained a genuine capacity for empathy which victims, witnesses and even certain perpetrators had enjoyed. The DCI was scrupulously fair, keen to curb the edge of resentment she sometimes felt towards pretty women, and she had learned to tame her short temper. The lack of serious crime in the district meant she would be closely monitored by her chief constable during the search for the McDowall girl. However, her good results had already earned her the admiration of her superiors, although they were slightly bemused by her detached air.

'Good morning, Inspector,' said Leo.

'Can I help you, sir?'

'As a matter of fact, I was hoping I might be of some help to you. Last night, after you left us, we were discussing Miss McDowall's disappearance, and something came to light. It might be entirely coincidental, but it transpires that another teenaged girl, by the name of Hazel Bannatyne, disappeared from this same vicinity back in 1979. On precisely the same date.'

'I'm already aware of that, sir.' Dalton went back to her map-reading.

Leo paused for a moment. Dogs barked in the middle distance. 'I wonder, Inspector, have you come across anything substantial yet? Footprints, for example?'

'We'll let the public know how we're progressing in due course, sir,' said Dalton with strained civility.

'Did Lauren have a boyfriend?'

'I can't divulge private information.'

Leo persevered. 'Her mother is a single parent, I believe. Does she or did she have a gentleman friend? Someone who might frequent the family home?'

'If I could just ask you to take your position with the search party, my sergeant is about to issue instructions.'

'I'd just like to let you know that my services are at your disposal. I don't know if you are aware, but I have certain psychic powers—'

'I'm fully aware of your alleged powers,' interrupted Dalton curtly. 'And of the embarrassment you brought on the force by discussing them at the inquest following the deaths up at Loch Dhonn.' Leo cringed at the memory. 'No, Mr Moran, we'll manage perfectly well by ourselves, thank you very much. I hold no truck for mumbo jumbo; I only believe in things I can punch. Now, let the experts do their jobs. And it's *Chief* Inspector, by the way.'

At that moment, Dalton's Nokia sounded, and, without a backward glance, she strode up the steps and disappeared into the summerhouse.

Leo, ever the opportunist, checked that none of the officers assembled nearby had their eye on him, then crept up to the veranda that encompassed the little building and sneaked round it to the rear. Through the thin wooden wall he could hear Dalton's telephone call quite distinctly.

'We're about to move off now, sir, but my officers have already done an initial recce . . . Yes. We believe Miss McDowall was wearing Converse High Tops, size six – Converse, sir. It's a brand of trendy footwear, a bit like sandshoes. There's a footprint matching them near to where Donald Kennedy saw her. We took a casting, and found it twice again by an old ruin known as Linn Priory. She was walking roughly westwards, but after the ruins we've drawn a blank. It's as though she vanished into thin air. Let's see what the dogs pick up.'

Vanished into thin air. Leo remembered Evelyn using the same words the previous evening to describe the disappearance of the Bannatyne girl. He heard Dalton sign off and then a knock on the door, followed by the words, 'PC McLellan, ma'am.'

'Come in.'

'The dogs have detected a scent trail, ma'am. After the priory, she cut south, through some fairly rough, overgrown ground. She climbed two barbed-wire fences, then a dyke, then walked west along the forest road for about half a mile. The trail then stops.'

'She must have got into a motor vehicle,' surmised Dalton. 'It's less likely that a commercial or forestry vehicle would be using a minor road at that time, but I want every conceivable haulier, farmer, and utility and delivery driver checked out.'

'Yes, ma'am. The scent ends at a lot the water board uses as a halting-place,' continued McLellan. 'It has a concrete surface so there are no tyre tracks, and you probably wouldn't notice a vehicle parked there from the road due to the greenery. So a perp may have seen her walking and pulled in there.'

'Or someone was waiting to meet her there,' speculated Dalton. 'Which would explain why she didn't simply go straight along the road from the village, and instead took the circuitous route via the priory. Perhaps she wanted to avoid being seen from houses on the initial part of road, if she was off for a clandestine liaison.'

'If she was picked up in a vehicle, it means she could be anywhere by now. Also, ma'am, she would have reached that lot, assuming she didn't delay, by around twenty-one thirty hours. Sunset was twenty-one thirty-one, and these summer nights are fairly light anyway, so she'd have been well visible had anyone been out looking for a victim. Also, we haven't found any of her footprints along the scent trail leading down to the road. The ground is dry from the weather, but there's the occasional muddy spot where we'd have hoped to have found another. There is the odd print from unknown adults in certain patches of soft ground, but they could be historical and belong to anyone.'

Dalton and McLellan then left the summerhouse and Leo had to clamber over the veranda's banister and through the pine trees – stinging his left wrist on some nettles as he did so – before sneaking back round to join the search party, who were being addressed by a police sergeant through a loudhailer, listing a series of instructions and prohibitions in monotone cop talk.

The party set off at a slow pace, two yards separating each searcher as they scanned the ground in front of them for clues. Beyond the foot of the lake they reached a wire fence that separated the lawns from the meadows, and had to regroup and funnel through a kissing gate, before splaying out again into their ragged line.

This rolling sheep pasture was punctuated by random copses of towering beech and was entirely invaded by buttercups. Larks twittered in the air above and the turf gave off a marvellous, sweet smell of dried soil. Leo tested it with his foot, to see if it would leave a print. Instead, the grass pretty much sprang back into shape. Now the instruction crackled over the megaphone for the line to alter its vector by ninety degrees in order to progress westwards, Lauren's approximate direction of travel when she was last seen. They passed through an avenue of trees, then into open grassland again, then through a belt of woodland and into a meadow. This was almost entirely enclosed but for a corridor at the southwestern extreme, a series of steep little bluffs that reached a saddle of land upon which sat the ruined priory. However, Leo, Fordyce and most of the searchers had to forgo this channel and instead negotiate the woods – difficult, broken terrain – and then clamber over a wire fence before ascending the steep slope, dotted with birch and bracken, to the higher ground. Beyond the priory to the west was dense commercial forestry, and to the south was the overgrown land riven with obstacles: ditches, more barbed wire, little defiles, a dyke and even a few lumbering Belted Galloway cattle which unnerved Leo. The searchers tried to maintain their loose line and inspected the uneven ground as best they could. Once they had reached the forest road they were instructed to return to base. The only item of interest that Leo saw was a dilapidated cabin in a clearing further west, which he'd noticed when standing upon a knob of raised ground. A police 4x4 vehicle sat outside it.

Fordyce and some of the men clambered into the coniferous screen to the west, shouting vainly for the lost girl, but Leo felt it unlikely that she would have entered that barely penetrable timberland. After a few minutes of gazing impotently into the wooded depths, he informed Fordyce that he was returning to the hall. His route was somewhat spontaneous, but he had a fixed idea of his destination: the so-called Enchanted Forest Fordyce and Evelyn had mentioned, where the sinister Talorc and his minions had held their weird ceremonies all those years ago. He clambered down the crags to the hidden meadow, through the trees until the land opened up, then skirted the woodland that clothed the higher ground until he was at the rear of Biggnarbriggs Hall itself. Then he walked through the orchard. Brian had planted primroses and rosemary to attract pollinators, and they would have a good crop of Galloway Pippins this September. It was warmer now, and Leo paused to drink in the fragrances of the place, detecting as he did a strain of coal smoke; he glanced up to see it scrolling from one of the hall's chimneys. Leo then strolled into what he presumed to be the Enchanted Forest, where he had been told the standing stones were situated. It was rich in its variety of deciduous species – oak, beech, larch and elm, some rowan and a few sycamores – and the canopy was spangled with sunlight. It was cooler here, and the perfumes sharper. A songbird emitted a haunting melody and Leo heard the plaintive call of a kite. A natural path took him to a small clearing where the circle was. It was a place of tall grass infested with thorny plants, although the area between the stones had been cut back. There were five of them, granite dragon's teeth, each the size of a man. The air buzzed with hoverflies and clegs. Leo spent a couple of fruitless minutes examining the vicinity, having no idea what he expected to find. He strolled under a bower into an adjoining glade, noting how the entire area seemed to vibrate with a strange, seductive energy.

A hawthorn tree stood in the middle of the golden grass, its branches dangling over a well. Coloured ribbons hung from its branches and coins were hammered into its bark. Perhaps some sort of fairy tree? Leo recalled Unity's children playing with a homemade kite with ribbon streamers. He photographed the tree and regarded it for a while. He succumbed to a need to urinate, his flow hissing into the dehydrated vegetation.

'These little trees can get quite old,' came Cynthia Blythman's voice from behind him. There was a pause, filled only with the drone of insects and the sound of Leo's water. He wondered if his ears had deceived him, but then she continued: 'This one, for example, is said to have been planted in the seventeenth century. Legend has it that they put a ball of soil and seeds into the belly of a hanged marauder. It's a shame you missed its blossom.'

'I beg your pardon,' said Leo as he glanced over his shoulder, apologising for his activity. Cynthia's jeans were clinging to her thighs, and the curve of her bosom was accentuated by her white vest top.

'It's a clootie tree,' she explained, a lubricious texture in her voice. 'People used to tie rags to such trees to represent a wish, and give gifts and baubles to appease the tree spirit or nature goddess. Or perhaps the little folk.'

'You seem to know a lot about these matters; you and Unity should chat. The ribbons and coins seem new. I wonder who put them there.'

Cynthia now brazenly stepped forward so that she was immediately behind Leo. Her voice was now a husky whisper. 'I saw you slipping away earlier, after we'd finished searching. I wondered where you were going.'

She seemed to exude an irresistible sexual force.

'Just felt like a stroll,' said Leo, a nervous catch in his voice.

'You were naughty to me last night, at dinner.'

Leo felt incapacitated by a surge of primal longing. 'However do you mean?' he croaked.

'Never mind, I forgive you. Do you want to hear something else?' Her voice was directly in his ear now, her breath hot, moist. He wanted to melt into her, into her beautiful, sexy ghastliness. 'In folklore, the thorn tree symbolised fertility; people would venerate it in order that their deepest desires would come true.'

Leo fixed himself and hobbled off, his temper fouled, leaving Cynthia smirking by the well.

As Leo arrived back at the hall, DCI Dalton and PC McLellan pulled up in an unmarked car. Leo took the opportunity to inform them about the wish tree, mentioning how it was situated near to a stone circle which had been the haunt of a cult who were suspects in the 1979 case. Considering this, perhaps the coinciding date of the year on which the two disappearances had occurred was some hallowed occult feast day. Dalton claimed she already knew about the items to which he was referring and Leo watched the officers walk purposefully towards the McGhies' cottage. He then wandered to the terrace, where his attention was arrested by the voice of Evelyn, chatting on a cordless telephone, her three spaniels excitedly circling her legs.

'I'm terribly sorry to hear that, Father. Yes, I shall tell him. Let us know if you need anything. Goodbye.'

'Is everything all right, Evelyn?' enquired Leo.

She sighed. 'I'm afraid it isn't. That was Father Larranzar from the Nain Community. Donald Kennedy was taken in for questioning early this morning. Apparently it was he who last saw Lauren.'

'Donald?' exclaimed Leo incredulously. 'A true gentleman – he wouldn't hurt a fly!'

'Indeed. Leo, I'm afraid I'm going to have to leave you – I promised to bring more coals to Jimmy's room, then the telephone rang. He's got a nasty chill.'

'Evelyn, before you go: do you know of a hawthorn tree, in a glade near to the standing stones? It sits by a little well.'

'Yes, I think I know where you mean.'

'Are you aware that it has recently been decorated with ribbons, and coins have been inserted into its trunk?'

'Gosh, no. It all sounds terribly pagan.'

With that, Evelyn and the dogs scurried indoors. Leo gazed over the great lawns. He could see police officers and the dregs of the search party sloping away from the summerhouse. Then he heard footsteps crunching on the gravel to his left, and walked back round from the terrace to witness Brian, his expression obscured to Leo's perspective, getting into the rear of the unmarked car, supervised by PC McLellan. DCI Dalton stood nearby, speaking in a calm voice to a tearful Unity, whose children clung pathetically to her skirts.

After the police had left, Leo comforted Unity then tracked down Evelyn, who was wiping coal dust from her hands in the kitchen, and informed her that Brian, too, had been taken in for questioning. Evelyn breathed deeply to steel herself, and then announced she was going to the cottage to give Unity some moral support. Leo informed her that he would visit Father Larranzar, and provide him with some of the same.

The Nain Community sat just north of Biggnarbriggs village. It was a Roman Catholic house of prayer with an ecumenical ethos which held retreats and youth residencies and sometimes provided a haven for alcoholics and drug addicts. It was under the stewardship of Donald Kennedy; during the early 1980s he and his late wife Edith had opened their farmhouse for the purpose. They spent their life savings on converting the house and constructing a modern dormitory. Its spiritual director was one Father Barnebas Larranzar, an ordained Capuchin friar who was whiling out his latter days there in semi-retirement. Leo had been honoured to have met these good people on previous occasions, and he knew the absurdity of Donald being suspected of anything foul.

The sun was fiercer now, and Leo was glad of the arbour as he walked, a pleasant mixture of ash, sycamore, young alder and the occasional elm. A road-killed frog was rolled out incongruously flat on the bitumen like a joke-shop trick. The hedgerow, interwoven with bramble, dog rose, nettles, fern and sticky willow, soon gave way to mossy drystane dykes.

To Leo's right, the shaded Biggnar Burn tumbled merrily over a bed of smooth stones, and birds sounded lazily from the branches. Just before the village he cut up a drive from where he could see Father Larranzar attending to his bees.

'Good day, Father!'

'Hello, Leo!' called the priest through his veil. 'I shall be with you presently.'

Leo leaned on the garden's stone wall and watched the little octogenarian at work, focused on a mass of bees clinging to an ash bole some yards from their hives. He used a mallet to strike the tree with a force that belied his advanced years, and gathered the insects in a wicker basket.

'The bees loyal to the old queen have left the hive with her,' shouted Larranzar, his undulating Spanish cadence still faintly discernible. 'I've had to despatch her, so that these workers will reintegrate. It's too late in the year to start a new colony – we wouldn't get any yield.'

Once the priest had deposited the bees back in their hive he walked over to Leo and removed his headwear. It was good to see his face: the bright brown eyes, the white hair swept back from weathered skin. He was bird-like in appearance and animation, a tactile person, often gesticulating and laughing.

'I heard about Donald being taken in,' said Leo.

'Purely routine, I'm sure.'

'How are you, Father?'

'I am well. I've had time for silence of late, *Deo gratias*.'

'I'm sorry to shatter it.'

'On the contrary, it's a pleasure to see you. Shall I fetch the board?'

'A splendid idea.'

They entered the old farmhouse by the rear door, and Leo waited in a lobby while Larranzar went to remove his apiarist suit. The place smelled of emulsion, and Leo had the feeling that nobody else was at home apart from Rupert, the community's Border Collie, who bounded in. Leo noticed scar tissue on his face, as though he had been attacked by a more powerful animal. He inexpertly tried to pat the creature to reciprocate its overenthusiasm. Leo then admired a Bible that sat upon a sideboard. It was decorated with reproductions of the Evangelists' symbols from the Book of Kells. The item was probably a gift, as such resplendence was unusual for the Nain Community, given Larranzar's Spartan ethos. The priest was one of a rare breed, a man palpably touched by the divine, filled with holiness and spirit, who exhibited sheer joy whenever he held the Eucharist aloft. People were drawn to him because he was a living miracle of goodness, a goodness expressed in kindness, patience and gentleness, and that goodness, when you experienced it, didn't disappoint because it did not glorify in itself. This, and the fact that Larranzar was a student of human nature, meant that people clung to him for advice and healing.

He entered the lobby wearing his friar's robes, carrying his chess set. He instructed Leo to fetch some lime cordial from the kitchen, and the pair installed themselves at a table in the umbrage of the ash tree with a view of the kailyard and the humming hives and the farmhouse beyond. The air was fragrant with honeysuckle, and Rupert lolled nearby, glad of the company.

They made a few cursory openers with their pieces, but they both sensed that this was merely the preamble to conversation.

'Something troubles you, my son,' ventured Larranzar.

'There is chaos in my soul.'

'Do you wish to confess?'

'Not really. It seems indecent to complain about my problems with this girl lost.'

'You must speak freely.'

'Do you remember my telling you that I killed a man at Loch Dhonn?'

'Of course. In self-defence.'

'It gnaws at me. I've seen him of late.'

'Within the visions you once told me of?'

'No, I mean he is become a revenant; I've actually *seen* him. Mocking me or trying to unnerve me.' A profound sadness filled the friar's eyes. 'I'm sorry, Father, I don't mean to upset you.'

'Believe me, my son, I've heard far worse.'

Leo moved a chesspiece. 'I think Gilbert's death has affected me quite deeply. Which is odd, really, as I didn't know him all that well and he'd had a reasonable innings.'

'The power of death is undone by the Resurrection, yet sudden loss can still broadside us, remind us of life's fragility. Particularly if we are in a vulnerable state. I am grieved to hear of your troubles, Leo, and I shall pray for you. And you also must pray. And receive the sacraments, to fortify you.'

Rupert began to bark excitedly, before shooting off to greet his master, who had appeared at the garden gate.

Donald Kennedy was a long-limbed man aged seventy with an air of eccentricity about him. His thin grey hair was always slightly unkempt, his clothing generally mismatched and threadbare, his wide-eyed expression intensified by the strong prescription of his metal-framed spectacles. His cheeks had hollowed with age, further pronouncing his large, intelligent forehead. He shook Leo's hand before seating himself.

'Donald, you poor chap,' said Leo. 'What a dreadful time you must have had.'

'It wasn't pleasant, I must say,' said Donald in his refined, gentle accent. 'However, the police must do their job. And we must pray to Our Blessed Lady to petition that poor Lauren McDowall is found safe.'

'Amen,' agreed Larranzar.

Leo asked Donald to explain what had occurred two nights ago. Apparently he and Brian had planned a night of fishing at Clugston Loch, about forty miles away. Donald was waiting to be picked up at the foot of drive. Brian was slightly late, and just after 9 p.m., through the trees by the roadside, Donald spotted Lauren walking across the meadow. He took little note of it, and didn't mention it to Brian when he arrived in his car a moment later. The pair then set off along the forest road, on which he saw nothing of further interest, not so much as another vehicle.

'I'm afraid DCI Dalton seemed unconvinced my story,' he added. 'They've taken Brian in too. Miss Dalton seems to think we abducted Lauren in his car, and that we could have buried her virtually anywhere within a wide radius.'

'She can't be too convinced, Donald; she didn't even hold you for twenty-four hours, which she would have been legally entitled to,' consoled Leo.

'I pointed out to her that if I was involved, why would I admit to having seen her? Also, I consented to provide physical samples to them for their DNA record. And I've given them permission to examine my clothes, plus they gave me a thorough bodily examination. Miss Dalton asked me why we went via the forest road, which is something of a detour, and I told her that it was because it is such a lovely drive of a summer's evening. She then grilled me about whether Brian and I regularly go off on such trips together. I confirmed that we do, now and then.'

It had already struck Leo that Donald and Brian seemed unlikely pals, but then he considered how the former could probably connect with just about anyone. It was as though Donald could discern in everyone what Thomas Merton had called 'the secret beauty of their hearts'.

Donald continued: 'I explained that I am an insomniac, and my response to the ailment is to perform the Stations of the Cross, which I installed upon Scoulag Hill a number of years ago; the Greatorixes, who own the land there, were most amenable. I sometimes use a head torch, but generally the starlight down here is more than adequate. Brian, too, suffers from insomnia and also finds going out walking eases the bleakness it inflicts. Our paths crossed on several such occasions and we got talking about our mutual love for fishing, and so organised these trips, every month or two. It was nice having someone to spend those waking hours with.'

'Would it be widely known that you are both insomniacs, taken to venturing out at night?' enquired Leo.

'Yes.'

'It all seems rather convenient, the two locals known for nocturnal rambling well out of the way.'

'Whatever do you mean?'

'I mean you two would have been a potential threat to the perpetrator or perpetrators, should they have had nefarious activities planned for a certain night in the locale.'

'Leo, we don't even know yet if Lauren was abducted,' interjected Larranzar. 'She may have run off. Or, God forbid, done harm to herself.'

'Whose idea was the trip this time?' asked Leo.

'Brian's, as it happens,' replied Donald.

Leo raised an eyebrow.

'You're surely not implying he was in league with someone who had targeted Lauren!' exclaimed Larranzar.

'I'm not implying anything, Father. Donald, you are certain you didn't see any other cars on the forest road?'

'Quite certain.'

'And no vehicle parked up?'

'No.'

48

Leo remembered PC McLellan saying that a vehicle parked in the water board's lot mightn't have been seen from the forest road anyway. Of course, Lauren could have been intercepted by or met a vehicle after McLellan's provisional ETA of 9.30 p.m. She might have dallied, sat around, smoked, drank or even slept.

'Not that it would prove your innocence, but were there were any witnesses to your being at Clugston Loch?' Leo asked Donald.

'No. We chose a deserted spot and the water baillie wasn't around to check our licence. However, I believe your fish course last night was our catch.'

'That proves little, I'm afraid,' said Leo. 'Tell me, are there any guests staying at the community at present?'

'No. We're currently renovating the place, so no one has stayed with us for a while.'

'I wonder if a previous guest could have taken an interest in Lauren and come back here.'

'It could just as likely have been someone who had once holidayed here, or a passing tradesman or driver,' observed Larranzar.

'Quite so, Father' said Leo.

Leo had a late luncheon at the community, and left for the hall in mid-afternoon. As he walked up the drive Brian's white Audi passed by, a policeman at the wheel. He happened across Mrs Grove, who informed him that there was no news regarding Lauren (who, upon enquiry, it transpired the cook barely knew), and that dinner would be served at seven. Leo napped for a while, then showered, dressed and went for a constitutional through the topiary. And – precisely as had occurred the previous evening – when he turned to regard the hall's grand south façade he saw Rachael. He felt his heart sing; Mrs Grove must have been mistaken when she had informed him that just he, Evelyn and Fordyce would be dining. Leo called out to Rachael, who was standing at the aviary, but she didn't seem to hear him. He realised she was acting peculiarly, gazing upwards at the eaves. Something in her behaviour stopped Leo from calling out again. Also, he noted, she wasn't dressed for dinner, just in jeans and a T-shirt. Now she reached up as though to adjust something, before walking round the side of the aviary and disappearing into the woods.

Leo marched over, and an inspection of where Rachael's attention had been focused revealed a small, oblong-shaped object, cleverly varnished to blend in with the wood to which it had been attached. Leo recognised it as an electronic bug, the kind a *bona fide* private investigator would use. Some instinct told him to leave it alone, for now.

Given Lauren's disappearance, dinner was an appropriately plain and rather sombre affair, a simple game pie served with Ayrshire potatoes and seasonal vegetables. Leo decided not to broach the subject of the bug just yet as he didn't want to give Evelyn any more cause for upset. He would tell Fordyce about it tomorrow. Leo was informed that Brian had been discharged by the police, and that he had permitted them to remove his car for examination. Leo told his hosts about his visit to the community and Donald's release.

After dinner, Leo resolved to spend the remainder of the humid evening in the coolness of the library, a room he had not yet got round to exploring properly. He had some research he wished to undertake: to try to flesh out the enigmatic Miss Kidd, and also to test a whimsical notion that the murder he had witnessed in his vision the previous night might be that of Fordyce's ancestor who was said to haunt the hall.

The library was a magnificent, high-ceilinged chamber of dark-varnished panelling, into which harmonised its centrepiece: a huge fireplace of exquisitely carved hardwood. A series of Phiz's Dickens illustrations hung on the walls. Leo almost wished it was wintertime so that he could pull up one of the room's Chesterfields and delve into a good ghost story, with a fir heartwood fire roaring in the grate and a good cigar for company.

Leo used the library's laptop computer to search online for Rachael Kidd, but drew a blank: no social media account, no professional profile – nothing. He then began browsing the room's collection, which included several rare and obscure items, as well as those *de rigeur* to a country house library. Many of the volumes had been rebound in beautiful morocco in the interest of uniformity, and classified by the possessor of a keen mind who had attached little reference cards at the end of each shelf, filled out in a remarkably precise handwriting. Leo sipped a brandy and perused. Curiously, the collection contained a section of distinctly Catholic works: Thomas à Kempis, Duns Scotus, Teresa of Ávila, Thérèse of Lisieux, Aquinas, The Roman Hymnal, and various ecclesiastical documents. Certain anonymous folios also caught Leo's eye; they contained beautiful colour pencil illustrations of local botany and zoology, with notes in the same meticulous script as on the reference cards. There were insects – including a particularly extensive section on butterflies, birds, mammals, reptiles and amphibians, superb renderings of wildflowers, and every tree of the locale from the blackthorn to the mighty Scots pine was drawn and annotated. Leo then came across three solander boxes bearing in gold leaf the inscription: 'Greatorix Archives'. He opened one of them to find that it contained letters, genealogical papers, sketches, photographs, bills of sale, and cuttings from journals in different hands, all chronologically pasted onto the pages of large exercise books, with explanatory notes in the same neat handwriting as before. He spent half an hour scanning these, but found nothing pertaining to the slain man in the plum coat from his vision or to the hall's ghost. However, there was a brief mention in a local history book about the eighth baron Greatorix being killed, possibly by rogue Jacobite soldiers, this being the time of Bonnie Prince Charlie's rising. Leo made a mental note to mention the subject to Fordyce, then retired to his room. Humid conditions always disagreed with him, heating his blood, turning his bowels to water and wrecking his slumber. He climbed into bed, pulling only a sheet over his naked body, unaware that sleep would bring the next instalment from whichever seraph governed his metaphysical gift.

The man who was attacked by the hooded, torch-bearing thugs from his vision of the previous night is summoning him, as though a spirit guide. He is wearing the same garb, including the plum coat. He evaporates as the image transmogrifies into a wooded scene. Leo walks through aromatic dells, colourful wildflowers sprinkled through the herbage like delicate confectionary. He spies a doe in the middle distance, standing upon the ridge of a little incline, her head tilted skywards. Leo is distracted by a sound to his left and sees a red squirrel dart up a tree. He looks up again and there is a vixen where the deer was. He walks towards it, but when he gets closer it becomes a serpent gliding through the undergrowth. It disappears over the knap of the slope. He follows upwards and when he gets to the top he notices a black pond in the glade below. A beautiful mute swan sits upon its surface. Leo is distracted by the mournful call of a kite, gliding on the thermals. When he looks back towards the swan it is standing upon the pond's far bank, except it is not a swan any more, it is a female human clad in brilliant-white robes. He is distracted by the flight of a butterfly, a gorgeous purple hairstreak. He looks back at the pond. The figure now wears the garb of a Celtic warrior princess. It is Rachael.

Now blackness, and then just a simple geometric shape emerges – two white columns supporting a crossbar. Now a rustic scene, Biggnarbriggs Hall in the backdrop, Lauren beckoning him. Then she runs off across a fair meadow, laughing, before drifting into the ether. Then the shape again, set upon a blank base and against a bruising sky. From between its vertical parts emerges a hooded figure clad in black robes, looking downwards as he drags a millstone tied by a rope to his neck. Nearer and nearer he gets, the robes sodden, slimy and stinking of the deep. Slowly he raises his head. His face is featureless – just skin stretched out across a blunt trellis of bone.

Leo woke up, sweating and panting. He clicked on his bedside lamp. A moth, that perennially fretful creature, began tap-tapping at the windowpane, some secret to impart. Then, like blessed relief, the rain. Gentle at first, merely suggesting itself to the dry darkness, then a heavier, soothing drumming. Leo gulped down a glass of water, then rose and filled a tumbler with Scotch and carried it to the window. He set it on the sill, opened the curtains, and hauled up the sash to let the cooler air in. The rain hissed on the lush canopy of Scoulag Woods, slaked the parched earth, and cleared the humidity as the air reoxygenised and the summer night perfumes ascended. Leo reflected upon the vision. It had signified that Rachael was not who she appeared to be. He recalled a Gaelic word, *ilchruthach* – a 'shapeshifter' in Celtic mythology. A despondency filled his stomach as he pondered the possibility that Miss Kidd was not going to fulfil a romantic role in his life after all.

Day Three

AFTER performing his morning ablutions, Leo noticed a text message from Fordyce informing him that he and Evelyn had set off early for Kirkcudbright on a couple of errands. Leo dressed in a pair of corduroy trousers and a short-sleeved shirt, then telephoned Frederick Norvell. He felt like a prize sneak, but last night's vision and the electronic bug had put him in mind of Rachael's furtiveness at dinner two nights ago regarding her place of employment. He wanted to check that she and Frederick did indeed work at the same government office. However, when he speed-dialled his friend's landline it rang out, and Leo remembered that Frederick, who stood defiantly against mobile phones, was holidaying in France. He rang directory enquiries and placed a call with the Criminal Injuries Compensation Board, but a tetchy receptionist would not confirm or deny that they had an individual by the name of Rachael Kidd working there, citing staff confidentiality.

Leo had no appetite and breakfasted on a couple of strawberries, accompanied by a large brandy to take the rawness off the vision's aftermath. He felt keenly he had to be doing something practical to help find Lauren. The only course of action he could devise was connected to the water flowing in the near darkness from his first vision in the church in London. He could start walking the watercourses in the locality, to see if he came across some clue as to the missing girl's whereabouts. Therefore he went into the library where he spread an Ordinance Survey map upon a table-top lectern. It revealed a confounding complexity of thin, snaking blue: rivers, tributaries, burns, ponds and lochs. Westwards, in the wider forest park area where Lauren could potentially have been driven to, the extent of these went into the hundreds of miles, sometimes flowing through difficult terrain; it would take someone weeks to negotiate them all. Still, he reflected, better to make a start than to do nothing at all.

He armed himself for the morning's adventure in the countryside: walking shoes, factor 30, summer spectacles, binoculars, and a knapsack containing the map, his hip flask, his aluminium water flask, a notebook and a leftover slice of Mrs Grove's game pie which he wrapped in a piece of greaseproof paper. As he strode out of the kitchen's external door he almost collided with a woman. She was aged in her late forties and wearing a grey tabard. She seemed harassed – perhaps she was late for her duties – but her stress lines, tousled brown hair and lack of make-up could not defy a certain persisting grace that inhabited her features.

'S-sorry, so sorry, Mr Moran,' she pleaded, barely making eye contact.

On previous visits to the hall, Leo had gently admonished Claire Hannay the cleaner for not calling him by his Christian name. He remembered her as a rather servile person, someone whose body language apologised for her very presence and spoke of having been defeated by life.

'It was entirely my fault, I do beg your pardon,' he said. She made to scuttle off, but Leo continued: 'Claire, you live in the village, don't you?'

'Aye, sir.'

'Do you know the McDowall family?'

'Aye. I chat to Anthea – Mrs McDowall. She owns the café.'

'Does anyone in the village have any idea what could have happened to her poor daughter?'

'No' that I've heard.'

'Do you happen to know if Lauren has a boyfriend?'

'She wasnae going steady wi' anyone to my knowledge. She's only fifteen, mind. She might have acted older and all worldly like, but you could tell she was just a wee lassie. Quite vulnerable in her own way.'

'I wonder why that was?'

'Her father left when she was just wee and I'm gey certain it hurt her deep, like. But she was fair independent. Had to be, I suppose – she was a bit of a latchkey kid, because Anthea had to be at the café so much of the time. As she got older she began acting up: you know, fighting with her mother, looking for attention from boys and men, spending far too long beautifying herself. But she had a different side to her. I once saw her break up a fight when some lassies were bullying one of their classmates. I used to wonder if Lauren might have been bullied herself, like, and felt sorry for the girl.'

* * *

The day was already warm and the land was drying out rapidly from last night's drenching; Leo concluded that the Ken Valley was in for another humdinger. He followed Scoulag Burn uphill through the greenwood as far as a place called the Cauldron, a churning pool beneath a little cascade of waterfalls. He crossed at a footbridge there and followed the burn downstream to Loch Grenoch. He was unable to survey a full circumference of that body of water due to the marshiness of its southern margins. He noticed police vehicles at a little car park; frogmen were searching the loch's reedy depths. Leo followed Biggnar Burn to the village, sometimes having to walk on the roadside due to the bank being steep or overgrown. He then consulted his map to locate a couple of watercourses south of the forest road: Carlin's Burn, and then at its confluence a stretch of the Water of Tarb. His progress was halted by a copper, who questioned him as to his business. Turning back northwards, Leo was buzzed by a drone that presumably belonged to the police. The sun was now tyrannical, so he sat down upon a tuft on the bank of Carlin's Burn in the shade of a solitary ash, where he consumed his slice of pie and drank from his water flask. The air was intoxicating with the fragrance of meadowsweet, and even the birds' chirrups seemed indolent in the sultriness.

'What happened to you, Lauren?' Leo uttered aloud, as he watched the peaty water flow by. He felt a curious whim to identify the etymology of the burn's name, so he fiddled inexpertly with the internet function on his mobile phone (the signal was strong hereabouts due to a mast at the village) and discovered that 'Carlin' means a witch or a hag in Lowland Scots. He refilled his bottle from the stream and set off. Once he had reached the forest road again he decided to head westwards, wishing to view where Constable McLellan had said that Lauren's scent trail had ceased, presumably because she had got into a motor vehicle. However, the area was still sealed off with police tape and an officer eyed him suspiciously. Defeated, Leo headed for home.

Once he reached the meadows he came across Jimmy Handley, Chas Shaw and the Major. They were armed with shotguns, and it transpired that a pheasant hunt they had planned had been kyboshed by DCI Dalton, much to the trio's chagrin.

'It's getting too bloody hot now anyway,' complained Jimmy, before explaining that they were instead setting off for a nearby farm, Lea Rigg, to practise against clay pigeons.

'These two need to keep their eye in for when the bobbies come for them,' remarked the Major, before laughing unkindly.

'The Major thinks it's most amusing that he's the only one of us with a firm alibi for when the McDowall girl went missing,' explained Jimmy irritably, before muttering, 'quite frankly, it's nobody's damn business where I was.'

'I was at home alone and I have no one to back it up,' announced Chas mournfully. 'A guilty man would have known that he needed an alibi and constructed one, wouldn't he?'

'Whereas I, my dear friends, was in the Rose and Crown in Castle Douglas with my man Lyle,' declared the Major smugly. 'With about forty witnesses to the fact!'

Leo, irked by the man's choice of humour, said, 'It's odd – you don't strike me as a public house sort of a cove.'

'I'm a firm believer in enjoying all of life's richly varied facets,' replied the Major with a wink. 'Now we must be off. And if we see any kidnappers or perverts lurking in the undergrowth, rest assured our aim shall be true!'

A little further on, Leo noticed some police personnel using a drag at the ornamental lake. The swans stood glowering from the bank, indignant at this invasion of their space. Leo gazed at the Temple of Venus sitting upon the tiny island and wondered if its portico, the two Doric columns supporting a lintel, could have been the geometric shape that had appeared in his vision of the previous night. Unfortunately, he couldn't explore it right now because of the police presence. As he skirted the lake he considered if its gently moving surface could possibly be the flowing water from his first vision. He felt the eyes of the cops on him, so he walked off briskly towards the hall. As he approached the porch his attention was arrested by birdsong coming from nearby, the distinctive piping of the bullfinch. He caught sight of a pink flash as the creature darted upwards from a shrub and perched itself upon the high wall of the kitchen garden. He gasped in delight and raised his binoculars. It was wonderful to see the gorgeous thing in close-up, even for just a brief moment before it took off. Leo lowered his binoculars and attempted to follow the trajectory of the bird's flight. As he did so, he noticed a figure standing on the battlement of the hall's tower, wearing distinctive plum-coloured garb reminiscent of the murdered man from his visions. Leo raised his field glasses again and adjusted the focus, but the figure was gone. A prickly chill crept up his back – had he just seen the hall's legendary ghost?

Leo noticed that Fordyce's car had returned. He located Evelyn in the kitchen, snipping the stems of a dozen soft-pink Falkland roses, her three spaniels lounging near her feet. 'Pardon me, Evelyn. I wonder, is there is someone on the tower's battlement?'

'I shouldn't think so. Folk seldom go up there.'

'I just fancied that I saw a figure there a moment ago.'

'Perhaps you've just seen our phantom!'

After Leo had tracked down Fordyce, the pair had installed themselves in the drawing room. Evelyn had gone to take the flowers she had been preparing to an elderly friend, therefore the men had stripped off but for their trunks, opened the French doors and drawn the net curtains, a thin gossamer to separate their near-nakedness from the world. Music sounded from two gramophone speakers they had rigged up. Fordyce lounged upon one of the sofas, a painting of Heracles and Hylas his backdrop. Leo reclined upon a wicker chair he had lifted in from the rose salon. On the carpet between them sat two pink gins and the sleeve of the record they were listening to. It featured an *al fresco* photograph of the conductor: fedora, overcoat and scarf tossed against the Central-European chill, his face intense as he presumably pondered the profundity of Bruckner's composition. That chill contrasted with the climate in the room, and beads of sweat lolled on the friends' skin. Leo's loins felt girded up by his chess victory. He regarded the noble board. *Attacking diagonally is a thing of beauty, Leo. A thing of beauty*, old Arnstein had advised him. Leo felt smugly proud of his quick victory and was glad Fordyce hadn't reset the pieces, instead leaving them in their glorious final attitude. There had been a time when chess was Leo's life. Studying it, thinking about it, playing it. Its countless possibilities beguiled him, sparkling alluringly like the infinity of constellations draped across the night firmament. Constantly he tried to find potential opponents who had a spare few hours. One adversary, who went by the name of Aubrey Garner, had to give the game up entirely after marathon sessions with Leo placed a strain on his marriage. Looking back, Leo now realised that chess had aided his recovery from mental breakdown, because its complexity had been a diversion for his otherwise complexly malfunctioning brain. God's wonderful grace working through prosaic means.

Leo then regarded Fordyce's kindly face and felt guilty for so savouring defeating him. He reflected on his friend's many qualities, such as not giving a stuff about petty competitiveness and always looking for the best in people. 'It's easier to love,' he had recently proposed. 'And if you are gentle with others, it's easier to treat yourself with gentleness.' Gentleness. The word epitomised the man.

'It has been such a tonic for me, meeting new friends,' Leo uttered into the stale, torpid air. 'I love you very much, Fordyce.'

'Why, I love you too, Leo! Look here, I'm fed up with gin. Care for a Pimm's?'

'Rather!'

'Which number?'

'Six, if you please.'

'Something to stiffen her up?'

'Why not!'

'One vodka sling coming up.'

Fordyce busied himself with the tongs, and the lemon, orange, cucumber and mint as Leo confided in him his vision of the dark flowing water. He speculated if the small quantity of light shining upon its surface was not from the moon but instead from another source, and that the conditions were dim because of being underground or in a culvert rather than at night. Fordyce replied that there were no major subterranean watercourses or culverts known to him in the area. Leo also asked his friend about the temple on the island, mentioning the geometric shape from his vision, but was assured that it was just an innocent folly, built in the early nineteenth century.

Leo tried a different tack: 'Fordyce, do you recall that yarn you told a couple of nights ago, about the hall being haunted?'

'That's all just tommyrot.'

'It's just that earlier . . . I thought I saw someone on the tower.'

'Perhaps Brian was up there, doing some odd job.'

Leo felt sure it hadn't been Brian, and continued: 'After we played the ghost game, do you remember I said that Rachael and I were hiding in the old attic adjoining the tower, and that someone came along the corridor and turned the door handle?'

'Yes.'

'When I mentioned it, you said it wasn't you. I assume you were just pretending that it wasn't you, for a lark?'

'But it *wasn't* me, old stick. I never went along that corridor.' Leo looked vexed. 'Neither was it a bogle, dear friend. It will simply have been one of the other players.'

'You said the ghost of the hall was supposed to be some Greatorix who was murdered in the eighteenth century. I believe one of my recent visions to have been of that murder. The victim seemed like the figure I saw on the battlement, although I didn't get a good look. Do you happen to possess a portrait of your ancestor?'

'No, I'm afraid not.'

'What exactly happened to him?'

'I'm hazy on the details. He was the eighth baron, I'm sure. You could try the family archives in the library; it's bound to be described in there.'

'I already did. No luck. Although a local history book says he may have been killed by wayward Jacobite troops.'

'Yes, that rings a bell – I seem to recall Father blamed the Jacobites.'

'But the thugs in my vision didn't have the look of Highlanders.'

'Look, old stick, I'm quite convinced that much of the ghost nonsense simply stemmed from Great Uncle Hugo, who died a number of years ago.'

'Do tell.'

Fordyce fetched a framed photograph from a console table and handed it to Leo. It was of an elderly man, a distracted expression on his thin features, his kind eyes not quite focused on the camera. 'Dear Hugo was quite the eccentric. He never married, and in his later years took to living in the tower, only occasionally flitting into our existence like an apparition. He was perfectly harmless, but no wonder people mistook him for a ghost – at night he could be glimpsed on the battlement wearing his nightgown, entreating the hills with *Laudes Creaturarum*. He would converse with things – actual inanimate objects, anything from a bookend to a snuff box. He would become immersed in some hare-brained project or other. Dissections, botany – even chemistry experiments; Father was anxious he would burn the place down. It was he who compiled the family archives, and rebound and catalogued the books in the library; he had a strong compulsion to classify things. When the

Longworth trap was invented he surveyed local small mammal populations; it was excessively thorough fieldwork, and it proved of great use to naturalists. He saw Leisler's bat a decade before it was officially first recorded in Scotland. He was a talented illustrator and there are folios in the library filled with his work, depictions of flora and fauna.'

'I saw those,' said Leo. 'He was obviously a skilled and sensitive man.'

'Hugo's quirkiness was because the poor chap had been in the thick of it in the trenches. Of course, there was scant therapy at hand for that wretched generation; poor old Tommy Atkins simply had to endure having his nerves shot to pieces. It wasn't just the savagery of war that offended Hugo, it was its absurdity. In that suddenly every man born west of the Rhine and east of the Oder was a defender of virtue, while every man born east of the Rhine but west of the Oder was dehumanised as a barbarian. Now this next part is relevant to the story: Hugo went over to your lot out there.' Leo's mind glanced to the Catholic books in the library. 'He seldom spoke of the Western Front,' continued Fordyce. 'And usually if he did it was to reverently describe unfearing Irish priests inspiring their Glaswegian flock to valorous feats. Of trenches flickering the night before a push from votive lights placed at tiny shrines hollowed into the earth walls, a faint anamorphosis of heaven in the teeth of hell. Combat so exposes life's fragility that it leaves a man gazing at his pure, denuded self and longing to survive so that he might forevermore live by that sublime version of his being. Therefore when the war ended Hugo resolved to love every human he met thereafter. However, that level of benevolence requires immense fortitude, and he was so broken he needed only the sanctuary of his home; he simply wasn't going to engage with that many new people ever again. As for his faith, he kept with it until the end with the ardour of the neophyte, albeit he became more reliant on sporadic visits from clergymen for the sacraments. That is until the Nain Community was set up, near to the end of his life. When the second show kicked off it was said he took to his bed for a month, such was his despondency, but his faith kept him from falling apart completely. He lived to a good age and became quite happy, in his way. As a child Evelyn adored him, and I believe she brought some true joy to his twilight years. At one point, I considered being received into your Church because of him.'

'Why?'

'Because when I witnessed Hugo performing his devotions I was so impressed by his solemnity and centredness that it occurred to me that this was the only part of his life that wasn't heretical.'

'The Catholic man,' interjected Leo, enthralled by this discovery of Hugo's conversion, 'believes his religion challenges him to a higher, better way of living. He aspires to tenderness and piety, but also to order.'

'Well, Hugo's piety could be cause for amusement: I was told that in the months following Vatican II he fell out with the priest in Castle Douglas because he obstinately continued to call out the responses in Latin. Anyway, one day – this would have been the best part of forty years ago, when Mummy was still alive – the ghost story grew new legs. A village girl had been working here for a few months. Margaret, her name was, a nervous little creature, but she seemed happy in her work and was a natural in the kitchen. Then out of the blue her mother telephoned to say she wouldn't be back; no notice, no explanation, nothing. Mummy was mortified they had perhaps offended Margaret, so Father resolved to get to the root of it. He set off for the village and returned an hour or so later, but despite my best efforts at eavesdropping I couldn't make out what he reported to Mummy. However, eventually I gathered that Margaret, who was required to work late some evenings when we had guests, had thought she'd seen a ghost on her final night at the hall, as she was fetching her coat to go home. She was terrified and vowed never to set foot over our threshold again. One day I asked Mummy, who was an eminently practical person, about it. She said that Great Uncle Hugo was most probably abroad in the house that night and had accidentally frightened Margaret. You see, it was an Easter Sunday, and my parents had spent much of the day trying to placate a particularly restless Hugo. He'd wanted to receive Communion in Castle Douglas and for some pious reason insisted upon walking there, which was quite out of the question. But apparently the girl had proved beyond persuading by this rational explanation.'

'What did your father make of it all?'

Fordyce paused before replying. 'Well, the funny thing is, old stick, I'm not entirely sure that Father *was* all that convinced it was Hugo who Margaret had seen. And I say this because one night, not all that long before Father died, we were sipping our after-dinner coffees when my brother brought the episode up. We three siblings then sat reminiscing, chuckling about the havoc the late, great Hugo had unwittingly wreaked, but I noticed that Father wasn't joining in. And then he said, "You do all realise that the ghost legend was around long before Hugo was even born?" And my brother said, "Father, you can't seriously be giving those silly tales any credence?" And my father was quite silent. Then I enquired, and I'm not entirely sure why: "Father, did you at any point encounter this spectre?" He did not answer my question, and instead said quite abruptly, "I do wish you would all stop treating the memory of poor Hugo with such levity, and now I ask that this conversation cease." And with that he shuffled off, telling Fotheringham (we still had a butler in those days) to serve his customary Madeira wine *digestif* in the billiard room, to where he would withdraw whenever he was cross, take up his cue and maltreat the ivory. Leaving us chastised offspring meditating guiltily upon the Meissen.'

Fordyce went to fetch some more ice, and Leo yielded to a vague notion to photograph Hugo's image with his mobile phone. As he did so a voice sounded from the direction of the French doors: 'Is this nudist bar members-only, or can anyone join in?'

Leo turned round to see a grinning Maxwell Blythman, his mustard-coloured shirt swathed with perspiration. He had stepped inside, uninvited.

'Just seeking refreshment from the dog day,' replied Leo stiffly as he pulled on his dressing gown.

The internal door opened and Fordyce bounded in, his corpulent gut swinging untethered over his trunks.

'Enter David,' sneered Maxwell.

Fordyce babbled an apology and slipped on his robe, and bid Maxwell be seated. He then prepared fresh vodka slings and passed them round.

'I require some advice,' began Maxwell. 'But the nature of my purpose is a little . . . delicate.'

'You can count on our utmost confidence,' said Fordyce.

'It's about the McDowall girl.'

'A truly beautiful young woman,' said Leo distractedly. The air was stifling, and he felt a trifle light-headed.

'She was indeed,' agreed Maxwell. 'And the police want to know where everyone was – where every *man* was, the night she went missing. Perhaps they should ask Jimmy Handley if they need any clues. He's always peering through his telescope from his attic in Scarrel House, to see what's on the horizon. Anyway, the thing is . . . I have an alibi. But it could get me into hot water.'

'Go on,' coaxed Fordyce gently, as he sat serenely in his robe like a Biblical figure.

'I was with someone.'

'Oh yes? Who, old man?'

'I mean *with* someone.'

'You mean, a woman?'

'Yes.'

'And not your wife?'

'Not my wife.'

'Out with it, man,' snapped Leo.

Maxwell read the look of distaste on his interlocutor's face. 'The woman who cleans the hall.'

'You mean Claire?' gasped Fordyce.

'Yes. At her place, in the village.'

'Well, tell the police then,' said Leo drily.

'I'm a married man!'

'I'm sure they'll be discreet.'

'I can't risk giving Cynthia grounds to take me to the cleaners, if you'll pardon the expression.'

'Well, you're simply going to have to,' stated Leo. 'What time did you leave?'

'About midnight, I guess.'

'Wasn't your wife suspicious that you weren't home until late?'

'We have separate rooms. There's not much intimacy between us these days.'

'Maxwell, I think Leo is right – just tell the police the truth,' counselled Fordyce. 'All will be well.'

Maxwell seemed unimpressed and rose to leave.

'Before you go,' called Leo, 'do you remember much about the case of the disappeared girl in 1979?'

'Merely its aftermath,' replied Maxwell a little testily. 'I was in France all summer with my parents.'

'You mentioned Lauren's blossoming beauty, old stick,' said Fordyce, once Maxwell had departed. 'I imagine the police will wish to interview her contemporaries – potentially spurned boys and jealous girls.'

'I expect so,' said Leo.

'Do you believe your visions to be tied up in some way with her disappearance?'

'Yes, although Dalton doesn't want my assistance. She flatly told me to keep my beak out. I'm going to have to investigate this case entirely independently.'

'Well, if you need any help, do ask. We made quite the team at Loch Dhonn – by Jove we set the pace up there!'

'Thank you, Fordyce, I shall be sure to do so,' said Leo. However, privately he had already resolved only to involve his friend in his sleuthing, particularly its more intrusive aspects, when necessary. Fordyce and his family were respected in the parish and the county, and it was far easier for Leo to tread on toes and poke his nose in where it wasn't wanted without fear of long-term repercussions. However, the electronic bug in the aviary was a direct incursion into Fordyce's privacy, and he had a right to know about it.

'Fordyce, I wonder if the case will be mentioned on the hourly bulletin on the wireless?' said Leo.

'Indeed. Let us sally forth to the kitchen.'

The Bush radio was of a vintage such that it had presumably announced JFK's assassination, and featured overlaid splatter from oils and sauces which if analysed would evidence a half century's evolution of culinary fashions. Fordyce fiddled expertly with the wonky controls until he located Radio South West. The story was the second lead item on the update, with DCI Dalton's media statement focusing on the possibility that Lauren had entered a vehicle – perhaps voluntarily – on the forest road. Once the broadcast had ended, Fordyce clicked off the set and then noticed his friend writing in block capitals on a piece of scrap paper with one of Mrs Grove's stubby pencils. Leo held up his production, and Fordyce read:

PLEASE REMAIN SILENT. I AM CONCERNED THERE MIGHT BE LISTENING DEVICES WITHIN THIS HOUSE – I SHALL EXPLAIN ALL PRESENTLY. IS THERE ANYWHERE YOU CAN LEAD ME TO THAT IS UNLIKELY TO BE BUGGED?

Fordyce fetched two iron keys from a drawer and used one to unlock a large green door at the eastern extremity of the kitchen. He opened it, stepped through and flicked a light switch. Leo followed to find himself standing on a landing from which stairs led downwards, the walls

64

crammed higgledy-piggledy with watercolours, photographs, etchings, maps and prints.

The duo descended, and at the bottom Fordyce flicked another switch, illuminating a long, tiled corridor with a high ceiling. They marched along it, their footsteps echoing off the stone floor as Leo glanced into old stores and utility rooms.

'From when this was a great house,' said Fordyce as he gestured towards numerous servant bells.

At the end of the corridor they came to a large, disused scullery where huge items of copperware still hung on the walls.

'Evelyn dislikes the ambience in here,' said Fordyce. 'It was used as an operating theatre during the Great War, when the hall had been turned over for use as a military hospital and sanatorium. Some men died in this room, poor fellows.'

Fordyce now approached a small door, black-painted with an arched lintel. He used the other key and opened it. 'My holy of holies,' he smiled, before pulling a cord that activated an array of electric light bulbs.

Leo followed Fordyce down a few rickety wooden steps and stopped to admire rack upon rack loaded with wine bottles, which cast fantastic shadows against the brickwork. Fordyce intuitively began quarter-turning some of the bottles to shift the sediment, and Leo followed suit.

'So, here we are. What's all this dastardliness about electronic bugs?'

'Fordyce, I feel compelled to inform you that I found such a device concealed at the aviary yesterday. I didn't want to mention it at dinner in case it further upset Evelyn. God knoweth how many other such articles may be secreted around the hall.'

'By Jove! Who could have planted such a thing – and why?'

'The why I cannot yet answer. As for the who, I hate to clype, but I'm afraid to say it was Rachael.'

'Rachael!'

'I witnessed her attaching it, then sneaking off. I am fond of the woman, but I have suspected something was up with her from the night of my arrival.'

'Pray divulge.'

'She seemed evasive when I asked her about her place of employment. She didn't know my associate Frederick, who would be her superior colleague there. I'm starting to doubt if she works at the Criminal

Injuries Compensation Board at all, although I'm currently unable to check because Frederick is unreachable. Then there was something she said after DCI Dalton had visited, when we were discussing the disappearance of the girl in the seventies. You said that some people had speculated it might have been Robert Black who abducted her. And Rachael said this was unlikely because Black tended to target younger girls, yet just before that she had made out as though she had never heard of the '79 case.'

'Meaning?'

'Meaning how did Rachael know that the Bannatyne girl was a young adult, and not a little girl? No one had hitherto mentioned Hazel Bannatyne's age. Also, I should mention that Rachael appeared in a vision I had last night, which seemed to suggest that she is in some way deceptive. I wonder, Fordyce, what can you tell me about this woman?'

'Well, she began holidaying locally a number of years ago, always on her own. Then, after she bought Sannox House, we got to know her better. Inasmuch as one *can* get to know Rachael.'

'How do you mean?'

'Only that she is something of an enigma. Sociable enough but simultaneously an intensely private person, elusive as to her life past and present. As you have indicated.'

'Why on earth would she bug the aviary?'

'Why indeed. Only Jimmy spends any amount of time there. You see, the birds were really Father's passion, although he noted that Jimmy, too, got pleasure from them. Therefore it was a deathbed request that henceforth he maintain the aviary, for the sake of the tradition of the hall and for Jimmy's contentment.'

Leo nodded thoughtfully, then said, 'I wonder, Fordyce, would you be amenable to leaving the bug *in situ*, just for the time being? I left it where it was, because I do not yet wish Miss Kidd to know that we are on to her.'

'Ah, good thinking. But surely you don't think she has anything to do with all of this dreadful business regarding poor Lauren?'

'I very much doubt it. But she evidently has *something* to hide.'

'Just like old Maxwell. That was a turn-up, him confessing to a rendezvous with Claire.'

'Yes. Alibis seem to be in great currency round these parts,' said Leo. 'I encountered Jimmy, Chas and the Major earlier. Chas was complaining that he doesn't have an alibi, and because he's innocent he hadn't constructed one. Now, this could be a sign of innocence or merely a double bluff. As for Jimmy, he was convincing in his own way, angrily saying his whereabouts at the time are nobody's business. Of course, it's conceivable that Lauren dallied somewhere and was only abducted at a later time. Thus rendering Maxwell's alibi, and for that matter the Major and his manservant's, rather less copper-bottomed.'

'But for goodness' sake, Maxwell has just confessed to us *adultery*. Why would he choose a lie so shameful and potentially self-destructive to cover his tracks?'

'He may indeed be entirely guiltless of anything other than infidelity. Or, alternatively, he set up a corroborating event – I'm quite sure he wasn't lying about his liaison with Claire – with just enough of a dash of scandal about it to give his claim to innocence of a greater crime that bit more substance. He said he had come here seeking advice, but he didn't seem particularly interested in receiving any. And if he really wanted counsel about so delicate a matter, why didn't he ask to speak with you, an old friend, in private, instead of airing his dirty linen in front of me, whom he barely knows? What I mean is that he might have visited simply in order to establish his alibi, to put me off the scent. What if Maxwell, and potentially other people in the locale are aware of my powers, and would go out of their way to convince me of their innocence?'

'Look, old stick, you heard the radio news. Lauren most probably got into a vehicle on the forest road, possibly belonging to a passing stranger. And is God knows where by now.'

'Where was everyone in 1979, when the Bannatyne girl went missing?'

'Maxwell was telling the truth – he spent the whole summer in France. I remember it clearly; he didn't return until school went back in late August. And anyway, he was surely too young to be murderer material. As for the Major, he was on a tour of duty in Northern Ireland. And that I know for certain.'

'How so?'

'Because he appeared on the television news at the time. One of his men was responsible for a civilian fatality at a civil rights march. The Major had to face the cameras.'

'What about Jimmy?'

'He was here. I recall him being on the search parties.'

'And Chas?'

'Yes, he was here too. He and I were both questioned by the police at the time. As for the Nain Community, it hadn't been established yet. And you know all about Talorc's lot being nearby.' Fordyce's brow furrowed. 'Leo, after you solved poor Helen Addison's murder up at Loch Dhonn, you told me in strictest confidence that you had enjoined in . . . communications with her.'

'Yes, that is correct.'

'And this time?'

'Nothing, I'm afraid.'

Leo spent an hour entering different web search criteria into the laptop computer in the library. He tried missing persons databases, scanning tragedies that went back to the 1950s in the UK and Ireland, many of which were high-profile. He felt moved by the troubled faces staring back at him from ancient photographs the desperate families had released to the media. There was scant information about the 1979 case, and he found no record of other similar incidents in the area. He tried googling the date – 25 July – on which Hazel Bannatyne and now Lauren McDowall had gone missing, to see if it was some occult feast day, but drew a blank. Then he googled all the local people he had come across, but retrieved nothing beyond the occasional professional profile.

He decided to ring Stephanie.

'Mr Moran!'

'Good day to you, Ms Mitchell. First of all, thank you for visiting my mother, who I telephoned earlier. Second, I wish to inform you that I am now toying with the idea of being buried at sea.'

'It could be arranged.'

'Please bear in mind that on no account must my body be embalmed, or the licence will not be granted. Lastly, I wish to check that you are still planning to attend the scattering of Gilbert's ashes on the morrow.'

By coincidence, Stephanie had vaguely known Fordyce prior to his meeting Leo, on account of her being acquainted with a cousin of his who was a QC. Leo had reintroduced the pair in Glasgow not long after the case up at Loch Dhonn, and they had become friends. Stephanie had subsequently joined Leo on one of his trips to Biggnarbriggs Hall, during which she had got on famously with Gilbert, who was also visiting at the time, and with Evelyn. She had been honoured when Fordyce had invited her to pay tribute to the Irishman's memory.

'*Should* I still come? It would feel a bit weird having these – what did Fordyce call them? – "summer skylarks" after that poor girl going missing.'

'The festivities have been cancelled as a mark of respect. Only the ashes ceremony, followed by a memorial dinner, will proceed. You simply *must* come; Fordyce and Evelyn would be cheered by your company. As would I.'

'Okay, but I can only stay for the one night. I'm baw-deep in a case at the moment,' said the ribald procurator fiscal. 'In other news: Jamie and I have separated.'

'Stephanie, I'm so sorry,' Leo began. 'Jamie—'

'Leo, it's all right,' she interposed. 'Honestly.'

What she could have said was: 'I know that as my friend you are indeed sorry for what I am going through, but you needn't pretend that you don't dislike Jamie or that you didn't believe our relationship to be overly founded on rivalry and lust.' Instead, she simply added: 'I didn't want to tell you at Gilbert's funeral. It didn't feel like the right time.'

It had irked Leo the way people hailed Stephanie and Jamie as the perfect couple, as though the beautiful lawyer and the darkly handsome actor were higher beings than everyone else, rightly destined to be as one. Leo remembered the wedding. He had felt like a Victorian uncle at the funky and lavish feast: single, uptight and scathing. He recalled how a buffet had been laid out later in the evening, the *smörgåsbord* chosen by Stephanie unconsciously reflecting her social aspirations, the fish and chips selected by Jamie, consciously in tribute to his fictional working-class origins.

Leo decided to change the subject. 'Stephanie, I need your help, in a professional capacity.'

'You're not getting involved in the case, are you?'

'I have little choice.'

'More visions?'

'Indeed. Now, listen carefully. In the summer of 1979 a sixteen-year-old female by the name of Hazel Bannatyne disappeared from near here, on exactly the same day of the year as this latest girl. She was never seen again. The police suspected it might have been the work of a druidic cult which at the time was ensconced in the area. It was run by some long-dead character who called himself Talorc. Yesterday I came across evidence of pagan activity, and I wonder if there is an occult element to this recent disappearance. I wanted to find out if there are any other historical unsolved disappearances or abductions or attempted abductions in the locality. I tried the internet but came up with nothing. Perhaps one of your police contacts could do a search of their records, going even further back. The chief bobby down here won't cooperate.'

'That's a lot to ask.'

'Please, Stephanie, it's important. I think I can make a difference to this case.'

'I'll see what I can do. See you tomorrow – and try to stay out of trouble.'

Later, Leo dined with Fordyce and Evelyn. A light meal of cold chicken in aspic with potato salad followed by peach melba was all they could manage after the torrid afternoon. Evelyn mentioned that before the previous day's search party had set off, she had entreated Rachael to stay at the hall until the case of Lauren's disappearance had been solved. Leo and Fordyce exchanged a meaningful look at the mention of Rachael's name. Earlier, they had resolved not to tell Evelyn about the device at the aviary for now.

'I can't help but feel anxious about her all by herself in that house in the woods,' she concluded.

'I'm sure there's nothing to worry about, dearest sis. But, of course, she would be most welcome to stay here.'

'She wasn't for persuading,' lamented Evelyn. 'She's such an independent sort.'

'I was planning to go for a meditative stroll after dinner,' said Leo. 'If you like, I could pop by her place and try to sway her.'

'That would be most kind of you, Leo,' said Evelyn. 'Perhaps a second opinion will do the trick.'

'Sannox House can be accessed by cutting north-northwest through the woods, old stick,' explained Fordyce. 'But that way's a bit overgrown and steep. The alternative is the longer route north – up the road and then onto a single-tracker that cuts across the top of Loch Grenoch before doubling back southwards. However, that round trip is the best part of five miles.'

'I could give you a lift to the top of the loch,' proposed Evelyn, who hadn't consumed any of the Sancerre that Leo and Fordyce had enjoyed with their meal. 'I'd have to leave you there, I'm afraid; I don't like driving those single-track roads. Then you could telephone me and I'll pick you up on the main road later. Although I'm sure Rachael will convey you home, hopefully with the intention of staying here herself.'

After Evelyn had dropped him off, Leo enjoyed a saunter over a charming little bridge and along the narrow road, a sports jacket draped over his shoulder, his white shirt brilliant in the dappling light. He was flanked by a woodland of hazel, sycamore and rhododendron. Birdsong sounded cheerfully from the thickets. As he strolled he picked wildflowers, the stems of which he wove together as a nosegay for Rachael. In spite of his burgeoning reservations about the woman's behaviour he was greatly looking forward to seeing her. A police helicopter throbbed in the middle distance and Leo could hear search dogs in the forest, yet these sounds were muted by the heavy air.

At one point the land opened up. A few farmhands rested by a tractor, passing a flask and admiring the bales their labours had extracted from the difficult, humpy field. Then he saw her, up ahead, ambling in his direction. She had her hair tied back and was wearing jeans and a white crocheted cotton summer blouse, with a necklace of colourful little beads.

They greeted each other warmly, and Leo bowed slightly and presented Rachael with the posy.

'Why, thank you,' she said with a smile, before sampling the flowers' perfumes.

'Out for a stroll?' he enquired.

'Yes. It's so beautiful.'

'Beautiful,' he uttered, regarding her serenely.

There was a strange quality to the thinning light, and a pause played out between them, an easy silence but with a tangible energy abroad.

'Look at our clothes, so white they could be luminous,' she observed.

'The golden evening softens in the west. And you are quite far from home, my dear.'

'So are you.'

'I'm on a secret mission.'

'Oh, really?'

'To persuade you to stay at the hall.'

'Evelyn worries so. She thinks something evil might be loose in these woods.'

'Do it for her, to stop her fretting. And to stop me fretting.'

'I can look after myself.'

'It might be fun; there was some talk of getting the Cluedo board out.'

'I'm sorry, Leo, but if someone has abducted that poor girl, I won't be terrorised by him.'

Day Four

I T was again balmy, and the treetops were profiled sharply against the cerulean sky. Leo, Fordyce, Evelyn and the spaniels breakfasted on the terrace and lamented Rachael's refusal to accept the hall's sanctuary. Constable McLellan came by with some missing person posters and Fordyce readily agreed to put them up at certain key locations on the outskirts of the estate. McLellan informed them that they had extended their search deeper into the forest and let slip that they were now using cadaver dogs. He also reported that they had finished their dragging of the ornamental lake, and so after the breakfast things had been cleared away, Leo excused himself and strolled towards it. He located a pole in the summerhouse and then, after some fumbling with his damaged hands, managed to untie one of the punts and work his way over to where the temple of Venus was. He stepped onto the island and opened an old wooden door that was located in the portico. The circular interior was blank, with nothing of note or out of order. The smooth stonework of the floor and the curving brick wall seemed perfectly solid. Leo then circumnavigated the tiny island itself, and found nothing of interest.

Having punted back, tethered the vessel and repatriated the pole, Leo walked in the direction of where Chas lived, in order to get an update on the repair of his Humber Hawk. He heard sounds of industry coming from the old stables behind the gatehouse, and there discovered Chas and Brian at work on the vehicle. Alongside it was parked Chas's restored Ford Sierra RS500 Cosworth in gleaming silver, and a 4x4 vehicle that belonged to the estate. Unity was also there, updating her husband on some domestic matter. Leo noted the way Brian merely continued tinkering under the bonnet as she addressed him, almost disregarding her presence. Unity left, smiling at Leo as she passed by. Leo called out a greeting to the men, and Nero began growling at him menacingly, but was silenced by an abrupt command from his owner. Chas then grinned at Leo, his eyes inscrutable behind aviators. What was this, considered Leo: mockery, amusement, sincere pleasantness? What do your *instincts* tell you?

'Howdy, Pilgrim,' said Chas. 'We ground the carbon off number two cylinder's valve. A fucker of a job it was. This vehicle's a nice museum piece, but for everyday driving you should think about getting a new one. I mean, there are classics, and there are classics.' He exchanged a smirk with Brian and then lit a cigarette.

'This car is a prime example of British workmanship. And it has sentimental attachments,' replied Leo, pretending not to be irked by the jibe and resenting Chas's presumption of using coarse language when addressing him.

Leo paid him for the job. The smell of fag smoke was obscene in the gathering heat. He regarded Chas as he departed: his gait consciously purposeful, a man's man, a fellow entirely at ease with his place in the world.

Brian continued tinkering.

'I was sorry to hear the police saw fit to take you in.'

'Over and done wi' now. Hopefully.'

'What did Dalton ask you at your interview?' ventured Leo.

'Och, nothing too interesting. "Did you and Donald Kennedy abduct and murder Lauren McDowall?"'

'Did you see Lauren, on your way to pick up Donald?'

'No. But I was driving, concentrating on the road. Anyway, I think the cops are easing off the idea that me and Donald had anything to do with it.'

'Why?'

'First of all, we're no' credible suspects . . . I mean to say, *Donald Kennedy* – you couldnae meet a nicer man. Secondly, I got clocked by a speed camera on the A75 near Newton Stewart. Donald's always telling me to slow down, but I like to open my beauty up a little. Anyway, it places and timestamps my car in the right place and direction of travel to concur wi' where we said we were going. Without allowing any time to, for example, bury a body. Now that alone doesnae get us in the clear, but the photo only has two figures in it. Dalton says we could have had the lassie stashed in the boot, but she's had a full forensic testing done on my car – which I didnae mysteriously have valeted or anything – and they've given me it back, wi' no' a trace. Also, Donald and me were swabbed and we handed over our clothing, which will also have come back clear of any trace of yon poor lassie.'

'That must be a relief. I wonder, could your wife have seen anything out of the ordinary of late, perhaps even on the night Lauren went missing?' enquired Leo, even though he had already heard Unity answer a similar question when DCI Dalton had first called at the hall.

'She was at hame watching the kids,' spat Brian, suddenly resentful of Leo's questioning. He closed the bonnet with a slam and wiped his oily hands on a rag. 'Now, turn the engine over and then take her out for a run. She should purr like a kitten now.'

Leo drove aimlessly through the bonny sunlit countryside, for once enjoying the simple pleasure of motoring. Chas and Brian had evidently done a sound job because the old Humber engine chattered away cheerfully, the pistons running smoothly. A distant blue hill with a long-sloping shoulder – which a local could have told Leo went by the name of Criffel and was visible from much of this part of southern Galloway – was his backdrop. At one point, he found himself puttering along King Street in Castle Douglas and he happened to notice the shop front for the *Kirkcudbrightshire Reformer*, a good-quality weekly title. On an impulse, he parked up and strolled inside, and asked a pretty young blonde woman on the front desk if he could speak with the editor about the case of the missing girl. The woman made a telephone call and there soon arrived a jaunty man aged in his later fifties, who was of diminutive stature and had a large, balding head and keen dark eyes. He wore a crumpled white shirt with its top button undone and his necktie was askew. He introduced himself as the editor, Des Fitzgerald. Leo, heartened at the small-town informality, found himself being escorted into the back office, complete with an actual traditional spike upon which to impale processed copy. There was an ambience of heightened activity on account of Lauren's disappearance. In response to a general conversational enquiry, Fitzgerald explained in rapid-fire speech the importance of local press speaking truth to power at micro-level within a healthy democracy, and lamented the increasing centralisation of regional newspaper production. 'Even subs should know the lie of the local land,' the little man concluded.

They sat down on either side of the desk in the editor's glass-walled cubicle. A framed front page announced the 1918 Armistice, while another described a visit to the county by Queen Victoria.

Leo explained that he was a friend of the Greatorixes and was staying up at the hall, and that he happened to be a private investigator who had helped the police with their inquiries before. He had heard about the case of Hazel Bannatyne who went missing in 1979 from the same area on the same day of the year as Lauren.

'Ah yes, a sad case, sad, sad, sad,' lamented Fitzgerald. 'Never found her. I remember it well – I shadowed old Ronnie Jardine on it. He's long dead now, God rest him. I'm the only one of the old school left. Ronnie did most of his digging down the local hostelries – but he got results, he sure got results. But there were no leads in that case, none at all. Wish I had a newshound like him on this story.'

'I expect it's keeping you busy?'

Fitzgerald's desk telephone rang and he signalled an apology to Leo as he gave his interlocutor a series of precise instructions in his fast-paced delivery regarding the reportage of a sheriff court case. He hung up abruptly and immediately refocused his attention on Leo, who felt he didn't want to encroach on the man's precious time for any longer than was absolutely necessary.

'I just wondered if the two cases might be connected,' he said.

'Doubt it; it's far too long ago.'

'Would you consider running a story about the '79 case? It might trigger a reader's memory of something important.'

Fitzgerald sucked his teeth, and then signalled through the glass with his fingers to someone positioned behind Leo that he would be available in two minutes. 'I don't think so. The trouble is, Mr Moran, I don't want to throw a red herring into our readers' minds. Apart from anything else, the police wouldn't appreciate it. They want the media's output to reflect their main lines of inquiry. It's at times like this that the local papers should in fact stand with the powers that be, in order to be of assistance.'

He signalled again over Leo's shoulder.

'I understand,' said Leo. 'I wonder, would it be possible for me to view your newspaper's archives from 1979, and any files on the story you might still have in your possession?'

Fitzgerald didn't answer directly, and instead picked up the phone and dialled an internal number. 'Iona, can you take Mr Moran down to the library and direct him to the bound volume for the summer of 1979. And show him any other files he wants to see.'

With that Fitzgerald rose and shook Leo's hand.

Iona was the young woman from the front desk, and she arrived and led Leo further into the building and down a flight of stairs into a quiet, windowless room. Upon several rows of racks sat massive volumes of previous editions of the *Reformer*, and Leo helped Iona to haul the relevant one onto a huge table, appreciating the way she pretended not to notice his gnarled hands. While he found the appropriate page at which to start, she began noisily opening and closing old grey filing-cabinet drawers.

'We don't tend to keep journalists' files from that far back. Oh, but hang on, you're in luck,' she said, handing a manila folder to Leo marked 'HAZEL BANNATYNE DISAPPEARANCE'.

Iona had to get back to manning the front desk, and so, in a demonstration of rural trustingness that amazed Leo, left him alone to browse. He spent over an hour turning page after page, and reading several articles regarding the case. Eventually, these evolved into down-page pieces, then wings, then shorts, then nibs. They elucidated little of interest in terms of fresh, hard facts, apart from the statement that the girl was last seen (by an elderly woman who happened to glance out of her cottage window) at the village crossroads, walking in a westward direction. From there she could have continued along the forest road, or entered the countryside north or south of it, or even doubled back and gone elsewhere. Of course, she could also have been abducted moments after the last witness saw her. The folder was similarly meagre, and contained mostly typed translations of reporters' shorthand notes, the salient points of which Leo had already read in the newspapers. One item did catch his attention, but more from a human-interest point of view. It was a reprint of a family photograph of the Bannatynes; the image of Hazel, a blonde-haired girl of some considerable beauty, was squared off in pen, obviously the source of the headshot Leo had seen several times in the old editions. There was something familiar about the disappeared girl's sister, who was aged about eleven, and on a whim Leo photographed the whole image with his mobile phone, before putting the volume and the folder back in their places, thanking Mr Fitzgerald and Iona, and leaving the building.

Leo drove back to the hall to find Evelyn and Fordyce greeting Stephanie, who had just disembarked from her Monterey Blue Nissan 370z. Leo parked the Humber, got out and embraced his friend. She popped her Ray-Bans onto her brow, her green eyes sparkling as she smiled effusively. Leo wondered if she had had her teeth whitened, and mused that every time he met her she seemed to have a different hairdo – today's variation was at the blonder end of her wide tonal spectrum. She looked glamorous with her denim dungaree dress accentuating her petite, gym-toned body and suntanned skin. The men carried her Burberry luggage inside while she chatted excitedly with Evelyn in her sexy, slightly husky voice. The Greatorixes installed Stephanie in the lavender room and left her and Leo alone. He noticed that she was not wearing her wedding ring.

'So. You left him.'

'Happy now?'

'For pity's sake, Stephanie.'

'I'm sorry. I need to stop taking it out on other people.' She walked to the window and gazed at the summer sky. 'Leo, some time ago I spoke in a TV discussion, defending the use of pornography. Afterwards, you criticised me for it.'

'Look, Steph, I don't want to fall out—'

'No, please hear me out. When I defended myself, you described an element of Jamie's and my relationship, our . . . lustfulness . . . as a kind of sickness.'

'I'd had a drink, I was being judgemental. Why cast that up now?'

'The reason I'm bringing it up is to tell you that you were *right*. I've thought about it a lot recently, and also about how there was too much competition between Jamie and me, too much ego, and – on both sides – too many unreasonable demands.'

Leo walked towards her and squeezed her shoulder. 'You do know that I care about you awfully, old girl,' he said gently.

She turned to face him and pecked him on the cheek, then changed the subject to Leo's request of the previous day. 'My Deep Throat at the police says there are no unsolved disappearances in this area since the Bannatyne case or for twenty years before it. He said it is unlikely a local serial killer would leave a gap as long as from then until the present day. He found no record of attempted abductions either. He said that the trouble with the Bannatyne case is that there is so little to go on. The girl just disappeared. There was no evidence or *modus operandi* with which to cross-reference it and link it with other cases or perps.'

'Well, thanks for trying, Stephanie,' said Leo with a sigh. 'I wonder if this place will ever give up its secrets.'

The scattering of the ashes took place after luncheon, at Loch Quien. This location was specified in Gilbert's last will and testament; he had spent many happy days fishing there. A little convoy of motor cars set off from the hall conveying Leo, Fordyce, Evelyn, Stephanie, Brian, Unity, Maxwell, Cynthia, Jimmy, Donald and Father Larranzar to the loch. Sadly, Gilbert's sisters were too frail to contemplate making the journey to Scotland.

'Is the Major not coming?' Leo asked Fordyce as they passed the gates to Maidenhead House, flanked by masses of rhododendron and above which towered an impressive monkey puzzle tree.

'I'm afraid not. He and Gilbert never quite saw eye to eye. Nonetheless, I thought he might have made the effort.'

The police had by now reopened the forest road which ploughed through cheerful glades. The branches formed a botanical vault, the foliage beautifully illuminated by the sun, abundant leafage spilling over drystane walls. After a while they turned off to drive a couple of hundred yards up a track, and then parked at a grassy lay-by near a white-painted house. Rachael had arrived from a different direction and was waiting for them there, leaning against her Mini Countryman, the windscreen of which had been turned into a lozenge of brilliant white light by the sun. Leo felt a thrill of elation when she smiled at him, but a sombreness descended on the group, and after Fordyce's initial instructions everyone walked on in silence. They traversed some glossy turf which smelled of mown clover, then climbed a stile and alighted in a broad stretch of blanket bog. The warm wind picked up, providing the solemn procession with a dose of atmosphere.

There were some dilapidated little boathouses and jetties along the loch's bank, and Fordyce stopped by a hut with a pier, explaining that it was Gilbert's favourite spot. He then made a moving tribute to his late friend, elucidating some of his many qualities and dropping in a couple of amusing anecdotes that gave the congregants some welcome light relief. Fordyce then asked everyone to bow their heads, unscrewed the lid of the lead urn he had been carrying, and shook Gilbert's remains out over the sparkling blue water.

Father Larranzar was next up. He donned his stole and led the prayers and blessings, using a thurible which Donald had helped him fire up. He then armed himself with an aspergillum and sprinkled holy water over the loch's blue surface and the mourners.

Then Unity, who was wearing a crown of moon daisies and looked almost transcendentally beautiful in a simple white calico dress, distributed candles which were duly lit, and stepped onto the decking to disperse rose petals upon the water. Making grandiose gestures, she uttered certain melodramatic pronouncements about the loch providing the forest's lifeblood, and entreating the guardian of the water to welcome Gilbert's spirit. Leo happened to be standing beside Brian, and thought he heard him sigh despairingly at his wife's performance.

It was all a bit too pagan for Leo, and on the way back to the cars he engaged Father Larranzar in conversation about what he saw as 'a feeble sort of obsequies'.

'I didn't know Unity was going to do that,' said the friar. 'However, Gilbert wasn't a big church man, Leo.'

'I thought the Vatican disapproved of these scatterings as pantheistic or naturalistic,' complained Leo a touch hypocritically given his recent fetish for leftfield forms of funerals.

'I don't particularly approve myself, but it was Gilbert's wish and I'd rather be here giving Christian blessing than sulking at home in the Community.' Larranzar laughed good-naturedly and added: 'Goodness, Leo, *I'm* the priest. Am I not the one who is meant to get vexed about canon law and orthodoxy?'

'I just find Unity's nature magic a touch tawdry.'

'Perhaps she experiences God in her own way. Sees Him in the natural world, hears the symphony of the Holy Spirit in the silence. Heaven forfend that Christ would refuse such a gentle creature.'

'Surely if Unity gives tribute to a god unknown then it is a false god, and *ergo* a potential for evil? The truth is, Father, I have noticed pagan imagery hereabouts of late. I'm worried that it might in some way be connected to the case of this missing girl. Not that I'm accusing Unity, of course.'

'I hear your concerns,' said Larranzar. 'But know that the Church used to distinguish between white and black magic, until the hysterical witch-burning one-upmanship that followed the Reformation.'

Leo decided to let the matter rest for the time being. 'Will you be joining us for the memorial dinner this evening, Father?'

'I'm afraid myself and Donald have a longstanding engagement in Ayr, a meal for clergy and certain laypeople hosted by the bishop.' He winked at Leo and added, 'I would never tell His Grace, but I'd sooner be feasting at the hall with you lot than discussing ecclesiastical matters!'

Having returned to Biggnarbriggs Hall after the ceremony, Leo, along with the other incumbents, felt the need for a nap. Perhaps the sorrowful nature of their outing had emotionally exhausted them all. Upon waking in the late afternoon, he found the place still silent and decided to stroll to the village pub, the Green Man, an institution he had never before visited. He wanted to check out the local characters, and he might even overhear a piece of gossip that could help direct his investigations into Lauren's disappearance.

He walked down the road to the village, the canopy and the gentle summer breeze softening the effects of the sun. The treetops billowed slightly, impossibly green and lush against the vivid ultramarine summer sky. To his right, the water of Biggnar Burn sparkled and danced over a mottled bed of polished stones. '"Glory be to God for dappled things!"' quoted Leo aloud. He entered the village, a comely place consisting chiefly of white cottages built around a crossroads with an old red GPO telephone box and pillar box. The road snaked a little and at one point it was skirted by quaint stone walls as it spanned the burn which had meandered eastwards, this being the bridge from which the village took its name.

The Green Man was the last building as one headed westwards out of Biggnarbriggs village along the forest road. It was a pleasant, low-roofed affair with white harling on its exterior walls. Leo entered and was presented with a cosy room with a large bar facing him and a charming fireplace to his left. Regimental emblems were pinned to the gantry, and other militaria decorated the pillars and walls. Old brass bugles dangled from the rafters, and a pair of blunderbuss pistols were perched on the mantelpiece. Leo took a moment to survey a couple of glass cases – one displaying a variety of bullets with their calibres and manufacturers detailed, the other containing different gauges of shotgun shells. He then approached the bar, conscious that the dozen or so male patrons were eyeing him, and ordered a pint of 70 shilling. He noted the blackboard, surprised at the exotic fare on offer at a humble country tavern. He attempted to make conversation with the landlord but received only cursory responses. He was a man aged around sixty with a bushy moustache to make up for his skull, which was shaved as smooth as a pumpkin. He had one of those West of Scotland brogues that rolled the vowels and softened the consonants due to its owner having lived for a prolonged period in the South East of England.

Leo installed himself at a table by the window, from where he could surreptitiously survey the punters. He recognised some faces from the search party. Several of the drinkers had accents from across the border, and Leo wondered if they concealed a sense of inadequacy with their laconic, monotone remarks about golf and rugby and damnable bus lanes and petrol prices and where best to exceed the national speed limit without being detected. They were bland men, bar-room bores, closet-Tories most probably, but intelligent enough to possess some glimmer of self-awareness that they were indeed buffoons. Leo detected an atmosphere of unfriendliness towards himself, and indeed some of the patrons slunk off during his brief stay. Perhaps he was being unfair; this was just a village pub, its brethren no doubt closed in on themselves at a time of crisis. Or perhaps his instinct was sensing something deeper.

Leo relaxed somewhat when a holidaying family came in and sat at the table beside him, glad of their unselfconscious West Midlands babble as they teased the father about the predictability of his menu choice. Leo supped up his pint and rose to leave, pleased that his friendly nod towards the Brummie dad was reciprocated.

On a whim, Leo decided to examine Linn Priory more closely, and he headed up the forest road. It occurred to him how he had been satisfied to consume just one jar in the pub, with no chaser, despite his inner troubles. Perhaps the thought of Rachael, shapeshifter or not, was now subconsciously moderating his usual rate of consumption.

He turned up the avenue of trees, and then cut through two belts of timber to the hidden meadow, which was fragrant with grass pollen, daisies, buttercups and cornflowers, and busy with bees. The crags leading up to the red sandstone ruins were sparsely covered in sun-goldened grass, and a few yards to the priory's north was a stand of ragged but lordly Scots pines; profiled against the electric-blue horizon, they were somehow evocative of Greece or the Holy Land. Leo ascended, and paused to look back and take in the view of the hidden meadow and beyond, where the parkland, its gentle ridges embroidered with tracts of mature trees, undulated harmoniously towards the ornamental lake and then the great hall itself, nestling serenely by the distant greenwood. Then he regarded the priory in close-up, its shadows cast on the flowering gorse and heather. The way the sun glowed through the ruins and softly lit the surrounding idyll put him in mind of the paintings of Samuel Palmer.

A plinth gave perfunctory details of the place's history. The Cistercian priory had been founded in 1190 by William the Lion, and its official title was the Priory of Our Lady and Saint Bride. It had been a daughter house to Dundrennan Abbey, which sat twelve miles or so south, and had been dissolved in 1588. Leo guessed that because of its obscure location, Linn Priory had been largely forgotten by the modern world. The dormitory was the best-preserved part; the only decent remnants of the chapel were the sacristy walls, and some good arches of the north transept with stone stumps of corbels and vault ribs incorporating interesting carvings of fruit and foliage.

Seventy yards or so from the ruins, Leo found a scattering of gravestones, some ancient and anonymous, most post-Reformation and inscribed with lofty sentiments. A cluster, including Great Uncle Hugo's with its distinctly Catholic character, immortalised Greatorix grandees. Another stone stood a way off from the others, and Leo stopped to inspect it. It was unmistakeably eighteenth-century, and curiously, it bore no name; only a heraldic winged lion and a year of death.

He returned by the way he had come, shrill house martins now manically tending to the eaves of the cottages in the village. The fierce day was surrendering to soft eventide as Leo traversed the road back to the hall.

Having dressed for dinner, Leo accompanied Stephanie to the drawing room where the guests were to gather for *apéritifs*. Privately, Leo felt proud of the very unlikeliness of his friendship with the fiscal, considering their differing worldviews and temperaments. Perhaps it was their mutual cleverness that drew them together. Fordyce, Maxwell, Cynthia and Rachael had already arrived, and then Jimmy appeared, having been out enjoying the aviary. Evelyn was helping Unity and Mrs Grove with the final preparations for the meal. The Major soon turned up and it struck Leo that he seemed happy enough to attend the more festive functions of remembrance. None of the guests, apart from Leo and Stephanie, were staying over at the hall that night, and apparently Chas was on taxi duties. Rachael wore an elegant dark-blue chiffon evening gown with an agate brooch, her chestnut hair to one side. Leo ached to gaze at her but didn't want to make her feel uncomfortable. The other ladies looked spectacular, glittering with sequins. Leo properly introduced Rachael to Stephanie, overemphasising the platonic nature of his relationship with the latter. He then introduced Stephanie to the Blythmans, and Cynthia remarked cattily, 'I saw your car parked outside. I had one of them, but in white. I thought the blue a tad garish.'

The dining table was beautifully dressed for the meal, and Evelyn had placed a framed photograph of Gilbert on a little stand near the door. Fordyce proposed the toast and Mrs Grove, who had been fond of the genial Irishman, honoured his memory with a menu of his favourites: Oscietra caviar, followed by oxtail soup with soda bread, trout caught from Loch Quien, fillet steak and a dessert of cabinet pudding with custard.

The first two courses were properly dominated by anecdotes about and tributes to Gilbert, but Leo knew he had to risk bad form by steering the conversation onto the strange goings-on of late, hoping that he might elicit something of interest. He deliberately chose his moment while Unity was serving nearby.

'I came across the queerest thing the other day,' he began, 'in the woods just north of here, near to the standing stones. There is a hawthorn tree in a glade with a natural well beside it. And the funny thing was, it had coloured ribbons hanging from its branches and coins embedded in its bark.'

'I already told you when I saw you up there,' said Cynthia. 'It's a clootie tree.'

'I don't suppose anyone knows who could have decorated it?' enquired Leo.

No one did, but Jimmy speculated: 'It was probably members of the local yeomanry, well fortified by a gallon of ale in each of their bellies, up to high jinks.'

'I hope a new cult hasn't sprung up,' said Evelyn.

'Talorc is long dead,' said Fordyce reassuringly. 'He surrounded himself with victims and sycophants – there was no obvious successor.'

Leo commented: 'The Belgian writer Émile Cammaerts inferred from the work of G.K. Chesterton a famous observation about our times: "The first effect of not believing in God is to believe in anything."'

Unity then spoke up: 'A wish tree is a beautiful, innocent old tradition. I'm certain whoever is responsible meant no harm.'

Cynthia, who looked affronted that the hired help had dared to speak, said to Leo, 'If you're concerned about it, can't you use your magic powers to find out who did it? Come to mention it, you could save the police a job by solving this missing person case. Is it true what they say about you, that you possess second sight?'

There was an awkward pause, before Leo said politely, 'I'm sure the extent of my talents are greatly oversold.'

Cynthia said, 'Do you know, the police even asked *me* where I was on the evening the McDowall girl went missing!'

'And where *were* you, darling,' asked Maxwell churlishly.

'Out riding at the other side of the parish,' she replied. Maxwell harrumphed. 'A fact to which I have several witnesses,' said Cynthia, glaring at her husband. Maxwell spluttered in faux laughter. 'I am refer-ring to people who saw me pass by.' Then she added sneeringly, 'Anyway, if the police want a suspect they should have a chat with Lauren's peers. I hear she was really *quite* the girl.'

'In what way is that relevant?' enquired Rachael.

'Only, my dear, that I'm sure she has offended a great many of them.'

'A young nympho, eh?' interjected the Major with a bang on the table. He had been greedily quaffing the Château Canon-la-Gaffelière. 'By God, I used to love a roll in the hay with a local scrubber!'

'Major, *please*,' implored Fordyce. 'There are ladies present.'

The Major, who was sitting to Leo's right, said conspiratorially to him in a low voice, 'What do you say, old boy? I remember my father took me up to a brothel in Jo'burg when I was fifteen – a high-class establishment, of course. Told me to fill my boots. I sampled every race of womanhood that night.' He lowered his voice even further. 'I bet the late baron wishes he'd done the same for Fordyce.'

Leo suspected that the Major was one of those tiresome characters who would make outrageous statements to cause a stir under the pretext of harpooning the sutras of political correctness. Generally, he found that the best policy was to ignore such histrionics.

Leo said to the company, 'I know nothing about the McDowall girl, but in general terms I do feel we need to provide our young people with a better example. What happened to innocence, restraint, chasteness, decency, faithfulness? People are afraid to speak up for these Christian values any more. We are reaping the whirlwind of sexual revolution. We adults have let down our little ones by putting ourselves first, failing to show a good example and justifying our selfishness via convenient, miserable systems of moral relativism.'

'I think you are canvassing for repression, darling,' said Cynthia loftily. 'I for one am delighted that we live in a more liberated age.'

'I bet you are,' muttered Maxwell.

'Is this liberation or enslavement to one's lower appetites?' proposed Leo, who was beginning to regret this digression. Rachael was sitting along to his left, and he was suddenly anxious that she might take him for a complete square, but he resolved to finish his point. 'Does it fulfil us or debase us and corrode our true self?'

'And what of gay people in your restrained world – are they all to march merrily back into the closet?' enquired Cynthia.

Leo was silent with embarrassment and stole a glance at Fordyce, who was studiously gazing at his cutlery. In truth, Leo was stumped; his argument was regularly beaten by this, and it was an issue – his Church's view of homosexual acts – that had troubled him recently. Yet Britain abounded with people like Cynthia who thought that by declaring themselves free of hatred against gay people or ethnic minorities it somehow rendered them paragons of virtue, when often their personal politics accommodated rampant materialism, sexual dissolution and an unthinking submission to instinctive selfishness.

At last, he said quietly, 'Perhaps the Christian revelation is still at a relatively early stage. I take the position of *mutatis mutandis*. Which means, broadly speaking, that we ought only to change the things that ought to be changed, and nothing else.'

'I *know* what it means,' lied Cynthia, irked by what she wrongly perceived as Leo's attempt to bamboozle her with classical phraseology.

'Religion makes me a better person,' continued Leo. 'I mean that at its most primitive level it is a deterrent from my giving into my every self-indulgent impulse. What I would be without it – what I *was* before it – I dread to contemplate.'

'You were always a good man, Leo,' said Stephanie gently.

'I would dispute that,' he responded.

'And what about reason?' said Jimmy.

'David Hume famously said that "reason is the slave of the passions",' replied Leo.

'And do you *ever* give into your passions?' enquired Cynthia.

'I didn't say that religion made me perfect. I am a sinner. The teachings of my Catholic faith enable me to recognise the fact that sometimes I will stray.'

'Do you know, I was almost court-martialled because of one of your priests?' interjected the Major drunkenly. 'There was this protest gathering in Belfast, in '79. Ballymonagh, to be precise. We used baton rounds. Supposed to bounce them off the ground, but one of our chaps gave it to this Romanist padre directly in the neck and he died. Next thing you know, yours truly is up against it, but I damn well always backed my men.'

Leo remembered types such as the Major addressing television cameras in Northern Ireland during the 1970s: olive-clad, stone-eyed men with Sandhurst accents trying to justify the behaviour of rogue squaddies.

'I told my colonel that very summer that the Micks needed to know who was boss, and I was proven right after what happened at Mullaghmore,' the Major blustered on. 'Told him they should have given the shooter the bloody MC, if they asked me. And let me tell you this: the next time that Larranzar fellow trespasses, I'll shoot straight for *his* blasted collar. And it won't be a plastic round, either.'

There was an excruciating silence. Fordyce would have spoken up to censure the Major, but in truth he was rendered mute by this last comment. Judging by her expression, only Cynthia seemed amused by the controversy.

Leo felt his late father's eyes on him. *Let it slide, son. Choose your battles carefully; this man is not worth showing yourself up for.* He took a moment to compose himself, and then said, 'Fordyce and Evelyn, I'd like to thank you both for this beautiful food and to apologise, but I feel I must take my leave.'

'Don't be like that, old boy,' said the Major. 'You must understand that back then we were at *war!* And not just against the Provos – there was also the enemy within. The Russians had cells in the unions, the Labour Party. The miners brought down the ruddy government. There were price controls, wages policies, ninety-eight per cent tax rates; a socialist state in all but name. The country was *finished*. You do know what happened at Heathrow in '74? I was there, and let me assure you, we weren't just serving the bastards a message – it was a dry run.'

Leo indeed knew to what the Major was referring: the unscheduled military operation at the airport that some had since speculated was an aborted *coup d'état* against the Wilson Government.

'If it had been up to me, I'd have gone the whole hog that very day and seized power,' continued the Major. 'Luckily, we did't have too long to wait until the Lady got in.'

Something extraordinary then happened. Evelyn rose and departed, leaving the connecting door wide open. A few moments later, some introductory notes sounded from the drawing room's burr walnut John Broadwood upright piano. Fordyce then got to his feet, brandishing his napkin somewhat foppishly before launching into the vocals of '*Largo al factotum*' from The Barber of Seville with considerable aplomb.

'*Figaro ... Figaro ... Figaro ... Figaro ... Figaro ...*
Figaro ... Figaro ... Figaro ... Figaro ... Figaro!
Ahimè che furia!
Ahimè, che folla!'

Leo was struck by the quality of his friend's amateur operatics, which, typical of the man, he had until now kept within his own breast. The impromptu performance reached its climax:

'*Sono il factotum della città,*
Sono il factotum della città,
della città, della città,
Della città!'

Fordyce finished with a flourish of his napkin to rapturous applause, having dispelled the frightful ambience of the Major's rant. Leo felt disappointed at Fordyce's choice of guest, but he knew the reason for it: sentimentality. The Major had been a friend of Fordyce's father, although

Leo now wondered if the old boy had merely tolerated his neighbour rather than actually liking him.

The guests now chattered away excitedly, and, as though reading his thoughts, Fordyce murmured in Leo's left ear, 'Look here, old stick, I know the Major can be a bit of a goose, but the truth is, somehow having him here brings back memories of Father.'

'There's no need to explain, Fordyce.'

After the coffee and mints had been served, Evelyn mused nostalgically: 'In Daddy's day, the gentlemen would retire to the drawing room or the billiard room after dinner to smoke, the ladies to the rose salon.'

'Yet on a balmy evening such as tonight, dearest sis, we shall take our *digestifs* on the terrace,' said Fordyce.

Leo watched Rachael standing at the balustrade. The air was as heady as wine. She caught his gaze, then walked down the steps towards the lawn. In a trance, he followed her to the topiary where she took her rightful place among the lithe figures from antiquity, the swirling sunset her glorious backcloth. He could hear the gentle water from where the stone Neptune was attended by his nymphs. She turned to face him, smiling puckishly. A fragment of Verlaine came into his mind: . . . *the fountains sobbing in ecstasy, The tall slender fountains among marble statues.*

Then Maxwell broke the spell. 'Off for a stroll? Mind if I impose – I need to get away from that bloody wife of mine.'

By the time he had extricated himself from Maxwell's company the moment with Rachael had passed, and a deflated Leo said his good-nights and retired to his bedroom. He performed his ablutions and donned his silk Paisley-patterned pyjamas and his dressing gown. He was about to put out his lamp when he heard a light tapping at his door. Excitedly, he strode over to open it.

'Don't look so disappointed,' said Stephanie.

She entered, poured them whiskies from the decanter, and then sat down. Leo slumped on the bed.

'Just wanted to check you were all right,' she said.

'Was the evening *that* dreadful?'

'Well, apart from that awful Blythman woman's incessant bitchiness, and the Major being somewhere to the right of Vlad the Impaler, and him, Jimmy and that creep Maxwell constantly leering at my cleavage, it was absolutely peachy.'

'Fordyce is a lovely, benevolent man, but it is precisely his amiability that can be his weakness. He's not discerning enough.'

'Totally. And why waste spending precious social time with arseholes when the majority of people in the world are cool.'

'Do you really think they are? How many people – percentage wise – would hand a mobile telephone they had found into the nearest police station?'

'A guy once handed me mine when he saw I'd left it on a table in a bar.'

'He probably wanted to get into your silken drawers. I beg your pardon, Stephanie – that was a vulgar thing to say. It's just that . . . when you have my powers, see the things I see, you tend to think the worst of mankind.'

'So, do you want to tell me what all that moralising was about?'

Leo pinched his temples and sighed. 'Could I have sounded any *more* like a maiden aunt? I guess I'm just expressing my disgust with societal permissiveness, which provided the no-doubt sordid context to poor Lauren's disappearance.'

Stephanie was glad to be able to steer the conversation onto something more substantial.

'What about the little hippie, Unity, and her pagan sympathies – could she fit into your theory of an occult angle?'

'She might well have decorated that tree but I doubt very much that she's a sociopath. However, I have to keep an open mind. She thinks she's got second sight, that she and I are birds of a feather, but she is merely a dabbler.'

'Ah, professional rivalry!'

'No, as I said: she is merely a dabbler.'

'You said on the phone that the cops down here won't cooperate with you?'

'Indeed. Which is a pity, because I'd love to firm up Cynthia's alibi. Did you notice how spiteful she sounded when she spoke of Lauren?'

'She's ghastly. Probably envied the girl her youth, now that her own beauty is fading.'

'There's a sexual coarseness about such upper-middle-class women that I find a tad jarring. I'm fairly certain she's involved in some adulterous intrigue with Jimmy.'

'I think you might be right there. Perhaps her husband or her lover was sniffing around Lauren, and she got jealous. She won't die wondering, will old Cruella.'

'Cynthia.'

'I'm calling her Cruella. I vaguely recognise her, a loudmouth shopper at Frasers, floating around as if she owned the place.'

Leo paused to take a sip of whisky, then lounged on his left side, in order that he could view his friend's facial reactions. 'Anyway . . . what about Rachael? What do you think of *her*?'

'You like her, don't you?'

Silence.

'You should discuss your feelings more openly.'

'I'm not a bloody American. What do *you* think of her?'

'She's nice,' replied Stephanie, surprised that she had to quell an obscure sense of envy. It was indeed notable, she considered, for her friend to be on the cusp of romance while she was uncharacteristically single. 'Except she isn't called Rachael.'

'What on God's green earth are you havering about?'

'I couldn't recall who she was until during dessert, and then it came to me. Her name's Elaine. She's a private investigator.'

'She told me she was a civil servant! I *knew* she wasn't telling the truth!'

'I saw her give evidence in court once; I was in the public gallery. She was very impressive. I enquired about her to a colleague and apparently she does a lot of good *pro bono* work for women's charities – gathers evidence for battered wives, that sort of thing. We've never been involved in the same case, so she didn't recognise me today. Anyway, you're going to be very interested to hear her real surname.' Stephanie paused for dramatic effect. 'It's Bannatyne.'

'Great Scott!' exclaimed Leo, leaping to his feet and spilling some Scotch onto his dressing gown.

Stephanie nodded.

Suddenly Leo recalled the image of Hazel's sister in the Bannatyne family photograph he had snapped earlier that day at the newspaper office. He snatched up his mobile phone from on top of the ottoman, brought up the image and studied it. 'Yes, Elaine is the younger sister!'

* * *

Much exercised by the revelation, Leo struggled to sleep. He kept switching his nightstand lamp back on and scrutinising the photograph on his phone, zooming in on Elaine Bannatyne's face. It was bladed by white, and not in a particularly high definition, yet he could make out the small birthmark on her cheekbone. The girl smiled uneasily at the lens, as though fearing disaster. Leo felt desperately sorry for this child, and the person she was about to become. Elaine Bannatyne's suspicious conduct was not entirely exonerated by this new information, but it certainly cast her in a more sympathetic light. She was surely here *incognito* in order to investigate the disappearance of her poor sister. And Leo could not help but feel relieved to possess this mitigating factor about a woman he held in burgeoning affection.

Day Five

DESPITE his lack of sleep, Leo rose with the buzz of his travel alarm feeling remarkably clear-headed and in good spirits. He threw open his curtains and surveyed the day – it was set to be another scorcher, the immense sky an enchanting azure, only the odd playful wisp of cloud smiling on the horizon.

After a fry-up breakfast, he helped Stephanie to her car with her luggage.

'You seem to have a spring in your step,' she observed, as they prepared to bid each other farewell.

'Just invigorated by the glory of the season,' Leo replied.

'Are you sure that's all that's invigorating you?'

'I'm sure I don't know what you mean.'

Stephanie smiled at him. 'Take care of yourself, Leo.'

He waved his friend off as she sped away in her sports coupé, then strode towards the Humber Hawk. Before he got in, he noticed Claire scurrying up the driveway. She was wearing a drab frock beneath her cleaning tabard. Leo called out a greeting, and as he approached her he tried to compose himself for what would be an awkward conversation.

'How does this beautiful day find you, Claire?'

'No' bad, Mr Moran. Yourself?'

'Fine, fine. Please, call me Leo. Only the police call me Mr Moran, and even then only when they are displeased with me. Which, admittedly, is quite often.'

Claire smiled politely at the lame joke. There followed a strained silence, but Leo knew he had no choice but to attempt to corroborate Maxwell's claim to an alibi for the night of Lauren's disappearance.

'Look, Claire, there is a question I have to ask you, and I truly hope that you are not offended by it.' Her eyes were downcast. 'It's just that I need to ask it, in an investigative capacity. Sometimes I perform investigations after something bad has happened. Now, I will strive to apply what discretion I reasonably can, should you be so good as to provide me with an answer.'

'Is it about . . . Mr Blythman?'

'Yes. He said he was . . . with you, on the night of Lauren's disappearance. Is this true?'

She nodded.

'Have you approached the police with this information?'

'No.'

'Why not?'

'Because I cannae.'

'Are you embarrassed?'

'Aye, but it's more than that. They might guess.'

'Guess what?'

'That he pays me.'

'The rotter! What time did he leave you that night?'

'Late-ish. Midnight maybe.'

'Had he arranged this assignation with you in advance?'

'Aye. A few days afore, as a matter o' fact.'

'Was this usual, for him to arrange in advance?'

'No. Usually he just texts me when he's feeling, you know, like he needs a bit, and comes on over if I'm available, which I usually am. I live by myself, you see. Look, Mr Blythman's got his faults, but he's no' capable of anything *really* bad.'

Leo motored towards Sannox House, a dozen Apricot Nectar roses that Evelyn had wrapped for him on the passenger seat. He had first detoured to the garage at St John's Town of Dalry to purchase some four-star and to compose himself for the coming *dénouement*. The upper valley had looked splendid in the sunshine, a verdant fertile strath where sheep safely grazed and the Water of Ken flowed proud and broad through huge rocks and flooded juniper. He turned off the Biggnarbriggs road and rolled over the quaint bridge that spanned the minor river which emptied into Loch Grenoch. He drove along the single-tracker, then swung south until he glimpsed the pretty chimneys of Sannox House through the trees. He glided the Humber between the gateposts and onto a little stretch of gravel on which was parked Elaine's green Mini. The house was isolated; after a ribbon of shrubs and flowers it was entirely enclosed by the woods. One seductive frond of pine breached the leafy curtain, a coniferous intruder to the soft border.

Leo approached the porch. It was a handsome nineteenth-century sandstone villa with red-painted sills, eaves and wrought-iron lacework, and sections of *art nouveau* stained glass. He pulled the bell. After a few moments Elaine opened the door. Her hair was up, exposing her slender, tanned neck. She wore old 501s and a faded blue V-necked T-shirt.

'Leo!'

'Hello, Elaine.'

For a moment all Leo could hear were the bumblebees lazily tending the blooms.

'Who knows?'

'Only Stephanie. It was she who recognised you. I only found you a touch . . . enigmatic. Here,' he said, handing her the bouquet. 'To demonstrate that I come in peace.'

'You'd better come in.'

She led Leo through the cool of the hall into a pleasant drawing room with bare floorboards, contemporary artworks on the white walls and an elegant blue-and-white suite.

'I guess I always liked the name Rachael,' said Elaine after she had brought through a jug of orange juice and glasses. 'Are you going to tell the police?'

'Why should I? You haven't done anything particularly illegal. And anyway, it appears the police aren't interested in anything I have to say. But you've been deceiving two dear friends of mine, and I think it's time for you to put me in the full picture.'

Elaine first divulged some generic information about her happy childhood, then took a sip from her glass and began relating the trauma that would always define her. Her eyes were unfocused as she spoke, revisiting the terrible countries of the past. Her face twitched at certain awful details, yet her voice stayed controlled. Sweet Jesus, what she has been through? thought Leo, his heart filled with pity. How has she coped?

'You probably know I'm not a civil servant and that my older sister Hazel disappeared from round here, presumed murdered. We used to take a cottage in the village for a few weeks of the summer holidays. Hazel's body was never found and the perpetrator never caught. I'm a freelance private investigator and paralegal. In my time off I try to find out who killed her. More and more it's become my life's work. A few years ago I started taking holidays down here under the name of Rachael Kidd, getting to know the local community with the hope of uncovering something: some conspiracy, some secret or lie. I thought that if people didn't know who I was then they would be more likely to let their guard down. The police stopped talking to me years ago, which made me suspicious that they were covering something up. I wasn't getting anywhere with my brief trips, so when Sannox House came on the market I decided to buy it, using an inheritance from my late aunt.

'Being down here makes me feel closer to Hazel. I can get back to Glasgow easily enough for work when I need to, and I've kept my flat on there. I honestly have the deepest regard for Fordyce and Evelyn, and it breaks my heart to have deceived them about my identity. When they started inviting me into their home for social engagements I felt awful, but I couldn't pass up the opportunity. By the way, I also felt rotten about lying to you, Leo. And not just because I did some research on you and discovered that you possess some sort of extrasensory power that you've used to fight crime. I thought you could be a useful ally, but I also like you and respect you.' Leo blushed.

'Anyway, I hadn't turned up anything, and then, that night, when I was sitting in the same room as you and that policewoman came in . . . God, it was like a re-run of our whole nightmare. I really believe the two disappearances are linked. I needed a break in the case, but not something like this. That is my truth, Leo and I hope you can forgive me.'

'Of course I do,' he said gently. 'I'm just so sorry for everything you've been through.'

Elaine smiled sadly. 'Hazel was extremely beautiful. She went out for a walk and vanished, just disappeared without a trace. It was as though the earth had swallowed her up. My parents were both dead within a few years. The doctors gave their cancers different fancy names, but it was grief, pure and simple, eating away at their insides. My younger brother Stuart and I stayed with my Aunt Joan for a while. She was a kind woman, but childless and elderly, and she struggled having two emotional adolescents dumped on her. As soon as he was old enough, my brother moved to Australia. He wanted me to come with him, but I wouldn't go, even when I was left with no one after Aunt Joan died. Something kept me here. It took me years to fully realise it, but I needed to at least try to solve the case for Hazel.'

'You said you were suspicious that the police were hiding something?'

'Archibald Strange, a DCI in the Dumfries and Galloway Constabulary was in charge of the investigation. He's still alive. He and his underlings were too quick to cut me out, despite my being the victim's sister. I'm in touch with the police in my day-to-day work and they usually tend to be far more cooperative. Other things made me suspicious too – reports and documents going mysteriously missing. Also, they were flogging the Talorc cult angle and I started to doubt it. The ex-druids I sought out in later years didn't seem the murdering type. And there wasn't any physical evidence up at the stones where they used to sacrifice animals. Sometimes the police care, consciously or subconsciously, more about getting a result – a conviction – than the truth. But this was something different.'

'But it sounds somewhat fantastic, a police cover-up.'

'All it would need is a few senior cops pulling the strings. The officers on the ground may be none the wiser. I believe our perpetrator is somebody powerful and connected. Of course, there could be more than one of them. It could also have been a woman, but that would be highly unusual.'

'Dalton is by-the-book,' said Leo. 'As I've mentioned, she doesn't want my help – told me to butt out.'

'Then she would presumably tell me to do likewise even if she knew my real identity,' said Elaine. 'Not that I trust the police enough to wish to work with them on this case anyway.'

'The fact that Lauren disappeared on precisely the same day of the year as Hazel seems highly coincidental,' said Leo, 'although we should keep an open mind as to the possibility that the cases are not, in fact, linked, or are linked only in an indirect way, such as a new perpetrator who had knowledge of the crime against your sister replicating it against Lauren. I wondered if there might be an occult significance to that date, and if the strange tree in the woods I mentioned at dinner might have any connection to the case.'

'The fact that our man chose the same date needn't have any significance other than the fact that he's honouring his past crime, creating some twisted narrative,' said Elaine.

'Still, I'd like to do further research. There are no similar unsolved disappearances in this area going back fifty or so years – I got Stephanie to check. It would be highly unusual for a typical serial predator to leave a long gap between crimes, which makes me wonder if there is indeed an occult motivation.'

'Sometimes I used to wonder if it was someone passing through who whisked Hazel away, and if I was just wasting my time on the locals. But I profiled all well-known killers from that time, and whether they could have been here on that day in July, and I drew a blank. Now, with Lauren's disappearance, I'm surer than ever that it was someone who lives around here.'

'Do you have anyone in mind?'

'Yes. Jimmy Handley. He was here in '79 – he gave me and Hazel horse-riding lessons – and he was really creepy towards her.'

'You said someone powerful and connected. How does Jimmy fit that bill, though?'

'He's got blue blood, albeit petty gentry. Merchiston Castle boy, the old school tie. You know how the system works.'

'Is the reason you bugged the aviary because you suspect Jimmy? I saw you planting the device.'

'I noticed recently that he talks to the birds. I know it sounds daft but I thought a bug might pick up a confession.'

'I'm afraid to tell you that I felt duty-bound to inform Fordyce about the item, although it's still where you left it. Is that the only one you planted?'

'Yes. There's something else about Jimmy. I kept an eye on him during the search party. When we got back I noticed him acting furtively; picking something up and concealing it on his person. Some clue, perhaps, which would have incriminated him in Lauren's disappearance. I lost sight of him in the throng, then he must have scuttled off somewhere. I considered telling the police, but I don't particularly trust them and I was terrified that if he got a chance to dispose of the item by the time they caught up with him, he'd know I suspected him. So I sneaked into his home. I searched the bins, everywhere, but found nothing.'

'I suspect that he burned it, whatever it was. You will recall he was staying at the hall the previous night. After the search party, I realised one of the chimneys was smoking. I then met Evelyn, who told me she was taking more coal to Jimmy's room because he had a chill. An unlikely scenario, given it's the height of a balmy summer. Anyway, we ought to examine that fireplace.'

'So, does this mean you're going to help me?'

'Only if you come clean to the Greatorixes.'

Elaine's brow furrowed. 'Yes, I suppose I must. Perhaps you could come with me, for moral support?'

'Of course.'

'It might help if I carry on pretending to be Rachael to everybody else for the time being, though.'

'Agreed,' said Leo after a thoughtful pause.

'So, tell me, Leo, how do these powers of yours actually work?'

'I see images, often moving ones, when my mind is in an unconscious or semi-conscious state. The vision can be of an event past or present or even future, and it may recur, perhaps with different details or from a different perspective. Or the content may be oblique or symbolic.'

'And have you experienced any revelations regarding Hazel or Lauren's disappearances?'

Leo told Elaine about his recent visions – about the water flowing in thin light, and how he had traversed nearby watercourses in search of clues. He told her about the scene he had witnessed in which the man in the plum hunting coat was murdered. And how he believed him to be the eighth baron Greatorix, whose discarnate spirit is said to haunt Biggnarbriggs Hall and who he thinks he saw on the tower's battlement and who Margaret, the young cook, may have been spooked by years ago. (Leo thought he discerned Elaine's expression glazing over at this talk of phantoms but he persevered.) He told her about the geometric shape that he thought could represent the portico of the temple of Venus on the island. And how he had punted over there to inspect it but it had yielded no clues. He told her everything else of note that sprung to mind about his recent stay at the hall, including his suspicion that Jimmy and Cynthia were having an affair (a notion that had also occurred to Elaine), about people's alibis and lack of alibis, about what he discerned from eavesdropping on DCI Dalton, and about his conversations with the police's initial suspects Donald Kennedy and Brian McGhie.

When he had finished his summary an idea occurred to him. 'Elaine, you said that this Strange fellow was still alive?'

'Yes. He lives in Drymen, north of Glasgow.'

'What if we were to visit him?'

'I doubt he would talk to anyone about Hazel's case.'

'He might be willing to open up in the light of Lauren's disappearance.'

'Well, there's no way he'll agree to see me. We didn't exactly part on cordial terms, albeit it was years ago.'

'Would he agree to see Rachael Kidd?'

'He'd probably still recognise me.'

'Not if Rachael becomes a blonde,' said Leo.

'You could visit him yourself,' suggested Elaine.

'No. You're the expert on your sister's disappearance. You've met him before and you're the one who would notice if something he said didn't add up. Stephanie is pally with quite a lot of coppers and ex-coppers. I'll see if she would be willing to try and get a message to him.'

Leo didn't want to disturb Stephanie with a call yet as she would still be driving back to Glasgow. Therefore he composed a text message, explaining that he had made alliance with Elaine, and that if Strange could be primed for a meeting to pick his brains about whether the current case had anything to do with the 1979 disappearance, she would pose as his assistant Rachael Kidd.

The pair then drove to Biggnarbriggs Hall where Leo wanted to show Elaine the fairy tree. As they stood regarding it, Leo wondered if the Enchanted Forest did in fact possess a strange, energising quality, or if it was just his being sexually drawn towards his companion in the intense heat.

'Unity seemed defensive when I raised the subject of this tree at dinner,' he said. 'And I saw her children playing with homemade kites with ribbons attached not dissimilar to these ones. But it's hard to suspect her of anything too sinister.'

They then headed to the aviary, where Elaine prised off the electronic bug using a cuticle pusher.

'Jimmy was here before dinner last night,' said Elaine. 'You never know, this thing might have picked something up.'

They entered the hall and ascended the servants' stairway to the first floor, passing through a sitting room that communicated with the so-called emerald room which Jimmy had occupied. Leo strode to the fireplace and crouched down at the hearth. The chalky coal ashes were still in the grate. He sniffed.

'Accelerant. Probably lighter fluid. I noticed he was in possession of an old-fashioned cigarette lighter on my first night here.' He stirred the ashes and inspected the rear of the fireplace. 'The coals are only partially burnt – and look at that dirty splash mark. This fire was doused with water, not allowed to burn out. So he got a blaze going quickly and then extinguished it suddenly, which increases my suspicion that he has incinerated something here.'

'Disposal of evidence,' surmised Elaine.

'Very possibly. Look, Elaine, I'm acutely aware I must not restrict my focus only on the people in the locality who I happen to know, such as those who frequent the hall. As for you – are you quite fixated on Jimmy?'

'There's one other guy.'

'Who?'

'One-legged Tam. The trouble is, I don't have a shred of evidence against him. I'm worried I'm being unfair, judging a book by its cover.'

'Who is one-legged Tam?'

'An ex-soldier. He came here in the late seventies after being blown up by an IRA bomb in Ulster. He was in the Major's company. He put him up in a cabin on his land.'

'Is it a ramshackle old cabin west of Maidenhead House, at the edge of the forest proper?'

'Yes.'

'I saw it when we were out searching. It's not that far from Linn Priory, where Lauren walked down to the forest road from. And your sister was last seen at the village crossroads walking west.'

'Apparently the Major said he could stay there *ad infinitum*.'

'I didn't think the man capable of such kindness. So, this Tam fellow – he was here when Hazel went missing?'

'Yes. He's deeply unpleasant. Irascible, unhygienic, misanthropic, quite the hermit . . . but . . .'

'But none of that makes him a killer.'

'Exactly. And I've dug around into his past. A few black marks on his military record but nothing heinous, and ever since he's been as good as gold. Sex perverts and psychos usually have something on their file, even a minor offence – animal cruelty or flashing or something. That's the thing about this case – none of the local men I've investigated have any prior of much interest.'

'Which could mean that the perp, should he be a local, is uncommonly meticulous in covering up his activities.'

'Meticulous and perhaps organised, in that if it's a group they work efficiently together. Or worse – are connected and protected.'

'By the way, does Tam own a vehicle?'

'No sign of one. He lives in abject poverty.'

Elaine steeled herself for the coming confession as she and Leo descended the grand staircase. The house was still and quiet, but then, through the French doors in the drawing room, Leo spied the Greatorixes. They were walking towards the hall flanked by the spaniels and coming from the direction of the lake, where, judging by Fordyce's straw boater and espadrilles and Evelyn's parasol, they had been punting. Elaine was grateful for the encouraging squeeze that Leo applied to her arm. She then stepped out to meet the siblings and requested that she speak with them inside.

'This sounds awfully serious!' remarked Fordyce as he sat down alongside Evelyn on one of the library's Chesterfields.

Elaine remained standing, and in the same dignified voice with which she had earlier informed Leo about her tragic backstory, she revealed her true identity and the extent of the deception she had inflicted upon the house of Greatorix. She explained her reasons and asked for forgiveness, and also admitted to planting a (now removed) listening device at the aviary.

The revelation was less of a shock to Fordyce, who was obviously already acquainted with the latter matter and with Leo's doubts about the former Miss Kidd. Therefore he explained in even tones that, while not approving of the subterfuge and lamenting the fact that she hadn't confided in him earlier, he perfectly understood her motives and had the utmost sympathy for she and her family for what they had endured. He added that he thought she was mistaken to suspect Jimmy and was glad to have been assured that the wretched bug had been removed.

As for Evelyn, she said nothing, but after a while she stood up, stepped towards Elaine and embraced her, her eyes brimming with tears.

Leo took the floor and explained that he and Elaine, both experienced investigators, had joined forces. They had been compelled into conducting their own enquiries into the disappearances of both Hazel and Lauren – which were probably connected – because DCI Dalton wouldn't cooperate with him and would doubtless apply the same unyielding attitude towards Elaine, even should she know her true identity. Leo humbly requested that the Greatorixes help maintain the Rachael Kidd masquerade for the time being. This triggered some soul searching; Fordyce had only just objected to the deception, and now he was being asked to be complicit in continuing to exact it on others. Leo promised it would only be necessary until the case was solved and that it could prove critical in their armoury. Therefore the Greatorixes acquiesced. Fordyce stood and shook Leo and Elaine's hands, and assured them that he and Evelyn would give them any help they required.

Leo then went to fetch his detective's kit from his bedroom before he and Elaine departed in the Humber.

'Why did they have to be so bloody *nice* about it?' said Elaine, her voice breaking as the old motor car rumbled down the drive. 'It makes me feel even worse.'

Leo glanced at her and felt a little guilty at having forced her into the trauma of the confession. In order to give her a chance to compose herself, he drove to a small car park by Loch Grenoch, where they gazed at the sparkling water for a while. After a few minutes, Elaine piped up with forced brightness, 'So, where to now, good sir?'

'I thought we might drop by this one-legged Tam's place.'

'That's the kind of boldness I like in a sidekick!'

'Hang on – *you're* the sidekick,' he joked. 'I'm Holmes, you're Watson.'

They exchanged smiles and Leo turned the key in the ignition.

Leo parked the Humber in a lay-by on the forest road. Tam's cabin was reached via a rough track that formed the border between the mixed woodland surrounding the priory and a section of Galloway Forest Park, which at this point was serried ranks of commercially planted conifers.

The wooden cabin was so decrepit that it almost seemed to be in some stage of collapse. It was quite a sprawling affair, single-storeyed and with various crooked chimneys protruding from a rusting corrugated-iron roof. The filthy windows were covered with sections of mismatching, sun-bleached fabric. There was a rickety veranda which, along with the dirt yard, was littered with junk. All was still, and Leo couldn't even hear a bird singing in the trees.

He stepped up and rapped sharply on the flimsy door. He tried twice more, the latter time calling out, but no one replied. He peered through the only unobscured window.

'I don't think anyone's home,' he said, then went back to the door. He tried the handle, and the door opened with an ugly squeak. 'Are you up for this?' he asked.

'You betcha.'

'Then let us see what we can find.'

They entered a gloomy little hallway and began exploring the hovel, Leo in particular baulking at its level of filthiness and disorder.

'What a *coup!*' he whispered.

To their right were Tam's squalid sleeping quarters, the unmade bed covered in stained old army blankets with dog hairs on them. A pail overfilled with ash and butts from roll-ups. The floor was strewn with well-worn prosthetic legs and cardboard boxes containing documents and dusty knickknacks. They entered a grubby kitchen that stank of roadkill and was cluttered with soiled dishes and saucepans, the walls streaked by years of slapdash cooking. Then they entered a living area, enough light coming through the window that Leo had looked through to reveal a mangy-looking, half-burst sofa facing a large television set, an old tea chest with a landline telephone and an overflowing ashtray upon it, and then more hoarder's chaos: boxes, tubs, piles of old newspapers and a preponderance of certain types of electrical junk, all stuff manufactured in the 1960s and 1970s. Obsolete items such as a Super-8 film camera and projector, an eight-track cartridge player, an absurdly oversized Loewy Dictaphone, an ancient compressor pedal. The objects were so outmoded and clunky as to resemble Soviet kitsch. The ceilings were nicotine-yellowed, the very fabric of the place wreathed with a cloying stale tobacco reek mixed with canine stink. The only ornamentation was an old 8x10 inch photograph, unframed and Blu-Tacked to a wall. It was of Tam's old army company, and Leo pointed out the scowling CO to Elaine: the Major.

Leo opened one of the cardboard boxes and was horrified to discover a trove of hard-core pornographic pictures. 'In this brave new anything-goes world, free as it is from respect for God, people will tend to dwell upon the profane in private until it devours them,' he declared. 'Morality is, after all, what we do when we think no one is watching.'

'Yeah, like non-Christians don't have a conscience, don't do good things,' retorted Elaine.

'Indeed they do, but as Chesterton said, the Christian virtues have now gone mad, wandering wildly, isolated from each other. To say nothing of the vices let loose.'

'Oh, Leo. There will always be wickedness in the world. People need to be free to make their own choices.'

'Quite so, but without the deterrent, the enduring standard, freedom is untrammelled—'

'Leo,' interrupted Elaine, but her companion, oblivious as he warmed to his moralistic riff, blustered on.

'I can only imagine that things will get worse, and societal breakdown will escalate—'

'Leo,' she said urgently.

'I think it was Thomas à Kempis who wrote—'

'*Leo!*' she snapped, nudging him abruptly in the ribs.

'What is it?'

'It's Tam,' she said, pointing at the window. 'He's coming.'

Leo looked out to see a man hobbling down the slope on the other side of the yard as he drew on a cigarette. He was a lank-haired, unshaven character with reptilian features.

'Quick – through there!' said Leo, grabbing Elaine's arm and dragging her to a nearby door, knocking against a pile of cardboard boxes as he did so and almost sending a false leg that was perched on top crashing to the ground.

It opened into the loo, a malodorous nightmare of mould and sinister staining.

Leo gingerly closed the lid of the WC, stood on it and reached to open a frosted-glass window. He helped Elaine to escape first, and held her beneath her armpits in order to aid her descent to the soft earth outside. He could hear Tam opening the front door and opted to simply dive through the aperture head first.

'It's no good,' he hissed as he struggled to force his shoulders through. 'I can't fit . . . I'll hide in the shower. I suspect he seldom utilises it so I should be safe there. Run for it – I'll see you back at the car.' He tossed the Humber's ignition key to her.

'No way – I'll be nearby. If he finds you, just yell, and I'll call the cops, in case he gets rough,' said Elaine before dashing the few yards to the tree line and concealing herself there.

Leo silently closed the window and pulled the mildewed shower curtain aside. He had to throttle a shriek when he saw a corpse there, propped up against the tiles.

He breathed a sigh of relief when he realised that it was, in fact, a life-size sex doll. He stepped in alongside it, muttering, 'Don't mind me, madam,' before pulling the curtain closed. He said a Hail Mary that Tam wouldn't enter the lavatory, and was relieved to hear him pick up the telephone receiver and make a call. He got out of the shower, crept to the door and listened in to Tam's half of the conversation, conducted in his throaty Ayrshire accent.

'Aye, it's Tam . . . We're on for the nicht. The cops have already finished searching that area . . . Look, you need to grow a pair. We must honour our rural traditions. The earth enfolds our rightful quarry . . . Aye, he's bringing a bitch, so we'll have fun aplenty . . . No, I'll walk there. Right, I'm away to find the dug. The daft bastard's fucked off after a hare again.'

With that, Tam replaced the receiver, and Leo quickly concealed himself again behind the shower curtain. A few moments later he heard the squeak of the front door. He carefully opened the loo door and through the window saw Tam's figure hirpling up the slope. Once he was out of sight, Leo walked out of the cabin and round to its rear, where he found Elaine. She embraced him with relief and Leo felt a little flutter of delight.

'He's gone,' he informed her. 'He only came by to fetch something.'

Leo told this lie because he was loth at this point to inform Elaine about the conversation he had overheard. He was already planning to follow Tam to his nocturnal engagement, whatever it was, and he didn't want her insisting that she come along, lest she be put in danger.

The pair stole back down the track to the car. As it was nearby, Leo suggested that they inspect the concrete lot where Lauren's scent trail had ended, but they found nothing of interest.

'Gosh, all this excitement has made me hungry,' said Elaine, as the Humber approached Biggnarbriggs village, sunlight flashing on the windscreen. 'Fancy a spot of early lunch?'

'We have someone to visit first,' said Leo. 'Lauren's mother.' Leo had been considering such a brazen approach for some time, but he had worried about upsetting the poor woman. 'In theory, meeting Mrs McDowall and seeing Lauren's home could stimulate my powers,' he explained. 'I've been dreading it, concerned that I might come across as a crank turning up on her doorstep. But with you, a sympathetic woman alongside, it might seem a little less . . .'

'Weird?'

'Yes.'

The McDowall home was easy to find on account of the police car parked outside it. It was the second-last house of the village as one drove eastwards, part of a plain 1960s terrace finished in roughcast; probably originally local authority housing. Leo always considered how incongruous such buildings looked when plonked down among rural Scottish cottages.

Three youths aged about fifteen loitered near the front gate. They were two girls with hooped earrings, who were chewing gum, and a thin, pimply-faced lad with sandy-red hair who was wearing a black T-shirt with a hip hop artist's logo on it and a rosary around his neck. The boy burped rudely as Leo and Elaine approached.

'Hi, guys,' said Elaine pleasantly.

The trio merely smirked.

'I take it this is the McDowall residence?' ventured Leo, addressing the boy.

'Aye.'

'It's such an awful time for everyone,' said Elaine kindly. 'Are you friends of Lauren?'

'Naw,' said the boy.

'You coppers?' enquired one of the girls.

'No. Just a couple of concerned citizens.'

'Well, fuck off then,' muttered the boy.

'I beg your pardon?' Leo snapped at him. 'And can I ask – why are you wearing a rosary around your neck like that?'

'It's a fashion accessory, for fuck's sake,' he sneered.

They left the surly threesome and walked up the garden path. 'A *fashion* accessory indeed!' fumed Leo.

He was about to address the policeman who was standing sentry when the front door opened. A woman, presumably Lauren's mother, was seeing DCI Dalton out. Leo braced himself.

'Mr Moran,' said Dalton grimly, 'what exactly is your business here?'

'I wish to speak with Mrs McDowall.'

'Why?'

'To see if I can be of assistance in finding her daughter.'

'By using your magic powers?'

'I just want to help, Detective Chief Inspector.'

'What powers?' asked Lauren's mother.

'Mrs McDowall,' began Elaine, 'my name is Rachael Kidd and this is my friend Leo Moran. Leo has a gift known as second sight. He experiences visions relating to certain crimes, and he's helped the police with their inquiries before, with some success. I'm sure that DCI Dalton is doing what she thinks best, but she has rejected Leo's help in solving your daughter's disappearance. Therefore we are here independently, to offer our services.'

'Have you had any visions about my Lauren?' Mrs McDowall asked Leo.

'I have had visions recently, madam, which I believe to be connected to this case, although they have been quite limited and oblique. I felt that by visiting the house and speaking with you, it might help point my powers in the right direction.'

'I'll have them moved on, Anthea,' said Dalton to Mrs McDowall.

'No, no. I've seen telly programmes about psychics and the like. I'm sure there's something in it.'

'I don't want them interfering with my investigation, Anthea,' said Dalton, her voice simmering with irritation, 'or upsetting you.'

'Thanks, Diane,' said Mrs McDowall. 'But it's my house and I dinnae see what harm it can do.'

The callers were therefore invited in, and Dalton shot Leo a furious glare as he stepped by her.

Leo and Elaine declined the offer of tea and were led into a living room, which had a lush carpet, comfortable cream leather sofas and a large plasma television set. Elaine admired a recent framed studio photograph of Mrs McDowall with her daughter. The place was meticulously clean and tidy, the antithesis of the Augean dwelling they had just poked around in.

'I must admit, I am a bit house-proud,' said Mrs McDowall in response to Leo and Elaine's compliments, before insisting that they address her as 'Anthea'. A cute little Westie by the name of Louis sauntered in, and Anthea placed him on her knee and began stroking him. She explained that she had shut up the café until Lauren came home; she couldn't face working at present.

Leo suddenly felt an inner panic at the situation, feeling intrusive and unworthy of witnessing the woman's private moment of vulnerability. He struggled to so much as glance at her countenance, and felt himself colouring with heat at his inner turmoil. He was heartily thankful for Elaine's presence. She slipped into the perfect mode, expertly calming and sympathetic, knowing just the right things to say. It was obvious that Elaine felt great empathy for Anthea, who in turn felt at ease enough to open up to her visitors at length.

She explained that she was Biggnarbriggs born and bred, and had spent her entire forty-three years in the village. Leo couldn't help but think that she looked somewhat older, probably due to years of smoking and tanning salons. She had evidently replaced the former vice with an e-cigarette, its blue tip glowing regularly as she sucked on it for dear life. She was tall in stature and a touch overweight, but had strong, attractive features and thick, long black hair. She wore a jogging suit and fashionable thick-rimmed spectacles, and spoke in a drawling voice that may have indicated some form of medication.

As her monologue touched upon the subject of her missing daughter, Leo suspected that Anthea was staving off her anxiety with not only prescription drugs but also the delusion that Lauren had eloped with a secret boyfriend.

'She didnae take her suitcase, but she might have been squirrelling things away wi' this fella, whoever he is, so that I didnae suspect her plans. He's probably bought her whatever else she needed. It won't be the first time I've been deserted.'

Elaine enquired if she had any family who could attend to her, and Anthea explained that her father was deceased, her mother an invalid living in Dumfries, but that her sister had been staying over – she was currently in Castle Douglas buying groceries.

'What about Lauren's father?' ventured Leo.

'The polis have traced him – he's on a rig in the Caspian Sea. No' that he would give a shite about comin' over. He did us a' a favour and buggered off when Lauren was six, the cheating bastard. Never to be seen again, and never so much as a penny in the way of child support. Now that the cops have located him, I'll need to get round to divorcing the sod.'

'Do you have anyone else to lean on, Anthea? A partner, a gentleman friend?' asked Leo, attempting to ascertain if there was a potentially wicked stepfather on the scene.

'No, my needs aren't being seen to at present, I'm afraid. No' for a long time.'

'Is there anything you could tell us about Lauren, to give us a clue as to what she's like as a person?' enquired Elaine.

'Let's go up to her room,' suggested Anthea. She continued speaking as they went upstairs. 'The polis kept asking if there was any way she might have been suicidal, but I told them: no way, no' my Lauren. She was full o' life, and she was in guid spirits the last time I saw her. She can be a difficult lass, mind. She can be cheeky and stay out late, y'know. I suspected she was drinking and smoking dope now and again. Mind you, she had a soft side to herself too. As a child, she was aye gentle wi' animals, and she'd greet if she saw a dying bird or beastie. And she's always been kindly towards wee ones, even when she was just a bairn herself. It would melt your heart, so it would.'

The entered Lauren's room, a riot of pink and boy band posters. A string of fairy lights in the shape of love hearts adorned the bedstead. Leo and Elaine nosed around, but the room seemed reasonably standard for a teenaged girl.

'Lauren was fair grown-up,' said Anthea. 'And no' always in a guid way. Sometimes I worry I didnae pay her enough attention over the years.'

'I'm sure it's been hard,' said Elaine reassuringly, 'being a single mum and running the business to provide for your daughter.'

'I remember Lauren's heid teacher called me in – this was when she was still in primary school. Some parent was concerned about emails between her and his lad. Lauren had been giving it all this grown-up talk, like "I feel we're both ready to be in a relationship together" and some such shite, even though they were only aged ten or eleven.'

'What did you do?' asked Leo.

'I told the heid to fuck off and mind her ain business. Anyway, I doubt you'll find much o' relevance in here. It's been thoroughly searched by the polis and by me.'

'Did Lauren keep a diary at all? Hidden perhaps?' asked Leo.

'No. But yesterday I found something interesting stashed in the loft. A collection o' expensive things: jewellery, a silver trinket box, a Gucci bag. She obviously didnae want me to see them. Gifts, I reckon. I handed them to the polis. Diane Dalton asked if I kent anything about a boyfriend who drove a green saloon car wi' tinted windows. Someone said they saw her getting picked up in it a few weeks back. I did have reason to think she might be seeing someone. She used to go out and come back late, and a couple o' times she caught herself out wi' lies. We had a couple o' rows; they weren't exactly blazing, but who knows, maybe that's why she eloped with this mystery fella. By the way, the polis and me reckon she had a second mobile phone.'

'Why do you say that?'

'Because we found an extra charger, and because there was nothing suspicious on her usual phone. She left that one in the house when she went out. And what young lassie goes out without a mobile?'

'Could any of her teachers have taken an unhealthy interest in Lauren?' asked Elaine.

'Diane said that they all checked out.'

'Could any of Lauren's peers have borne a grudge – felt jealous or scorned, for example?' enquired Leo.

'No' that I know of.' Anthea sat down on Lauren's bed and sighed, a desolate look upon her face. She took a couple of puffs on her e-cigarette. 'It seems like everyone kent, apart from me.'

Elaine sat down beside her and took her hand. 'Knew what, Anthea?'

'What Lauren was *like*. I've only just been told by Diane that she'd been prescribed contraceptives even though she's underage. They had no right to do that without me being consulted, surely. Before the polis took her computer awa for analysis I found dozens o' porn searches on it. So many things make sense now: nasty comments across the street from her schoolmates, sleazy remarks from men in the café.'

'Which men?' asked Leo.

'Thon Jimmy Handley for one. Aye drooling over her and making innuendos. It put that snooty bitch Cynthia whatshername's nose right out o' joint. She was in wi' him a couple o' times; I reckon they're having a fling. You could tell she was jealous o' my Lauren.' Anthea took another long draw of vapour, then fixed Leo in the eye. 'This second sight thingy o' yours. Tell me the truth – is my daughter still alive?'

'I'm sorry, Anthea, but truly I do not know.'

And Anthea McDowall began weeping gently, and moaning, 'Please, darling, please just come home,' and Leo thought his heart would break.

Leo and Elaine walked down Anthea's garden path in solemn silence. The three youths had moved along the street a little, to where a hedge obstructed the police sentry's line of vision. As the pair passed by, the boy spat on the pavement.

'That's a charming repertoire you have, burping and expectorating,' observed Leo. 'What do you do for an encore – fart to the tune of *The Flight of the Bumblebee*?'

As they walked off, the lad muttered, 'That wee slag's probably just getting pumped by her sugar daddy.'

Leo turned on him. 'Do you know his identity?'

He was met by a smirk. A red mist descended upon Leo, and he ripped the rosary from the boy's neck and grabbed him by the throat, the unfettered beads pinging as they landed on the pavement. One of the girls murmured something impudent about Leo having 'weird hands', but a glint of fear sparked in the boy's eyes.

'Have you lost your tongue? I asked you a bloody question!'

'I dinnae ken who he was. I didnae see him. Just saw her getting into this green car wi' tinted windows a few weeks back.'

'What type of vehicle was it?'

'I dinnae ken. It was too far away.'

'Where was this?'

'Up the forest road a bit. I've already telt the polis a' this.'

Leo and Elaine climbed into the Humber and sat for a few moments, collecting their thoughts.

Elaine was first to break the silence: 'Let's head to mine and use the computer – there are a few things we need to check. And before that, I'll make us some lunch.'

Leo started the engine and swung the car left up a residential road that led back into the heart of the village. Leo noted Andrea's shuttered café and a bonny little white-painted kirk in which the police had set up their incident room.

'Thank you, by the way,' he said.

'What for?'

'For being the compassionate person that you are. You were so kind to that poor woman.'

'I feel so sorry for her.'

'I can't help think that Lauren has been let down somehow, that she was denied the proper innocence of childhood. She should have been better protected from the corrosive influences of this rough old world.'

'By her mother?'

'Not necessarily. Anthea alone had to work hard to provide for her daughter. Her father should have done his manly duty and stood by them, shown a good example. Yet even the most conscientious of parents face a tough task nowadays, considering the slurry of sexualisation and pornography raining down from all sides. When you think about it, Lauren just did what all little girls and boys do: they ape adult behaviour. It's just that nowadays grown-up behaviour is a diet of melodrama, vanity, selfishness and carnality. Lauren was deeply unfortunate if some older person latched onto her worldliness and encouraged it.'

'You really are quite the moralist, Leo. Perhaps she simply had a high sex drive.'

'Sex drive! She was a *child*, for God's sake!'

'She was fifteen, and mature for her age.' A few moments of frosty silence played out between them, and Leo inwardly lamented how he had simply never *got* the modern world. 'Leo, regarding what you said back there to Anthea – do you really not sense if Lauren is dead or not?'

'There are several explanations for the disappearance that must be considered,' he began. 'First, an accident, and second, suicide. We have just discovered there was bullying – the verbal abuse in the street which Anthea mentioned might have been the tip of the iceberg, but Lauren did not seem in any mental distress when last seen. If it was either an accident or suicide then she would most probably have been found by now, and also, why would my powers be stimulated to investigate such an open-and-shut case? And finally, why did her scent trail end abruptly at the forest road? The third possibility is that Lauren ran away, but that seems improbable because none of her personal belongings were missing from her home. That leaves abduction, resulting in captivity or murder.'

'I agree. By the same guy or guys who kidnapped my sister.'

'Let's keep an open mind about whether the cases are linked or not. Although if I was a betting man, I'd say they are.'

'You didn't answer my question. Do you really not sense if she is dead or not?'

Leo pondered, and then replied, 'I worry that she is . . . beyond us.'

'What does that mean?'

'I don't know. I sense we aren't going to find her alive.' He paused for a moment. 'Do you mind my asking, when did you accept that your sister—'

'Was dead? In a fit of rage, rage at myself for keeping the dream alive for three years. October the fifth, 1982. No particular reason it should have been that day, but the dam just burst.'

Upon arrival at Sannox House, Leo checked his mobile phone to discover a text message from Stephanie, stating 'Strange will C U', with a landline number at the end. He created an entry for Strange in his phone's contacts and strode into the large, sunny kitchen to inform Elaine, who was preparing lunch.

'You won't believe this – Stephanie has come through, Strange is happy to meet us!'

'My goodness,' replied Elaine. 'Perhaps Lauren's disappearance has piqued his interest after all.'

Leo and Elaine agreed that they would visit Strange in Drymen tomorrow, if convenient to him. He then rang the number that Stephanie had sent him and found himself speaking to a laconic, elderly man who confirmed he'd been expecting the call and would indeed be amenable to a visit tomorrow, at any time during the afternoon. He stated his address, and Leo provided him with his mobile phone number in case there was a change of circumstance.

After a pleasant lunch of Parma ham, scrambled eggs and asparagus, Leo wondered if Lauren had been active on social media, so Elaine led him into a little study where her laptop computer was kept. 'Do you know what social media actually *is?*' she enquired, her lip curling slightly as she guessed at Leo's level of technophobia.

'I know *of* it,' he replied, rolling with the jibe.

'Bingo! She has an account and it's still live.'

'What are you doing now?' asked Leo as Elaine tapped the keyboard some more.

'Just a spot of hacking. I'm sure you agree that the modern PI should be something of a computer expert,' she teased. 'Lauren's settings are such that we can't see much of her account, but I want a peek behind the curtain.'

Leo stood behind Elaine and watched her as she typed, her head thrust towards the screen, the attitude embodying the determined, serious, self-possessed way she pursued justice and hunted her sister's killer. He gazed at the exposed nape of her neck and felt a longing to kiss the soft skin there. He regarded her chestnut hair, the pattern it made as it wove around her scalp. The careless manner in which it had been piled on top of her head was somehow endearing. He wondered at the pain that had endured inside that kindly cranium, what wisdom had been earned at an awful price. He wanted to help make things better for her. Suddenly, Leo felt a thrilling sensation that he hadn't experienced in half a lifetime: that he was *meant* to be here – in this place, with this person, at this moment.

'Elaine, may I ask you something?'

'Fire away.'

'Do you believe I can help you? What I mean to say is, do you truly believe that I have the gift of second sight, that such a power exists?'

'Generally I'm a sceptic, Leo. However, I don't believe that you are dishonest or that different police officers would have worked with you had they not felt there was some value in it. I would reject any meta-physical explanation, however. I simply believe there are some powers as yet unexplained by science.' She typed a little more, before declaring, 'We're in!'

They read Lauren's final status update, a banal item posted on the morning of her disappearance with her profile photograph alongside; it hung tantalisingly in cyberspace, so recent and fresh that Leo felt he could reach out and touch her. There followed a message from a class-mate, posted after Lauren had gone missing. It, too, was banal, because the girl had been then still ignorant of Lauren's disappearance. What had come to pass between those two communications was seismic such that they now stood as a wholly inadequate digital representation of a lost life. It put Leo in mind of an airliner that had gone off the radar over the mid-Atlantic. The television news had shown the arrivals board in the destination airport with the entry 'Cancelled' alongside the flight number. It was a pretence, a bromide, a euphemism to stave off panic until the families could be gently informed that there were not expected to be any survivors.

Thereafter, the social media messages – many from Anthea – became appeals to Lauren to come home. There were also postings from the police, hopeful ones requesting that the girl get in touch, and others directed at her cyber friends, requesting information. Elaine then scrolled back and they saw other, spiteful messages from before Lauren had gone missing, referring to her alleged promiscuity. These were posted along-side profile pictures of adolescent females pouting and posturing in suggestive ways.

'It is notable how even in these modern times a female is still slandered for her proclivities whereas men would be lauded for their conquests,' observed Leo. 'The inglorious sexual revolution abolished chasteness but kept other things exactly the same as before.'

'They seem like proper brats, mind you,' commented Elaine.

'The youth wrecks because he or she naively believes in the durability of his or her world. However, although it is important not to rule anything out – and I'm sure the police will be checking out all her peers – the expensive gifts, the second mobile phone . . . these all point to an older, grooming lover. I suspect that Lauren used to meet him up on the forest road where he waited in his car. That nasty lad who was wearing the rosary said he saw Lauren get into a green saloon there a few weeks ago, and of course the scent trail picked up by the police dogs ended there, albeit in a lot just by the road. Perhaps Lauren went up there as usual on the night she disappeared, but unbeknownst to her this time her fella had something different in store for her.'

'What about Jimmy? Anthea thought he was a sleazebag and I told you that I suspected him regarding Hazel.'

'We must keep an open mind,' replied Leo. 'And Jimmy's car is, in fact, brown.'

'Which could easily have been mistaken for green in a certain light,' said Elaine.

'Also, Jimmy's car doesn't have tinted windows,' observed Leo.

'But car windows can appear as if they're tinted when in shadow. Remember, the boy said he only saw the vehicle from a distance.'

Leo told Elaine that he was expected to dine at Biggnarbriggs Hall that evening and he first wanted to prepare for tomorrow's trip north to meet with Strange. In fact, his purpose in returning to the hall as early as he did was to try to get some sleep, because he planned on spending at least a portion of the coming night tracking one-legged Tam.

Leo did indeed manage a couple of hours' nap during the late afternoon. There was a slightly awkward atmosphere at dinner, with Fordyce and Evelyn still adjusting to the strange revelation of that morning and regularly having to correct themselves whenever they referred to Elaine as 'Rachael'. Leo, mindful of his resolution not to drag the Greatorixes unnecessarily into the case, fended off any queries regarding their investigations with bland responses. He most certainly was not going to tell them of his plans for that night, although he did inform them of the meeting arranged with Strange, which would mean he would be absent from the hall for a day and a night.

After dinner, he said that he felt sun-tired and was going to retire early, declining Fordyce's proposal of a frame or two of snooker. Once in his room, he changed into his tweed trousers and looked out the things he required. A lambswool jersey with a cravat underneath and his Harris herringbone sports jacket should be sufficient to keep him warm. He decided against his windcheater, which he feared would make a *swishing* noise as he moved and could therefore give him away. He looked out his deerstalker and his walking shoes, and placed his detective's kit, his aluminium water flask, his mobile telephone and a crocodile-skin notebook into his knapsack. He would carry his Stanley torch – heavy enough to make any ruffian think twice – and be ready to dial 999 on his mobile should anything too sinister unfold.

Leo set off just after 9 p.m. He could hear Fordyce and Evelyn conversing in the drawing room, so he slipped out of the kitchen door and dashed for the tree line, hoping no one happened to be looking out from the McGhies' cottage. He followed the darkening woods as they skirted the great lawns, then entered the hidden meadow and climbed the crags to the priory. The setting sun drenched the ruins and the Scots pines in honeyed light. A gnarled and warty oak looked particularly resplendent, as though intricately gilded. Leo then approached Tam's abode, keeping himself concealed amid scrub as he descended the final slope.

Electric lights burned from the cabin's windows, and Leo ensconced himself behind a pile of rotting timber at the other side of the yard. He unpeeled a tube of orange creams for sustenance. Leo's penchant for this confection was rooted in his childhood introduction to the Fry's Orange Cream by his Aunt Francesca. He had been devastated when he heard rumour that the line was to be discontinued, and a flurry of letter writing and protest ensued. But his taste had refined to encompass a whole host of brands of luxurious dark chocolate and orange fondant medleys. There had been the occasional affair with the strawberry and the lime cream, and an insane dalliance or two with the floral fancies of the violet and rose varieties; however, he would inevitably return to the parlour of his beloved, with her bitter-sweet, zesty tang.

He had to endure forty minutes of being eaten alive by midges until he heard the trademark squeak of the cabin door, followed by the pattering of canine feet coming in his direction. This was an eventuality that Leo had overlooked. The animal halted just shy of the woodpile, then emitted a low growling sound. Leo held his nerve and speculatively threw three orange creams to the side of his position, and the dog began munching greedily upon them. Leo gave thanks to the Iraqi chocolatier in Glasgow's West End for the irresistibility of his candies.

'Bandit!' called out Tam, and the creature sloped off to his master's side. Tam was wearing a shabby field jacket and carrying an electric camping lantern, and as Leo watched him limping up the slope he noticed that he also had a shotgun cradled in the crook of his arm. He considered his rubber torch – it seemed an inadequate weapon in comparison. Although he generally objected to firearms, part of him now wished that he had confided his plan to Fordyce; the loan of a 12-gauge Westley Richards would have brought him some comfort right now.

Leo crept though the summer night, which was fragrant but for the odd whiff of his quarry's cheap tobacco smoke, keeping a safe distance lest he alert the dog to his presence. After the hidden meadow, Tam wove a path roughly northwards. Leo couldn't risk switching on his torch, but light filtered down from the half moon and the stars sprinkled across the firmament. Tam entered Scoulag Woods, which had turned to shadow. He waded through Scoulag Burn, carrying his dog across it, and after a while Leo likewise forded its cold flow. Visibility became far more restricted in the depths of thickly planted conifers, and Leo, often having to feel his way forwards, dreaded giving himself away with the snap of a dry twig underfoot. Ahead lay a section of natural, mixed woodland, and in its midst was the glow from a floodlight which had been rigged up. Tam joined a little assembly gathered there, and Leo crept forwards and concealed himself behind the upturned roots of a giant fir which had been felled by a storm. He peered out. He reckoned that there were about eight men standing around a slight bank. They were leaning on spades or wooden stakes, smoking and passing a bottle as they chatted. Two or three of them, like Tam, carried shotguns. Leo couldn't make out the words of their conversation, and the glare of the light, shining directly into his eyes, made it difficult to pick out facial features with any precision. Behind them were parked two 4x4 vehicles; evidently there was a stretch of track leading from the road down into this grove. At one point, one of the men, who was wearing a muscle vest, walked over to where Leo was crouching. He began to urinate, the steaming yellow stream bouncing on the compost a yard to Leo's right. Leo stayed perfectly still. The man's face was in shadow but the artificial light did illuminate a singular tattoo on his right shoulder. Its main component was a geometric shape, two columns supporting a crossbar, like the one in Leo's last vision. The urinator rejoined his confederates and then a third truck arrived. At this point Tam called his dog – which Leo reckoned was a bull lurcher – towards him and attached a leash to his collar. A man, whom Leo recognised from his blunt profile as Chas, got out of the newly arrived off-road vehicle and dragged Nero from the boot on a chain lead. Nero and Tam's mutt Bandit strained at the leash and began barking aggressively at each other. Then a third dog was brought out on a short leash. This animal was taller and muscular, and evidently a female given the way the other two dogs behaved towards it. Three of the men then began digging at the bank, and after twenty minutes or so of industry they passed the spades to some of their comrades, who took over. There was a second change in shift, and after almost an hour the diggers cast aside their spades as an excited babble immersed the assembly. They vied for better viewing positions and aimed camera phones at the pit as the dogs were brought forth, one by one, and the angle of the floodlight adjusted to optimally illuminate the depths. Some of the men aimed their stakes into the hole and leaned on them as though to drive them into the soil.

Leo would never be able to un-hear the dreadful squealing and screaming that emanated from that wretched pit and sounded above the whoops and laughter of the onlookers, as the badger was baited. He felt sick to his stomach and terribly sorry for the poor creature, and regretted being unable to intervene on its behalf lest he blow his cover; these men were armed and evidently sadistic. Leo considered how cruelty to animals is often a sign of antisocial personality disorder, but beyond this abstraction and the tattoo, he realised his nocturnal mission had in fact been unrelated to Lauren's disappearance.

The cacophony at last ceased, and the men toasted their endeavours with fresh bottles and showered the attack dogs with booze and adulation. Eventually they switched on their torches and lanterns, killed the floodlight and dispersed, most of them in the 4x4s. Leo lay flat on the ground as Tam hobbled past, Bandit padding tiredly in his wake, too blood-sated to notice or care about a stranger's scent. Leo waited for a safe pause, then switched on his torch and slouched off in the general direction of the hall. He miscalculated his trajectory and arrived at the woods' border three hundred yards south of where he had anticipated, and then trudged across the great lawns towards the civilised outline of the darkened Biggnarbriggs Hall, overpowered by the need to sleep.

Day Six

THE day was generally sunny, but clouds processed across the sky in a stiff breeze. Leo enjoyed the gear changes and the roar of the engine as the Humber held the country roads faithfully. *This* is proper driving, he thought to himself, dreading the uncouth velocities of the motorway which lay ahead. Elaine, who looked lovely in a floral-print shift dress, privately regretted not having suggested they use her Mini, and had insisted they join the M74 rather than take the picturesque route which Leo had favoured.

Elaine's misgivings about her driver's penchant for scenic detours were increased when he suddenly swung the Humber off the trunk road and headed in the opposite direction.

'You know, I've never been to Sweetheart Abbey,' he said.

'Leo, we've got more pressing priorities than the tourist trail. Can we just get on?'

'To be honest, it's not actually sightseeing I have in mind. I want to take the B roads to see if the car that's been behind us pretty much since we set off continues to follow.' He looked in his rear-view mirror. '*Et voilà*, there she is.'

Elaine glanced in the wing-mirror. A black saloon was two hundred yards behind them. They continued negotiating the narrow roads lined with abundant hedgerows of gorse blossom, herb Robert and moon daisies. The fine granite profile of Criffel near New Abbey was the backdrop, which to its south gave way to the salt marshes and golden sands of the inner Solway Firth.

The saloon continued to follow, keeping its distance. When they reached Sweetheart Abbey Leo pulled in at the side of the road. He and Elaine disembarked, and a few moments later watched the black car round the bend, slow down and then roll on by. It was a big, powerful Mercedes with tinted windows and mud-sprayed licence plates.

They took a few moments to admire the ruined red abbey, Leo mourning the annihilation of the Reformation.

'It wasn't just the loveliness of these places that was wrecked. They were powerhouses of prayer, and there were dozens upon dozens of them, even in a poor and sparsely populated country such as Scotland. They were the welfare state of the Middle Ages, providing broth, medicine and shelter, wiped out in a spiteful rage. This one was built by Lady Dervorgilla in memory of her late husband Lord John Balliol in the thirteenth century.' He glanced sideways at Elaine and added coyly, 'Would you commission an abbey in mourning for me?'

'Possibly.'

They drove towards Dumfries, checking a couple of times that the Merc hadn't doubled back and picked up their tail again. Elaine fiddled with the archaic radio to get the hourly news bulletin; the police were now appealing to the public for information about the mysterious green saloon. Once they had joined the M74, Leo's usual motorway stress was compounded by Elaine's reaction to his confession that he had followed one-legged Tam after overhearing his telephone conversation in the cabin. She was angry that he had shut her out. Leo explained that he would have been concerned for her safety had she come along, but promised that from now on he would be fully up-front with her.

Once they reached Glasgow, Leo parked in the Merchant City and, as an apology, treated Elaine to a spot of lunch at a charming Italian restaurant he sometimes patronised prior to attending concerts at the City Halls. It felt thrilling and novel not to be dining alone there for once. They then visited a boutique which Leo had in mind where Elaine pinned her hair up and selected a blonde wig with a low fringe. It was remarkably realistic and Leo was bewitched by the transformation, particularly when it was accentuated by her donning a pair of non-prescription lens spectacles from a dressing-up shop. He kept glancing at her as they took a rustic route to Drymen. They passed through pretty villages which nestled in the gentle pastoral tract that lay between the city and the Campsies. These fells, the beginning of the West Highlands, looked resplendent in the afternoon light, sweeping mightily to their volcanic meridian. Each settlement possessed towering cypress trees, a kirk with high windows through which summer sunsets would gently refract, and a sad obelisk bearing appalling ledger to the Great War.

They located the Strange abode in Drymen, a pleasant little bungalow with a white-painted roughcast exterior, a neat lawn and a well-tended herbaceous border. Elaine felt a sense of trepidation as she walked up the pebble path; Strange might recognise her, and if he didn't she was about to revisit the trauma of her sister's disappearance. Leo, intuiting her unease, gave her arm an encouraging squeeze and stepped forwards with some brio to ring the doorbell. A soft chime sounded from behind the frosted glass, and after a few seconds a white-haired woman opened the door. Leo introduced himself and Elaine – or rather Rachael – to Mrs Strange, who said that they were expected and made some small talk about the recent heatwave as she showed them into the front room, a pleasant parlour of Parker Knoll furniture and framed photographs of grandchildren. They sat down on the sofa, and a few moments later the retired DCI Strange shuffled in. He wore a golf shirt and steel-framed bifocals and was frail and silver-haired, but he still possessed a noble imprint of his handsome younger self. He shook hands with his visitors, thankfully showing not a glimmer of recognition when introduced to 'Rachael'.

They had already decided that Leo should do the questioning, for fear Strange would remember Elaine's voice. Leo admired a medal of commendation that was housed in a glass display on the mantelpiece. Strange explained that it had been awarded for a brilliant arrest made in the early 1980s of a pair of violent desperados who had been robbing post offices in rural areas throughout Northumbria, Cumbria and into southern Scotland. 'So much of police work is about instinct,' he remarked, as his wife brought in a tea tray. 'Tapping into your experience, trusting your gut.'

Leo brought the subject round to the McDowall missing person case, which Strange had indeed read about. Leo explained that he was investigating the matter in a private capacity, and that he was concerned that Lauren and Hazel Bannatyne's disappearances were connected, not least because they had occurred on the same day of the year.

'Am I right in saying that the police investigation in 1979 was focused on the druidic cult run by the character known as Talorc?' he asked.

'I would concur that it was our primary line of inquiry,' said Strange, still beholden to dour police-speak after all these years.

'Did that chime with your viscera?'

'We weren't fixated on it,' replied Strange bluntly. 'If the two cases are connected, then the fact that the McDowall lassie disappeared on the same day of the year would suggest that there is a pseudo-religious aspect to that date, aligning with our suspicion of a cultish motive. Is there any sign that a group similar to Talorc's could have returned?'

'Not that I know of,' said Leo. 'In 1979, there was no forensic evidence found at the standing stones just north of Biggnarbriggs Hall. Did that not undermine your theory that the cult had murdered Hazel Bannatyne?'

'We did not believe she had been killed at that locus. Often abduction victims are taken away and despatched elsewhere.'

'But the cult did sacrifice animals up at those stones,' said Leo, feeling wretched to be discussing poor Hazel's demise so clinically in front of her sister. 'Surely that was their sacred place, where they would also sacrifice a human?'

'But that would have led to their detection.'

'But they were doing it for a mystical purpose; logical considerations would have been less significant.'

Strange shrugged. 'There are two types of crime: ones of impulse and ones of calculation. Sex crimes tend to fall into the former category, but the Bannatyne one seemed to fall into the latter.'

'Why?'

'Precisely because there was so little evidence anywhere – not just at the standing stones – and no body. Also, that lack of evidence might well point to more than one perpetrator, as it is difficult for a lone felon to commit a crime so cleanly.'

Leo decided to go for broke. 'Could the general lack of evidence have been because of a police cover-up? An element of the investigation team in some way connected to the crime? I was told files went missing.'

'Certainly not,' snapped Strange. 'Hazel Bannatyne's sister – what was her name? – Elaine, she gave me a hard time about that. Nippy sweetie, she was. Wouldn't let it go.'

Leo sensed Elaine prickle. 'They can be like that, bereft relatives,' he stated.

'Have you discovered any occult significance to the date of July the twenty-fifth?' asked Strange. 'My men couldn't, back in '79.'

'Not yet. I'm looking into it. On the way up here we decided to visit the Mitchell Library.'

'I suppose the dates could just be a coincidence,' mused Strange, before venturing, 'I wonder if the police have any current suspects who were also present in 1979?'

'I really don't know,' replied Leo.

They conversed for a while longer, and Leo rose when he sensed that he wasn't going to ascertain anything further of note. 'You have my number,' he concluded. 'Please ring me if you think of anything else that may be of relevance.'

'So, Miss Nippy, did you find him Strange?' asked Leo, once they were motoring through the lovely countryside towards Glasgow.

'I found him to be a liar.'

'Why?'

'An unconscious non-verbal cue. When you asked him about police collusion his hand went to his ear lobe.'

'Well spotted. Also, he asked *us* quite a few questions, as though he's more than passingly interested in the current case. I think he's hiding something. Which is presumably why he wouldn't see you for all these years. He did say one or two things of value, however: his contention that Hazel's abduction was calculated and very possibly committed by more than one perpetrator.'

The Mitchell Library would be closing soon, so the investigators decided to pursue their research there tomorrow. Elaine asked that Leo drop her at her city apartment at Glasgow Harbour. He pulled up outside the modern edifice and they sat pondering the river for a while, the clang of industry sounding from the opposite bank as a massive grey military vessel took shape.

'Leo, does your gift ever make you feel like an outsider?'

'Yes. But if I'm being honest, even as a child, before I fully realised that I possessed second sight, I never really knew how to connect with other folk, how to share their interests, how to make conversation with them. It's hard to put into words . . . life seemed to be something that was going to happen to other people.'

'I was the same. People think I'm standoffish, a bit of a loner, and they assume it's because of the trauma of losing my sister. And that definitely had a big, detrimental effect on me. But I'm ashamed to admit that sometimes I've used it as an excuse so that I can be left alone. You see, when I was young, when Hazel was still alive, I already felt left out, always on the periphery of things or wanting to plough my own furrow. Whereas she . . . she shone like a *star!* I resented her sometimes, even when I was wee, because deep down I knew I would never sparkle like her. It wasn't all plain sailing in our house.' Elaine began taking the wig off. 'Don't want the neighbours thinking I've gone barmy!' she quipped.

'No, leave it on. Just for a moment longer,' said Leo. She obeyed, and he leaned over and kissed her.

That physical act and its reciprocation had a deep impression upon Leo, and it was clear that he had reached one of those moments in his life that was both an ending and a beginning. The depression which had been a living cancer in his cranium these last few weeks, a vice fastened to his skull, seemed to abate. And something of the goodness and purpose that underpins this world reasserted itself to him.

Leo savoured the sweet agony of parting as he drove the short distance to the sheltered housing complex, stopping at a florist to buy an extravagant bouquet for his mother. Her wise, pale-blue eyes twinkled when she noted her son's moonstruck state.

Leo ascended the stairs and entered his apartment. The old place seemed different somehow, the furniture and antiques smiling at him in the summer dusk. He felt a profound sense of wellbeing, as though at last his trajectory was towards a meaningful end. Everything seemed exalted, in stark contrast to his recent state. A remembered fragment floated out of the haze, a telephone conversation made to Stephanie from some cheap boozer. He feeling utterly desperate, but his friend not listening properly, at the end of the line in body only.

'For pity's sake, Stephanie . . . can we not just have a proper conversation?'

'We're having a proper conversation.'

'No, we're not. You're distracted, I can tell. Plus I suspect I am currently on speakerphone. Come on, I need someone to talk to.'

'Okay, what do you want to talk about?'

'Anything. Which way the wind doth blow, Celtic's new centre-half, the price of fish fingers, how much I detest the music of George Gershwin. I just need to engage with another humanoid.'

'You're pished. I can hear it in your voice. You're drinking too much.'

'Don't you understand? I am self-medicating. I am not an alcoholic, I am a melancholic. And sometimes whisky brings powerful clarity. For example, I have just decided I wish you to be a legal witness.'

'To what?'

'My burial plans.'

'Leo! Do you realise how narcissistic fantasising about your own demise is?'

He ignored the jibe. 'I wish to be buried in the soil, and a tree planted upon me.'

'Are you serious?'

'Certainly. There's a place by Loch Lomond that does it. That tree will sprout from my very mortal remains; people shall enjoy the shade of my leaves, children will play among my boughs.'

'Isn't that all rather . . . pagan?'

'Not in the least. It is a highly environmentally-friendly choice; and what could be godlier than nourishing His earthly estate as my final act?'

'Right. So what kind of tree do you fancy? Maybe a weeping willow?'

'I believe that if asked, people generally would associate me more with an oak: constant and magnificent.'

'Do you realise that the Tory Party's logo is an oak? I'm worried about you.'

A text message had come from Stephanie half an hour later: 'I meant it. I'm worried about you.'

'I am in booze, Stepp'd in so far,' he had replied self-indulgently.

Leo was jolted from the reminiscence by knocking. He walked to the front door and undid the bolt. It was Rocco from downstairs.

Leo ushered him in, went to the kitchen, lit the gas burner and put the kettle on, while Rocco, wearing sandals and an emerald tracksuit with gold Adidas trim, padded into the drawing room and sat down. Leo always found the way Rocco's Britpop-era mop top clashed with his prematurely aged face to be faintly comical, and he couldn't resist smiling at his neighbour when he arrived with the tea tray.

'I had a feelin' you'd be up the road tonight,' began Rocco. 'Then, right enough, I heard ye comin' up the stair. Maybe I've got a dose o' thon second sight thingy too?'

'Perhaps.'

'I heard some lassie's gone missin' down there. I suppose that would put the kibosh on a holiday. Is that why ye came home so soon?'

'In a manner of speaking. Although I'll be going back to Kirkcud-brightshire on the morrow.'

'You certainly seem in better spirits.'

Leo smiled serenely.

'Leo, you've no' . . . *met* somebody, by any chance?' enquired Rocco excitedly.

'A gentlemen never tells.'

A broad grin broke out on Rocco's features. 'In that case, I'm comin' in,' he said, as he rose and made to embrace Leo. These prolonged, skunk-perfumed bear hugs were experiences which Leo had found unnerving when he had first known Rocco, but had privately come to enjoy.

'I am truly stoked you're feeling better, pal.'

'Thank you, my dear friend.'

Day Seven

LEO felt in holiday mode and whistled to himself as he showered. He then donned a pair of grey trousers and an open-necked peach-coloured shirt, beneath which he arranged a spotted damson cravat. He repacked his bag and set off to pick up Elaine. Notably, he wasn't waylaid by his customary need to compulsively check time and time again that his apartment was safe and secure.

The day was cloudy and muggy, so Leo motored along the Clydeside Expressway with his window open, the moving air fluttering Elaine's chestnut hair. She wore light Capri pants and a sleeveless top with a bohemian design. Leo resisted telling her how adorable she looked. Best not to come on too strong.

'Leo, why do you keep looking in your rear-view mirror?'

'I thought I glimpsed that black Mercedes.'

Elaine looked in the wing-mirror. 'You're imagining things. And anyway, there could be any number of black Mercs on the roads of Glasgow.'

They parked at a meter and walked towards the grand, domed Mitchell Library, an institution which used to overlook a fine terrace until it was demolished for a stretch of the M8. Just before they turned a corner, Leo glanced back up the street they had just walked down.

'Not more black cars?' teased Elaine.

'Sorry. I'm being paranoid.'

They entered the library and made their way through a series of arched corridors with waxed chequerboard floors until they arrived at a building guide fixed to a wall within the institution's modern extension, a soothingly beige world of blond wood and muffling carpets. They walked to the lifts and pressed the button for the fourth floor. A pleasant, bearded young man behind the counter there helped them wrestle with certain oversized geological maps of the Stewartry. Leo ascertained that there were no major culverts or subterranean caverns or watercourses in the vicinity of Biggnarbriggs Hall, nor indeed did the wider Kirkcudbrightshire-Wigtownshire region seem like much of a potholers' paradise. This seemed to put paid to Leo's speculation that the water flowing in near darkness from his vision might have been underground.

'The religion section is on this very floor,' he said after they had returned the maps. They sat down at a computer terminal and Elaine started entering different search criteria into the library system, bringing up various books on the occult while Leo filled in the results on little chitties. The bearded librarian sighed involuntarily when he saw the stack of paper, then retreated to a dusty vault to retrieve their requests.

Twenty minutes later, Leo and Elaine wobbled with their books to a deserted corner where there was a large glass-topped table and comfortable chairs. Among their finds was Charles Godfrey Leland's *Gospel of the Witches*, Sir James George Frazer's *The Golden Bough* and *The Encyclopaedia of Modern Witchcraft and Neo-paganism* by Shelley Rabinovitch and James Lewis. There was Heinrich Kramer's notorious 1486 treatise *Malleus Maleficarum – Hammer of Witches* and *Capitulum Episcopi*, a piece of medieval canon law based on surviving pagan customs in Francia.

'Now, select your chapters carefully and skim, my dear, *skim*,' urged Leo.

He jotted in his crocodile-skin notebook, intrigued by the subject of Witches' Sabbaths, on which the Sabbatic Goat, a horned idol, was often revered. These *soirées* could be held for a variety of reasons, such as a full moon or a sacred day, but Leo found no significance to the date of 25 July. He researched the Wheel of the Year, which detailed the main pagan festivals, but again drew a blank. Despite their sombre purpose, Leo had to inwardly admit he was enjoying himself, simply because he liked being in Elaine's company. At one point they took a break for brunch in the library's refectory, where they shared anecdotes about favourite childhood foods and drinks, enjoying that camaraderie found through mutual points of reference with a person from one's approximate own generation. Yet, Leo reflected, what they had in common was less interests or background but something ethereal and unspoken. A cool, tranquil pool of mutuality bathed in soft glade-sharded light in which they could both repose. A connection as though you had known this person all your life, or that you had simply been waiting for them all along to arrive.

About a half hour after they had returned to their task, the relaxed mood was broken. Leo became aware that Elaine had stopped turning the pages of her latest and final book. She was staring into the middle distance and the colour had drained from her face.

'Elaine, whatever is the matter?' enquired Leo.

She simply pointed at the page before her. The book was a newly acquired translation of *Compendium Habentis Maleficia*, which was composed in 1614 by one Br Jose Antonio del Nido. It was in part a witch-hunter's manual, and detailed much about alleged ceremonies and spells. Leo began reading in a soft voice from the opened page, which outlined various rites observed in parts of the Celtic North on certain hallowed days. These included Lammas Day, August 1st, when most of the population gave thanks for the harvest in church. An editorial note explained that the feast day was called Lùnastal in Scotland and Lughnasadh in Ireland by the pagans, some of whom were said to ritually sacrifice a young woman at dawn, as a blood offering to the 'horned god' for a bountiful crop. Significantly, the victim had to be procured several days before Lùnastal – for 'preparation', which was evidently a medieval euphemism for repeated sexual assault. Precisely seven days before.

'Which is . . .'

'July the twenty-fifth,' gasped Elaine.

'The date on which Lauren and Hazel went missing,' said Leo. 'So there *was* an occult angle to that day of the year.'

'This means that my sister was . . . *abused* for a week before being . . . slaughtered!'

'We don't know that for sure, Elaine,' said Leo weakly.

'Oh, Leo – *today* is August the first!' wailed Elaine.

Leo felt a terrible nausea in the pit of his being. 'Which means that poor Lauren has already been slain, at dawn this morning,' he concluded grimly. 'Which concurs with my instinct that she was beyond our rescue.'

'If only we'd been quicker.'

'You mustn't let yourself go down that road,' said Leo, although he himself suddenly felt a familiar pining for alcohol, dreading the possibility that he could have done something more to save Lauren. But what, within reason, *could* he have done? 'We won't be able to establish anyone's alibis for this morning, because at this time of year the sun rises at the back of five; everyone would simply claim they were abed.'

'Hazel and Lauren must have been held somewhere for those seven days,' said Elaine. 'Probably in some sort of secret chamber. But the police will have searched everywhere.'

'I wonder if the location could be related to the flowing water I saw in my vision. Perhaps it is close to water – some cabin or cellar or outbuilding, for instance. I'll tell you something else that this discovery means: the folk who had alibis for Hazel and Lauren's abductions needn't be innocent of their deaths. If some coven was in operation they could still have been present a week later, at the actual sacrifice.'

'Which means that, for instance, the Major and Maxwell might have been there.'

'No, not Maxwell; not for Hazel at least. He was abroad on the day of, and for some considerable time after, her disappearance. As for the Major, let's see if we can ascertain any more about his movements during that long-lost summer.'

However, Elaine, considerably troubled by the revelations that Lauren was most probably dead and that her sister had been held and abused before being murdered, told Leo that she first required some fresh air.

'I need to be alone for a wee while. I'll see you here in half an hour.'

Leo felt wretched that he had not undertaken this research trip by himself, given its propensity to throw up something upsetting. He jotted down some notes and subjected the remainder of *Compendium Habentis Maleficia* to a fruitless scan.

Elaine then returned, raw-eyed but composed.

'Remember, this doesn't necessarily mean that the perpetrator or perpetrators of Lauren's abduction are all or any of the same as those who took your sister,' said Leo, as they ascended a flight of stairs to where the newspaper archives were kept.

'You *know* this is all connected, Leo, so stop trying to be so bloody *reasonable!*'

A microfiche machine soon confirmed Fordyce's memory that the Major had been serving in Ulster at the time of Hazel's disappearance. In fact, he was photographed giving a news conference defending his men's use of baton rounds in an edition marked 26 July – the picture was from the day before, the very day Hazel went missing. Furthermore, when Leo checked the microfiche for a week ahead, he discovered a photograph of the Major dealing with the media after reveille on his base's parade ground, on the day they supposed Hazel would have been sacrificed at dawn.

'You know what this means – that Major Jock Lindsay Balfour-MacWhinnie, DSO, while guilty of being an objectionable, reactionary old buffoon, must be innocent of your sister's abduction and murder.'

They endured a miserable, humid car journey back to the Ken Valley, Leo sensing, correctly, that Elaine didn't want to talk. He prayed silently for her as she faced a new inner abyss in the wake of the revelation about her sister's final days. When he dropped her at Sannox House she informed him that she was going for a nap, such was her emotional exhaustion. Leo then drove to Biggnarbriggs Hall where he unpacked his bag and sought out the Greatorixes. They were in the rose salon, the spaniels lazing at their feet. The chamber was named because of its dominant tone and its fine views over the rose garden. Fordyce had nearly licked the *Times* crossword and Evelyn was fanning herself while re-reading *Jane Eyre*. Leo got the impression that their enquiries regarding his and Elaine's trip north were deliberately generic, as though they had sensed his desire not to be interrogated on the case's specifics.

Leo then drove to where the police had set up their incident room in the village. He parked and walked towards the kirk, exchanging a friendly nod with the local minister who passed by, a thin, middle-aged, grey-haired gentleman.

Adjoining the church was its little hall, which smelled sweetly of dust and varnished wood, evocative of sunny school gymnasiums and halcyon Scout huts. A couple of desks and laptops had been installed, with Dalton sitting at one and PC McLellan at the other. Dalton looked as though she was toiling in the day's torpor, and her mood descended a further league when she looked up to acknowledge her visitor.

'I come in peace, Detective Chief Inspector. Just to share some informa-tion.' She regarded him in perfect silence with a glare so glacial it threatened to melt the humidity. Leo felt slightly unnerved, and began blurting out the headlines of his recent sleuthing. 'I have undertaken research into the occult at the Mitchell Library, and I discovered a significance to the date of July the twenty-fifth. It precedes Lammas Day, on which a ritual dawn human sacrifice was made by certain pagans of old, by exactly a week, which is the length of time the victim was to be held in preparation. I'm afraid to say that Lammas is today, August the first. I believe Hazel Bannatyne and Lauren McDowall were kept somewhere, possibly close to dark, flowing water. Also, there's this black car that was—'

'That's enough, Mr Moran. Suffice to say, you're not my favourite person right now. I am still beyond pissed off that you imposed yourself on Anthea McDowall two days ago. You took advantage of a desperate woman's need to hear something positive to impose your weird, self-indulgent claims to some sort of some extrasensory perception. You raised her hopes—'

'I beg to differ. I did *not* raise her hopes.'

'You raised her hopes that something beyond solid, painstaking police work will solve her daughter's disappearance. Now, Anthea, in her bereft state, may have bought into your peculiar brand of psychobabble, but I will not countenance it. If you approach me or any of my officers again, I will have you arrested for wasting police time.'

Defeated, Leo slouched back to the Humber. All he wanted from what was left of the day was a gill of Scotch.

Day Eight

LEO overslept and when he woke felt jaded because of the numerous whiskies he had consumed the previous evening. He prepared himself for the day, descended the grand staircase and, finding nobody around, entered the kitchen. He had a terrible drouth, and took a moment to gaze at the glass of orange juice he had poured, savouring the anticipation before consuming it in a single draught, four thousand hours of Florida sunshine exploding inside his head. He went out through the French doors and strolled along the terrace, and upon reaching the hall's south-eastern extremity saw Elaine standing ahead of him.

'Elaine!' he called out.

She shot him a look of fury, and as he turned the corner he realised why. Leaning against the porch was Cynthia Blythman, her horse tethered nearby. Leo nodded towards her politely. Evelyn was also there, circling nervously as she chatted on a mobile phone, her spaniels running excitedly around her.

Elaine strode over to him and hissed, 'For Pete's sake, Leo, why did you call me by my real name? Cynthia might have heard you!'

Leo sensed that she was still under great stress from the previous day's revelations and offered an apology.

'That besom could tell Jimmy, assuming she's having an affair with him, or Maxwell.'

'Please, do forgive. She's unlikely to have heard and, even if she did, she won't know who Elaine is. She'll think it was just a slip of the tongue. Anyway, what are you doing here?'

'Evelyn texted me earlier, to ask me over for coffee. I found her out here on the phone, quite upset.'

Leo tuned in to Evelyn's conversation. 'I'm so dreadfully sorry, Donald. I'm going there right now. No, I insist; it's about time we got all this sorted out . . .'

Cynthia walked over to where Leo and Elaine were standing. She was swishing a riding crop, and her boots crunched cruelly on the gravel. She smiled serenely when she noticed Leo admiring how superbly her jodhpurs sculpted her legs.

'Whatever is the matter, Cynthia?' enquired Leo.

'There's been another incident over by Maidenhead House,' she began. 'I was out riding and came across the aftermath, on the bridleway, the old right of way. Apparently Donald was taking Rupert for a walk to the ruined priory. Lyle, the Major's butler, came past on a quad bike and ran him over.'

'Ran Donald over?' asked Leo, aghast.

'No, Rupert. I'm afraid he's dead. There was a terrible argy-bargy going on. The butler said it was an accident, but Donald didn't seem to think so. He's insisting Lyle swerved deliberately to hit the poor thing. It was quite something to see Donald so animated; he's usually such a peaceable chap. I thought I'd better come over and tell the Greatorixes. Evelyn is on my mobile to Donald now.'

At that moment, Evelyn finished her call and approached the group, looking decidedly harassed. She handed Cynthia her phone and thanked her. Cynthia said her goodbyes, untethered her horse, mounted it and set off at a trot. Leo had to admit that she looked magnificent on the chestnut thoroughbred.

'Cynthia told us what happened,' said Leo to Evelyn. 'Are you all right, my dear?'

'I told Donald I'd go over and have a word with the Major right away,' she stated, breathing deeply as though to steel herself. 'Our lands are in many ways mutually managed, so I feel responsible, somehow, when such things happen.'

'What about Fordyce?' asked Elaine.

'He'll be in Dumfries on business for most of the day.'

'Well, please let me accompany you, Evelyn.'

'And me,' added Leo.

'Thank you both, that would be most welcome. Let me just leave the dogs with Unity.'

It was cloudier than it had been of late, although the humidity wasn't as high as the previous day. They walked across the great lawns past the ornamental lake, through the kissing gate and towards the old bridleway that cut through a ribbon of woodland. Evelyn named wildflowers as they journeyed a stretch of sweet meadow – silverweed, vetchling and milkwort – as though to occupy her mind with pleasant pursuits.

'Forgive my ramblings – dear Great Uncle Hugo's influence, I expect,' she said. 'He so loved the natural world.'

Leo observed Evelyn for a moment as she strode forth in her odd, loping gait, dreading the coming encounter yet quietly determined to do the right thing. In truth, she could be as fragile as the petals she was describing and seemed out of context in this wide-open space, exposed to a world which had wounded her. Evelyn felt secure only in the tree-bound Arcadia of the hall and its immediate precincts, and only as long as she repressed the more evocative textures of existence. The wrenching loss of her mother had been particularly acute. Evelyn had been young, a mere child of nine, when she had died. It was no surprise that she had found a kindred spirit in her reclusive great uncle. During her mid-twenties Evelyn had been jilted by a cad, the adult trauma counterpart to her childhood bereavement. However, as for crime: it had generally seemed a distant evil. And the closer and higher the ramparts, the more traumatic the breach, and Lauren's disappearance, like that of Hazel in 1979 when her eleven-year-old self had gazed horror-struck for hours from the window of the rose salon, hoping to glimpse the missing girl, had pressed the sky downwards upon Balmakethe Parish, rupturing its pleasant pastures and pulverising its kindly gables.

Yet there was a paradox within Evelyn Greatorix. It was easy to misjudge her, to underestimate her as flimsy or dizzy or anodyne. In fact, in many ways she was the load-bearing member of the family and had a remarkable ability to accept that which is unalterable and proceed in the most practical way, even if all the while such a course of action grieved her to the roots of her soul. She lived as though in an early-Victorian novel, an unfulfilled yet heroic protagonist who goodness went right through and who prevailed with a kind of gentle stoicism.

'Evelyn, forgive me, but earlier Cynthia said there had been *another* incident over by Maidenhead House. What did she mean?' enquired Leo, as they entered the cool woodland arcade of the bridleway.

'Unfortunately the Major and the Nain Community are at constant war. Donald and Father Larranzar were probably too polite ever to mention it to you.' Leo recalled the off-colour remark the Major had made at dinner about shooting Father Larranzar. 'I shall give you the long story short,' continued Evelyn. 'Maidenhead House was originally built as a dower house for Biggnarbriggs Hall. In 1917, a couple by the name of Gordon purchased it and the surrounding land – including Linn Priory and beyond, and several acres south of the road – from my great-grandfather, who needed the funds. The Major had spent much of his childhood in this parish – his father was a gentleman farmer a couple of miles eastwards – before the family upped sticks and left for the Transvaal. He came back to Britain to join the army, then his parents died and he inherited a fortune, thanks to his father's diamond mining interests. In the mid-seventies, the Major bought Maidenhead House from Mrs Gordon, who was by then an elderly widow. To the Major's chagrin, Mrs Gordon insisted on donating the pocket of land on which the priory sits to the National Trust. When she lived here, Mrs Gordon never obstructed use of this bridleway, which runs roughly parallel to the forest road and to the rear of Maidenhead House, as it is by far the easiest and safest way of accessing the priory. But the Major quickly reneged on this custom and would be unpleasant to ramblers, and, once the community was established, people staying there who would visit the priory for religious purposes. The Major put up a fence, but this is an ancient public right of way and locals would often damage it. After the Land Reform Act, court officers removed the fence but the Major still made life difficult. He says that the bridleway is too near to his garden and therefore it's a privacy issue. However, although there's the rear gate, the Major's garden is quite enclosed.'

'Folk with such an excessive need for privacy are often hiding something,' speculated Leo.

'Surely you don't suspect the Major had anything to do with poor Hazel and Lauren's disappearances?' asked Evelyn, clutching Elaine's arm after she mentioned her sister.

'I have reason not to suspect him,' replied Leo. 'However, I intend to make sure his alibi stands up for the night Lauren went missing.'

Evelyn continued: 'After my father, who had been supportive of the Nain Community's cause, passed away, the Major's campaign went up a notch. For example, a few months ago Chas's dog Nero attacked Rupert. Chas was accused of setting the animal loose, but he denied this.' Leo recalled the scarring on Rupert's face. 'Oh, and one time, when there was a youth pilgrimage group staying at the community, the Major even let off a shotgun.'

'Great Scott!' said Leo.

'He wasn't aiming at anyone, just trying to scare folk away. There was something else . . . but there's absolutely no proof.'

'What, Evelyn?'

'Donald installed the Stations of the Cross on Scoulag Hill, just plaster statues. He goes there most mornings at dawn, to pray. Anyway, last autumn they were desecrated. Donald was terribly upset.'

'And you think it might have been an act of malice on the part of the Major?'

'Oh dear, I shouldn't have said anything; there's absolutely no reason to believe that. Aren't the forget-me-nots lovely? Is it just me, or have they become more abundant in recent years?'

This news about the vandalism of the Stations of the Cross disturbed Leo. He speculated inwardly that if Lauren and Hazel's disappearances had an occult motive, then there could be a connection with the desecration of sacred renderings.

They arrived at the rear of Maidenhead House. A high, mossy stone wall closed off its grounds from the wider world. The gate was painted black and featured a two-headed hound in the wrought-ironwork.

Leo tried the handle. 'It's locked . . . Hang on, I think I can hear somebody moving about. Hello! Is anybody there?'

After a few moments the gate opened, and a man wearing a sober black suit with a work apron over it appeared, carrying a dust shovel. He was aged about fifty and had a blank, pasty face and a receding hairline. Leo recalled Brian identifying him as Lyle, the Major's man, before the search party had set off. He regarded the visitors superciliously.

'The Major has one of his headaches. He is not receiving at present,' he said.

'Actually, it was you we wanted to speak with, Mr Lyle,' said Leo.

'If it's about that dog – it ran directly in front of my vehicle.'

'Donald doesn't seem to think so.'

'Well, he is mistaken. If he wishes, he can report the matter to the police and discover that they have more pressing matters on their hands.'

'Look here, Mr Lyle, this war of attrition has gone on long enough,' interjected Evelyn, her voice quivering with emotion. 'My father knew your employer, and he wouldn't have tolerated—'

'I'm afraid I have nothing further to say on the matter. Good day to you.'

With that, Lyle shut the gate on them, and the trio began trudging back towards Biggnarbriggs Hall.

'Did either of you notice the motto above the back door? *Pulsanti operietur* – "To him who knocks it shall be opened",' said Leo. 'I believe it is commonly used on Masonic temples.'

'How on earth would you know such a thing?' asked Elaine.

'Know thine enemy,' replied Leo.

Leo was pleased when Elaine agreed to stay at the hall for luncheon, as he felt that being in other people's company was the best thing for her. She looked pale and drawn as she sat at the kitchen table and picked at her potato salad, and he felt moved with pity for her. Leo, mindful of his promise to keep Elaine abreast of any investigating he had planned, informed her of his intention to have an early dinner at the Rose and Crown in Castle Douglas, in order to probe the Major's alibi for the evening of Lauren's disappearance. Elaine left the hall for Sannox House in the mid-afternoon, and Leo spent an hour strolling around the topiary and the maze, meditating upon the case's clues. He then drove to the Nain Community, intending to offer his sympathies for the death of Rupert, but there was no reply when he knocked the door. He jotted down a note and pushed it through the letterbox. Leo drove slowly through the village and then eastwards, lost in admiration for the soft countryside, the grey ridge of Criffel as its background. An impatient Flash Harry overtook him – presumably a local who knew the road – irritably sounding the horn of his canary-yellow Reliant Scimitar and making Leo swerve slightly. A half mile further on, Leo noticed that Flash Harry had pulled in at a rough-cast double garage, with redundant FINA petrol pumps faded blue and orange. Leo slowed down for a look. Chas and a couple of his pals glanced up from tinkering under the bonnet of a 1969 Ford Mustang Fastback with a gorgeous aqua metallic paintjob and black over-stripe. Leo speculated that these fellows gunned the vehicle up the old Ayr road between St John's Town of Dalry and the county border north of Carsphairn, and could almost hear its throttle gargling through the ascending gears. Flash Harry stood alongside his car, regarding Leo disdainfully. Leo jabbed a two-fingered salute at him and then accelerated, instantly regretting such uncharacteristically coarse behaviour.

He arrived at Castle Douglas and left the Humber in a municipal car park across from the Rose and Crown. He wanted to buy a present for Fordyce and Evelyn as a token of gratitude for their hospitality. However, he suspected that his hosts now privately desired a greater gift from him: the solving of the disappearances of Hazel Bannatyne and Lauren McDowall. He wandered into a gallery and chose an agreeable water-colour by a local artist, *Colours from the Shore, Mossyard*, which he thought would nicely adorn one of the hall's bedchambers. He also bought kites for the McGhie children from a toy shop and two delightful old-fashioned flip-top bottles of pink lemonade for Elaine from a delicatessen.

He deposited these goods in the Humber, then approached the Rose and Crown, which was a modest hotel with a public restaurant and bar. The white harling and black paintwork were in good trim, and Leo found the interior to be similarly appealing. A cheerful, pregnant young Gallovidian waitress appeared, who upon his request directed him to the restaurant.

A large retirement luncheon was in its boozy latter stages, and Leo felt slightly self-conscious as he sat alone at a little table. He was pleased the waitress wasn't one of those overbearing types who would by her effer-vescence unwittingly draw further attention to his solitariness. After a minute or two of studying the menu, he realised that the party were lovely, salt-of-the-earth types. He considered the polite people who had served him in the shops, and was relieved to remember that in spite of certain unpleasant recent encounters, the lieutenancy of Kirkcudbrightshire was generally stocked brim-full of solid, decent, courteous folk.

Leo ordered prawns followed by the Balmoral chicken, which was served with clapshot and drizzled with whisky sauce. It was tasty repast, and he engaged the waitress, whose name he learned was Heather, in conversation as she served. He mentioned Lauren's disappearance and asked if she remembered the Major and Lyle being at the hotel on the night of 25 July.

Heather replied, 'Aye, they had a slap-up dinner. I mind it well, because that auld bugger kept trying to grab my bum whenever I served his food!'

'The barbarian!'

As he ate, Leo pondered the sense of entitlement wealthy men like the Major possessed, and the resentment he felt towards them. He contrasted their easy plenty with his own threadbare childhood. Some summers, when his father was ill and there was barely any money coming in, in lieu of a holiday the Moran family would occupy themselves with daytrips to different municipal parks (of which Glasgow was amply furnished). He recalled the touching little plaques on wooden benches, remembrances to a late dogwalker; *Jeannie Mackinnon, 1882–1965. She loved this place.* Sloping arched beds spelling out a church centenary in flowers, or the honour of the local Boys' Brigade Company or Co-operative Women's Guild. There was something humble and quietly heroic about the way they would content themselves with these modest adventures; Leo's mother preparing a picnic of egg-and-tomato sandwiches, tinned pilchards, Kia Ora and Tunnock's Caramel Wafers. She would have amassed the exact bus fares required and the fees for the day's 'special treat' – a go on the boating lake or the putting green. Leo had a mental picture of himself solemnly focused as he and his mother endeavoured to finish their round before the rain came on, his father watching from a bench, quietly unwell, several layers on despite the season.

After Leo was served his coffee the cook came out to help Heather clear the tables that had been vacated by the retirement party. She was a diminutive, rotund woman aged around sixty with a kindly face.

'Did you enjoy your meal, sir?' she happened to ask.

'It was delicious, thank you.'

'Castle Douglas is kent as the "Food Town", so a' the produce is the best o' stuff. Makes my job gey easy.'

'You're just modest, Margaret,' interjected Heather. She looked at Leo and said with a wink, 'Everybody kens she's the best cook in the Stewar'ry!'

Suddenly Leo recalled what Fordyce had told him about the young woman from the village who had worked at the hall but who never returned after she thought she had seen a ghost. Her name was Margaret and she was a talented cook, and this lady's age profile seemed to fit.

'I beg your pardon, but did you ever live in Biggnarbriggs?' enquired Leo of her.

'I was born and bred in the village. I moved into my daughter's house in Castle Douglas about five years ago.'

'And did you happen to work at the hall during your youth?'

'I did. Wonderful place it was, but it didnae last.'

'She was too feart o' ghosts!' teased Heather.

'Look, I have no wish to be impertinent,' said Leo, enthused by the brilliance of the connection he had made, 'but I'm residing at the hall at present, as a guest of the Greatorixes. Fordyce told me about you, the experience you had. And this ghost, I feel I may have seen it too; or at least glimpsed it in my dreams.'

'A shiver runs through me every time I think o' it, sir.'

'Some people think you might have seen the family's reclusive Great Uncle Hugo.'

'Naw, sir, this was a real apparition.'

'Would you mind if I showed you a photograph of Hugo?'

Leo fiddled with his phone, and then displayed the picture to Margaret.

'No, sir, that's no' who I saw. The fella I saw was a young man, wi' different features altogether. He was wearing verra old-fashioned clothes. And a purple coat. He didnae gie off a bad feeling, but it was gey frightening a' the same.'

Leo paid his bill, leaving an extravagant tip, and then sauntered into the cramped public bar. The landlord, an overweight red-headed chap in his late forties, welcomed him pleasantly. Leo complimented him on the variety of whiskies and real ales available, and apologised for only being able to sample a half pint of IPA because he was driving. He treated the man to a dram, and continued making small talk, eventually steering the subject round to the Major and Lyle's alibi.

'Aye, they were in here till late that nicht, right enough,' the landlord responded. 'Took a right good drap the pair o' them did. And that Major fella made a pest o' himself wi' Heather through in the restaurant when they were havin' their dinner. I had to have a word.'

'Do they often come in?'

'Never seen them in here afore or sinsein.'

*   *   *

Leo drove to Sannox House but Elaine didn't answer when he pulled the doorbell. He concluded that she was resting or out for a walk, so he left the lemonade at her door with a note. He returned to the hall and telephoned his mother, then spent some time in the library, dipping into *Ivanhoe* and sipping a Whisky Mac. At one point he placed a record – a classical compilation – on an ancient gramophone turntable and set the needle. Leo transposed the tender feelings he felt for Elaine upon the swelling sensation the soaring strings invoked within his breast. He could recall the precise moment in his youth when he fell in love with this music. One summer evening his parents had switched the wireless on to listen to *Your Hundred Best Tunes*, and Alan Keith had introduced Mozart's *Laudate Dominum*. Leo had stood transfixed, staggered that something could exist on this earth that sounded so unspeakably beautiful. The soprano was like an angel descended from heaven. When the piece was finished Leo had discreetly retired to his room, sat down upon his bed and wept.

He decided to go for a stroll before he repaired to his bedroom for the night, wishing to enjoy the rose garden for a few moments. The gloaming created a cinematic effect inside the great hall as his clipped footsteps echoed through the space. He walked through the porch and towards the front of the house, noticing that Fordyce, who had been away all day, and Jimmy's cars were parked there. The cloud cover had much receded and he stepped into the gorgeous light radiating from the heart-breaking sunset, as though he was entering a landscape painting. Rabbits playfully chased each other on the great lawns, and the birdsong was as though guided by some unseen celestial conductor. He ambled past the topiary and reached the roses, and began reading the tabs that bore both the English and Latin names in Evelyn's meticulous handwriting. She had evidently specialised in traditional Scottish varieties: Old Yellow Scotch, pink and white Mary Queen of Scots, delicate pink Falkland, light pink Alba and bright pink Ayrshire Old Lavender. There was a nice floribunda called Apricot Nectar and some good, full-headed hybrid teas.

Leo's attention was drawn by a voice and he glanced up to see Jimmy, who apparently hadn't noticed him, up at the aviary. He regarded him for a few moments as he spoke tenderly to the birds and puffed on a cigar. There was something melancholy in his disposition that moved Leo a little.

'A beautiful evening!' he called out.

Jimmy gazed down at him and then gestured at the sky, where the waxing moon was summer gold. 'The stars are wonderful down here at this time of year,' said Jimmy. 'Look ye to the north: Cassiopeia, Polaris and the Plough are already visible; I'll be using my telescope tonight. We're fortunate in this part of the country – there's hardly any light pollution. Plus Scarrel House is on a raised bit of land, which helps.'

Leo walked towards the aviary and into a cloud of smoke as Jimmy relit his cigar. Leo privately disapproved of his not having removed the band from it first, as befits a gentleman, to say nothing of his casual discarding of the spent match.

'I thought there was a new pope!' he jested.

'It's to keep away the midges, mostly. Little bloodsuckers. Did you know it's the female of the species who does all the biting? Typical, I suppose.'

'I'm told you are the keeper of the aviary.'

'Indeed. I look after it in honour of the late baron. Although it is a pleasure, to be honest. You should have seen the exotic birds I had when I was in Papua New Guinea; *extraordinary* specimens!'

'There were peacocks perambulating the grounds last time I was here,' said Leo. 'I haven't seen them lately.'

'Chas reckons the foxes must have taken 'em. Or perhaps the Major bagged them for his pot. It wouldn't surprise me.' Jimmy's mood suddenly turned glum. 'Anyway, what's a lost bird or two compared to a lost girl? Do you think they'll find her . . . alive?'

'I'm afraid I do not.'

Jimmy sighed. 'I have a daughter myself, you know. Or had, I should say.'

'I'm so sorry.'

'Oh, she's not dead. She hates me, is all. I haven't seen her in six years, but I miss her every damn day. She got in with this crowd, you see – suddenly she thought me a terrible reactionary. They turned her against me, said that because I was a tea grower in New Guinea for a while it made me some sort of latter-day colonialist. Ask the native people who worked with me out there, who played cricket with me, who dined at my table if I was in any way a racist. I bent over backwards to accommodate my daughter's behaviour, even when I found it downright gross. I tried to pretend I agreed with her views, even though deep down I thought they were empty-headed. But none of it did any good. Bloody Marxists! They are so angry at God knows what they poison everything that's sacred with their gender politics. The poor old nuclear family is finished in this country, thanks to those damned man-haters.'

Leo felt that Jimmy's defence of traditional values was a touch rich, considering he was most probably involved in an adulterous affair with Cynthia Blythman. 'But hatred of women – that is also a serious issue these days, wouldn't you agree?' he ventured, pretending to examine a hangnail as he spoke. 'Some men feel angry at what they perceive as being left behind, as we progress to a more equitable society.'

'Equitable – don't make me laugh! You should try spending some time in a family court.'

'Granted. But what about men who might feel frustrated if they cannot possess an object of their desire. I wonder if some such fellow harmed poor Lauren.'

Jimmy bristled. 'What the hell are you getting at? Speak plainly, man!'

Leo cleared his throat. 'Was Lauren an object of *your* desire? Did you ever show an interest in her, in the café?'

'Look, Malone—'

'Moran.'

'Moran then. I'll level with you – I liked the girl. She was beautiful, she had plenty of spirit. And she knew that men were drawn to her sexually. And she was more than able to stand up to a bit of flirtation. I'll admit it, I like to flirt with younger women – it makes me feel young myself. But I wouldn't *do* anything with them. Sometimes I have a problem with communication; perhaps I come across as prurient. And maybe – just maybe – I did want to bed her, but if that were the case then I wouldn't be particularly proud of it. I certainly wouldn't have harmed a hair on her – or any girl's – head.'

Jimmy cast his cigar away and stormed off towards the terrace.

Leo followed him. 'Look, Jimmy, I want to make myself clear. I wasn't accusing you. It's just that a young woman has gone missing and we can't leave any stone unturned.'

'Who's *we*? You aren't the bloody police,' he barked over his shoulder as he ascended the side steps to the terrace.

'Quite so, but I'm taking an interest in the case. I happen to know that you took something from the lawns. During the search the morning after the inspector called at the hall.'

Jimmy stopped and slowly turned around to face Leo. He sighed, then said, 'I reckon this could land me right in it.'

'I just need to know all of the facts. I will be the soul of discretion, if at all possible.'

'It was an undergarment.'

'It didn't belong to Lauren, did it?'

'No. Oh, what the hell, it's a bloody open secret anyway. It was Cynthia's. We met out there; we both love that wide-open space. We thought it might be fun to have a jolly good fuck under the starlight.'

'When was this?'

'A couple of weeks ago, before all of this kicked off. The lingerie had nothing to do with the police investigation and it wouldn't have done to have it all come out, so I just decided to swipe it.'

'What did you do with it?'

'I returned it to Cynthia, pretty much straight after I found it.'

'You didn't burn it?'

'Of course I didn't bloody burn it!'

'Were you with Cynthia the evening Lauren went missing?'

Jimmy sat upon the balustrade. 'Yes. There's an old cottage on the other side of the parish which belongs to the Blythmans. She rode over on her horse to be with me there. We meet there quite often.'

'How long have you two been . . . seeing each other?'

'Nigh on two years, off and on. Look, I know you probably don't approve, but it's not just hanky-panky, you know. Damn it, Moran, I actually love that gal. Cynthia's a wonderful woman, despite having been put through hell during her fucked-up childhood. As for that bloody drip of a husband of hers, *Maxwell*, he's not worthy of her!'

Leo doubted this impression of Cynthia, but decided to keep his counsel on the matter. 'All the same, it seems a tad harsh: dishonouring him with his wife in one of his own houses.'

'Do you know that Cynthia or Maxwell often do not spend the night at the Ridings?' said Jimmy. 'One of them will arrive back at dawn and not even bother to offer an explanation to the other. They tell their servants their separate rooms are due to his snoring, but that's entirely contrived.'

Leo felt a little sorry for Jimmy. He was deluded as to Cynthia's character, and beyond a cheap thrill she wouldn't be interested in him – an ageing man falling into penury.

Jimmy made to leave, and Leo rolled out the Columbo routine, just to check the veracity of his version of events. 'Just one more thing. A week ago, the night when DCI Dalton called – after the ghost game you said your drink was "purely medicinal". You literally meant that, didn't you? I mean, you have recurrent malaria, and Dubonnet contains quinine.'

'Yes. Sometimes, such as on that night, I can anticipate an attack coming on. I become all hot and bothered, like a tremor before the quake. So I get thoroughly soused in Dubonnet. God knows if it has any real effect or not, but it seems to take the edge off.'

'I expect among the symptoms of an attack is that you get uncomfortably cold, then uncomfortably hot?'

'Yes.'

'So you sometimes need to build a hot fire, then extinguish it quickly.'

'Correct.'

Leo watched Jimmy walk off in the direction of his car. He placed a hand on the masonry of the hall; it felt pleasantly warm, still retaining the energy of the daytime sun. It was the blue hour now, and the strange light soothed his mood. He thought he could detect music floating through the drawing room's French doors. He ambled along the terrace and realised it was the *Evening Prayer* from Humperdinck's Hansel and Gretel. The floor-length curtains moved a little in the slight breeze, and Leo paused for a moment to regard Fordyce inside alone, tired from a day's business, sipping a port and ginger. He was wearing his tubeteika – what he called his 'thinking cap' – and pondering his unlit calabash. Leo wondered what his host was brooding upon, but sensed not to disturb him.

He would have been thoroughly intrigued by the topic of his dear friend's deliberations: a brief telephone conversation overheard three days ago which had drifted through these same opened doors, and what to do about it.

It had been the voice of Elaine Bannatyne, the woman until only a few minutes earlier known to him as Rachael Kidd. After the *dénouement*, which had taken place in the library, Fordyce had gone alone to the drawing room to fix himself a drink and digest the news. Prior to leaving on their investigations, Leo had gone upstairs to fetch some item or other, and instead of waiting in the car, Elaine had taken a stroll along the terrace when her mobile phone rang. She paused serendipitously just at Fordyce's vantage.

'Wee brother! It must be getting late in Melbourne . . . Of course I've thought more about it, but emigration is such a big deal.'

Fordyce normally wouldn't have countenanced eavesdropping, but this first instalment had incapacitated him and stopped him clearing his throat to announce his presence. His friend had seemed invigorated ever since he'd set eyes upon Rachael – or rather Elaine. The thought of a chance of joy being snatched away filled him with reflected dread.

'I know Sarah and the kids would love to have me there. I'd love to be with them. It's just . . . I think I've met someone. What I mean is, I think I've got feelings for him . . . Look, I sense Hazel's disappearance might soon be solved at last. And then . . . then my head will be clearer.'

Fordyce had always liked Rachael, and was sympathetic to her reasons for concealing her true identity. Nonetheless, he and Evelyn could hardly be blamed for feeling somewhat perturbed by her unmasking. They had, after all, still been victim to a rather lengthy deception. Now Fordyce found himself in a quandary. He was keen to warn Leo, who was already in a fragile mental state, that he might face heartbreak should he become romantically entwined with Elaine, but he had garnered this information illicitly, and to share it would offend his sense of honour. Also, Leo might object to his interfering; the chances were that Elaine was planning to tell him of her potential plans for emigration anyway. For him to wade in clumsily could cause more problems between the two. Poor Fordyce was such a conscientious man. He simply could not endure the thought of causing hurt to a fellow human being.

For her part, Elaine, already upset after her confession to the Greatorix siblings, had felt even more wretched due to the telephone call, anxious that she might have used Leo as her latest justification not to join her brother's antipodean life, a self-deception which would have been disrespectful to both men. Since then, she'd had misgivings about her and Leo as an item. Now that they had kissed, things seemed to be hurtling towards an escalation which thrilled her but also scared her. It was not unusual for two people on the north side of forty to meet and quickly take up together, and doubtless there was a strong unspoken connection between them, to say nothing of their mutual attraction and respect. However, something hindered her. She was so used to a solitary existence and was so set in her ways that she was concerned about how much of herself she could now bequeath to a partner. Moreover, she had started to suspect that her peculiar make-up combined with her unusual life – the early trauma and the subsequent obsession with finding her sister's killer, the way it had driven her and kept her alone – had caused a vital portion of her heart to ossify. Perversely, a part of her wanted Leo to recognise this in her and hold it against her, instead of purely fostering desire for her, which was evident despite his inexpert attempts to restrain it. Elaine felt that she might soon finally find out what had happened to her sister, and perhaps even obtain justice, an outcome that would bring immense satisfaction. However, the uncomfortable fact remained that she would then also have run out of excuses about how she wished to spend the remainder of her time on this earth.

Day Nine

As though telepathically tuning into Elaine's misgivings, Leo suffered anxious dreams and awoke at dawn dimly aware of a sense of pessimism regarding their fledgling relationship. He got up, opened his curtains and gazed out, pleading for the gloom to lift: '"With my soul have I desired Thee in the night; yea, with my spirit within me will I seek Thee early."'

A thin drizzle was descending over the maze, lawns and lake, melancholy in the haggard light. At least a blackbird had the decency to sing out. Leo wondered whimsically if the one he could hear was descended from the 'merle' immortalised in verse by Robert Burns. He noticed a tall figure in a hooded yellow waterproof jacket using a staff striding across the grounds. It was probably Donald on his way to his Stations of the Cross statues on Scoulag Hill, but what if it wasn't? Leo thought of the fairy tree: what if this was someone out to place new pagan iconography in the vicinity, or perform some other mischief? The figure paused, just abreast of the maze, and stooped to tie a shoelace, buying Leo a vital few seconds. He pulled on trousers, windcheater and shoes, and dashed downstairs and along the terrace in time to see the man enter the tree line beyond the tennis court.

Once in the dripping woodland Leo felt nervous as his eyes adjusted to the light. Then the robins began repeating their musical phrases at each other from their little territories, and a thrush uttered its song, alternating between the morose and the comical. Leo was heartened by this dawn chorus, and gave thanks that grace operated in such mysterious ways. He picked up the yellow-clad man's tail, traversing the border of Scoulag Woods and what was known as the Enchanted Forest. The man was heading up the incline towards Elaine's home and Scoulag Hill, and therefore away from the weird energy of the standing stones and the fairy tree, so Leo concluded that the figure most probably was Donald en route to his early-morning devotions. However, he realised he had now lost sight of his quarry. He walked on and paused by a prone beech, ancient and rotting. His attention was arrested by an extraordinary *churring* sound just to his left and he swung round. It was a nightjar, not two yards away, which had now risen in flight with its trademark white tail and wing spots in perfect view.

Leo's sudden movement meant the weapon that had been aimed at his skull made merely a glancing, rather than a fatal, collision. His knees weakened and his vision blurred, and as he sank to the ground he saw his father's smiling face saying, 'Come with me, son. I'll look after you now.'

No, Daddy, not yet – there's things still need doing.

His sight returned as the assailant, who had no face, raised his weapon to strike the final blow. But another, yellow-clad, figure had appeared and a staff flashed through the air.

Leo passed out and saw water flowing in the near darkness and then the countenance of Gilbert Doyle, horribly afraid.

Slowly, he became aware of Donald Kennedy, who indeed was the man in the yellow jacket, gently coaxing him back to consciousness. Warm blood was trickling down the side of his face from a wound above his left ear. He felt nauseous and giddy when he stood up, and Donald slowly walked him towards Sannox House, which was the nearest abode.

'What happened?' asked Leo groggily as Elaine's Mini bumped up the rutted road that skirted Loch Grenoch.

'You were attacked,' replied Elaine. 'Donald intervened, then woke me.'

'He was wearing a ski mask,' said Donald, who sat alongside Leo, holding a towel to his wound. 'He scarpered, but left his weapon behind. It's in the boot. When you came round you were mumbling something about the birds being the "intervening angels of the Almighty".'

'Of course! The song of the blackbird, the robins and the thrush fortified my spirits, and then the nightjar distracted me, such that my attacker only struck me a slight blow instead of braining me. The nightjar is rare in Scotland and well camouflaged and therefore seldom seen; in spite of its unjustly sinister associations it was utilised as an instrument in a miracle!'

Leo spent the rest of the journey to the Accident & Emergency department at the Royal Infirmary in Dumfries drifting in and out of sleep, at one point being vaguely aware of Donald using Elaine's mobile to report the incident to the police. In spite of the profuse bleeding, the head wound was not deep; it was cleaned and a few absorbable sutures and a dressing applied. Leo underwent a CT scan because of his sickness and loss of consciousness. The registrar urged him to stay in for observation as she feared he might have concussion, but Leo, who had a profound aversion to hospitals, signed himself out, much to the consternation of his friends. Elaine's concerns were assuaged by her being permitted to install him in the guest room on the ground floor at Sannox House, where his immediate needs could be attended to. She then telephoned Evelyn and told her about what had happened and that she would host Leo until he was steady enough on his feet to tackle the hall's grand staircase. In fact, Elaine simply wanted to look after him.

Leo slept until late afternoon in Elaine's deliciously soft guest bed. His resting consciousness drifted through weird and lovely realms. His dreams then suddenly shifted to the romantic – to Maddi, his long-lost love.

'And lo, this is heaven!' He laughed out loud. 'So I wasn't such a bad fellow after all.'

His laughter must have woken him, but he realised that a component of the dream had persevered – a pleasurable sensation, a rhythmic movement. He saw Cynthia sitting at the bottom of his bed, her breasts jiggling beneath her orange summer top as she vigorously massaged his feet.

'Nice?'

'Most rejuvenating,' murmured Leo.

'Merely an act of kindness for a wounded soldier,' said Cynthia. 'I'm trained in reflexology. Did you know that nerve endings in your extremities connect to various internal organs – *all* the organs, as a matter of fact. You simply manipulate them to promote bodily health.'

'Fascinating, I'm sure.'

'I've brought you flowers.'

Leo noted a spray of orchids with a little card. 'Thank you kindly.'

'I just wanted to pay my respects. I was out looking for Maxwell earlier when I came across Fordyce, who told me you'd been hurt.'

'Is your husband missing?'

'His bed hadn't been slept in.'

Leo mused that it was almost as if Cynthia was trying to drop her husband in the soup. Elaine entered the room carrying a cardboard box and Cynthia let go of Leo's foot and got up to leave. She flashed a false smile at Elaine as she departed. Leo smoothed down his blankets guiltily.

'Leo, what the hell is going on?' demanded Elaine.

He sighed. 'I awoke and she was . . .'

'Engaged in foreplay with your feet?'

'Administering reflexology.'

'While you were sleeping, Fordyce and Evelyn came over with gifts and some of your things.'

With that, Elaine angrily dropped the box on the bed, accidentally striking Leo's right big toe with it, and stormed out.

'Bloody *Cynthia!*' he exclaimed as he rubbed his tender digit.

He took an inventory of the items in the box, then read a note from his best friend.

Old stick,

Grieved to hear of thy tribulation. Myself and Ev popped by, but you were conked out and we didn't wish to disturb.

Please find herein some necessities and also a tea loaf and a flask of sis's restorative rosehip syrup. A leather case contains one 1917 British Army issue Webley MK VI service revolver, unloaded, replete with a box of 12 rounds. It was last fired in anger at the Hindenburg Line by Great Uncle Hugo, but is oiled and properly maintained. My brother kept it as an antique when the law changed in 1997, properly surrendering its ammunition. However, this morning a singular thing occurred. I was searching the wood-drying shed for some trout flies I had tied as a youth when I happened across this long-forgotten box of .455. Ordinarily I deplore firearms, but my discovery felt providential. We can turn the bullets over to the authorities after the present emergency is passed.

Rest up, my friend.

Yours affectionately,

F.

Leo suspected that his own abhorrence for guns exceeded Fordyce's. However, he reluctantly broke the revolver, filled the six chambers and put the weapon back in its case.

A while later, Elaine entered the room in sulky silence, carrying a tray bearing a pot of tea, buttered toast and two soft-boiled eggs; she had reckoned accurately that it was about all her patient had an appetite for. She noisily arranged these things on the bedside table.

'Do you wish me to cut your toast into soldiers?' she asked eventually.

'Please.'

She proceeded without speaking further, the only sound that of the butter knife traumatising the tea plate.

'I love the crockery, all the little bunnies and chickens. Puts me in mind of Easter. And I love that ship in a bottle on the windowsill. There's a pleasant nautical feel to this room.'

Elaine didn't respond as she brutally decapitated the eggs.

'You realise she's trying to sow discord between us, by using her tender weapons?' said Leo. 'That's what people like Cynthia do.'

'I'm not remotely interested in the woman,' said Elaine as she poured the tea. 'Although you clearly are – you weren't exactly fighting her off. Plus I saw the way you were staring at her yesterday in her jodhpurs.'

'May I ask you something?' ventured Leo.

'What?'

'Will you hold off the investigating until I'm recovered? This case has violence at its pips, and it's safer to work as a team.'

'That's rich. Three days ago you promised you would tell me in advance of any investigations you had planned.'

'But last night was entirely exceptional. I just happened to wake at dawn and look out of my window, at which point I saw someone – I didn't know it was Donald at the time – walking across the grounds of the hall. I had to act instantly or I would have lost his tail. Little did I realise that someone else was following *me*.'

'DCI Dalton came over earlier and took the horrid weapon Donald retrieved,' remarked Elaine. 'She told me to let her know when you were awake. Are you ready to speak with her?'

'Yes.'

'Then I'll give her a call.'

Leo first described his visit to the Rose and Crown, how he had met Margaret the cook and shown her a photograph of Hugo, who wasn't the same individual she had been frightened by in her youth. 'I'm now convinced that Margaret encountered the same ghost I saw on the hall's battlement, the man in the plum coat from my visions,' he concluded.

'Leo, all this talk of spooks . . . I'm unconvinced.'

'Fair enough. Anyway, concerning the Major and his man Lyle's alibi – they were definitely in the hotel on the night of Lauren's disappearance. The Major was a pest towards the waitress there. Now, this is a long shot, because the evidence seems to put him in the clear and I know he makes a habit of being lecherous towards younger women, but it is just possible that the Major had been bothersome towards the waitress in order to make his presence all the more memorable and thus reinforce his alibi.'

'Leo, the Major is a complete arse, but he's innocent in all this. We've cleared him for '79, remember? Let's stop pussy-footing around and admit Jimmy is most probably the perpetrator. The bastard was creepy towards Hazel when we were kids and then swiped something at the search party.'

'I was about to come to the subject of Jimmy. Last night I happened upon him at the aviary, and we had a direct exchange, which culminated in him admitting that on the night of Lauren's disappearance he was with Cynthia for an adulterous assignation. You'll remember we suspected he had destroyed by fire in his bedchamber whatever item he had taken from the lawns. A fire lit in summer is a dead giveaway of disposal of evidence, and I thought it fishy his claiming to have a chill on such a balmy morning. But I now know that Jimmy got a hot fire going quickly and extinguished it instantly due to a malarial paroxysm.'

'How do you know?'

'Because I guessed it and he confirmed it. Last night, he reminded me he'd lived in Papua New Guinea for a while, which I know is a malarial country. After we played the ghost game on that evening of the first dinner party, I noticed he was sweating profusely, although I initially assumed it solely due to a passionate intrigue with Cynthia. He then started gulping down Dubonnet and mentioned it being "medicinal", but as it happens he didn't mean that jokingly; I recalled that the beverage actually *does* possess a medicinal quality – quinine, used to treat malaria. The fire in his bedchamber was lit with accelerant because he quickly needed ample heat due to his chill, and then suddenly put out with water because the fevered stage of the attack was then setting in.'

'But I saw him picking something up.'

'Yes, evidence of a tryst. It was an undergarment belonging to Cynthia, left there by mistake two weeks ago. He restored it to her possession.'

'A very neat explanation.'

'Elaine, don't turn your justice into poison. It's time for you to shed your prejudices against Mr Handley. Have you analysed the bug you attached to the aviary?'

'Yes.'

'And?'

'Nothing of note. Just Jimmy Dolittle talking banalities to the birds.'

A half hour later, Leo heard the doorbell sound and DCI Dalton and PC McLellan were shown into his room. Elaine brought a couple of chairs in for them, and after they declined tea, she left.

'How are you, Mr Moran?' enquired McLellan.

'I have endured the Torments of Tantalus,' declared Leo melodramatically. 'But *nil desperandum*, Dunkirk Spirit and all that.'

'I suggest that when you're feeling better you go home to Glasgow, for your own safety,' said Dalton.

'I'm not prepared to do that, Chief Inspector,' replied Leo.

'Well, let me detail a police protection officer to you. And you must not go out again at night.'

'No and no,' stated Leo defiantly.

For a few moments there was only the sound of the birds chirruping softly in the early evening sunshine in the woods to the rear of Elaine's property. Dalton broke the silence, requesting Leo's version of events from early that morning, and he provided her with a brief summary.

When he had finished, Dalton said, 'There were no fingerprints on the weapon other than Mr Kennedy's, who picked it up after the attack. He says the assailant was wearing gloves, and of average height and build. Mr Kennedy took us to the locus earlier. We found footprints belonging to a third party. A size-nine, man's outdoor shoe. Our dogs picked up a scent, which doubled back and terminated at the car park by Loch Grenoch. The suspect must have had a vehicle waiting there, and that usually breaks the scent trail. Anyway, I thought you might be interested in seeing the item that almost killed you.' Dalton reached into a canvas bag and withdrew a heavy, varnished object approximately a foot in length and wrapped in polythene. It had been skilfully turned from a single piece of mahogany. The lower two thirds were a beaded handle, and the upper portion a bulbous head, which had a flat top with intricate symbolism upon it.

'It's an ugly-looking thing,' said Leo. 'On the night you told us of Lauren's disappearance, I had a vision of a gang of thugs beating a man to death using clubs. I believe it was a flashback to an incident that actually took place hereabouts during the eighteenth century. I wonder if the clubs were similar to this one, and if there's still more than one of them in this locale.'

'As it happens, this item does date from the eighteenth century. We took it to an antiques expert who confirmed it, although he said that the markings were added much later. And neither he nor anyone else has a clue as to what they mean.'

Leo studied the symbolism, which was carved into the wood and inlaid with white enamel. He was greatly intrigued to see that the main component was two vertical lines supporting a crossbar. The bottoms and tops of the vertical lines were slightly splayed. Above this shape was a little circle with a dot within it. At the bottom was an inverted triangle, with a vertical line descending from its lower point, and another, longer vertical line descending from its left-hand point. All of this detail was enclosed within a circular band, embedded into which were five tiny obscure characters, perhaps from some ancient script.

'We believe it may be quasi-Masonic.'

'Well, you ought to know, officer,' said Leo, but Dalton didn't appear to like the joke. 'You do realise that this thing is a setting maul?'

'Yes. As used in Masonic rituals.'

'Indeed. In Masonic mythology such an item was used to assassinate Hiram, King Solomon's architect. By the way, I noticed a Masonic motto engraved above the rear door of Maidenhead House. However, assuming the cases are related, Major Balfour-MacWhinnie couldn't personally have been present for the abduction and murder of Hazel Bannatyne, or the abduction of Lauren McDowall – as long as she didn't loiter prior to getting into the vehicle on the forest road, as I have firmed up his alibis. An ancient symbol might suggest an occult sect and therefore multiple offenders, like the thugs in my vision. The enclosing band probably illustrates the closed and hugger-mugger nature of the sect.'

'Possibly, although it could be a sect of one.'

'What do you see when you look at the shape in the centre?' Leo asked Dalton.

'Perhaps Doric columns supporting a lintel.'

'Yes, it might represent a classical temple. I have seen such a shape twice before. First of all in a vision during which a shadowy, ghastly spectre appeared to me. Then, four nights ago, I saw it on a badger baiter's arm in upper Scoulag Woods. His tattoo was an abbreviation of this symbol.'

'Can you describe the man?'

'No, I didn't get a look at his face. But Chas and that one-legged Tam fellow were there. You might wish to question them as to this tattooed man's identity. There is a temple of Venus on the island in the ornamental lake near to Biggnarbriggs Hall. Now, I have had a recurring vision about flowing water in dim light, and that lagoon is syphoned from Scoulag Burn. The water in it therefore flows slightly, although I admit that my vision had faster-moving water. But sometimes the visions are oblique or symbolic representations of reality. I believe it a distinct possibility that Lauren's disappearance has some connection to that island temple. It's situated not far from where she was last seen. Perhaps there's a chamber beneath it where dastardly deeds have been done, although I couldn't see anything untoward when I visited it.'

'Neither could my officers.'

'Detective, I need your men to re-examine it. Take it apart brick by brick if necessary. See if it yields some clue, no matter how small.'

Dalton motioned her head towards PC McLellan and the two of them left the room; the detective obviously valued the input of her uniformed sidekick. While they were in conference, Leo took the opportunity to photograph the maul and the symbol it bore several times, from different perspectives.

The police officers returned, and Dalton sat down again and said, 'All right, Mr Moran. I'm going to take a chance on you – one chance, and that's your lot. We will have another look at that island. But understand this: no one – and I mean no one – must know that I'm acting upon your advice.'

'My lips are sealed.'

'Now, tell me everything you know that might be of interest to this case.'

Leo told Dalton about his recent visions and the clues and information he had gathered. However, he didn't reveal Elaine's identity or the fact that they had visited Strange in Drymen and believed there may have been police collusion in a cover-up at the time of Hazel's disappearance. He also didn't bother mentioning Jimmy removing Cynthia's undergarment from the lawns. He told her in detail about the research at the Mitchell Library, including the consequent theory that Lauren had already been killed as part of an occult ritual (a notion now reinforced by the strange symbolism on the maul), after having been, like Hazel, kept in a secret location for the previous week. If it wasn't at the folly then it was likely some other chamber near flowing water. Dalton interjected to assure him that a thorough search had been made of the locality, including of all properties, and that all householders had been most cooperative, although she acknowledged the fact that Lauren could have been driven further afield. Leo informed her that he had personally walked most of the nearby watercourses, and that his research in Glasgow seemed to rule out any major subterranean cavern or watercourse in the vicinity. He told her in more detail about his vision in which the man in the plum coat – presumably the eighth baron Greatorix – was murdered. The ghost of whom he believed he had glimpsed standing on the tower's battlement and who Margaret the cook had encountered years ago. Dalton clicked her pen impatiently at the mention of phantoms, so Leo moved on, and told her everything else of note that sprung to mind about his recent stay at the hall, including people's alibis and rivalries. He mentioned the desecration of the Stations of the Cross and the mysterious black Mercedes.

'On the subject of sinister cars, has the green saloon been traced?' he asked Dalton.

'No.'

'Do you suspect any of Lauren's peers could have been involved in her disappearance?'

'No.'

'I think you're right not to. What do you make of this one-legged Tam fellow?'

'Rather unpleasant, but probably harmless.'

'Is he a suspect? He seems a very unsavoury type. Furthermore, he was here in 1979 when Hazel went missing, and Lauren disappeared not far from his hovel.'

'That's all true, but there's not a shred of evidence against Tam McEwan. He readily gave us permission to search his cabin when we were looking for Miss McDowall. Now, if that's everything, your girlfriend can stop eavesdropping from behind the door and we'll be on our way.'

Dalton took a note of Leo's mobile number but significantly did not offer him hers, as though to curb his expectations as to the extent of their collaboration. After she had left, Leo and Elaine sat together and digested what had been discussed, in particular the setting maul and the symbolism carved into its head. Leo worried about the pervasive influence of the global secret society within the police force, and he wondered if the Masonic flavour to the weapon could in some way validate Elaine's theory about a cover-up of her sister's abduction.

Elaine took her leave of Leo, and he sent a lengthy text message to Fordyce to reassure him that, although tired, he was well enough, and to thank him for the gifts. He also advised him to ensure the doors of the hall were locked at night. Lastly, he asked if he would mind checking on Maxwell's whereabouts, remembering what Cynthia had said about having been unable to locate him.

The reply read: 'Rest thy gentle head – I shall visit on the morrow. Maxwell here at this very moment, playing tennis with Evelyn.'

So he hasn't scarpered, thought Leo. And thinking of Elaine, sweet sleep overcame him.

Day Ten

L EO woke at 8 a.m. with the daylight streaming through the upper window of the guest room and the birds singing cheerfully in the sunny trees outside. He felt dizzy and nauseous when he rose to use the water closet. Elaine heard him moving around, and helped him back to bed. Her manner had softened, and Leo realised her testiness of the previous day was more rooted in the recent revelation about her sister's final days than Cynthia's touchy-feeliness.

'How do you feel?'

'Fine. Just a tad woozy when I first stood up,' replied Leo, forgoing his customary hypochondria.

Elaine didn't want to say but her patient looked fairly awful, and she was ready to veto any plans he might be hatching to be up and about sleuthing prematurely.

'Well, you have a snooze and I'll ring the doctor, just to have you checked out.'

The GP, a chirpy man called Doctor Monteith, arrived at around noon. He cleaned and inspected Leo's stitches and told him not to keep the wound covered any longer. He was concerned Leo had concussion, and instructed him to stay abed for another few days. Leo was frustrated by this interdict, and by the fact that he had again missed a visit from Fordyce and Evelyn, who had come by in the late morning while he was asleep. He ate a light meal and as Elaine was taking the tray away the doorbell rang. She checked if Leo felt like receiving visitors and then showed Donald Kennedy and Father Larranzar into his room.

'How are you feeling, Leo?' asked Donald.

'I shall toast another Christmas or two yet – and all thanks to you, Donald.' He revisited the incident: 'I happened to awaken and look out of my window, and I saw you walk by. I wondered if it might have been someone else, up to no good, so I followed. Then I lost sight of you and was attacked.'

'It was the most curious thing,' said Donald. 'I was on my way up to Scoulag Hill and I suddenly felt this need to pray, right there and then. I knelt on the turf amid this green grove, and said the Prayer to Holy Michael the Archangel. As I stood up I heard this sound – it was you crashing to the ground, only a few yards away. The assailant was preparing to strike you again with his bludgeon, but I managed to dash over and get my staff in the way just as it was coming down. The thing went flying out of his hand, and he ran off.'

'It sounds as though your sudden urge to kneel and pray was a miracle, otherwise you would have strode on ahead and my brains would currently be fertilising the herbage of Scoulag Woods. The next miracle was the arrival of a nightjar that startled me enough to make me avoid the worst of the weapon's blow. Tell me, Donald, have you ever seen anything strange in these parts on your nocturnal walks?'

'No, although Gilbert, may he rest in peace, felt there was something odd going on around here. He said he once saw people moving around at night.'

'When did he tell you this?'

'A year or so ago.'

'Could it have been badger baiters?'

'Who knows. There was another thing – last year the statues I placed on Scoulag Hill were desecrated.'

'Evelyn mentioned that to me.'

'Some of them were inverted, and all of them were splashed with red paint.'

'Did you inform the police?'

'No.'

'Did you happen to take any photographs of the vandalism, for future evidence?'

'No. I was so upset I just wanted to get it sorted and move on. The paint came off easily enough, and I said a prayer for the culprit.'

'Who could have done such a thing?'

'I wouldn't like to accuse.'

Donald then discreetly took his leave, and Leo noticed that Larranzar was tying a clump of small yellow flowers to the bed frame.

'Pretty, isn't it, for something so tiny?' said the friar.

'Is that herb Bennett?'

'Well noted. Herb Bennett or *Geum urbanum* or St Benedict's herb. It wards off evil spirits.'

'It sounds rather pagan. I'm beginning to worry about you, Father. I'll have to report you to the bishop,' joked Leo.

'I happened across them on my way over here. The species has five petals which are said to represent the Five Wounds of Christ.'

The friar then laid his hands gently on his friend's head, taking care to avoid touching his wound, and said a prayer.

'Thank you, Father. I hope your blessing will keep me strong enough not to booze excessively.'

'Your drinking concerns you, doesn't it, Leo?'

'Yes. But my current hostess makes me want not to drink. Yet conversely, because my keenness for her is reciprocated, I am horribly afraid. Such that sometimes I want to drown myself in alcohol.'

'What are you afraid of?'

'I don't know. Happiness. Blowing it. Losing her.'

'At some point you're going to have to get off this rollercoaster, and with Christ's help face down your demons. It sounds as though this woman has inspired you to take the first step.'

Leo spent the afternoon trying to view the case through a wider aperture and to puzzle out the significance of the setting maul, occasionally gazing out through the opened curtains at the finches whirring their wings in the sparkling water of Elaine's birdbath. He sketched out the recondite symbol on an A4 pad and stared at it for a while. Some fancy compelled him to draw inner lines between the five characters embedded in the outer circular band. As he expected, this created a pentagram. Leo used the internet browser on Elaine's laptop to research this shape, and spent hours filtering out scholarly work from an ocean of balderdash and oddball conspiracy theories.

When bound within a circle, like this one, the pentagram is often known as a 'pentacle'. The pentagram is used in magic, the five points referring to the five Platonic elements, the top one being aether or spirit. In black magic the pentagram was inverted, aether downwards pointing to denote the transgression of the natural order of things. Leo noted that the pentagram he had drawn based on the symbol on the maul was itself inverted.

In the nineteenth century, the pentagram became associated with Baphomet, and the deity's goat head was represented set within an inverted pentagram. It was speculated that Baphomet represented the so-called Sabbatic Goat worshipped at pagan ceremonies and Witches' Sabbaths, and Leo recalled research he had undertaken into this subject in the Mitchell Library. Baphomet was also said to be the horned god glorified during the ancient cults of the Goat of Mendes and then Pan, and later the horned fertility god cults in parts of the Celtic north, where Herne the Hunter or the Green Man were idolised. Many of these cults were said to have involved acts of sexual perversion and even human sacrifice at their ceremonies and festivals. The nineteenth-century rendering of Baphomet's goat's face within the pentagram was often enclosed by a circular band with Hebrew lettering inside that spelled out 'Leviathan', the water monster from the Book of Job. Leo realised that the five tiny characters embedded within the outer band of the symbol on the setting maul were also Hebrew – אַחְדוּת, which translated as the word 'oneness' or 'solidarity' or 'unity'. Leo knew someone called 'Unity' who was interested in the mystical and whom he had seen wearing a pentacle medallion, but of course his attacker had the height and build of a man, whereas Mrs McGhie was decidedly petite.

Leo shared his discoveries with Elaine, who, like him, doubted that Donald could have mistaken little Unity for a grown man or that she could be the leader or member of some terrible cohort. The information was nonetheless intriguing.

The police's search of the temple of Venus drew a blank. During the late afternoon, Leo awoke from a snooze to find he had missed a call from a restricted number. He dialled his voicemail to hear DCI Dalton's voice, straining with irritation. Apparently, frogmen had double-checked the ornamental lake and Forensics had crawled all over the island and the folly itself. They had even taken out interior brickwork and drilled holes in the floor to confirm it wasn't false. It had achieved nothing, only a massive diversion of resources. Also, the men Leo had named – Chas Shaw and Tam McEwan – flatly denied having anything to do with any badger baiting or knowing anyone with a tattoo like the one Leo had described. He was instructed not to contact DCI Dalton again, and encouraged to 'bugger off back to Glasgow'.

Leo's appetite began to return, and by suppertime he was complimenting the risotto Elaine had served him as he sat up in bed. She was perched on a chair, her own bowl balanced on her lap while her patient finished off his last few mouthfuls, an easy silence stretching out between them.

'Leo, when were you first aware that you had second sight?' asked Elaine eventually.

'There was a singular incident that occurred in Baghdad, where I was holidaying with my parents when I was five years old. A dervish identified me in the street as a brother mystic. Later in my childhood, I started experiencing certain dreams and imaginings that possessed a specific intensity and a peculiar quality I cannot put into words. Eventually, certain events coincided with these visions, and it was clear to me that there was a purpose to them. My mother explained to me that second sight ran in her family (although she herself did not possess it). Apparently her aunt, when a teenager, had been mistrusted and shunned due to her accurate foretelling of someone's imminent death.'

Elaine finished her risotto and placed her and Leo's bowls on the dressing table. She then slid onto the bed beside Leo.

'What is it that haunts you, Leo Moran?'

'That, my sweet, is a long story,' he said as he stroked her hair.

'That night we first met, at dinner, you drank like a fiend. What was troubling you?'

'You were. You made me feel even worse about myself. Your beauty, your goodness, the attraction I felt towards you; and all the while I was feeling wretched.'

'Why?'

'Different reasons . . . for starters there was the usual background noise of self-loathing and loneliness.'

'What else?'

'Two winters ago, up at Loch Dhonn in Argyll, I solved the case of the murder of a young nurse by the name of Helen Addison. In self-defence I was forced to take the life of the perpetrator. His spirit started tormenting me, and it's been affecting me badly. Then Gilbert died suddenly and it tipped me into a depression.'

'Gosh, you *killed* a man! That must resonate, psychologically.'

'Indeed. But I'm still glad I moved to defeat Helen's killer. On the one occasion when I didn't act decisively on the content of my visions, I ended up with these.' He held up his gnarled, purpled hands.

'What happened?'

And so it was that Leo related his tragic backstory to Elaine: 'As I indicated, fragmented visions had visited me from time to time during my childhood. They seemed random and meaningless, until the long hot summer of 1976, when I was fourteen years of age. A nine-year-old boy, Hugh Renton, had gone missing from my neighbourhood. Privately, the police weren't overly concerned as the lad had ran off before, due to a troubled home life, and always returned. But I had this vision which suggested that Hugh was, in fact, in danger. I went to the police but they didn't take me seriously. However, the vision had given me clues as to Hugh's whereabouts, and I located him in a derelict tenement apartment. It turned out that he had been taken captive by a paedophile, who had by now taken his own life. Upon Hugh's rescue, the cops suddenly took an interest in *me*, and began grilling me mercilessly; how had I come to know so much about the abduction? Was I an accomplice of the dead perpetrator? It was *horrible*, and although the police couldn't pin anything on me, rumours spread around my community about my involvement in the crime. I was roundly abused and ostracised. I became quite the loner.'

'Oh God, Leo. I'm so sorry you had to go through all of that.'

'It gets worse, I'm afraid. And the next chapter doesn't exactly cover me with glory.' Leo took a deep breath. 'The following year I had another vision. This one referred to a girl I knew a little, who was my age. The vision suggested her being assaulted by some teenaged males. By now, I had become so introverted that I couldn't bear the thought of bringing more attention upon myself. I also wanted to avoid suspicion should a crime actually be perpetrated of which I again would have specific knowledge. So I took the coward's way out: I repressed the vision. I didn't speak out, I didn't warn her. I did endeavour to track her movements, particularly when she was walking to and from school along the canal towpath, promising myself that I would intervene should anything unfold, and lying to myself that the vision was probably just a random dream, not an omen. And then, one day when I was unable to follow her home, the vision came true. She was gang-raped. In the aftermath she simply fell to pieces as a human being. The next vision I experienced occurred late one night, and was of her trapped alone in her house as fire ripped through it. I awoke and ran over to her place, and, lo, it was ablaze. I burned my hands as I tried to get inside to aid her, but it was too late. Two firemen had to drag me away from the inferno. It was never proven, but it was suspected that the lassie had self-immolated, such was her trauma. And the part I played – or rather failed to play – in her sad story has racked me ever since. I would drown the consequent shame and guilt in a sea of alcohol but eventually, at the end of my time at university, my past caught up with me and I spent a spell in a mental hospital. And my relationship with my beloved was wrecked. Ever since that terrible fire, my greatest fear has been not acting to save someone.'

For her part, Elaine had listened aghast, not least because she realised that their backstories had at one point overlapped. She vividly recalled the Hugh Renton case from the newspapers, because at the time her family had realised that his abductor had also attacked a neighbour of theirs, the summer before. She explained this to Leo and for a long time they held each other tightly.

'Fordyce claims that the sunsets here are the greatest in the three kingdoms,' said Leo eventually, sighing and groaning like an old man as he raised himself from the bed. 'Let us go then, you and I, and experience it.'

Elaine draped a blanket over Leo's shoulders and helped him towards the front door. Outside, the martins had come up from Biggnarbriggs Hall to wheel and screech and gorge upon the midges; then it was the pipistrelles' turn. Generations of both species had nestled in the tower's eaves and nooks for so many centuries that should a particularly learned little bat have taken the task upon him and donned the wig, he could quite reasonably have litigated for their inclusion under the illustrious Greatorix patronymic. The high land, majestic and abiding, darkened solemnly against the bloodshot sky. The moon glowed impossibly as the sun gave forth its glorious final blossom, before taking its stately leave of the ancient and lonely mountains. Coolness descended and then, quite suddenly, there arrived a strange mist, smoking from glades in the forest. On the other side of the Biggnarbriggs valley it crept ghostly upon the hillocks and meadows. And as the bats flitted thrillingly within inches of his face, Leo held Elaine's hand and wondered how in the face of such beauty there could be any evil in the world, any lass ever snatched away in the first flush of her youth.

Day Eleven

Elaine let Leo sleep until mid-morning, and when she brought him in a light breakfast he declared himself recovered and announced his intention to visit the hall that day. He wanted to browse certain books he had spied in the library, and more importantly engage the help of Fordyce in unravelling the symbolism carved into the setting maul. Leo was a little envious of the cryptographic cast of Fordyce's mind which could with ease complete crosswords, unlock codes and solve puzzles. However, Elaine was adamant that he remain in bed, so they struck a compromise whereby Fordyce would come over to visit him after luncheon.

Leo was delighted to see Fordyce, who arrived wearing a rather striking pair of scarlet trousers and armed with the requested items: J.D. Buckley's *History of Freemasonry* and *Ancient Alphabets and Hieroglyphic Characters* by Bin Wahshih Al-Ani. Fordyce had brought over a few other volumes he felt might be of help and Elaine provided the men with her laptop in order that they could also research online.

'Confucius proclaimed: "Signs and symbols make the world, not words nor laws",' said Leo. 'So let us decipher, my dear fellow.'

Leo was comfortable with Fordyce assisting in the case like this, from a safe distance, and felt it proper to update his friend on certain developments. He told him that when Margaret had thought she had encountered a ghost she had not, in fact, seen Great Uncle Hugo but a younger man in a purple coat like the individual from his visions and the figure he had espied on the battlement. He told him in detail about his and Elaine's visit to Strange in Drymen and how they believed there may have been a cover-up at the time of Hazel's disappearance. He summarised the research into the occult that he and Elaine had undertaken at the Mitchell Library, and to Fordyce's horror told him about their theory that Lauren had by now been killed in a ritual, after being kept prisoner somewhere for a week, probably in a chamber near flowing water. He said that this was the same fate which likely met Hazel in the summer of 1979. He also mentioned the mysterious black Mercedes, but Fordyce didn't know of anyone in the locality who owned such a vehicle. Leo told him about the badger baiting, and Chas and Tam's untruthful denial to DCI Dalton that they were present there. When probed, Fordyce admitted that Tam McEwan was an unpleasant, irascible man, but stated that he had no reason to suspect him of anything sinister.

'Old stick,' he continued, 'there was something regarding Great Uncle Hugo which has only just now popped into my mind. In his final months, with his dotage well advanced, he would haver about "the lanthorns". He would plead: "Why aren't they abed?" A lanthorn being an old Scots word for a lantern. Perhaps he was simply referring to the stars. He was quite wandered in those last years, I'm afraid.'

'I wonder if he saw something from his tower,' suggested Leo.

'Perhaps it was Talorc's cult, or badger baiters,' proposed Fordyce. 'That cruel practice may have gone on in Hugo's day.'

'Donald told me that Gilbert saw strange goings-on at night only a year or so ago. What if it was a group somehow linked to the men with torches I saw in my vision, who were responsible for both girls' abductions?'

'It's possible, I suppose. Although the population round here is much altered over the last few decades. There have arrived incomers from far and wide in the UK.'

This statement made Leo recall the mixture of accents he had heard in the Green Man Inn. He updated Fordyce on the research he had undertaken the previous day on the symbolism on the setting maul, and showed him the photographs he had taken when Dalton and McLellan were out of the room, explaining that the central shape was the same one he had seen in a vision. He also showed him his sketch of the symbol, and explained how he had superimposed an inverted pentagram which could be related to the deity Baphomet, and mentioned the tattoo he had seen on the shoulder of one of the badger baiters.

'I've never seen such a tattoo, although as it was on the man's shoulder I would be unlikely to have ever glimpsed it. Do you think the man who struck you was this tattooed chap?'

'It's possible. But if we're dealing with some sect, then it could have been any one of their number. This Hebrew word on the symbol certainly sounds like the motto of a group, requesting "oneness" or "unity". Of course, we both know someone called Unity!'

'It wouldn't be anything to do with young Unity, my dear fellow,' said Fordyce. 'She's a trifle unorthodox, but fundamentally a very sweet person, and she would not be in alliance with violent men.'

'I happen to agree. And anyway, these translations are merely approximations. However, I'll be sure to follow the matter up with the woman.'

Fordyce gazed intently at the photographs on Leo's mobile telephone of the maul.

'The bludgeon is an antique setting maul, as used in Masonic rituals,' said Leo. 'The antiquarian the police consulted stated that it's eighteenth-century, but that the symbol was added later, which is borne out by the fact that it was adapted from nineteenth-century imagery.'

'Could a cult of Baphomet really be alive today?' proposed Fordyce.

'It's a distinct possibility.'

The books and the internet bequeathed information. About how panic and persecution had spread through mediaeval Europe after the Knights Templar were alleged to have been involved in Baphomet worship. About how the Templars were said to have spawned both the Illuminati and the Freemasons. About how the Masons were accused of Baphomet-worship and then of devil-worship.

'I mistrust the Craft, but some of these anti-Masonic websites smack of conspiracy nuts,' said Leo, looking up from the laptop.

'Perhaps we're dealing with a Baphomet cult who heard of and bought the conspiracy theories and therefore chose to adopt quasi-Masonic symbolism,' suggested Fordyce.

'Or the other way round: Freemasons who chose to believe the theories and start worshipping Baphomet,' said Leo. He regarded his sketch again and said, 'What about the item above the central element, the circle with the point inside?'

Fordyce consulted the book by Bin Wahshih Al-Ani and another thin volume on esoteric symbolism. 'It can denote many things in alchemy and the occult,' he stated. 'Gold, the sun, air. The Masons use it. Some think they borrowed it from Eastern religions and that it represents the penis within the vagina – a tribute to nature's reproductive powers.'

'Or it could symbolise how mystical knowledge and dire initiations within the Craft are kept secret by those in the inner degrees,' said Leo, paraphrasing as he scanned another anti-Masonic website. 'The circle within the circle.'

'Leo, let's focus on the central shape, the two columns supporting a crossbar.' Leo's mind glanced guiltily upon the folly which the police had wrecked. 'What if it's the capitalisation of the Greek character *Pi*?' proposed Fordyce.

'Of course – so it could be a mathematical clue.' Leo tapped at the laptop. '*Pi* has significance to Freemasons. They're interested in its relevance to construction, and on the cosmic plane the building work of the Almighty – the Great Architect. They also believe the constant to be a transcendental number because it is infinite.'

'What if *Pi's* significance applies to the circle with the dot in it,' suggested Fordyce. 'In that the constant refers to the ratio of a circle's circumference to its diameter. Or it could be the Greek letter *Pi*. Or it could denote the written Greek numeral of eighty.' Fordyce flicked through a numerology book. 'According to this, eighty symbolises power, dominance and control.'

'We're doing well, Fordyce. We have a translation for the Hebrew word in the outer band. We have the significance of Baphomet in the pentagram. And we have several solid suggestions for the circle with the dot and the *Pi* shape. Now, what about this strange item at the bottom: the upside-down triangle with a vertical line descending from its lower point, and a longer line descending from the left-hand point?'

They referred to the Bin Wahshih Al-Ani book and tried numerous internet lists. They wondered if it was a letter from an alphabet. They tried ancient Hieratic, Hebrew, Ogham, Phoenician and Sanskrit characters but drew a blank. They considered that it could be an obscure alchemic, astrological or planetary symbol, or a hieroglyph or a rune, but again found no match. A web page stated that some occultists simply create their own bespoke symbols, and Leo and Fordyce agreed this was the most likely scenario.

Elaine came in with lemonade and biscuits.

'I say, old stick, you and Miss Bannatyne seem to be getting on famously!' observed Fordyce after she had left.

'I've only known her a short time, but I must confess we have a strong connection,' replied Leo bashfully. 'She somehow makes me feel calmer within myself.'

'And she seems . . . keen as mustard too!'

'I think so.'

'I take it she has no . . . plans for the future that could prove an obstruction?'

'What do you mean?'

'Oh, nothing. Could you do something for me? Promise you'll take things slowly, in case – heaven forfend – things don't work out.'

'Of course, my dear friend.'

Elaine invited Fordyce to stay for dinner and telephoned Evelyn, who, keen to check on the patient, also came over. Leo, fed up with being confined to bed, insisted that they sit at the kitchen table. Elaine had prepared a delicious carbonara in the belief that the pasta would fortify her house guest. Leo sulked a little when she refused him wine due to his head injury. The other diners also abstained, in solidarity, and Leo soon warmed to the conversation as Fordyce began outlining the afternoon's research.

Despite Elaine being younger than him, Leo felt like the junior partner in their fledgling romance, but he didn't mind. There was a natural symbiosis to their interactions, and despite his throbbing head he'd loved his time at Sannox House. As well as mothering him, Elaine was tolerant of Leo's foibles and would smile forbearingly when he expounded one of the offbeat observations about life he had nurtured in the febrile solitude of his usual existence. Meanwhile, she remained as self-contained and restrained in her responses as she was in control of her intakes. She did, however, issue malapropisms so endearing that even the pedagogic Leo couldn't bring himself to correct them – 'stigmata' instead of 'stigma'; an acquaintance who was 'lactose intolerable'. And she had a charming way of regarding a person, thoughtfully, silently, a slight sparkle in her eye, the faintest trace of a smile forming upon her lips as though she was connecting with and savouring their unique essence.

For so long, any sort of a life with a lover had been anathema to Leo. In his youth he had woven romantic little futures, until tribulation had put them unreachable as the moon, and survival had become his only objective. For consolation he had convinced himself that seclusion, in fact, suited him. Now, completely unexpectedly, he had met Elaine, and sharing her habitat for a brief few days had exploded this as fallacy; in fact, he liked immensely the presence of another human being nearby.

Yet the prospect of companionship still terrified him. Sometimes, when he regarded her and detected the trace of the first loveliness of her youth, the old demons of self-loathing would taunt him and a familiar feeling of unworthiness would swell up in his breast. He wanted more than anything to expel these moments with gill after gill of Scotch, but then the feeling would pass because Elaine was unlike anyone else he'd ever met. He felt comfortable around her; she wanted to soothe his wounds and insecurities.

Leo knew it was seemly to hold back, but he was ready to insinuate this inamorata into his routine and he could not help but dream of a simple existence with her, their mutual commitment to privacy and quietude sanctified in this pretty house in the woods. They could tend vegetables, wash their faces in the dawn dew and assuage the aftershocks of each other's youthful traumas. They had different aesthetic tastes but the same commitment to domestic hygiene and order that prolonged solitary living breeds, and he would gladly overthrow the lavish accoutrements that adorned his apartment, sell them off for the poor. And whenever they wanted company, Fordyce and Evelyn would be just through the trees.

Leo adored the Greatorixes, but he wasn't from the same world as them. He hailed from that most uncherished echelon of Britain's caste system, the upper-working/lower-middle-class. He was bereft of a classical education, of teenage skiing holidays and school trips to the battlefields and temples of Antiquity, of October mists upon the rugger fields, of the cut-glass diction which inhered self-confidence and commanded respect. He came from streets just as bland, albeit shabbier, as the ones Elaine had been brought up in, and one fibre of his attraction to her was precisely her comforting familiarity, her girl-next-door ordinariness, even though her right to suburban ordinariness had been brutally denied by the murder of her sister when she was aged eleven.

Once Fordyce and Evelyn had left, Elaine escorted Leo to the guest room. At the bedside he turned to face her, and moved by some sudden foreboding uttered the words: 'You do not want to get close to me.'

And she kissed him and then whispered, 'Why?'

'My soul is harrowed right through with shadow.'

'You get to a certain age and you realise everyone's weird, everyone's messed up.'

And they lay together and that experience of her was heavenly balm for every moment of pain and obscurity he had ever endured, every suffering his visions had inflicted on his consciousness. And the loneliness of ten thousand nights was gilded with meaning as they sank into each other's arms, in mutual recognition; *at last, I have found you, fellow lone wayfarer, dear heart*.

And for a moment Lauren was returned safe to the bosom of home, and Hazel and her parents smiled down from paradise. And through the woods, softly gorgeous did the late sun rest upon the cloistered pale stone of Biggnarbriggs Hall, and lo, the thrush throated his full-hearted evensong which echoed through embowered glen and o'er brook and hearth-farm and fragrant meadow, and rang to the very heavens. And all the trees of the forest rejoiced for Leo and Elaine's love, and the hills sighed with a peace that would last a thousand years.

Day Twelve

LEO rose early, showered, dressed in his outdoor clothes and pored over an OS map as he distractedly ate toast and marmalade. He informed Elaine that he was feeling better and that he was going to explore as many stretches of the watercourses in the area as possible that very day. 'Twice I have glimpsed flowing water in my visions. I have already examined the local spots; now it is time to move further afield.'

'Look, Leo, I hate to be blunt, but we are only looking for a corpse now, remember? Why not just wait until you're fully recovered? Also, it's going to be a humid day.'

'I'm not sitting around in bed any longer,' he stated firmly. 'We can find clues with which to trace Lauren's killer or killers, before they strike again.'

Elaine sighed defeatedly. 'What was the dark water in your vision like? Was it a broad or narrow stream, was it a waterfall, was it rocky, was it foamy?'

'It was in close-up. Quick, fast-flowing, I think. But the visions are often merely oblique approximations of reality.'

'That doesn't give us a whole lot to go on.'

Leo went to pack his knapsack. He slung the leather case containing the Webley revolver over his shoulder; hopefully Elaine wouldn't enquire as to its contents. He still felt a little unsteady on his feet, and was privately glad that she would be driving.

The first port of call was the upper reaches of Scoulag Burn, from the so-called Cauldron westwards to Loch Quien. They parked by the forest road and followed a track through a pine wood until it skirted the burn. It was beautiful here, the hazy sunlight filtering though the verdure and glancing upon the water as it chattered over a bed of smooth stones. They tried to walk the bank itself, however, sometimes it became impassable and they had to revert to the track. Also, the burn had so many tributaries it would have been impossible to follow them all. At one point, they heard a four-stroke petrol engine nearby. It echoed loudly around the wooded depression, making it impossible to know where it was coming from. Its pitch and movement made Leo suspect it was a quad bike. He withdrew the Webley from its case.

'Leo, where the *hell* did you get that?' asked Elaine.

He disregarded the question. 'The Major's man Lyle uses a quad bike,' he said as he scanned the undergrowth for the machine, its engine gurgling now as it idled. Then the throttle opened and the vehicle snarled off into the distance.

Further up, they had to cut through some birch woods to follow the burn, which was now flowing black and brown over ugly dark rocks. They crossed a strange, wicker-like bridge to where the rusting carcass of a 1960 Vauxhall Cresta grinned at them from the shadow, implausibly placed in this remote thicket. Nearby were mossy bricks and collapsed timbers from some abandoned abode. At one point, Leo thought he heard the quad bike in the distance, but he didn't tell Elaine.

After they reached Loch Quien they returned to the Mini, where Leo examined the map and announced that they would drive to Glen Trool, declaring he had 'a feeling' about the place. They descended into Gatehouse of Fleet, thrilled by the prospect of an abundant valley, its sloping pastures blessed with clumps of furze and then ancient woods, and criss-crossed with drystane dykes, the sea sparkling in the distance. Beyond Gatehouse Leo thought he glimpsed a quad bike in the wing-mirror, which was slightly askew, but when he turned around the Mini had gone into a curve, and he didn't see anything of further note.

They parked at a woodland hamlet and started walking the Water of Trool. After its confluence with the Water of Minnoch its flow became so imperceptible that pond skaters were able to crouch upon its surface tension. The path cut inland for a while where the bank was impassable, and there were pools in which Lauren's face threatened to gaze up from amid ghostly fronds of submerged sedge. They passed through a wood of rowan, birch and oak, and then enjoyed a glorious descent through majestically tall pines to the banks of Loch Trool, the wild heart of the huge forest. They walked the lochside for a while, then took a different route back to the car as the sun reached its zenith, the sibilance of water ever nearby. Sometimes it was a cataract, sometimes a river, sometimes a burn. Sometimes it flowed quickly, sometimes slowly, sometimes not at all. Sometimes it ran tea-brown and curdled to thick foam where it eddied, or languid willows dipped their leaves where it crawled. Serried pines stood starkly silhouetted on a hazy ridge or on the brow of a moor as a crow cawed above a deposit of desiccated branches, bark-denuded, sun-bleached, bone-brittle. The yammer and gnaw of a tree harvester (at first Leo thought it was the dratted quad bike) drifted over the land, a police helicopter vibrated above, and a pair of officers strode past wearing boiler suits, thrashing with sticks through the wilting weeds and crackling brake.

They replenished their flasks with fresh water as the heat and humidity built, and stopped by an old stone bridge for a repast of cheese savoury sandwiches and boiled eggs. They took off their shoes and dangled their feet in the river. Already they had formed their own club, with its own humour and terms of reference, not so much against the world as apart from it.

They returned to the Mini, and Leo obsessed over the map as they drove. Elaine became frustrated because she had to execute complex manoeuvres in the tight roads whenever her passenger had an impulse that they turn back to examine the ground surrounding some obscure burn, only to find the sallow alluvial ribbon of a dried-up stream bed or banks hopelessly overgrown or uneven. They walked a stretch of the Big Water of Fleet to find a rough, bleak glen, the aesthetics of which depressed Leo, where sheep bleated miserably amid the tussocks and flies of evil metallic beauty rose in filthy swarms from lumps of dung. He was again haunted by imagining the sound a quad bike engine chattering in the distance. Then, to Elaine's irritation, Leo requested that they double back along a difficult little single-tracker and then up a lovely tree-canopied road, following the Cree upstream as it meandered through wood and meadow.

They drew up on a grassy strip near to a tributary that Leo wanted to explore, which cut through a sloping area of mixed forestry called Wood of Larg. First, Elaine requested a look at the map. She regarded the maze of curling blue lines with exasperation.

'Leo, this is hopeless. We've only scoured about one per cent of these watercourses. Do you realise this is the largest forest park in Britain?'

Leo sighed. 'I've been hoping I'd been acting on some extrasensory instinct, but it's starting to feel like blind guesswork.'

'Well, why don't we give this area a thorough once-over, and then we'll call it a day,' she said gently, gazing into his eyes.

Leo was glad to agree because the exercise and the humidity were tiring him. However, something coquettish in Elaine's manner stirred vigour within him. She then said obliquely in a low voice, 'I'll see you in there,' got out of the car and walked towards the tree line.

He entered a belt of pine woods and was drawn by the distant sound of gushing water. The fragrance was sweet, the shade providing some succour to the heat. Leo realised that the depression that had persecuted him of late had waned to a mere membrane which filmed the periphery of his perception; only an echo, a vestigial imprint of his recent state. Suddenly, a noise: two beautiful roe deer breaking cover, startled by his presence. His heart soared as he followed them upwards through the sloping thicket. He reached the brown water, foaming and thundering downwards through the living rock. A dipper perched amid the slight mist thrown up by the tumult. Mosses and alien-looking liverworts gave off a strange, delicate aroma.

The ground up here was small hillocks which nestled secret dells enclosed by virgin woodland, chiefly stunted, mossy oak. Redstarts and warblers sang to the glory of the season. The understory, too, had changed as the earth became shallower and less base rich. A carpet of bilberry and sphagnum, dotted with tiny flowers: the mauve of wood cranesbill and, everywhere, yellow blades of cow wheat.

It was then that he saw her, standing upon one of the little ridges, her red clothing framed by a leafy ellipse. She regarded him, then turned and walked off solemnly.

He followed her. He was in a state of heightened consciousness such that he could discern the wingbeat of a bird, perceive the intricate texture and grain of lichen and bark and stone, stone so ancient that it had known his love at dawn of the earth.

She was standing in a sun-dappled hollow. A single ray robed her in light, summer was her crown. Her clothing nestled on the spongy, fecund floor. He proceeded, stroked her face; she recoiled in the ecstasy of touch. He drew her towards him, and the sound of the water in the middle distance came louder and louder and louder until it was a deafening roar.

* * *

At one point as they were driving back towards Balmakethe Parish, Elaine said, 'Leo, I've had an idea about part of the symbol on the setting maul – the wee circle with the dot inside it. Could it refer to the ring of standing stones in the Enchanted Forest?'

'Good thinking! Perhaps the dot denotes something hidden at its centre.'

'Yes. And there were five Hebrew characters in the outer band, which could also represent the five standing stones. Why don't we have a poke around this afternoon?'

'I think we should leave it until tomorrow,' said Leo, frowning at the horizon. 'There's a thunderstorm brewing.'

After they arrived back at Sannox House, they rested together in the guest room. Leo quickly drifted into a blissful sleep. He woke in the early evening with the humidity peaking. Elaine was nowhere to be seen. She wasn't in the house or the garden, yet her car was parked where she had left it. Leo regarded the sky with foreboding; black clouds were piling up in the west. There was no note anywhere and no message on his mobile, and when he rang Elaine's phone he heard it sounding on the kitchen table where it had been left alongside the keys to the Mini. He rang Biggnarbriggs Hall but neither Fordyce nor Evelyn had seen nor heard from Elaine.

Leo recalled her theory that part of the imagery on the setting maul might represent the stone circle. Perhaps she had felt impatient to investigate the place. The trouble was that Leo wasn't sure of the way through the woods from his current position. He went to the front room and anxiously regarded the sky again. Elaine's safety was at stake. Therefore he strode to the kitchen and picked up the car keys. He would drive round to the hall and reach the Enchanted Forest on foot from there.

It felt peculiar operating such a modern vehicle, the pedals so much more sensitive than he was used to with the Humber. It transpired that Elaine wasn't off to the standing stones. Beyond the top of Loch Grenoch, near to where he had chanced upon her on the evening he had set out to persuade her to stay at Biggnarbriggs Hall, Leo spied her. She was standing at the edge of a field, beneath the branches of a lovely horse chestnut. She looked vulnerable in the gathering gloom, wearing only her light summer clothes. He brought the car to an abrupt halt in a little passing place and got out.

Leo felt the initial suggestion of moisture on his face and could detect the earthy scent of petrichor rising as the first drops ticked on the undergrowth. 'Elaine!' he called out, but she either ignored him or was oblivious to him; she seemed transfixed by the sky, He clambered over a wire fence and walked towards her.

The temperature was dropping and the first gust insolently buffeted them. The trees' lush foliage began to boil in the thickening breeze, exposing the pale undersides of the leaves.

Leo reached her and said, 'Elaine, there's a storm approaching, can't you tell? We need to get back to the house. What on earth are you doing up here?'

Her voice came out monotone, robotic. 'I had an awful dream about Hazel being snatched and held captive. I woke up and had to get outside . . . I just found myself here. It was just like this back then . . . so green and fragrant. So many wildflowers that July; in my mind's eye it was ablaze with colour. I made a daisy chain that day. Yet I don't remember it being the best of summers. Some sunny days, but cool and cloudy a lot of the time, and in August it got quite wet, or else it was grey and mild. We had the usual cottage in the village. Do you remember when it happened, in the news I mean?'

'No, Elaine, I don't,' said Leo gently. He felt somehow guilty saying this, admitting he had no connection to, no memory of the seismic event of his lover's life.

'She was going for a walk. She asked me to join her. But I was in one of my moods. Greta, Dad used to call me when I was like that. You know, as in Greta Garbo: "I want to be alone"? The thing is, we hadn't fallen out, and my mood was borderline . . . I very nearly *did* go with her, but some obstinacy held me back, some wee bit of theatricality, some wee desire for attention. Or maybe it was that resentment I always felt towards her, that envy which was never far beneath the surface. So I stayed behind and read my Nancy Drew book.'

'For pity's sake, Elaine, you were a *child* – you must forgive yourself!'

'Look who's talking! You can't forgive yourself for the girl who died when you failed to act as a youth.'

'I know. That's why it hurts me to see someone else put themselves through this purgatory. Someone I care about.'

'It's not just a question of saying "I forgive myself" though, is it? You need to *do* something. Achieve something. Atone. I've played that day back to myself a million times. And often I make-believe a different version of it in which I *do* go on the walk, and Hazel and I chat as we go our merry way, like we used to; just about sisterly things, you know. Then the man approaches, but we are *together* so we're all right. Better than all right – we're Charlie's Angels; we bash the bastard over the head and tie him up and call the police, and he goes to jail. I was about to enter that fantasy just a moment ago. But I'm glad you interrupted me, because although it gives me momentary liberation, when I come back to reality I always feel worse.'

The eye of the vortex, enthroned upon the baying, silver Irish Sea, swirled ever darker. File of thunderheads shirred upon gigantic file, pausing as though to display their colossal latency before the awful charge. It will break over the Galloway Hills, Leo thought. 'Elaine, the storm's nearly here. For God's sake let's get back to the house.'

They climbed over the fence and began walking along the single-track road towards the car, but instead of getting in Elaine crossed to the other side and scaled a mossy drystane dyke and picked her way through a brake of rhododendron. Leo followed her. She waded through a burn and strode into a wood of hazel and sycamore.

'Things look different over time: cars, haircuts, clothes, the way we age,' she said. 'But the countryside pretty much stays the same. Walking here, it could be thirty-odd years ago. Hazel could still be alive.'

The cloud mass began to flicker with its terrible energy. Leo remembered that if there are fewer than thirty seconds of a gap between lightning and thunder then there was real danger, so he started counting, *one elephant, two elephant, three elephant* . . . He also knew that they had to get away from the taller trees, and try to find a hollow.

Elaine stopped. 'She was only sixteen . . . I wonder what she went through that week she was kept prisoner, what she felt. How *terrified* she must have been.'

'You must take comfort. I sense she dwells in a state of radiance, on the shining fields of immortality.'

'And now poor Lauren is dead. This thunder is her funeral dirge.'

It got darker, and the breeze picked up another notch, yet still Elaine walked, further away from the car. The compressed light made every outline sharpen in definition, and the landscape prickled with static. The coolness was accompanied by the scent of fir needles and soil and ozone and then the ocean herself. All birdsong had ceased. They walked through a pine grove and by a miracle they came across a bothy. Leo insisted that they take shelter and guided her inside.

The thunder was now a booming fusillade and then a colossal ripping sound, as though the very fabric of the firmament was being torn asunder. The rain came on heavily, whipped up by the wind, and soon the lightning earthed itself nearby with great violence.

Leo held Elaine tenderly as the water drummed heavier and heavier upon the flimsy roof.

Back at Sannox House they bathed, ate a simple meal at the kitchen table, and then made love in the guest room. Afterwards, they lay together, listening to the gentle rain, the birds' song tentative as they re-emerged after the clamour. Leo filled their goblets with claret, and considered how Dante had conceived romantic love as a preparation for and a taste of the unimaginable love of the Almighty.

At one point, Elaine said softly, 'Leo, I feel a little guilty for this, for our pleasure. What with poor Lauren presumed dead.'

'I do, too, my sweet.'

'Do you often think about death, Leo?'

'All the time. Yet I start to see death not as an ending or a failure, but as a beginning, as the dawn of a place where one can be free of one's anxieties, of whatever glitch of unworthiness that curtails one, where the individual can be his or her true self and experience joy in a pure way. Perhaps death as something beautiful, to be prepared for, even looked forward to. What is your idea of heaven, Elaine?'

'I don't believe in it.'

'Then make-believe.'

'I've always been drawn to time travel. Can you imagine seeing Glasgow in Victorian days?'

Leo took a sip of wine, then shifted tack. 'So, you're a non-believer?'

'I don't believe in heaven, or God, or that my sister is anywhere other than oblivion.'

'What if, for argument's sake, I could provide you with a glimpse behind this temporal veil – would that open your mind to the possibility of what we refer to as God?'

'But you can't. And your power, this so-called second sight – there will be an entirely rational explanation for it. Look, Leo, I'll grant you that my atheism is probably mostly rooted in the abject suffering of losing my beloved sister, but it's also down to simple credulity. Take my latest bugbear: Christianity teaches that people are damned to hell forevermore because they've broken certain rules during their brief stay on earth. A tad disproportionate, don't you think?'

'Hell must exist on logical terms, as a counterpoint to heaven and in that our actions must echo in eternity. The Catholic Church admits she lacks competency to say for certain if anyone is in it. Yet in a sense hell is something we create for ourselves, even while here on earth, through sin, by estranging ourselves from goodness.'

'And what of sin? Even Christians can't decide upon a fixed moral point any more. For example, what about you, Leo, and what we just did together. Wasn't that sinful?'

'I am a man of some considerable passion,' he retorted feebly.

Day Thirteen

ELAINE had errands to attend to in Castle Douglas, so she made an arrangement with Leo that they meet at the stone circle at 11 a.m. to investigate the theory that a clue might be concealed there. She gave precise instructions about how to find the stones from Sannox House by cutting through the woods towards Biggnarbriggs Hall. The weather was fine and Leo left with time to spare, ambling through the pleasant, sun-dappled glades. He felt physically recovered, however Elaine's confirmation of her atheism and the debate that had ensued into the wee small hours had Leo worried. A strain had been introduced into their nascent romance, and he wondered if their opposing worldviews didn't spell some incompatibility. After a while, he spied the gaunt tower of the hall and cut through the shrubbery towards it. He emerged to see Unity staring directly at him from the other side of the tennis court through two layers of chain-link fencing. She beckoned to him solemnly, so he walked round and greeted her.

'It is providential you have appeared,' she announced portentously. She was wearing the pentacle medallion Leo had noticed before. 'I've found something.' Without another word she began walking away, and Leo followed. Some way along the natural path that led through the Enchanted Forest, she paused and pointed at something dangling from a rowan branch stump. It was a weird, repellent object, some sort of amulet or talisman. Its centrepiece was a smooth wooden disk about four inches in diameter, upon which were painted three matchstick human figures holding hands. It was suspended by a length of rough string, which was threaded round five polished pebbles. Leo wondered if they could refer to the five standing stones in the nearby clearing. Below the centrepiece was attached a faggot of straw. Leo noted that the item was in full view, able to be seen by anyone walking along the trail. He examined it closely; it was unweathered, so must have been hung from the tree only very recently, probably after the electrical storm. He took several photographs of it with his camera phone.

Leo thought of Unity's Wiccan religion, and recalled seeing her making corn dollies and her children playing with homemade, beribboned kites. He regarded her a little suspiciously. 'When did you find this?'

'Just before I met you. I walked back and saw you come out of the woods. I felt you would come.'

'Have you any idea what it symbolises?'

'No, although it has a Wiccan feel to it. I've a book at the cottage which we could consult.'

'Right-o. But let's leave the thing *in situ*, in case it's evidence.'

As they walked, Unity chattered on about her preparations for that night's full-moon celebration. Leo recalled reading in the Mitchell Library that esbats in modern paganism could be held to mark a full moon.

'What, precisely, do you intend to do?'

'Visit the stones, of course! And there cast a circle, and make spells to garner blessings. The folk from Piperhall should be there.'

'I beg your pardon – who?'

'They're a collective a mile or so east of here, just half a dozen of them. They were originally New Age travellers but were forced to settle down after all the new laws and bother during the nineties. One of them, Florence Learmonth, inherited her parents' house, Piperhall, and a few acres of land, and they established a commune there. They try to be as self-sufficient as possible.'

'I wonder if that icon was placed in the Enchanted Forest in advance of the full moon?' he asked. 'Perhaps by these New Age types?'

'I've no idea,' said Unity.

Brian was crouched over a tap at the rear wall of his cottage, and the two men exchanged a perfunctory greeting. The McGhie children were playing happily nearby. Brian was evidently uninterested in Leo and Unity's purpose, and resumed his task of cleaning animal tissue and blood from a pair of butcher's knives. Leo was led inside and installed at a large oak kitchen table, politely forgoing a dandelion tea. Unity went to fetch the book and Leo took in the old-fashioned room, surmising it was his hostess's domain. He noticed a rendering of the Wheel of the Year hanging on one of the white-painted gypsum walls, and shelves crammed with jars of homemade preserves, pickles and herbal remedies – feverfew, chamomile, deadly nightshade and sage. In a corner, a shaft of sunlight illuminated bubbling demijohns containing different-coloured liquids: viridescent, plum and amber. There was a gigantic range and cookware dangled from the ceiling beams. Spread across the table-top was a variety of paraphernalia presumably looked out for the coming esbat, including thick candles of various colours, a broom, a steel chalice, an earthenware incense burner and a purple glass vial of oil. Leo couldn't help but wonder what Brian made of all of this hokum, of his wife preparing to leave the family home in the dead of night to engage in bizarre ceremony. He noticed that the chalice had a pentagram engraved on it. Unity returned and sat beside him, showing him the book, a second-rate self-published effort authored by one 'Orianna' and entitled *Wiccan Rites, Rubrics and Symbolism*. They scanned its pages together, but found no icon similar to the one in the forest.

'Now, Unity, this is of great importance: you must tell DCI Dalton about what you have found, in case it has anything to do with Lauren's disappearance.'

Unity nodded, and then on Leo's request furnished him with precise directions to Piperhall.

'Before I go, I need to speak frankly with you. I notice you're wearing a pentagram, and that there's also one engraved upon your chalice. You'll doubtless be aware of its association with a horned deity?'

'In these instances they don't denote the Horned God – apart from anything they're not inverted – although we Wiccans do honour him when he is known as Cernunnos or Herne the Hunter, embodying among other things male virility. The pentagram on the cup suggests the harmony between the five Platonic elements, each point representing a different one. Aether is the top point to embody our ability to bring the soul to earth. As for the medallion, it's a pentacle, not a pentagram, and simply a beneficent amulet.'

Leo gazed at her fixedly. 'All right. However, there was the suggestion of a pentagram on the weapon which nearly dashed my brains out. Now, I'm not accusing you of anything, but the Hebrew characters which would be the five points of that shape approximately translate as your name.'

'But . . . I'd nothing to do with that!' she faltered. 'I even invoked a healing incantation when I heard you'd been hurt.'

'Let me put to you another question. Have you been planting this pagan iconography – the ugly thing you just showed me and the coins and ribbons at the fairy tree?'

'No.'

'These activities are transgressions against God and Nature.'

'Gosh, you're *such* an Aries!' she declared, suddenly and oddly amused by the interaction. Leo felt irked by this empty-headedness, but she ploughed on, explaining the significance of the hawthorn tree (she referred to it as a 'whitethorn') in folklore. 'They were believed to have been inhabited by the Little People, and were associated with the Fairy Queen. Priestesses often held nature goddess worship within groves of whitethorns.'

Leo glanced at the kitchen clock – it was approaching eleven o'clock. He rose to leave, but Unity grasped his arm, a wild expression in her brilliant blue eyes. 'You disapproved of my rituals for Gilbert, I could tell. But your and my beliefs have more in common than you think. Jesus' great-uncle planted his staff at Glastonbury and there sprouted a whitethorn. You worship "I Am that I Am", that which revealed itself to the prophet Moses. We, too, hold with Prime Mover. And I have seen it: the higher truth of this world, the glory of the Unknowable, the meaning of things, the way we are supposed to live. And it is twofold.'

The ticking of the clock seemed to decelerate.

'What is it?'

'It is love and flow.'

'I will accept that, as long as you mean by love, seeing God-ness in every human being, and by flow, being attuned to God's grace as it operates in this realm.'

'We are all children of the light.'

'Indeed we are. However, men still herded the platform at Treblinka, and right now a girl has been stolen. That, too, is the reality of this valley of tears: children of light becoming vessels of darkness, all the time, in ways great and small, usually through self-deceit, as though we have a predilection towards it.'

With that, Leo gently shrugged off Unity's grip and took his leave.

* * *

Leo borrowed a heavy hammer and an old iron fence paling from Brian. Elaine appeared, and they made their way into the Enchanted Forest. Elaine seemed distant as Leo soliloquised on the sun-spangled canopy under which they walked. Leo worried that she was preoccupied with the nature of her sister's final days, or that she felt alienated from him after their exchange of views the previous night. However, her interest was aroused when Leo told her about the pagan icon Unity had shown him, and he took her to it. They then headed towards the stone circle.

'Let's stop by the fairy tree first,' suggested Leo.

They noted that fresh ribbons had been tied to the hawthorn's branches. Leo suddenly felt charged by the strange energy that seemed to inhabit the glade. He sidled up to Elaine. 'You will recall that the ribbons represent wishes,' he said softly. 'It could be for a successful harvest, good weather . . . even a lover.'

She turned away from him.

'Elaine, what's wrong?'

'Just before I came here I went back to Sannox House to leave the groceries. Cynthia arrived, asking for you. I told her you weren't in, and let slip that we were to visit the Enchanted Forest together. And she said, "Watch out, when I was down there he was exposing himself to the fresh air." What did she mean by that, Leo?'

He sighed. 'I was here on the day of the search party. I felt the need to urinate and suddenly she was just *there*, behind me. She was behaving quite wantonly, whispering in my ear.'

'What did you do?'

'Nothing. I simply left.'

'God, how can you like her? She's such an *asshole!*'

'But I don't like her, and nothing happened. Elaine, for pity's sake, how can you allow that *succubus* to come between us?'

They walked through to the standing stones.

'She is very beautiful, I suppose,' said Elaine sulkily.

'Vulgar is the word I'd use,' said Leo, attempting to assuage her jealousy. There was a loud cawing sound as several crows took flight, and Leo noticed Elaine draw up short, a horrified expression on her face. He followed her gaze, and there upon the turf between the westernmost two stones was a dead fox. It was lying belly up, and its paws had been pinned out with six-inch nails such that it struck a horrible attitude. Furthermore, its stomach had been slit to expose its innards.

'What new knavery is this?' said Leo as he approached the humiliated cadaver and knelt down.

'Don't touch it, Leo, for Pete's sake!' Elaine cried out.

'I'm not going to.' He sniffed, and announced, 'It's fresh.' He took several photographs and then walked back over to where Elaine was standing.

'Elaine, you must inform DCI Dalton about this and indeed the fresh ribbons, because she won't speak to me. You might also mention the icon I showed you. I told Unity to tell Dalton about it but I'm not sure she will.'

'Why – do you think Unity might have had something to do with all of this?'

'It's a possibility. She claims she found the icon, yet she has a keen interest in Wiccan handicrafts. And earlier I saw Brian cleaning blood and flesh from a pair of knives. Furthermore, their cottage is the nearest abode to this area.'

'But, Leo, a while ago you said you didn't think that Unity could be mixed up in anything sinister.'

'She probably isn't, but we must keep an open mind. It might simply be she's indulging in mischief-making, perhaps trying to promote her folk religion. I challenged her earlier, asked her directly if she had planted the icon and decorated the fairy tree. I also enquired about her fondness for pentagrams and the fact that the setting maul bore an approximate translation of her name, but she denied any involvement. The fact is anyone could have planted the ribbons and the coins and the icon and now this poor dead creature; for example, at the last dinner party the fairy tree was broadly discussed, and Cynthia seems to know a lot about such trees. By the way, tonight is a full moon, and Unity intends on marking it up here with some squalid ritual. She said that residents from some commune called Piperhall might also be here. I intend to visit them today.'

'I wouldn't bother, they're just a bunch of harmless hippies.'

Leo then adopted a gentle tone, and asked, 'Elaine, you mentioned that you came to doubt that the druidic cult were responsible for your sister's abduction. I wonder, could you expand on that?'

She sat down upon the turf, took a deep breath, and began: 'I'd been trying the cult angle for years. Those old members who I traced and who agreed to speak with me denied having anything to do with human sacrifice and I believed them. I've become a pretty good judge of a liar. They were all just sad, damaged individuals. Mixed-up kids or acid casualties from the seventies who wanted to "find themselves" by communing with the land and such nonsense. If they had killed Hazel then I'm sure one of them would have confessed or let something slip. The cult felt they had to move on after my sister's disappearance, but they claimed they weren't actually in the parish on the day she went missing, and the cops couldn't find a witness against this. By all accounts Talorc was a strange piece of work. He died in 1981 and I never met him. With his death the cult broke up and the case went cold. Everyone just assumed that he'd been responsible, and the police seemed too content to let the matter rest – why, for example, didn't they continue to pursue his possible accomplices from the cult? Eventually, I started to doubt the whole cult theory. If Hazel been sacrificed it would very probably have taken place here at these stones, and the cops would have found *some* scrap of physical evidence. It was the seventies, so forensics weren't that advanced and there had been a bit of rain, but the place would have been drenched with . . . blood.'

'Did you ever wonder if this Talorc might have acted alone, without the knowledge of his minions, not to perform a sacrifice but for his own gratification?'

'I did consider that, but for all his sins the cult members I spoke to said that Talorc didn't ever demonstrate lecherous or sexually perverse behaviour.'

The duo paced out the precise centre of the stone circle, and Leo drove the paling Brian had lent him into the turf using the hammer. It was sweaty work in the intense heat, and Leo prayed that the harsh light wasn't being overly unkind to his features. His hope was that he would come across either an obstruction – a buried clue – or a cavity, but instead all he plunged was soil and clay.

'So my idea was wrong,' observed Elaine.

'It looks like it,' said Leo. 'Which means that perhaps one of my or Fordyce's theories regarding the circle with the dot in it were, after all, sound.'

*　　*　　*

As they drove back to Sannox House, Leo told Elaine of his intention to move back to Biggnarbriggs Hall. Privately, he didn't want to impose himself on her hospitality any longer, particularly as she still seemed resentful over Cynthia's flirtatious behaviour. Also, now that he had recovered from the attack, it would be bad form not to return to the bosom of the Greatorixes, with whom, after all, he was supposed to be spending the summer. Furthermore, he had hatched an idea to that night survey the locality from the hall's tower, to see what suspicious activity the full moon drew out; perhaps he would see who was planting the pagan iconography hereabouts. Elaine thought this was a constructive idea but out of concern for his safety urged him to telephone the police if he saw anything sinister. For his part, Leo was worried about leaving Elaine alone at Sannox House and encouraged her to stay at the hall until the case had been solved. Elaine said she would consider it and in the meantime agreed to take the Webley for her protection.

After a rather dismal lunch during which conversation was strained, Leo packed his belongings and Elaine drove him over to the hall. He pecked her on the cheek, got out, and removed his possessions from the boot. Then Elaine opened her door and placed something on the ground alongside the Mini. She called out, 'I've left you that damn gun. I appreciate your concern but I don't want it. Don't worry, I'll be fine by myself – I always am.'

She closed her door and began turning the car on the gravel, leaving Leo at the mercy of his thoughts. What did her final words mean? Was it a simple, innocent remark? A statement, accidental or deliberate, of her future intent? An unconscious wish? An omen? He picked up the abandoned pistol case and made to wave at the Mini. But it was already moving on, Elaine's closed face set directly ahead.

Leo walked strange, hillocky fields, feeling dangerously exposed to the intense afternoon sun in spite of his Panama. Insects seethed among swathes of prickly weeds and a raven's caw mocked a tattie bogle that slumped crippled upon a little ridge. High above, a red kite hovered in suspended animation. The land, which was spiked with thistle, Rosebay willowherb, gorse, foxglove and the odd ancient hardwood tree, seemed to vibrate with portent. Unity's directions to Piperhall were sound, and soon he saw the old grange at the bottom of a gentle slope, nestling amid agricultural land, much of it lying fallow. He entered a rambling yard, which had gone to seed and was punctuated by corollas of daisy, buttercups, dandelions and flowering clover. Antiquated vehicles slouched in different stages of disintegration, relics of the residents' days on the road. There was a rusting Bedford S-type truck and a once-lovely Seddon coach. Leo stopped to admire a two-tone Albion Victor bus which was still in decent nick.

'That old girl survived the Battle of the Beanfield in '85,' came a charming West Country voice.

Leo turned to see a bearded middle-aged man with sparkling green eyes smiling at him. He wore a tie-dye T-shirt, decrepit denim jeans and Dr Martens decorated with a rainbow design.

'She's a beauty, and I'm proud to say she was built in my home city,' stated Leo, before introducing himself.

'Everyone here calls me Morph,' said the man, shaking Leo's hand. 'Welcome to our little community.'

'This area seems to attract communal living; I don't know if you are familiar with the Nain Community, just north of Biggnarbriggs village?'

'Indeed I am. I usually don't have much time for organised religion, but they're copacetic.'

Leo resisted the temptation to enquire if Morph preferred disorganised religion.

'Morph, I'm currently a guest of the Greatorix family over at Biggnarbriggs Hall, and I've taken an interest in the case of the missing girl, Lauren McDowall.'

'Dreadful business.'

'Have the police been round to speak with you?'

'Yes. Detective Daltrey, I think her name was.'

'Dalton.'

'Yep, that's it. She wanted to know if we'd seen or heard anything of interest, and where we were at the time of the disappearance. As it happens, we were all together in the big room that night, sharing a bong.' He winked at Leo and added, 'Although I left that last detail out.'

'Has she spoken to any of you again?'

'No.'

'I wonder, Morph, might I run a couple of things by you and your friends?'

The hippie shrugged in agreement and led Leo round the side of the house. The red sandstone building was in need of much attention, but at the back there was at least some evidence of industry: a few glasshouses and polytunnels loaded with crops – no doubt some of which were illicit – and a couple of tracts of land which had been half-heartedly put to the harrow and planted. The rest of the scruffy residents lounged around on hammocks and deck chairs, passing a joint or whittling what Leo assumed to be pagan handicrafts. Morph introduced them and Leo doffed his Panama politely. There was Florence, a jolly, red-cheeked woman who Unity had mentioned and who Leo guessed was Morph's partner, two other scraggly ladies, Marjory and Willow, a man by the name of Robin, and a surly youth called Lucien with shaggy blond hair. The adults were all aged in their fifties, and apart from Florence and Lucien everyone possessed English accents. Leo was invited to be seated and accepted the offer of some homemade ginger beer rather than nettle tea, and declined a draw on the spliff. Privately, he longed to be given some 'proper' working-class tea; Elaine had only stocked herbal varieties and everyone else seemed to be simply infusing boiled water with the local undergrowth.

Leo stated that he was here regarding Lauren's disappearance.

'Over to check us out, are we?' remarked Lucien from his berth beneath a rowan tree as he studied the strings of the guitar on his lap.

'Lucien , don't be rude!' rebuked Florence.

'I was chatting to Unity McGhie earlier,' continued Leo. 'She's hoping to see you all over at the standing stones later, for the full moon.'

'We'll be there,' said Florence. 'Dear Unity, she's such a sweet wee thing.'

'And talented too,' added Willow as she let out a stream of sweet-smelling smoke, some shadow of youthful beauty momentarily inhabiting her weathered features. 'There's no one I know can carve as well as her. And she makes my corn dollies look like they've been made in nursery school.'

'On that note, Unity happened across an icon this very morning, in the so-called Enchanted Forest,' said Leo as he took out his camera phone. 'I wondered if any of you might have deposited it there?'

The glare from the sun was such that he had to take the phone into the shade of the rowan in order that the hippies could see the photograph on the screen properly. They gathered round, but none of them had seen the item before.

'Does anyone know what it actually is?' enquired Leo.

'It's a gillygog,' said Marjory, a rotund woman with long, raven-black hair who until now had maintained a grumpy silence. 'Don't ask me what it was used for, though, because I can't remember. It's Wiccan, I think.'

'That's odd. Unity didn't recognise it, and she's a fully-fledged white witch. And neither was it in her book on the subject.'

'Probably because it's so obscure,' said Marjory.

'I wonder if it might have been placed in the woods in advance of the full moon?' asked Leo.

'No idea,' replied Marjory flatly.

Leo then showed the assembly the photographs he had taken of the fairy tree and the dead fox, and although Marjory knew the genus of both items (the crucified fox was apparently a druidic Harvest offering) they denied having planted them. Also, when asked, they said that they had only vaguely heard of Talorc and his cult.

Morph accompanied Leo to the front-yard gate. They shook hands, and as Leo turned to leave Morph said, 'It's terrible about that poor girl going missing. You can't help but worry that she's been abducted by some sod. It just goes to prove what Florence always says: people need to start learning to love each other again or this old world is doomed.'

Normally, Leo would have had little time for such anodyne hippie pronouncements, but today as he walked away from the faded grandeur of Piperhall, he felt that the fellow had a point.

The balmy night was clear but for a piste of surf-white cloud rimming the horizon. The sky was bejewelled with stars, and the full moon, which had a reddish harvest tint to it, illuminated the landscape to the extent that Leo had to remind himself that it was, in fact, 11.30 p.m. He hadn't told Fordyce or Evelyn, with whom he had earlier shared an excellent welcome-home dinner prepared by Mrs Grove, of his plan because he didn't want to get them involved, and had sneaked his binoculars and the Webley from his room. He gained access to the tower by locating an ancient brass key beneath a nearby plant pot. This unlocked a black-painted door on the tower's exterior, and Leo climbed a tight turnpike stair to the battlement. As he opened the trapdoor at the top, he recalled with a shiver the day he had witnessed the ghost in the plum coat standing up here.

Leo took an occasional sip from his hip flask to top up his alcohol intake from dinner. He missed Elaine and the beautiful night somehow intensified his lonesomeness. Soon he saw Unity leaving the cottage for the standing stones. She was wearing a flowing green dress and carried a bundle presumably containing the accoutrements for her weird rituals. Leo decided to follow her, but just as he was about to descend he noticed another individual leaving the cottage. This person strode off in a different direction – eastwards – from Unity. Leo trained his binoculars on the figure and confirmed it was Brian. Obviously this was a man known for his insomniac nocturnal walks, but there was something furtive in his body language and furthermore Leo found it odd that he would leave the children alone for the sake of mere sleeplessness. Therefore it was Brian's trail that Leo picked up once he had rushed down the stairs to ground level. He kept to the turfy edge of the driveway lest his feet crunched too loudly on the gravel, and soon discerned his quarry up ahead. At the junction of the drive with the Biggnarbriggs road, Brian turned northwards, creeping along the shadowy verge and once concealing himself within the screen of birch that lined the highway when a car happened to drive past. Soon he dashed across the road and Leo kept pace as he walked up a track with a sign announcing 'Lea Rigg Farm' at its mouth. Instead of continuing towards the farmhouse, Brian clambered over an old drystane dyke to his right and out of sight.

Leo followed, peered over the wall and discerned only trees and the overgrown ruins of some mill buildings. He swung his legs over and landed soundlessly. He stole over the soft ground, the air thick with the herby perfumes of the season. He could hear a burn tinkling nearby, sheep bleating in an adjacent field and the distant mournful barking of a dog. His attention was then arrested by different, human noises, and he tiptoed towards their source, crouching behind a thicket of bracken. He gazed into a grove of elder, hawthorn and a huge spreading ash which canopied the brook. There, in the silver light, upon a carpet of crane's-bill and hazel seedlings, was Brian, in a passionate naked clinch with Cynthia.

Leo was startled by a sinister sound from behind him. He swung round to see Bandit, one-legged Tam's bull lurcher, staring at him and emitting a low growl. Judging by the escalating emissions of ecstasy from the stream bank, the growling was not audible to Brian or Cynthia. Leo carefully unpeeled the remainder of his tube of orange creams and cast them towards the dog. Bandit set upon these with relish, and Leo dashed past him, hurdled the wall and walked briskly down the track to the road.

Leo knew Bandit had a habit of running off, so he may have been without his master. However, he had the feeling he was being watched as he walked back to the hall, and a profound anxiety inhabited him, aggravated by the fact that in his haste he had left the Webley sitting alongside the binoculars on the tower's parapet. He fancied enemies lurking in the murk of foreboding thickets, and at one point he wondered if he saw a dark figure hobbling through the birches in pursuit, so he dashed the final few hundred yards back to safety, his heart fluttering in his chest.

He was asleep as soon as his head hit the pillow, unaware that the next vision had been waiting for him in the aether.

It is daylight. The man in the plum hunting coat is smiling and beckoning to Leo, leading him through sublime woodland. Leo regards the green carpet of grasses, wood garlic, dock and sorrel, dotted with white enchanter's nightshade, yellow pimpernel and willowherb. He listens to the mellifluous birdsong, and looks up at the towering sun-kissed boughs and is blessed with a glimpse of a pied flycatcher. The man walks several yards ahead, through a dipping path, the canopy forming a tunnel. Black hairstreak butterflies and dragonflies flicker in the glades, which are little lime-lucent galleries, the overhanging branches' cheerful curtains announcing the next and the next. Leo pauses in one and gazes at the floor, which is rich with hazel and ash seedlings, bracken and shamrock. It is also alive: an intricate, purposeful machinery of moving ant parts, many bearing insect limbs or harvested fungus or vegetation. Leo considers the glorious forest, how it is burgeoning with life, yet also how its gorgeousness conceals a million little murders. Much of the matter surrounding him is withering, flaking, dead or in the process of dying. But this atrophy would sustain new life; death as a part of the cycle of life.

Leo is now led out of the greenwood, across sweet meadowland. They clamber up the crags to Linn Priory. The man in the plum coat walks to where the graves are located. He gestures towards one which sits apart from the others, his face now wearing a grim expression. Suddenly the land seems to darken and a feeling of foreboding grips Leo's heart as he approaches the dreaded stone.

Day Fourteen

L EO awoke after 9 a.m. He opened the curtains. It would be another dog day, although regions of the sky were dirty with cloud. Beethoven informed him that a text message had arrived. It was from Elaine, enquiring as to his wellbeing. Leo stated that he was fine and that he would update her later on his night-time mission but she didn't respond further. As he prepared for the day he began fretting again that a distance had come between them. He tried not to ponder the gathering ache for alcohol, which manifested itself physically as a sickness in his belly and a queer taste in his mouth. Something else perturbed him. Leo was a courageous man, but the order of fear he had experienced the previous night had been peculiarly visceral, and had sent him scampering back to the hall. He worried he was up against forces that were quite simply beyond him. He poured his rosary into his trouser pocket. And he would keep the Webley strapped to his person from now on.

He went downstairs and spied Evelyn in the rose salon, petting the spaniels. A pensive expression inhabited her countenance. Leo entered the room and greeted her, and she snapped into her usual cordiality.

'Leo! Let me prepare you some breakfast.'

'No, thank you, Evelyn; I feel a touch seedy. Actually, I could murder a cup of tea. Do you happen to have a common-or-garden variety?' said Leo, dreading his hostess's preference for Earl Grey.

She smiled and said, 'I think we have breakfast tea hidden away somewhere,' and then led him to the kitchen, the dogs following faithfully at her heels.

She chattered as she prepared the pot. 'I always insist on plain, traditional biscuits – Scotch Abernethy, Rich Tea, Arrowroot and the like; don't you find them so comforting?'

'Indeed. I'd go so far as to say that the Scotch Abernethy is a heartbreakingly neglected creation – the unsung hero of the biscuit barrel! As for the demise of the Royal Scot and the Barmouth, it ought to be a national scandal.'

'Quite!'

Leo lifted the tray and they went back to the rose salon and sat down. Evelyn had placed roses everywhere in the room: in bowls, in vases, in baskets – even tied by their briars round pillars. A cabinet displayed her antique doll display, and on the facing wall were some art nouveau folk-lore illustrations by Glasgow Girl Jessie M. King; she had resided in the county capital, long renowned as 'The Artists' Town'. There was also a series of glass paste medallions by the eighteenth-century engraver James Tassie, portraying the ninth baron and his wife and offspring.

'Evelyn, when I first saw you a few minutes ago you seemed to be fretting about something. Were you upset about Lauren?'

'Actually, no, I was vexing over poor Gilbert's death. I can't help worrying that he over-exerted himself during his last stay with us, which as you know was just before he died. He had an underlying heart condition. He seldom complained, but everyone knew about it. I should have been more *heedful*, rather than organising fishing and walking outings. To say nothing of the fatty foods, cigars and drink we plied him with.'

'My dear, I'm sure Gilbert was most glad of your generous hospitality. I know I am. Did he seem particularly unwell to you during his visit?'

'No, although at the funeral one of his sisters said he didn't seem himself when he arrived back in London. As though he was brooding over something. She was displeased with him because he had driven all the way without a proper rest; in his latter years, since his diagnosis, he would stay in the Peak District overnight to break the journey. His sister asked me if anything had happened up here, a falling out or something.'

'Had it?'

'No – everything went splendidly. We all got on famously, as usual.'

Leo remembered something he'd been told at the funeral and the sense of foreboding he had experienced when he'd heard it: that Gilbert's death mask of sheer terror had put the kybosh on an open casket. And then Leo recalled seeing, while semi-concussed after being struck on the head in Scoulag Woods, a flashing vision of Gilbert's face, horribly afraid – surely there was significance behind this image being relayed to him?

After tea was finished, they noticed Fordyce through the window, feeding the birds in the aviary.

'He's a sterling chap, your brother,' said Leo as he observed Fordyce with affection.

'But lonely.' Evelyn sighed. 'Sometimes I fear it's the Greatorix curse, to be unlucky in love. I think Fordyce wishes he was different, in terms of his . . . preferences. He loved our father, but there was always a certain distance between them. I think Daddy had an inkling, and perhaps showed too much favour to my eldest brother on account of his being heir. Fordyce therefore had a close bond with Mummy.'

Leo took his leave of Evelyn and walked outside to greet Fordyce. He brought up the subject of Gilbert's demise.

'Evelyn said that, according to one of his sisters, he arrived back in London after his last visit to the hall not quite himself. Perhaps something had happened to upset him up here. Could he, for instance, have decided to explore the strange night-time goings-on he had mentioned to Donald?'

'But he left in perfectly good spirits, old stick. Maybe he took a funny turn on the way down.' Fordyce paused. 'Unless . . .'

'Unless what?'

'Gilbert had a tradition. On his way back to London he would take a detour to the Cauldron, further up Scoulag Burn. He thought it a lovely, secluded spot. He'd stop by and smoke one of his little cigars. It's a long shot, but I wonder if he witnessed something there.'

'I was told his face was deformed with terror upon his passing. Which is why his family couldn't have an open casket.'

'I daresay folk perish with all manner of unfortunate expressions graven on their phizogs. As for cases such as the late lamented Gilbert: well, I doubt the initial tremors of heart failure fill a chap with anything other than mortal dread.'

'Fordyce, I recall Gilbert's London home from the wake. It's a neglected old place; someone could break into it quite easily. He lived with his elderly sisters, who are as deaf as posts and wouldn't have heard a thing. And anyway, Gilbert lived in a kind of separate wing.'

'What are you driving at, old stick?'

'What if he saw something at the Cauldron that upset him and precipitated a heart attack, or worse, that whoever was up to no good up there wanted him silenced. It was common knowledge that Gilbert had a dicky heart; what if he was murdered – frightened to death?'

'By Jove, that's fantastic!'

'Can you remember if any local people were absent at the time of Gilbert's death?'

'Well now, Chas and the Major weren't here when we got the news that he had died in the night. They had gone up north early the previous morning on a fishing trip. The Major has a holiday cottage on one of the Slate Islands.'

'Do you know if there was a postmortem?'

'Why, yes, one of the sisters happened to mention it.'

'Was it a clinical PM?'

'Actually, no. The death was reported to the coroner.'

'Intriguing.'

'I shouldn't read anything into it, old stick; these things can be fairly common following sudden death. It was only conducted because Gilbert's usual physician had been unavailable to attend after the death, and also hadn't seen him for a while prior to his passing, because he was up here with us.'

'Fordyce, I had another vision last night. The man in the plum hunting coat – the chap I believe to be your ancestor, the eighth baron – was showing me a grave at Linn Priory, one that is set apart from the rest up there. I'd noticed it before; it has a heraldic winged lion on it but no name.'

'It belongs to the so-called Black Earl. Apparently he was a villain who roamed hereabouts during the eighteenth century, a man so black-hearted that the locals insisted his grave be dug away from those of decent folk. Who he was precisely, and where he was the earl of, and even if he was a proper earl, I'm afraid I don't know.'

Leo went to the library and consulted a couple of local history books, but found no mention of this Black Earl, and various internet search criteria brought up nothing of relevance. He then used the browser to establish which jurisdiction Gilbert's autopsy would have fallen under.

His next task, that of confronting Brian, was one he dreaded, and he spent a minute or so composing himself.

It had always struck Leo as highly coincidental that Brian had suggested taking fellow night owl Donald well out of the way on a fishing trip on the very night that Lauren went missing. It could have been sheer chance, but Leo felt that statistically this was unlikely. Brian could have been a fully-fledged confederate in the plot to kidnap Lauren, his particular duty being to remove Donald from the scene of the crime. However, Leo's instinct told him that the man wasn't made of such material. Therefore he favoured a third possibility: that Brian had been *forced* into organising the fishing trip, probably ignorant as to the heinous nature of what was actually about to take place, perhaps blackmailed by someone who had knowledge of his affair with Cynthia.

Leo had to be careful about the psychology he would employ. If his favoured theory was wrong, he didn't want to mention it to Brian lest he give him the idea of clothing himself in it as cover for the far more serious crime of being a willing accessory to the abduction. Therefore he would accuse Brian of that greater crime, and see what emerged. And Leo despised the prospect, as he himself knew what it felt like to be falsely accused.

He located Brian behind his cottage, moodily mashing potash into blood and bone for rose garden feed.

'Good morning, Brian,' said Leo.

Brian grunted a greeting, barely looking up from his task.

'Where are Unity and the children?'

'Awa' for a walk.'

'Good, because there's a delicate matter I wish to discuss with you.'

'Oh aye?'

'Whose idea was it to go fishing on the night Lauren went missing?' asked Leo, already knowing the answer.

'Mine. So what? We've been nicht fishing together afore.'

'It all seems rather convenient, the two folk in the area known for nocturnal rambling absent.'

'The lassie was last seen at just after nine o'clock. Assuming she was taken thereabouts, it was hardly the deid of the nicht, was it?' said Brian, squinting in the sunlight as he looked up at Leo.

'There might have been other dastardly operations planned, for later on in the locale.'

'What are you getting at?' demanded Brian as he stood up, his hands splashed with gore.

'Were you party to the villainous plot to abduct poor Lauren?'

'Fuck off.'

'It was a neat idea, removing Donald. You could let your pals kidnap Lauren, and have your own fun with her later.' Brian walked away from him, his jaw set in stone, but Leo followed. 'I know all about your affair, by the way. Your *insomnia* is just a ruse to allow you to venture out at night and meet Cynthia.'

'Fuck off,' said Brian again, as he turned on the wall tap and began rinsing the blood from his hands.

'I saw you together out by Lea Rigg Farm last night. Talk about the madness of the full moon – what kind of a man are you, leaving those kiddies alone in the house, especially after everything that's happened around here?'

This last statement was designed to strike home, and it provoked the most extraordinary effect: Brian began weeping. Leo held off his attack. After a while, Brian rinsed his face in the tap water.

'You disapprove, I suppose. But I needed the other. You cannae imagine what it's like living wi' Unity – her heid's in the clouds. I cannae connect wi' her. Even when we're making love, it's like she's no' really present. I needed the other, a *real* woman. I really *am* an insomniac, and my nicht walks were and often still are because o' that. One nicht, I was out walking along the Biggnarbriggs road and this car pulled up. It was Cynthia. She'd stayed late at some party in Kirkcudbright. She asked me to get into the car. It all just started from there.'

'When did this occur?'

'A couple o' years back.'

'Did you confide your affair to anyone?'

'No.'

'You're going to have to tell me everything, Brian.'

'I swear I'm no' part o' any plot to kidnap that poor lassie – no' willingly anyway. A week afore she went missing, there was an envelope left in my tool shed. Inside were sex photos of me and Cynthia together. Someone must have been spying on us one nicht. There was also a printed note.'

'Do you still have the note or the photos?'

'No, I burned them.'

'What did the note say?'

'I was instructed to take Donald fishing at nine o'clock on July the twenty-fifth. If I did this, then the photos would be destroyed; otherwise my marriage would be destroyed. I decided to play along (sod's law – the car wouldn't bloody start and I was a wee bit late), thinking maybe someone had a big housebreaking planned. It wouldnae be the first time one o' the rich places hereabouts had been hit.'

'Really? You thought a mere housebreaker would go to the trouble of photographing your bare bahookie?'

'Aye. Here's a for instance: local legend has it that the Major has a bunch o' diamonds stashed at Maidenheid House, from his South African days. If an organised mob from Glasgow got a whiff of that, then they certainly *would* go to a whole lot of trouble. I reckoned jewels might be precious, but no' as precious as a marriage. Then, the nicht after, I was told the McDowall girl had gone missing – how the fuck was I to ken *that* was what was going to happen?'

'You indeed were not to know, but you are culpable for not subsequently telling the police about the blackmail.'

'I didnae tell them as there was no clue to who was blackmailing me. It was fair professional-looking and I'd already burned the evidence. What guid would it have done, going to the polis?'

'Not good enough, Brian. There's a girl missing. You will tell DCI Dalton everything, right now, otherwise I will. There's a chance she'll keep it discreet until you confess to your wife yourself.'

Leo now intended to inspect the grave of the so-called Black Earl, in response to the previous night's vision. He was perspiring profusely when he arrived at the priory. Leo abhorred Celsius; the scale meant nothing to him. Due to his mother's descriptions of childhood summer days, Fahrenheit had lodged, and right now he reckoned that the mercury was nudging eighty. He examined the ground near the grave and felt around the granite headstone, checking for hidden cavities or items of interest. Then he studied the simple inscription, the winged lion with the year of death in Roman numerals. He had initially presumed that the winged lion was an element of family heraldry, but an idea occurred to him. He recalled the beautiful Bible at the Nain Community, with its reproductions of the Evangelists' symbols from the Book of Kells. One of them was a winged lion, which Leo believed was the symbol for Saint Mark. The numerals on the stone were separated by the winged lion, with V, for 5, to its left, and IX, for 9, to its right. Leo had assumed that this meant '59' as in 1759, but he was being a damned fool; the Roman numeral for 59 was LIX, not VIX. So what if the engraving was, in fact, a Biblical reference – Mark 5:9? Leo fiddled inexpertly with the internet function on his phone to discover that chapter five of the Gospel of Mark opens with the telling of the possessed man who lived among the tombs at Gerasenes. Leo scanned forward to verse nine and a shiver crept up his spine as he read: 'And Jesus asked him, "What is your name?" He replied, "My name is Legion, for we are many."'

Leo now wondered if the murder of the man in the plum coat from his visions, presumably the eighth baron Greatorix, had anything to do with this Black Earl. Perhaps he was the leader of the torch-bearing, club-wielding band, the tall, well-built fellow wearing the tricorne hat whose face Leo couldn't see. Leo thought about Great Uncle Hugo's 'lanthorns' and Gilbert seeing strange goings-on at night, and the other clues and symbolism that pointed towards more than one perpetrator in the abduction of Lauren, and for that matter Hazel. Could there be a revival of whatever group this Black Earl had led? The design of the symbol on the setting maul was more recent than the eighteenth century, but that could merely have been a modern addition.

Leo re-read the verse on his phone and was startled when it leapt to life, the word 'Strange' displayed. He greeted the retired copper.

'Look, Moran, something's been bothering me that I didn't tell you when you came by.'

Leo suspected the man had been drinking. 'You have my attention.'

'There had been an attempted abduction in the area two summers before the Bannatyne girl went missing. The lassie was also a holiday-maker and of a similar age profile – she was fifteen.'

'What happened?'

'Two men pulled her off her bicycle and tried to drag her over a wall into some woods. A couple of foreign tourists happened by in a car and the suspects made off. The lassie was shaken but all right. It all happened so fast that none of them were able to give precise descriptions of the attackers.'

'Where was this?'

'On the forest road that leads to Biggnarbriggs village.'

'Why wasn't it publicised when Hazel went missing?'

'We thought it would interfere with the case, give a confused message.'

'Why?'

'Because Talorc's druids couldn't have been responsible for the first abduction attempt. They didn't move to the area until '78. And we were fairly sure it was them who had abducted Hazel.'

'Mr Strange, I realise British police methods in the seventies could rather tend to obsess upon one line of inquiry. However, when I spoke with you in your home you denied that your investigations back then were fixated on the druidic cult. Now, what you have just said to me is false. So I will ask you again: why was the lead not followed up and made public?'

'I already told you.'

'I've had a search done by a police operative of old records, and this incident didn't come up.'

'The files were . . . mislaid.'

'*Mislaid*, my backside. Also, when I visited your home you denied any files had gone missing.'

'That is all I have to say on the matter,' slurred Strange. With that, he broke the connection.

'So, indeed there *are* more than one,' Leo said aloud. 'And I'm going to unmask every man Jack of you.'

As Leo walked back to the hall, he telephoned Stephanie and told her about Strange's call and his suspicion of police involvement in a cover-up at the time of the disappearance of Hazel Bannatyne.

'Strange must think I came up the Clyde on a banana boat; there are Masonic aspects to this latest case, and we all know how the Craft infects our forces of law and order,' he concluded.

'Not you and your obsession again. Look, Leo, I understand you caught a bad break off the cops when you were a kid, but that doesn't mean they're all part of some global Satanic-Masonic conspiracy.'

'Pope Clement the Twelfth said of the Freemasons in *In eminenti apostolatus*: "if they were not doing evil they would not have so great a hatred of the light". Now listen carefully, my dear. I have another soupçon of detective work for you to undertake. It is my suspicion that Gilbert was deliberately frightened to death because he witnessed something in the Stewartry which someone wanted kept quiet.'

'Witnessed what, exactly?'

'Alas, that I do not know. It was well known that Gilbert had a serious heart condition and would therefore have been vulnerable to any type of shock. What I require from you is to find out if anything suspicious was brought to light by Gilbert's postmortem. The medical report will be held at St Pancras Coroner's Court.'

'That would require formal authorisation. Haven't you heard of patient confidentiality?'

'Can't you use your charms?'

'You seem to think I have connections with every authority across the land. Okay, I'll do what I can. Now tell me, how are things going with sweet Elaine?'

'That is my business.'

'Don't get coy with me, young man – you've been kissing her, haven't you?'

'Stephanie, please don't tease me.'

She detected the anguish in her friend's voice. 'I'm sorry, Leo. Are you all right?'

'I'll survive, old girl. Always have, always will.'

'Leo, will you reach out to me if you need someone to talk to? I don't want you bottling things up again.'

'Look, Steph, I've got to go. Bye for now.'

'Be careful, Leo.'

Beyond the hidden meadow, Leo came across Unity out with her children. They were laughing and chattering as they took the spaniels for a walk across the great lawns. Leo tipped his Panama, and Unity greeted him cordially, seeming not to hold any grudges over their existential contretemps of the previous day. Her daughter Branwyn, a beautiful, golden-haired child aged six, handed him a 'delescope'. It was, in fact, a kaleidoscope and Leo made great play of enjoying gazing into the multi-coloured, tubular universe, all the while feeling guilty about the *dénouement* that augured for the McGhie family in the wake of his uncovering of Brian's infidelity. The toy – its rattling beads, and the smell and texture of the plastic – evoked a nebulous rising of pure, uncomplicated childhood joy within Leo, a sense of laughter drifting over some forgotten lawn, and then a feeling of longing for that lost and innocent world.

He handed the item back to the girl, then enquired of Unity: 'How were the festivities last night?'

'Awesome,' she replied. She addressed the children: 'Now, what do we say to Mr Moran for the kites he gave you?'

'Thank you, Mr Moran,' said the kids in unison.

'You are most welcome. And please, call me Leo.'

As he walked off, Leo reflected upon the thrill, the delight and fulfilment that parenthood must bring. The fascination of watching young lives develop. He ruminated morosely if such a process would have had a softening, focusing influence on him. Then he noticed the temple of Venus on the ornamental lake. Bricks and rubble that had been removed from its interior lay piled upon the little island, evidence of the fruitless search he had persuaded the police to undertake. Another cause for guilt, he mused. *Leo Moran Inc., Demolition Expert: Marriages and Nineteenth-century Follies a Speciality.*

Leo felt overcome by a sense of lassitude and decided to rest amid the sanctuary of Scoulag Woods. He felt drugged by the afternoon heat, the soporific drone of honey bees. He entered the Edenic greenwood, his footsteps thudding hollowly against the rooty earth. The light slanted through the towering wych elms in great shards, brightening the verdant floor, the high leaves shimmering ecstatically. A blackbird, invisible amid the cool roots of the flowering rhododendron and azalea, rustled through last year's leaf litter. Leo rested upon a shaded bed of sphagnum and gazed at where the lush tree branches framed the lake, upon which the pair of mute swans romanced. The undulating surface sparkled in the sunlight. The male dismounted in a flurry of spray and beating wings, and as he did so the female wheeled around to face her mate. As if in slow-motion and in perfect unison the pair reared in the shallow water and arched their slender necks forwards until their heads touched, forming a perfect love heart.

Having been excluded from courtship for so long, having pined after it, Leo, ever prone to despondency, no longer dared to hope for it. He would marvel at the routineness of other people's affairs; to him a romance was rare, and therefore seismic. Then, out of the blue, Elaine Bannatyne had happened along. She was his last chance. And now angst had crept into their fledgling relationship. It wasn't only their differing worldviews or the obstruction caused by Cynthia's irksome flirtatiousness – it was a sense of remoteness brought about by Elaine reasserting her independent self. Perhaps he had come on too strongly, too quickly.

Perhaps Fordyce had sensed he was doing this when he advised him to take things slowly. 'Well past the halfway point in life and I'm still a naive fool, rushing in,' said Leo aloud. To think he had speculated that Elaine was curing him of his drinking, whereas all his flesh craved right now was whisky. The swans parted, and sailed off to different extremes of the lagoon where they languished alone.

Leo dreaded the rest of the day: the necessity of putting on an agreeable face, pretending he was interested in banality when all he wanted was to be with Elaine. However, as it happened he wouldn't have to endure even the afternoon without her, because at luncheon Evelyn stated that she was coming over to play her at tennis. Leo's heart rose in his chest. He had to update her on his latest investigations anyway, which provided the perfect reason to seek out her fragrant company. In the meantime, he decided to check the Greatorix family archives more thoroughly in case he had missed anything on his initial sweep, specifically anything relating to the Black Earl and the eighth baron's extinction.

Leo entered the library and fetched the three solander boxes to the table-top lectern. He admired Hugo's fastidiousness as he slowly browsed the contents. He found the exercise book that documented the first half of the eighteenth century and carefully inspected it, but again drew a blank. However, he noticed that towards the end there protruded the stumps of three pages which had been neatly razored out close to the spine. Obviously someone who had access to this room wanted a piece of Greatorix history deleted from the record.

As Leo replaced the boxes he noticed a shelf he hadn't previously explored. It bore mainly Evelyn's scrapbooks and flower pressings, but also a 1950 tome entitled *Codex Arcadia: An Index of Folk Ritual and Symbolism in Rural Britain and Ireland*, authored by one Lady Edith Grey. He opened its musty pages and successfully located an entry for 'gillygog'. Apparently it was 'a folkloric hex sign based on an old Scandinavian tradition, symbolising regeneration and sexual potency, favoured by certain modern pagans, such as in the novel Wicca movement'. Further perusal confirmed that the crucified fox at the standing stones was indeed simply a druidic Harvest offering as Marjory at Piperhall had suggested, and Leo also certified his understanding of the origins of the wish tree.

He considered the fact that these clues seemed to point in different directions: the gillygog was Wiccan, the mutilated fox druidic, and the wish tree Celtic pagan. All of these traditions were related, but the clues themselves felt tenuously linked, and were moreover utterly distinct from the quasi-Masonic flavour to the setting maul. That item had been left in the fleeing assailant's haste only because the attempt on Leo's life had failed, whereas the other things had been left in plain sight. Leo deduced that false trails were being set, in order to suggest the revival of a druidic cult and/or in an attempt to place various local pagan misfits into the police's frame. He recalled something that Sun Tzu, the ancient Chinese philosopher and military strategist had said: 'All warfare is based on deception.' And he *was* engaged in warfare. Not primarily against people, but against sin and demonic forces.

He headed aimlessly to the billiard room. Snooker balls were splayed across the baize of the full-size table, which dominated the fine chamber. Leo's eye glanced upon the varnished wooden scoreboard fastened to the wall. One of the brass sliders happened to be set at the number eighty. *Eighty*, the Greek number *Pi*, the character for which was on the setting maul. Thoughts crowded Leo's mind as he strained to slice through the Gordian knot of the riddle. Could it be something to do with the numerological properties of the number eighty, as Fordyce had suggested? Or could the Greek character in this instance refer to the mathematical constant *Pi*? Did it indeed have something to do with a circle, perhaps the standing-stone circle or the circle with the dot in it that was engraved on the setting maul? What about other uses for the mathematical constant? *Pi* continually crops up in the natural world, and often appears in equations describing fundamental principles of the universe. He walked back to the library and consulted an ancient almanac, but the mathematics therein made his head ache.

He went to the kitchen to refresh himself with a glass of water and through the open window heard the steady report of a tennis ball being thrashed across the court. Leo stepped over the threshold and saw Evelyn and then Elaine. He suddenly underwent physical manifestations of longing: a tightness in his chest and a constriction of his throat. He wandered to the perimeter of the court, which was shaded by the fringe of Scoulag Woods, trying surreptitiously to glance at Elaine's bronzed legs. She completed her two-set demolition, blotted the perspiration from her brow with a towel, and drank from a water flask. Evelyn tactfully took her leave, and as they strolled into the Secret Garden Leo began updating Elaine on the latest theories and developments. When he mentioned Brian and Cynthia's affair, and the former being blackmailed with it to get him and Donald out of the way, Elaine wondered if it could have been a honey trap. Could Cynthia have been luring Brian out so that incriminating photos be taken and used against him?

'I don't believe so,' countered Leo. 'The intrigue began in the relatively distant past – two years ago – and Cynthia still meets Brian for trysts even now. The level of enthusiasm which she demonstrated last night suggests to me it is a matter of carnal pleasure.'

He left the matter of Strange's phone call until last, and first entreated Elaine to sit upon a wooden bench in the shade of a cherry tree. 'Strange rang me earlier and told me the most damned thing: there was an attempted abduction of a fifteen-year-old girl on the forest road in 1977 by two men, who were never identified. They were foiled by some passing tourists and fled. Talorc's cult didn't arrive in the area until the following year. Strange claimed that the reason this incident wasn't publicised was that they didn't want to muddy the waters in the wake of your sister's disappearance, and that the file on it went missing. I called him a liar. You were right about a police cover-up.'

'Those . . . *bastards!*' Hot tears welled in her eyes and she broke down.

After Elaine had composed herself, Leo accompanied her to her car via the kitchen garden. Chas was there, lighting a bonfire of horticultural refuse, his dog resting sullenly on the ground beside him, a pile of latent muscle and fangs. Leo noticed raw perforations on the animal's shoulder.

'Howdy, Pilgrims!' called out Chas with dubious bonhomie as he wiped his forehead with a greasy tweed cap. They returned the greeting, and as they were passing he muttered, 'How was the bare-arsed boxing up at Wood of Larg?'

They walked on a few paces, mortification compounding Elaine's rage. Leo clasped her arm sympathetically and collected himself. He spun round and said, 'That's a nasty wound on Nero's shoulder.'

'Aye. He ran off a few days back. Must have got himself nicked on barbed wire.'

Leo pretended to examine the beast and said, 'No, that's a bite from a mammal with a long jaw.' He fixed Chas with his gaze and added, 'A badger, most probably.'

Chas just smirked.

Leo tried in vain to comfort Elaine as they walked on.

'Leo, for Pete's *sake*, someone was *watching us* together!' she sobbed.

'Chas or someone known to him must have been on that quad bike we heard. Perhaps Lyle, the Major's man; he uses such a vehicle.'

Poor Elaine's tribulations were not yet over. Beneath one of the Mini's windscreen wipers was pressed a bunch of lilies with a small card attached. It read: how is your sister?

'Oh my *God!*' she exclaimed.

'Oh dear.'

'That's Cynthia's handwriting! That pretentious flourish – I saw it on the note with the bouquet she left after you were assaulted. She must have heard you calling me Elaine and worked out who I am.'

'Surely she wouldn't be so foolish as to incriminate herself so clumsily?'

'Incriminate herself with what – knowing my identity? Knowing that my sister is dead? Being a cruel bitch?'

Leo picked up the card and examined it, taking care to hold only its sides lest he leave fingerprints. 'Elaine, Cynthia did not leave this message,' he said.

'Oh, for Pete's sake! We're no closer to finding the bastards responsible, and she's making these . . . *passes* at you, and now she's put this horrible thing on my car and you're trying to stick up for her!'

'I don't even like the woman – I have no interest in sticking up for her.'

'No, but you fancy her, maybe more than you fancy me. I thought we had a *connection*, you and me. Like we were two lone wolves destined to cross paths.'

'And I sensed those things between us too,' said Leo gently, slightly gratified by her admission; perhaps there was hope for their relationship after all. 'But Cynthia Blythman did not leave this message.'

'How do you know?'

'Observe – this note was originally written on paper, good-quality writing paper, and then *pasted onto* the little card.' Leo held it up to the sunlight. 'I propose it was snipped from a letter, a phrase plucked from its innocent context in order to create this beastly message. The piece of paper has been scissored closely, because the words it bears were surrounded by a full text. Also, the first letter is lowercase – the words have been extracted from the midst of a sentence.' He held the card out carefully to Elaine, saying, 'I'd hand this over to DCI Dalton for analysis.'

She snatched it, then grabbed the lilies and strode back in the direction from where they had just come. Leo followed her.

'Elaine, that's *evidence!* What are you doing?'

'I'm going to send a message that I won't be intimidated.'

She marched into the kitchen garden and Leo watched as she hurled the lilies and card into the bonfire and then glared at Chas. He regarded her impassively.

'Look, Leo, I've got to get out of here. I'm going for a drive in the forest,' said Elaine, turning on her heel.

'You're not going to see Cynthia, are you?'

'No. You're right. She probably didn't leave it. I just need to burn some rubber.'

'Let me drive, you're not fit.'

'No. Come with me if you want, but make your mind up now.'

The Mini rumbled down the driveway, Elaine going too fast and glowering when Leo instinctively put his foot down to push a phantom brake pedal. She turned north, and after three miles or so, as Leo had dreaded, hung a left up the Raiders' Road. This ancient artery, which ran through Kells Parish, was so rough that it was only open during the summer months. It was an old drove road and had featured in a swashbuckling romance by a local author of the Kailyard School. In the story, rustled cattle were driven along it, then on into the remote Galloway Hills. The Bruce hid amid the brake and won victories in those wild glens.

They drove past Slogarie Hill, Airie Hill and Carin Edward Hill, the road approximately following the Black Water of Dee. The rubbly surface was rutted and pitted, and Elaine was taking it too quickly, throwing up an impressive amount of dust.

'Elaine, this is a single-track road,' said Leo. 'You need to slow down. I know they hold rallies round these parts, but what if a vehicle comes the other way?'

'Oh, hark at you, Miss Marple.'

They proceeded in miserable silence. Adjacent to Shaw Hill they passed a sign saying 'Otter Pool – 200yds' and Leo implored Elaine to pull in. With a sigh she acceded and rolled the car into a little grassy car park amid a towering grove of lordly fir and Scots pine. As they ambled towards the pool they glimpsed a pair of red deer disappearing into the thicket. It was an idyllic place, the Black Water of Dee broad here and formed by a series of shallow waterfalls. A heron stood transfixed on a boulder, poised to strike. Elaine sat on the flint bank and gazed at the rapids. Leo patted her shoulder sympathetically then settled down beside her. She smiled thinly at him.

Nearby, a powerful black Mercedes with tinted windows had crawled into the shadows, its engine idling in a low growl.

After a while, they returned to the Mini and began motoring towards Fell of Fleet at a more sedate pace. Elaine noticed Leo staring into the wing-mirror and then looking behind him.

'Not seeing black cars again, are we?'

'Whatever it was it took a right at that last fork.'

The road climbed somewhat and parted with the river, and there was now a steep earthen drop to their left.

'Elaine, you're going too fast again,' complained Leo.

Suddenly, two hundred yards ahead, the black Mercedes burst from an unclassified road and raced towards them at speed, its headlights on full beam.

'Great Scott! Look out, Elaine!'

She braked violently and took evasive action, bearing left as the Merc occupied the entire middle of the road. There was a skidding sound as Elaine lost control, the wheels hammering over the rough surface. Loose aggregate whipped up by the Merc as it passed by pinged against the Mini's bodywork. They veered leftwards, leftwards, all the time slowing, but it was too late, and the passenger side left *terra firma* for thin air. There was a violent sound of pine branches lashing the windscreen. Leo murmured *'God help us!'* and waited for the falling sensation, but then the miracle arrived.

The Mini came to a halt, the wheels on the driver's side resting upon the verge. Leo's flank was cradled by the branches of a sturdy pine tree rooted to the floor of the canyon. Leo made the Sign of the Cross in thanksgiving. Elaine killed the engine and for a moment there was only the sound of birdsong and the creaking of branches.

'Leo,' whispered Elaine, as though to speak at a normal volume would send the vehicle careering down the drop. 'We're going to have to both get out of the car at exactly the same time. If I get out first, then your weight might . . .'

'Tip me over the edge,' he said, completing her sentence.

She nodded solemnly. Moving cautiously, she arched her body in order to let Leo haul himself over the gear stick and sit with her on his knee, her tennis skirt riding up to reveal the tops of her thighs.

'Let's stay like this for a wee while,' he whispered in her ear.

'For Pete's sake, this is no time for kidding around! Now, I'm opening the door . . . On the count of three we're both going to leap out . . . One, two, three!'

Elaine tumbled onto the ground and Leo landed upon her a moment later. The Mini stayed perfectly still.

'We did it!' they said in unison. They embraced and gazed into each other's eyes, but the moment was spoiled by the whine of a gearbox in reverse.

Leo scrambled to his feet and withdrew the Webley. 'I'll pretend to aim at him, but shoot wide. That should scare him off.'

He pointed the pistol slightly to the left of the black car, which was some distance away, and fired. The bullet thumped into a pine bole. The kickback was only moderate but still sent a shard of protest though his damaged right hand. Leo double-gripped the pistol and adjusted his stance. He fired one, two, three shots more, the final one whanging off the Merc's rear offside wheel arch. British lead on German steel after all these years.

'Oh dear, I didn't mean to do that!' grumbled Leo.

The Merc sped away amid a cloud of grit.

'I got the licence number,' said Elaine. 'T44 WTB. I'll see if I can get a trace on it later. There's a hacker who posts stuff from the DVLA's database.'

Leo nodded vaguely, then broke the Webley to eject the spent cartridges, withdrew four new rounds and inserted them into the empty chambers. 'It looks like we're walking back,' he said. 'We can call the garage in St John's Town and arrange for them to collect the keys from you. Hopefully they can then tow the car out of the tree without its getting written off.'

They began the long walk back through the weald, traversing sunny heaths, negotiating green thickets and fording cooling streams. They kept the road in their vicinity for orientation, occasionally crouching down when they thought they heard an engine. Eventually they reached Sannox House. Elaine consulted her computer and informed Leo that the Mercedes' registration number was 'unassigned'; therefore it had been wearing a false plate. Sun-tired and dusty, they collapsed onto the drawing-room sofa and held each other tenderly. He begged her to return with him to the Greatorixes for safety's sake, but she refused.

Day Fifteen

L EO woke with a thumping hangover, having consumed far too many *digestifs* with Fordyce the previous night. After Evelyn had retired, Leo had told his friend about the incident on the Raiders' Road. He ascertained Chas's innocence in the matter – Fordyce had seen him still working in the kitchen garden at approximately the same time as the Mercedes almost sent him careering to his death.

Leo rose, prepared a seltzer remedy and gazed out of his bedroom window. It was raining lightly, which would clear the humidity, and he suspected the sun would break through soon enough. He resolved to engage in a spot of birdwatching to take his mind off the case (and let the clues percolate in his subconscious), and indeed Elaine, and his desire to drink. He used to dabble in this meditative pursuit from time to time, and made a little vow to renew his membership of the British Trust for Ornithology.

After breakfasting with Fordyce and Evelyn, Leo gathered his outdoor things and his grandfather's birding journal (with its heinous 'egging' column), to which his father and then Leo had appended their own ledgers. He then went to the library, from where he borrowed *British Birds in Their Haunts* by the Reverend C.A. Johns.

He drove the Humber through the village and up the forest road. As he motored the rain abated and the sun began winking through the hazel canopy. He parked on the verge, grabbed his knapsack and strode into the sylvan realm.

Leo savoured the smell of a fir thicket, droplets glittering on the needles. To his right was the laughing water of Scoulag Burn. By its steaming banks flourished shamrock, sphagnum, water mint and liverwort. The sun had now fully established itself in the firmament, glancing gloriously upon the towering pine trunks of a grand timberland. Finches, pipits and tits chattered in the high branches where a slight haze had formed. Leo peeled off his windcheater and walked further in, enjoying the sensation of his feet on the carpet of fresh herbage. The sparkling forest was a gallery of song, an avian ensemble. The wood pigeon's drowsy five-note refrain provided the baritone. There was the complex silvery liquid trill of the goldfinch, the cheerful abstract notes of the robin and the gorgeous warble of the blackbird. A carrion crow crouched on a low bough in begrudged silence like an atheist in a cathedral, secretly impressed and just gracious enough not to mar the sublimity of the chorus with an abrasive croak or caw.

Two hours later Leo sat by the brook, washing down a slice of Mrs Grove's pork pie with a flask of lemonade, and added the rest of his sightings to the journal: jay, chaffinch, great spotted woodpecker, siskin, coal tit, great tit, blue tit, linnet, wren, spotted flycatcher and house sparrow. Yes, the trip had proved to be the perfect tonic, Leo meditated, unaware of the dark figure watching him from the trees.

Leo took a notion to visit the Cauldron again, which was a mere knight's move away, on the off chance that Gilbert's favourite beauty spot might yield some clue. After a fruitless scan of the area, he gazed at the cascades which tumbled into the frothing pool, noting the considerable volume of water even in a dry summer such as this; in spring it must be a veritable torrent. He imagined Gilbert resting here, smiling at the sheer gorgeousity of the place, Irish whimsy flashing through his mind.

'What did you see here, Gilbert?' he asked aloud.

Leo mused that a 'linn' is the Scots word for a waterfall. Therefore the ruined priory probably took its name from this place; a slightly tenuous nomenclature given that it was situated a mile away. He walked downstream a little and considered that perhaps the burn became influent because below the Cauldron its progress seemed more genteel, as though its spirit softened as it glimpsed the tender country beyond the tree line.

Leo then doubled back and walked in the direction of Loch Quien for a while. He noticed a thin tributary flowing down into the burn through a grassy gorge, and on impulse decided to explore it. It was queer inhabiting this enclosed, primeval place; a moist, dank world of cushion and swan-neck mosses, shamrocks and fern. Sunlight slanted through the pine branches on the higher ground down onto the gorge's floor. Leo happened to glance upwards and observed a dark-clad figure, the size and build male, standing at the top of the slope, framed by two fir trees. He was wearing a black hood with eyeholes cut into it, and stood perfectly motionless. Leo produced the Webley and fired a warning shot into the heavens. A surge of pain jarred his damaged hand as the bullet ripped through the canopy, twig splinters and droplets of rainwater falling through the air and landing on his scalp. The report echoed through the noble pines and birds flew away in panic. The watcher melted into the greenery. Leo replaced the round and walked smartly back to the Humber, dreading that some mischief had been done to it by the creepy man, but the trusty old vehicle sat on the verge unmolested.

Leo drove down the forest road, sunlight flashing on his windscreen as he considered the hooded figure in the woods. The sinister incursion into his idyll had disturbed and offended him. As he approached Biggnarbriggs village, a black Mercedes with tinted windows swung out from the Green Man Inn and drove on ahead of him. Leo drew close as the two vehicles slowed to a halt to give way at the village crossroads. He noted a patch of fibreglass which had been hastily patched onto the rear offside wheel arch in order to cover Leo's bullet hole. Suddenly the Mercedes, its driver presumably now aware of Leo's presence, sped off, the powerful German engine roaring ferociously. Leo put the Humber into low gear but he brought the clutch up too quickly, causing it to stall. By the time he had restarted, a sluggish tractor, followed by a convoy of frustrated motorists, had taken up the highway. Leo slammed the steering wheel in exasperation, then placed the car into reverse and rolled it backwards, and parked outside the Green Man between Maxwell's E-Type and the canary-yellow Reliant Scimitar that had cut him up several days before.

As he entered the tavern, the conversation among the all-male patrons abated. Leo took a good look round, recognising a few faces from his last visit here and from the search party. He also noticed the Reliant Scimitar-driving Flash Harry.

'Who was in the car that just pulled out from here?' Leo asked the landlord.

'The black Merc? No idea – it was just using the yard to turn in. I've never seen it before.' He called out to the pub: 'Anyone know anything about that Merc?'

Silence.

'That's Maxwell Blythman's Jaguar parked outside,' said Leo. 'Where is he?'

'Oh, I noticed him parking it there earlier. He didn't come in. Perhaps he was off for a ramble.'

Leo picked up a lonely glass, sniffed its contents and then placed it back down upon the bar. It was Bénédictine and brandy, Maxwell's favourite poison. 'Whose drink is this?' he enquired.

'That would be mine,' replied the landlord, who took a sip from it. He then held Leo's gaze, the slightest suggestion of insolence inhabiting his features.

Leo returned to his car and swung it left at the crossroads, then parked near to the bridge that spanned the Biggnar Burn and gave the village its name. He got out and gazed down at the flowing water for a while, but failed to extricate himself from the little dungeon of foul temper into which he had descended. He was about to get back into the Humber when DCI Dalton approached him.

'Mr Moran. I was chatting to the driver of a garage truck earlier, which had your girlfriend's Mini on the back. What's this I hear about it being plucked out of a fir tree?'

'It was a pine, as a matter of fact.'

'So you were in the vehicle at the time?'

'None of your business.'

'I'm making it my business. Failure to report a road traffic accident—'

'I'm not interested. I'm tired of you people. I don't trust a damn one of you.'

'Let me remind you that I happen to be leading a missing person inquiry.'

'You lot don't give a tuppeny fart about poor Lauren, any more than you cared about Hazel Bannatyne.'

'Mr Moran, you will adjust your—'

'Which of the brethren are you taking your orders from?'

Dalton pulled herself up, took a breath. Placed her hand on the driver's door as a signal that Leo should not proceed. 'Women are not permitted in the Craft, as I'm sure you know.'

'Am I required by law to speak with you? Otherwise, I shall wish you good day, Inspector.'

Dalton took her hand from the car and Leo made to get in.

'Strange is dead,' she said.

Leo straightened up. 'What happened?'

'Whisky and pills, the copper's favourite.'

'May the Lord have mercy on his soul.'

'There was a letter, addressed to you. I have a copy of it here,' said Dalton as she produced an A4 sheet. Leo reached out but she held it back. 'I've already read it.'

'You had no right.'

She handed Leo the document. He scanned the text while she provided a summary. 'He says he told you in a phone call that at the time of Hazel Bannatyne's disappearance the police didn't make public an attempted abduction of a teenage girl in the area in the summer of 1977. He says he was instructed not to. Masonic stuff, he felt sure, but more. There were mutterings about protecting someone key to Defence of the Realm. Strange genuinely believed Talorc's sect were responsible for the Bannatyne girl, but nonetheless all these years he felt shitty that an attempted abduction had been covered up; it should have been properly publicised in case the cult theory was wrong. It always gnawed at him, as did loads of other crappy compromises he made throughout his career. When Lauren went missing he got worried, what with Talorc being dead for thirty years. Perhaps it wasn't the cult that had done for Hazel after all; perhaps it was these men who tried to abduct the first lassie in '77. He says that's why he agreed to see you. He was trying to work out if he'd made a terrible mistake back then, by following orders. He's spent these last few days fretting over what other victims there could be. I think at some point last night it just became too much for him.'

'This Defence of the Realm stuff – Major Balfour-MacWhinnie boasted to me that he was at Heathrow in 1974. Are you familiar with the alleged attempted *coup d'état*?'

'Yes, I watched a BBC documentary about it.'

'However, as I told you before, the Major appears to have cast-iron alibis.'

'Right, Mr Moran, I think it's time for us to cooperate. And for you to tell me everything you know.'

Leo walked with Dalton to the incident room where he informed her about his latest theories and investigations, including the notion that

Gilbert Doyle had been frightened to death, his and Fordyce's ideas about the symbol on the setting maul, and his observations about the strange gravestone and his thoughts about the Black Earl and the possibility that Hugo and Gilbert had glimpsed a revival of the scoundrel's clique. Some details had already been provided to the police detective. Brian had confessed to holding back the details of his being blackmailed. Unity had led her to the pagan icon in the Enchanted Forest. And 'Rachael Kidd' had told her about the fresh ribbons on the wish tree and the crucified fox. Dalton mentioned that these items had as yet yielded no forensic clues, suggesting, Leo posited, a professional job. He didn't unmask Rachael as Elaine, or mention his possession and use of a handgun, which thankfully he'd left in the Humber. However, he did tell Dalton about the black Mercedes with the false licence plate running them off the Raiders' Road, and that he had just seen the same vehicle pull away from the Green Man, but that the landlord had claimed it had only been using his yard to turn in. He also mentioned the hooded figure in the forest, and seeing Maxwell's car parked outside the Green Man, and his trademark tipple, a Bénédictine and brandy, sat upon the bar.

'But Maxwell was nowhere to be seen,' concluded Leo. 'The landlord said the drink belonged to him, but I'm certain he was lying. B&B is not exactly a common-or-garden daytime beverage.'

'Do you think Maxwell was the hooded individual you saw in the woods?'

'It's possible. The B&B had fresh ice in it, meaning it had only been recently served. I've a feeling Maxwell was hiding in the back or something. I just found it all a touch suspicious.'

'I wonder where that Mercedes is being kept,' wondered Dalton.

Leo was lost in thought for a moment, then said, 'Hang on – do you know a derelict petrol station on the B road between here and Castle Douglas?'

'Yes.'

'A week ago I saw Chas Shaw and his chums there. It's quite out of the way, and has a double garage.'

'Let's go.'

They climbed into an unmarked Mondeo and first traversed the short distance to the Green Man – Dalton wanted to establish whether Maxwell had been avoiding Leo earlier, and, if so, why. However, the

Jaguar had gone and the landlord claimed he'd just seen Maxwell return and drive off. They sped to their next destination, police despatch messages crackling from the Motorola. Dalton rolled the powerful vehicle onto the lonely stretch of oil-stained concrete, and the pair disembarked.

The sun was quite strong, and insects sounded noisily in nearby thorns. The place seemed deserted. They approached the garage and Dalton tried the two up-and-over doors, but they were both locked. Leo stood on his tiptoes to peer through a high slit window.

'Anything?' asked Dalton.

'The glass is covered.'

Dalton tried a side door, which was also locked.

'Can I help you?' came a voice.

Leo and Dalton spun round. It was a man aged in his early sixties wearing agricultural overalls, muddy Wellingtons and plastic-rimmed spectacles. He had thinning grey hair and wore a scowl on his tired, lined face.

Dalton produced her ID and said, 'I beg your pardon, Mr . . . ?'

'Moffat. I'm the farmer,' he said, jabbing his thumb to indicate the land over a nearby wall.

'And I'm DCI Dalton. I'm trying to trace a black Mercedes car with darkened windows. Who owns this property?'

'Me,' said Moffat. 'I let folk keep their vehicles here sometimes, for a wee fee. There's no Mercedes in there.'

'Do you mind if I take a look?' asked Dalton.

Moffat obliged ungraciously, selecting a key from a large bunch he had withdrawn from his pocket, and muttering that the policewoman should bring a warrant next time.

Leo and Dalton stepped into the cool, gloomy interior. All that was parked there was the Ford Mustang Leo had seen on the forecourt a week ago.

'You see?' said Moffat.

The place smelled of motor oil and paint primer. There was another, fresher, plasticky odour which Leo couldn't quite place. As he was leaving he scanned a shelf and realised its source: a tin of fibreglass resin, its seal broken.

* * *

Dalton dropped Leo where he had left the Humber in the village after providing him with her direct number. Leo returned to the hall and repaired to his bedroom. He rang his mother, and then digested the day's events along with a few orange creams. After a few minutes his mobile rang. Stephanie.

He answered, and they chatted for a while about the decline and fall of his friend's marriage. Leo didn't mention it, but he couldn't help but wonder that if folk like Stephanie and Jamie hadn't abandoned old-fashioned values of fidelity then they would have been a whole lot happier.

'I got Gilbert Doyle's PM report,' she said eventually.

'Well done, old girl! How on earth did you manage it?'

'There was no way other than approaching the family. So I rang the Doyle residence and spoke with one of the sisters on the pretext of offering my condolences. I managed to steer the conversation to the matter of Gilbert's cause of death. And guess what – the sisters had themselves already requested a copy of the medical report. They had got to talking after the funeral and were a little concerned.'

'Really?'

'I'm not saying they suspected any dark deeds, just that they had general misgivings about their brother's end. Anyway, I explained that I'm a legal professional, experienced in examining such documents, so the old dear got a neighbour to fax me the report summary. Also, I've been researching your theory of foul play. Have you heard of the term "psychogenic death"?'

'No.'

'It's the notion that sudden death can be brought about by a colossal emotional shock. Also known as "voodoo death". At such times our bodies are programmed to go into fight-or-flight response, which is activated by the central nervous system sending a large dose of adrenaline through the body. Adrenaline is toxic in large amounts, and can damage, among other organs, the heart, making it go into irregular rhythms. Adrenaline makes the cells produce calcium, which causes the heart muscle to contract. Now these processes, in someone with a cardiac condition, can be fatal. And Gilbert's medical report stated that there were raised levels of adrenaline in his urine and large calcium deposits in the heart ventricles.' Leo whistled. 'This means that it *could* have been a psychogenic death,' continued Stephanie, 'but there's no definitive way of knowing.'

'So someone who knew about Gilbert's state of health could have deliberately given him a terrible fright.'

'Indeed.'

After he had hung up, Leo telephoned Dalton and told her about Stephanie's research. He then showered, dressed for dinner and rang Elaine to brief her on the day's developments. She was shocked to hear of Strange's demise, and told him that the Mini had been salvaged and restored to her possession after only a minor repair.

Leo enjoyed a hearty meal consisting of a magnificent platter of langoustines, mussels and cockles, followed by stovies accompanied by an excellent Château Latour, and then brandied pears and whipped cream. Evelyn drove Mrs Grove home, and when she returned, having enclosed the spaniels in the gun room, found that the gentlemen had repaired to the drawing room to consume their *digestifs*. She announced her intention to retire to her bedroom, and bid them goodnight.

'I fear poor Ev is suffering from nervous exhaustion,' said Fordyce. 'What with all the high drama of these last weeks.'

Leo, too, felt drained by recent events, and as he relaxed in the leather embrace of one of the Chesterfields a great weariness overcame him. Fordyce went to the kitchen to fetch some ice and Leo dozed off.

A large attic room, seemingly interconnected to multitudinous other chambers. There is a lumbering ogre, a seven-foot biped with a muscular body clad in rough black garments and the head of a large pig. The grinning monster is chasing Leo around the room, much to the glee of a gibbering mob of sycophants: odd, scrawny, barely human creatures dressed in filthy rags who sit on or swing from rafters. The pig-man catches his quarry and bites into his back, evoking delighted squeals and yelps from the gnomish spectators. It occurs to Leo that this vision is long-standing, one first experienced during his childhood.

The horrific scene fades and he sees the kindly face of the man in the plum hunting coat who he believes to be the eighth baron Greatorix who haunts Biggnarbriggs Hall. He leads Leo to another attic room. Leo realises he's been here before – it's the chamber where Elaine and he hid during the hide-and-seek game. The man points towards the door they had tried

to open, with its distinctive, archaic, arched design and its extravagant,
S-shaped handle.

A sound snapped Leo from his slumber – it was Fordyce returning with
the ice.

'By Jove, old stick, you look like you've seen a ghost!'

'In a manner of speaking I have – I nodded off and experienced a
vision.'

Leo took a gulp of whisky and then divulged the details of the
pig-man, the ghost and the locked door in the attic room.

'That door leads to the rooms in the tower,' said Fordyce.

'Shall we take a dekko?' suggested Leo.

Fordyce withdrew two torches from the dining-room sideboard and a
heavy iron key from the kitchen drawer, and after Leo had fetched his
detective's kit the duo ascended the grand staircase to the attic level,
walking towards the sixteenth-century wing of the great house. They
entered the old chamber, switching on their torches as it wasn't wired
for electric lighting. Leo felt uneasy stepping into the place after having
just experienced it in his vision. They strode across the boards and
Fordyce unlocked the door and opened it with a creak worthy of any
Hammer film.

'Gosh, it's been *years* since I've been up here,' he said as they ascended
a steep stone stairway.

They came to a little landing with a wooden door which Fordyce
opened. He fumbled for an old Bakelite switch and a bulb illuminated
the most curious of rooms.

'This is where my dear great uncle spent so much of his time,'
explained Fordyce.

The lancet windows were shuttered and a musty atmosphere prevailed.
A large oak table dominated the floor space, on which sat some of
Hugo's scientific apparatus, thick with dust. Against the wall was an
extraordinary piece of furniture, a Rococo walnut cabinet with a kneeler
and a crucifix, Christ carved from ivory. Hundreds of books and papers
were piled up in places, and charts and diagrams were pinned to the
walls. There was also a portrait, unmistakably a Ramsay. It was of a man
with handsome, kindly features, aged approximately thirty. He was
wearing a plum hunting coat with big golden buttons, an ivory satin

waistcoat and a lace cravat. Unlike the man from Leo's visions, he was wearing a periwig, but it was undoubtedly the same individual. A small brass plaque on the frame read: 'James Alexander Torquil Greatorix, eighth baron Greatorix of Biggnarbriggs'.

'Fordyce, I do believe we've found your ancestor! The man I dreamed of in the plum coat, the ghost I saw on the tower and who Margaret the cook met. There must be a reason he instructed me to come here.'

'Do forgive, but I have no memory of that portrait being here!'

Instinctively, Leo hoisted the picture from its hooks, dislodging ancient stour and cobwebs, and placed it on the table. He examined the exposed wall carefully, tapping it and running his hands over the plaster, but there seemed nothing untoward. He moved his attention to the picture itself. He turned it over, placing it face down.

'I hope you don't mind Fordyce,' he said, as he withdrew his penknife.

'Not at all.'

Leo prised out a series of pins to release the mount. He removed it, and there, resting against the back of the canvas, was an old, yellowed document bearing a steady, plain hand:

M'Lady Baroness,

Further to our Discourse this is my written Testament according to your wish, given on this Sixth day of January in the Year of Our Lord 1746.

On December 21st last, Baron Greatorix rode out to Dumfries to meet the Prince. The Baron was no Jacobite, he did not hold with the Hielanmen's Popish ways, but he fear'd havoc now that the Army had return'd to Scotland, and wish'd to entreat Charles to peaceful Settlement. The Prince gave him due Conference, but being a rash and proud young Fellow refus'd the Baron's pleas. That nicht on his return home the Baron spy'd a strange sight, lights moving by the auld Priory. Upon inspection it was a weird Procession, men clad in black with torches, a dozen or so, with a fell feart lass in bonds as though she was to be deflower'd by those men. As Baron, yer Gudeman had right to impose the King's Laws and punish ill-gait'd Folk, and he was a Noble Laird with a soothfast sense of Duty. Therefore he intervene'd, but was attack'd and clubb'd most treacherously, after being telt that the lass was for their Yule Revelry that very nicht, it being the longest ain. They telt him they were of the Freemasons, yet their Leader had been cast out for his Debauchery, so they had set up their own unco Temple, a "Hell-fire Club", with their ain Rules and Rites whereby they gie'd worship to the Horn'd Idol just as did the Witches and afore them the Pagans of auld. The Baron had been left for dying all nicht in the raw cold until I, Malcolm Tywnholm, Shepherd, of Balmakethe Parish, found him on my way down from my shieling on the high pasture abune Loch Quien. Before he pass'd away he relat'd to me of these details regarding the terrible Attack upon his person, saying the men were hood'd but for the Leader, Walter the Bastard, the Black Earl, one of the most powerful Noblemen in the Kingdom. It is said he was once ain of a Hell-fire Club in England, and that now he rides from his Ancestral Lands twenty miles further to this airt to meet other ill-gait'd men for debauchery. The maiden Jean Hannay of the wee mailin at Sannox has not been seen since that dreadful nicht and is fear'd perish'd.

M'Lady, since we last spake, innuendo has fester'd in the Parish that his Lairdship had been plotting with the Pretender which is why he was kill'd by some outrag'd Carl, but this is a lie doubtless commenc'd by the Guilty Men. Or that the Murder of the Baron was commit'd by marauding Jacobite Renegades, who also made off with the maid Jean, but this too is a lie. Though I was first feart to widely refute these false-hoods, I have come resolved to make this Testimony, and I swear upon the Holy Book that what is screive'd herein be soothfast.

Malcolm Tywnholm.

'I wonder why the Baroness hid this document rather than take it to the authorities,' mused Leo.

'I seem to recall she died of a broken heart soon after her husband's death,' said Fordyce. 'The country must have been in turmoil at that time due to the rebellion. I'll wager she concealed it behind her late beloved's portrait, waiting for law and order to be restored, at which time she would approach the sheriff.'

'But then she herself passed away.'

'And it has been left here, forgotten about, ever since.'

'That vision must indeed have been of the eighth baron's sad demise,' said Leo.

228

'And the setting maul with which you were attacked and the symbolism on it chime with the quasi-Masonic aspect of the Black Earl's so-called Hellfire Club,' observed Fordyce. 'And the mention of the horned idol chimes with the Baphomet worship implied by the pentagram.'

'Meaning that there most certainly has been a revival of this Hellfire Club, which will be the lanthorns Hugo saw, and the nocturnal goings-on Gilbert witnessed.'

'And will probably be the same men who tried to snatch the girl in '77, and took poor Hazel and Lauren.'

Leo took photographs of the document using his phone, then said, 'Come on. Let's go to the library; we've research to do.'

As they walked, Leo informed Fordyce about the three missing pages from the Greatorix family archives. They entered the library, sat at the table and switched on the laptop. Leo keyed 'Walter the Bastard + Kirkcudbrightshire' into the search engine. It brought up an eighteenth-century portrait of the most extraordinary-looking creature: a well-built man of anaemic, porcine features, his black hair and tricorne hat barely concealing the irregular contours of his skull. Malevolent green eyes were set beneath the grisly frown of his brow.

'How queer!'

'What, old stick?'

'I saw a man who looked rather like him at Gilbert's wake. I popped into the back garden for some fresh air and he was staring at me from across the fence. He had different-coloured hair and eyes, and the features weren't *exactly* the same, but he's similar. Incidentally, the leader of the thugs in my vision of the murder of the eighth baron was wearing a tricorne hat.'

A couple of amateur history websites filled in some of Walter the Bastard's backstory. He belonged to a clan of high nobility whose ancestral lands lay twenty miles or so to the north of Biggnarbriggs. He was the black sheep of his family, whose sobriquet originated in his illegitimacy but also aptly described the fellow's character. As a young man, he spent much of his time drinking, fornicating, and squandering his fortune while a member of a London society for licentious noblemen, and was an acquaintance of Sir Francis Dashwood, who would go on to found the most infamous of the Hellfire Clubs. Walter returned from the capital and upon his accession – which, it was strongly rumoured, he gained by disposing of his half-brother – he became known as the Black Earl, and not just on account of his preferred colour of clothing. He died from syphilis, and apparently his family chose to bury him down by Linn Priory because he had brought such disgrace upon them with his debauchery, not least at a Hellfire Club he had launched in Balmakethe Parish.

'Forgive me, Leo, but what's all this Hellfire Club business?'

'I believe they were sort of bacchanalian societies set up by toffs, chiefly during the eighteenth century.'

Leo knew he had once possessed far more information on the subject, and cursed years of boozing for his poor recall. However, the men's internet searches divulged much of interest. Particularly, that the original Hellfirers were often prominent Freemasons who incorporated those influences into their proceedings. They saw themselves as freethinkers who sought to rebel against the established moral order, yet they also wanted to enforce and enjoy the privilege of the upper classes.

The original club was founded by the Duke of Wharton in London in 1718, and it spawned numerous imitations, most notably the one set up by the aforementioned Dashwood that operated in the mid-eighteenth century. Wharton's club held sham religious ceremonies to mock Christianity, but their main interests were drinking, gluttony and proto-intellectualism. Dashwood took things a step further, creating a club in man-made caves beneath an old Cistercian abbey in Medmenham, Buckinghamshire. Proceedings were strongly influenced by classical paganism, replete with a River Styx and ferryman Charon, and a chamber called Venus's Parlour. Dashwood was one of several so-called 'friars' who indulged themselves fulsomely beneath the earth, enjoying dressing up, melodrama, drunkenness, feasting and depraved orgies with prostitutes and servant girls. Rumours abounded that Black Masses were held and even human sacrifice. These latter tales were probably apocryphal, but some of the Hellfire Clubs founded in Scotland were most certainly Satanic in ethos.

'These powerful men felt entitled to exploit the weak and vulnerable,' said Leo mournfully. 'And I do not doubt that our present-day gang are inheritors of their callous, hedonistic proclivities.'

'I say, old stick, all of this talk of hellfire has made me think of something regarding the shape that you dreamt of, the one at the centre of the symbol on the setting maul. You may recall I mentioned it could be the Greek letter *Pi* rather than the number or the mathematical constant. What if it stands for the ancient Greek word for fire – *pyr*?'

'Why, that's quite brilliant, Fordyce! And could the lower component of the symbol – the upside-down triangle with the vertical line descending from its lower point and a line descending from the left-hand point – represent another element?'

'But it's not a Greek letter, Leo. Unless . . .'

'Unless what?'

'The other classical elements are air, aether, earth and water. What if the other component is an amalgam of uppercase gamma and upsilon, one beneath the other? Gamma standing for *ge*, which means earth, and upsilon standing for *hudor*, which means water.'

'And the fact that the water symbol is under that of the earth is significant. Thus Hellfire, where water flows under the earth, like Dashwood's Styx. Which would be the dark flowing water in my visions,' said Leo excitedly. 'Now, Dashwood's caves were under a disused monastery – what if there was a deliberate significance in placing a club below a former place of devotion to profane Christianity, and if our mob's lair is therefore beneath Linn Priory? Perhaps Walter the Bastard wrote to his friend about his subterranean pleasure palace, which sparked the ideas for Medmenham Abbey. Maybe there were cellars or catacombs dug out beneath Linn Priory which had been long forgotten, after the place was left to ruin following the Reformation. Earlier in my investigations I ruled out any underground watercourses to explain the water in my visions. However, it occurred to me earlier today that a linn is a waterfall in Scots, hence Linn Priory. But it struck me that the cascades flowing into the Cauldron are a good mile away from it. Then I realised the water level of Scoulag Burn is lower downstream from the Cauldron. What if the burn splits there, perhaps a distributary flowing underground? And if the miners of any catacombs came across such a subterranean stream, then perhaps the priory didn't originally take its name from the cascades at all, but from some waterfall *underneath* the priory.'

'But surely the police would have found something suspicious at the priory?'

'The bold gendarmes were deflected by a scent trail that led down to the forest road. Perhaps the latter part of it, after the ruins, was falsely laid. I'll tell you something else, my friend: if my theories are correct, it could explain why a certain gentleman is so keen to keep people away from that priory.'

'The Major.'

'Quite. The trouble is that not only does he have a cast-iron alibi for the time Lauren was last seen, but he was in Ireland when Hazel went missing and when she would have been killed. Behold,' said Leo, fiddling with his phone and showing Fordyce an image file. 'This is a photograph of a newspaper microfiche I took in the Mitchell Library. It's of the Major addressing journalists at his base on the very morn Hazel would have been ritually sacrificed at dawn.'

Fordyce took the device from his friend and stared intently at the picture of the young Major on the parade ground. He used the zoom function to enhance a detail. 'But this photograph wasn't taken in Ireland, old stick. Look, that's Criffel in the background.'

'Criffel?'

'It's a hill near New Abbey.'

'Good God, you're right – I recognise it!'

'The photo must have been taken at the Kirkcudbright Training Area, down by Dundrennan. Lots of the military visit there. There's an artillery range too.'

Leo stood up and paced around. 'The first statement the Major made to the media, which took place on the day Hazel went missing, regarding his men's use of baton rounds, was definitely from Belfast; there were RUC officers in the room. When I first saw that photograph of his second news conference I made an assumption – the worst thing a detective can do – that it also took place in the Six Counties.'

'But you weren't to know, Leo. The newspaper report simply refers to the venue as the Major's company "base", and you can hardly see Criffel in the photo. I'm local to these parts and more familiar with the landscape.'

'Probably after what had happened at Ballymonagh they were pulled out of the action – they would have been marked men – and sent to do exercises for a while on the mainland,' said Leo, sitting back down. 'The media would have been instructed not to reveal their location for security reasons. Anyway, the point is that this blows the Major's alibi apart – he could easily have been present for the dawn murder of Hazel, and then driven down to the Training Area in time for reveille and then the news conference. There is a strong suggestion there was a cover-up, and Strange, the man who headed the investigation into Hazel's disappearance, felt that it was Masonic but more than that – Defence of the Realm stuff. He was ordered not to publicise an attempted abduction on the forest road in 1977. He has just committed suicide, because of the guilt he felt about the case. Now, I recall the Major boasting to me that he'd been in Heathrow in '74.'

'I remember him doing so. To be honest, old stick, I didn't know what he was referring to.'

'The army occupied the airport. The official explanation would be that it was a training exercise, but Harold Wilson, who was Prime Minister at the time, later said he had never been informed about it. Some have speculated it was a dry run for a *coup d'état* or a show of strength aimed at certain parties perceived as disloyal to the country. Others said it might have been the actual start of a coup which didn't gather the necessary momentum. Back then there was a dirty tricks campaign initiated by Special Branch in Northern Ireland called Clockwork Orange. It fed disinformation: Wilson being a KGB agent, his secretary being an IRA sympathiser, Marxists lurking in every Whitehall department. The trouble was that MI5 and to a lesser extent MI6 had fascist elements within them, folk who believed that Britain was headed to the dogs, and they didn't realise it was all black propaganda. And the spooks were in league with key business, armed forces and establishment figures, all willing to overthrow the government.'

'So, what are you saying?'

'I'm saying that the Major would have had friends in very high places. The Major with the Masonic motto above his gate. The Major who could have pulled strings to ensure the police didn't follow up on the '77 attempted abduction.'

'You surely can't mean that dark powerful forces covered up the Major committing *murder*, just because he was one of their own?'

'That's precisely what I mean. Think of the historical context: there was a war going on in the Six Counties, bombs in the capital. The miners had just brought down a Tory government, the Cold War was raging and there was paranoia abounding about KGB influence and infiltration . . . one dead girl could be considered collateral damage to keep a key player on the team.'

'It's just too fantastic. They would have thrown him to the wolves.'

'These wars are dirty, and operatives work by possessing dirt on enemies, rivals and even allies; knowledge about their darkest vices so that they have leverage when required. And a dissolute scoundrel like the Major must have witnessed powerful men in some fairly compromising scenarios. Who knows what scandal he could have dished if he hadn't been offered immunity for his own perverted pursuits, on the proviso that he would be a good boy and not do it ever again? Remember, Fordyce, such a conspiracy would only require a few participants to pull strings and put the kybosh on lines of inquiry. The vast majority of the investigating police officers involved might be entirely innocent. I shall ring Dalton first thing.'

'I'm not sure she's going to buy all this conspiracy stuff.'

'You'd be surprised,' said Leo. 'It was she who showed me Strange's suicide note. But let's nip down to the ruins now and see if we can find anything more substantial for her.'

'Are you sure that's a good idea? It's getting late.'

Leo read the slight expression of concern on Fordyce's face, but curiosity had overcome him. 'There's still a bit of light in the sky,' he said. 'Let's have a butcher's.'

They fetched their jackets and Leo slung the Webley case over his shoulder. Then they set off, two decent men tiny on the face of the earth and innocent to the ordeal that was about to engulf them.

The stroll over the lawns and meadows was deceptively pleasant. Bats flitted in the soft gloaming, which accentuated the whiteness of the men's shirts and their sun-browned faces. The ruined priory was gently backlit by the summer dusk sky, the deepening azure clear but for a cloud band of supernal purity to the south and west. The moon was a ball of burnished gold as the first stars winked out.

'Why, this is just like old times up at Loch Dhonn, old stick! You and I off adventuring together, me as *aide-de-camp* to the great sleuth!'

'Indeed it is, my friend.'

'What exactly are we looking for?'

'I don't know, Fordyce. A way in, perhaps.'

They walked towards the graves, which were located seventy yards or so from the ruins, on slightly lower ground. Leo scanned the area around the Black Earl's final resting place again. They inspected some of the other graves, and Leo spotted a tomb he had not noticed before. Partially obscured by bracken, it was evidently dug into the face of a ten-foot earthen dip where at one point the higher ground fell away abruptly. It was marked with a large stone that was embedded in the near-vertical scarp.

'Look at this one, Fordyce. There's no Christian symbolism upon it,' said Leo. 'But there is a graven inscription: John Nemo, seventeen forty-four. The surname is significant.'

'Why, Leo? It's a touch unusual, I grant you. But I'm sure it's just a variation of Nimmo, an old Stirlingshire name.'

'Perhaps, but what does *nemo* mean in Latin?'

'No one.'

'Precisely. I'll wager this man didn't exist, and "no one" is interred here. And the date, 1744 – that fits in with when the Black Earl was roaming these parts.'

'Look, there's a smaller inscription towards the bottom: *Facilis descensus Averno.*'

'Easy is the descent to Hell,' translated Leo.

'That's Virgil,' said Fordyce.

'Well, let's see just how easy the descent is.' Leo felt around the edge of the stone. 'Fordyce, I've found something . . . hinges . . . and a latch, I think.' Leo pulled and then heaved the stone, which was only a couple of inches thick. It yawned open.

'By Jove, it's a door!' exclaimed Fordyce.

Light came from within the entrance. Leo withdrew the Webley and stepped over the threshold. 'Into the maw of hell,' he muttered.

They entered a rough-hewn circular chamber, about fifteen feet in diameter. To their left was a strong door and ahead was a passageway. The room and the corridor were lit by strings of battery-powered electric bulbs which nestled in ancient sconces that had probably once housed oil lamps. The walls were decorated with faded murals of priapic classical figures in various positions, and a goat's skull was mounted prominently with a little inscription beneath it: *Bibamus, moriendum est.*

'Let us drink, for we must die,' translated Fordyce.

They walked carefully up the passageway for thirty yards, to where it forked into two different routes.

'Leo, the fact that these lights are burning means that this place is currently in use,' said Fordyce. 'Let's get out of here and dial nine-nine-nine.'

'Very well. I suppose there's no sense in placing ourselves in unnecessary danger.'

The two men turned back. As they emerged into the quickening twilight, they almost tripped over a dark heap.

'Dear God!' exclaimed Fordyce. 'It's Jimmy!'

Leo knelt down. A cricket bat lay beside the man. 'Bludgeoned to death. Just like your ancestor, Fordyce. God rest your soul, Jimmy.'

'L-L-Leo, look!' said Fordyce in horror.

Ahead of them, through the woodland, processed the Hellfirers, walking slowly towards them. They funnelled into the open, fanned out into a rank twenty yards from where Leo and Fordyce stood, and halted. There were twelve of them, all clad in pitch-black robes and cowls, and cloth face masks bearing the same symbol that had been engraved on the setting maul. Each figure carried a maul in one hand and a fiery torch in the other. Out in front was an unlucky thirteenth figure, Maxwell Blythman, who was wearing a dishevelled suit and whose hands were bound with cord. He looked battered and defeated. In unison, the Hellfirers raised their masks. They were all men, and included one-legged Tam, the landlord from the Green Man, the Flash Harry Scimitar driver and Moffat the farmer. Leo also recognised several other faces from the pub and/or the search party. Some of them were quite young but most were middle-aged – doubtless the original members. Leo raised the Webley and was about to utter a threat when he felt an agonising blow as the pistol was knocked from his grip. He clutched his right hand as Chas – it was he who had sneaked up alongside and struck him with his maul – retrieved the gun from a clump of weeds. The Major and his manservant Lyle also appeared from Leo's right. This latter trio wore the same garb as their brethren. Before Leo could react, Lyle raised his maul and brought it down violently. Leo felt a rush of pain in his head and then collapsed to the ground, a strange light flooding his vision.

Leo awoke to a curious chafing sound. The crown of his head ached, and his right hand throbbed mercilessly. He was lying on his side, and as his eyesight focused he discerned a light bulb berthed in a sconce set upon a stone wall. He was in a small, windowless room, a cell really. On the other side of the floor knelt Maxwell, working the binding on his wrists against a sharp little outcrop of rock. The shredded cord gave way and he shook his hands free.

'That's better,' he said, noticing that Leo had regained consciousness. 'I didn't want to spend my last minutes on earth in discomfort. That bastard cord was really digging in.'

Leo patted himself down with his left hand; his mobile phone had been confiscated, as had his detective's kit. He checked his wristwatch; he had only been out cold for a few minutes.

'Where's Fordyce?'

'Dead by now, most probably. Cast into the Styx in the lower cavern where the waterfall is. It is the way of things; how we sacrifice people.'

Leo groaned, bereft and sick at heart for the plight of his friend. He castigated himself for dragging Fordyce into such peril.

'I shouldn't mourn too much – we'll be joining him soon enough,' said Maxwell. 'We'll never be found, you know. The Styx flows all the way underground to the sea. It is cursed; in medieval times the nuns had the tunnels sealed off due to some witchcraft committed down here by a hag.'

Leo struggled to his feet and tried the door with his good hand.

'I wouldn't bother; it's bolted fast.'

Leo gazed through a grille in the door into the entrance chamber; he was therefore locked behind the strong door he had noticed when they first stepped into the catacombs.

'Why did they turn against you?' he asked as he slumped to the ground.

Maxwell merely stared forlornly at a fixed point in space.

'Your alibi for the time of Lauren's disappearance, of sleeping with poor Claire was particularly sly. Shameful to admit to and therefore more plausible.'

Again, Maxwell ignored him. A moment later the bolt began sliding. Leo composed himself; he wanted to make a good death, even though he'd always envisaged seeing a priest first. The door creaked open, and a figure wearing a grey jogging suit stepped inside.

It was Elaine.

Leo breathed a sigh of relief, then said, 'I'm so glad you decided to pop by, my dear. I was finding Maxwell such *tiresome* company.'

'Leo, there's blood on your collar!' exclaimed Elaine.

'Yet another blow to the Moran noggin, I'm afraid to report. And my hand took a whack too. Now, there's no time to waste – we must save Fordyce. We were right to suspect a group of perpetrators. They're going to cast him into a stream somewhere in this hellhole.'

'What about him?' said Elaine, gesturing towards Maxwell, who seemed wholly indifferent to her arrival.

'He was one of the cohort, but he seems to have fallen from grace.'

'Shall we keep him locked in here?'

'No. If they get to him first they'll kill him.'

'But the bastard is guilty!'

'I don't much care whether you lock me in or not,' remarked Maxwell. 'I'm all done in.'

'Elaine, I beg of you – time is of the essence,' urged Leo.

Maxwell got to his feet and addressed Leo and Elaine. 'Should you enter those catacombs you shall perish. For we worship and are favoured by the Hidden One, the One who Dwelleth in the Void.'

'Baphomet,' said Leo.

'The Major is getting more and more connected,' continued Maxwell. 'He can become some sort of avatar-host by binding his spirit with that of the Black Earl. His actual head . . . it transforms.'

'Utter twaddle,' sniffed Leo, although he couldn't help but recall the striking-looking fellow with the porcine head from the wake in London who had somewhat resembled the Black Earl. *That* must somehow have been the Major, perhaps there to gloat at poor Gilbert's demise! Only now, with hindsight, as he reflected on the face of the man, did Leo discern certain underlying physical characteristics of the army man. And the pig-man from his last vision must have been a representation of this monstrous Walter the Bastard–Major hybrid.

'I saw poor Jimmy's body outside,' said Elaine.

'They were careless to leave it *in situ*, and for not posting a guard at the cell,' said Leo.

'They were all too high on booze and coke – and the prospect of sacrifice – to care about such practicalities,' muttered Maxwell before shambling out of the cell and into the night.

'I'll explain everything later, but the important thing is that the police are on their way,' said Elaine.

'Then go and wait for them at the road. I need you to lead them to the entrance. I'll try to find Fordyce.'

'No chance. I'm going in with you.'

'Elaine, I must insist—'

'No, Leo – you can't stop me. The police will find us all right. Jimmy's body will draw their attention to the door. It's wide open, and they'll see the light.'

Defeated, Leo went outside. It was night-time now, but the countryside was discernible in the moonlight. He picked up Jimmy's cricket bat from where it still lay nestled in the turf and stepped back over the threshold. He handed the bat to Elaine, saying, 'Very well, we'll both go, but you're taking this.'

They walked briskly down the corridor. Leo clutched his painful right hand. He still felt woozy from the blow to his head. They came to where the passageway forked, and Leo declared that he would take the left route, Elaine the right. He didn't mention it to her, but Leo had calculated that his way would take him to the lower cavern where the Hellfirers lurked; Elaine's would hopefully be safe. They touched each other's fingertips and held eye contact for a moment. Then they parted.

As Leo walked he noticed alcoves containing couches, gaudy draperies, opium pipes and sex paraphernalia. Occult statuettes were set in little altars. He became aware that the passageway was sloping downwards, and he muttered a verse: '"I sank to the foundations of the mountains, the earth's gates shut behind me forever! Then you raised my life from the Pit, Lord my God!"'

About forty yards from where the passage had forked, he arrived at the cavern, which was illuminated by electric floodlights rigged up to heavy-duty batteries. He stepped onto a stone shelf above a thirty-foot wide gorge. To his right, the linn ejaculated from an aperture; this subterranean distributary of Scoulag Burn must have been fed by other runlets and fountains to create such a fierce flow. The waterfall tumbled into the ravine beneath him, which contained a deep, boiling reservoir that drained out through a narrow tunnel at the other end of the cavern. Some outer reaches of water flowed less fiercely and were thinly lit; it was perturbing to view the precise image from his visions.

On the other side of the chasm, the dry rock was on two levels. Straight ahead was higher ground, upon which was a large idol of a

Sabbatic Goat and a simple granite altar. To the right was the mouth of a passageway. To the left, this stratum was split by a cleft of sheer smooth walls and of similar breadth to the gorge. It was spanned by a little bridge. The subjacent ground, lapped by the water, was to Leo's far left, and connected to the higher territory by a stairway hewn into the rock. It was on this lower level that the Hellfirers were congregated around a banqueting table laden with sumptuous food and wine.

Leo gave thanks to God when he saw that Fordyce was still alive. His hands were bound, and a red rope was tied round his waist and attached to a ceremonial belt which the Major wore. The Major had donned red robes decorated with occult symbolism, and was seated at the head of the table on a carved throne like an African chief.

Leo called out over the sound of the flowing water, 'All behold the goblin king enthroned in his fetid cave, surrounded by his foul host!'

'You denigrate the echelon within the echelon, the circle within the circle,' returned the Major. 'However, I welcome you to the inner sanctum, to witness its full majesty: the casting of your friend into these anointed waters. But first, pray indulge me: how did you get loose?'

Leo had to think quickly because he didn't want to alert the Hellfirers to the fact that Elaine was abroad. 'Maxwell must have been worried about your plans for him, because he had a hatchet concealed in that cell. It would be best for you lot to give it up – he'll have alerted the police by now.'

'No, he won't,' said the Major.

'Wanna die by your own gun?' shouted one of the men. He raised the Webley and Leo flung himself behind the lip of the passageway as the report of all six rounds resonated around the chamber, the bullets sparking up rock fragments and powder. The men laughed as the echoes of the shots died away.

'You shower of bastards!' yelled Leo.

He stepped back onto the ledge and scanned the cavern, desperately trying to work out a way to get down the cliff so he could rescue Fordyce from the rapids once he was thrown in. He noticed that the bridge that spanned the cleft had a swivel mechanism, which meant it was designed to reach across the main gorge too. Therefore, even if Leo managed to scramble down to the water to aid his friend, doubtless the Hellfirers would turn the bridge ninety degrees, cross it and have them surrounded.

Furthermore, the blow from Chas's maul meant that he had only one functioning hand – inasmuch as his burned hands ever functioned adequately. Leo felt a peculiar despondency bloom within him.

As though reading his thoughts, the Major shouted, 'I can see you looking for a way down to try and rescue your friend once I cast him into the waters. Such heroism will be irresistible, and it will prove your demise. Now bear witness to my transmogrification!'

The Major produced a ceremonial knife and spoke with four of his men, who then followed him up the steps. The Major, grinning like a satyr, moved with a savage energy as he prodded Fordyce upwards and then across the bridge with the knife. His entourage sojourned on rocks across the bridge from their leader – a good vantage point for the coming drama.

Tears began to stream down Leo's face as the Major nudged Fordyce towards the rim of the ledge above the gorge. He withdrew his rosary from his pocket and held the little crucifix up in the direction of the Major. His antagonist noticed this and laughed cruelly. The Major then busied himself with certain items on the altar, muttering incantations and at one point throwing brightly coloured powder into the air. Then, while making elaborate hand gestures, he declared loudly, 'I honour by sacrifice the Diadem and the Basilisk, and the Mystery of Mystery, the Androgyne who is the symbol of arcane perfection, and his renowned name Baphomet! And upon this hallowed promontory, I thy servant call upon the unknowable power to compel my master Walter to dwelleth now within me.'

Suddenly, there was a loud report followed by a surge of red smoke that entirely engulfed the Major. The electric light seemed to dim somewhat and Leo detected a peculiar sulphuric odour. As the smoke cleared, Leo realised that the Major had undergone a terrible transformation. His countenance, awful of aspect, bulged and rippled, the Black Earl's features merged with his own. Even his minions further along the high bank cowered and retreated a little at this new, misshapen physiognomy of their wizard.

'You've got a face like a Hallowe'en cake,' shouted Leo. 'It's a big improvement!'

The Major stepped forwards, his eyes blazing a supernatural blue, and raised the knife to cut the bond that linked him to Fordyce.

The next events happened in a blur.

Elaine appeared from the mouth of the passageway to the Major's left, and, seeing the raised knife, assumed he was about to stab Fordyce with it rather than cut the rope that connected them, which she hadn't noticed. She rushed forwards and whacked the Major on the wrist with Jimmy's cricket bat. This disarmed him and the blade clattered to the ground. She then struck the Major in the stomach, winding him. Throwing aside the bat, Elaine then heaved the fulcrum so that the bridge swung outwards, leaving the flabbergasted Hellfirers stranded on the other side of the cleft. One of their number, Lyle, made a leap for the retreating bridge, but clutched at thin air and fell into the cleft, where he lay injured and writhing in agony. The bridge continued to swing by its own momentum, and as it reached Leo and spanned the gorge, he noticed that the Major had recovered himself and was rushing towards Elaine, aiming to bowl her over the edge.

'Look out!' called Leo.

Elaine stepped out of the Major's trajectory and kicked his backside as he passed her, sending him tottering on the lip of the abyss.

'He's attached to Fordyce!' yelled Leo in panic.

Elaine made a desperate snatch for the Major's belt, but it was too late. The fiend toppled over the edge, battered his head on the cliff face and disappeared under the effervescence. She then made to grab Fordyce, but the rope tautened and he was yanked over the side.

Leo dashed across the bridge and gazed down in horror at the frothing surface of the water. Then, miraculously, Fordyce's face appeared; he was clinging onto a little outcrop of rock, despite the fact that his hands were bound together and the dead weight of the Major was dragging him down. Leo managed to scramble down a depression in the cliff face and position himself on a flat rock by the water's edge. He grabbed his friend's wrists and held him steady for a short while, but then he slipped, slipped, slipped.

'Hang on, my friend. Help is on its way,' said Leo above the roar of the linn.

'It's no good, old stick,' said Fordyce, through mouthfuls of fluid. 'I'll see you on the other side. Do not fret: *non omnis moriar*.'

Leo's injured hand seared with pain as he lost his grip and Fordyce's kindly face submerged beneath the seething water. Leo prepared to jump in after him but at that moment he felt Elaine's restraining hand. She had picked up the Major's knife, and located a length of rope and tied it round her waist, then clambered down to where Leo was positioned. She now shouted at Leo to bandolier the other end of the rope round his body, which he did. She then ordered, 'Get ready to take the strain,' leapt out and disappeared beneath the surface.

And so began the longest moments of Leo Moran's life. In his mind's eye the illustrations Great Uncle Hugo had made of the local flora and fauna came to life within the sacred night, and he imagined that he could tune in to the soft tread of the fox in the scrub outside, rabbits going to ground just in time. A stately brock foraged, unmolested tonight by cruel baiters, and a weasel raced up a tall pine. Lime trees shimmered in their gowns of moonlit leaves which reached down to the verdant floor, the forest magnificent and eternal in the vestigial light. Wildflowers gave off their delicate nocturnal fragrance and looked sublime silhouetted atop the bank of a laughing brook. A trout broke the film of Loch Quien as it leapt in slow-motion for an insect, and field mice settled safely into their nests as an owl swooped like a phantasm against the golden moon.

Leo, dimly aware of the stranded Hellfirers making a vain attempt to ford the torrent, resolved to give it another five seconds, after which he would jump in after his friends. At least I will make an honourable death, he thought to himself.

But they surfaced, Elaine struggling for breath, Fordyce half drowned and unconscious.

'I've cut the rope,' Elaine gasped, 'but I can't hold him, Leo. He's too heavy.'

'Get the rope about him and I'll haul you both in.'

Elaine managed to lash the rope around Fordyce, and Leo began to heave the pair towards him, looping length after length around his left forearm. His right hand screamed in agony as it took its share of the tension and he thought he would pass out with exhaustion, but he tuned into the Almighty and felt a surge of strength. Eventually, the stricken duo reached the water's edge and Leo grasped Fordyce as Elaine clambered onto dry land. Then, together Leo and Elaine pulled Fordyce onto the rock. Leo was vaguely aware of police officers storming into the cavern as he watched Elaine trying to revive his beloved friend. She managed to expel an amount of liquid from his lungs and then began performing mouth-to-mouth resuscitation.

When Fordyce finally opened his eyes, Leo, relief tearing through him like a narcotic, could not resist kissing his friend's forehead, which was bloodied from lacerations. He unbound Fordyce's hands, then peeled off his jacket and placed it over him.

'I could see this light, old stick. I was moving towards it. It was so *beautiful!* I was not afraid.'

'Rest easy, dear friend.'

With her head craning upwards, Elaine conducted a shouted conversation with PC McLellan, giving a brief summary of what had happened and explaining the urgency of Fordyce's situation. She also told him the location of Chas, whom she had earlier knocked out with a blow from Jimmy's cricket bat. The policeman ran off to obtain a rope and harness from his vehicle with which Fordyce could be hoisted up, and to radio for back-up and ambulances.

As they waited, Leo said to Elaine with gravity, 'You saw it.'

'Saw what?'

'That man you tackled – it was the Major.'

'I know, I recognised him.'

'But you saw the way he looked.'

'Some trick, special effects make-up perhaps.'

'No. He transformed, in front of my very eyes, before you came in! There was this big puff of smoke—'

'Puff of smoke indeed! And did he use mirrors too?' enquired Elaine mordantly. 'Leo, his get-up was very convincing, but you only *think* you saw him transform. And you've taken quite a bang to your head.'

'But the smoke was only there for a few seconds. How could he have applied stage make-up in that time?'

'He could easily have had some sort of latex prosthesis already concealed on the altar. All he would have needed to do would be to pull it on.'

Leo felt a little foolish. Elaine told of how she had come to arrive on the other side of the gorge. The passageway she had taken had led her to a smaller cavern upstream where the water was far less turbulent. She had spied Chas up ahead, standing by a little cable ferry, and had sneaked up behind him and knocked him out cold with the cricket bat. She then winched the ferry the few yards over the water. Once there, she noticed a passageway to her left, which took her directly into the main cavern. It was then that she saw the Major wielding the knife and ran to Fordyce's rescue.

'But how did you come to be at the priory tonight?' enquired Leo.

'I was at home taking a bath, and when I got out I noticed I'd received a message on my landline. It was from Jimmy; I think he'd had too much to drink. He said he knew my real identity, because Cynthia had told him she had heard me being called Elaine by you, and he'd remembered that Hazel had a sister of that name. He said he thought that I suspected him of Hazel's abduction because of the way he'd caught me looking at him at times, but he assured me he'd never harmed a hair on her or any other girl's head. But he said he felt guilty that he hadn't ever had the gumption to investigate the Major, whom he'd tolerated but never fully trusted. He happened to know that the men under his command hadn't liked him, that they thought he was a bastard who had brought dishonour to their regiment at Tumbledown. Now poor Lauren was gone and he'd just glimpsed strange lights at Linn Priory through one of his telescopes. He said he was going to bloody well drive over and sort it out, once and for all, with his trusty cricket bat. Anyway, I rang him back but he didn't answer, so I dialled nine-nine-nine and told the operator to despatch the police to the priory immediately. I threw on some clothes and drove here as fast as I could, hoping to head Jimmy off and get him to wait for the cops, in case he became the next victim. By the time I got here he was already dead. Then I noticed light coming from behind that gravestone door. I looked inside and heard your voice coming from the cell. So I unbolted the door . . . and there you were.'

After a few minutes PC McLellan returned, and let down a rope and harness with which Fordyce was gradually hauled out of the gorge by three burly constables. Elaine and Leo, in spite of the latter's injury, managed to clamber up the cliff face back to where the altar was. Leo took a moment to regard the Hellfirers, stranded on their rocky outcrop and being watched by an ever-increasing number of police officers. He shook his head in disgust.

Outside the entrance there was a buzz of activity as the forces of law and order took charge of the locus. Leo was impressed to see through the trees that two police 4x4s had made it along the old bridleway to where it terminated. A floodlight had been hastily rigged up to illuminate the area, and Elaine clutched her lover's arm and pointed towards the spreading oak Leo had noticed on a previous visit to the priory. Two policemen were cutting down the corpse of Maxwell Blythman which dangled from a bough.

Paramedics were now strapping Fordyce onto a gurney as PC McLellan and another copper observed.

'Well, old stick, it would appear my prediction of my early demise was much exaggerated,' croaked Fordyce.

'I am truly glad to know it, dear friend.'

'As for my esteemed ancestor, the eighth baron, I will extract his portrait from the tower and hang it in pride of place in the great hall. And forevermore we Greatorixes shall honour him by regaling guests with tales of his goodness and courage.'

A paramedic fitted an oxygen mask to Fordyce's haggard face.

'We'll come with him in the ambulance,' said Elaine.

'I'm sorry, ma'am, I can't permit that. My boss will want to speak with you both,' said PC McLellan, nodding to where DCI Dalton was in conference with a colleague.

'For pity's sake, man!' said Leo.

'Mr Moran, three men are dead. I'm sure you can go to the hospital once you've made a statement.'

With that, Fordyce was hoisted and taken to where an ambulance was waiting.

Elaine noticed a policeman reverently covering up Jimmy's body. 'I feel terrible for suspecting the poor man,' she said.

'Jimmy Handley is gone to glory,' said Leo.

'You're sure about that?'

'Of course. His final act was most certainly honourable,' replied Leo. 'I just hope his daughter can take some pride in his memory,' he added obliquely.

Elaine sighed. 'If you don't mind, I'm going to go over to have a quiet moment with him and pay my respects.'

Another ambulance crew and several firemen arrived on the scene to attend to Lyle. The firemen and one of the paramedics disappeared into the catacombs. The remaining paramedic had noticed Leo wincing in pain and insisted on checking him over. Leo sat on a mossy stump as the woman used a pencil torch to first inspect the crown of his head, to which she applied antiseptic and then a dressing.

'Will it need stitches?' he asked.

'I shouldn't think so, but you should really attend hospital after any significant blow to the head.'

The paramedic then gently held Leo's injured hand, touching it delicately to ascertain the source of his pain. 'It's your second metacarpal, I reckon. Although I can't tell if it's broken or not. You'll need an X-ray.'

Leo thanked the woman and promised to seek further medical attention in the morning. As she walked off he noticed a figure emerging from the hidden meadow. It was the ghost of the eighth baron. He ascended the crags and walked towards the stones that marked where the ancient grandees of the Greatorix clan were interred, some twenty yards from where Leo was seated. He paused there, his plum hunting coat resplendent, and nodded at Leo. The apparition became more and more radiant with luminescence as though transfigured, then disappeared to nothing. Leo looked around – apparently no one else had seen it.

DCI Dalton then approached and enquired after Leo's wellbeing. He was then debriefed as to the night's events, and Dalton concluded: 'I'm sorry to tell you that there's no sign of Chas. He must have come to and sneaked away.'

'Dear God!' said Leo.

'Don't worry,' said Dalton. 'We'll catch him. In the meantime, we'll post guards at the hall and your girlfriend's house, just in case.'

DCI Dalton was wrong: Chas Shaw did escape the grasp of the police. However, he did not avoid the grasp of justice.

Three days later, wearing a brilliant disguise, he strolled a wild, remote beach beneath Cumbrian cliffs. He congratulated himself on having got away with all his years of perversity. The night the catacombs had been raided he had regained consciousness and found himself lying on the gravel apron that skirted the stream. The cable ferry was on the other side of the water, so someone had obviously sneaked up behind him, bashed him over the head and crossed. He had crept down the passageway in the direction of the entrance and, upon hearing footsteps coming swiftly towards him, had flung himself into a dark alcove. It was coppers – two of them – and they ran straight past him. He had to move quickly before reinforcements arrived. He dashed out of the catacombs (noticing with satisfaction that Maxwell had done himself in) and raced over to one-legged Tam's place. For a number of years Chas had stored a trail bike in an outhouse that abutted Tam's cabin for precisely this type of eventuality, and he always kept the ignition key with him. He knew the precise escape route off by heart: a series of farm tracks, forestry trails and B roads. He had to swing north and enter civilisation at Dumfries, then it was a dash for the border, which he crossed near a hamlet called Milltown, then south, and then west to the bolthole he and the Major had been told about by some of their wider brethren.

He reminisced about rare delicacies enjoyed beneath Linn Priory and grinned as he considered his plan to hook up with one of the English chapters. As a loyal, long-standing member, he could rely on being looked after.

But the rhythm of the waves and the screech of the seagulls started to get on his nerves, like an accusation of mortality. He began yelling at the damned birds in defiance. On and on he ranted, his eyes heavenwards, circling ever closer to the water's edge.

The first he knew of any peril was the softness of the sand sucking him downwards. He was almost amused at first, and began hauling himself back towards the dry shore. But the waves began to press in, swelling and swelling, the tide working quicker than he could negotiate the morass. He cursed and fumed, the water now lapping his crotch. By the time it reached his abdomen, Chas realised he was in real danger, but the more he struggled the more he seemed to be engulfed. Soon his feet were rooted to the spot, and at that point the surf calmed somewhat, as though to toy with him. Then it surged forth with fulsome rage.

He was drowned while standing up, then dragged out to the depths.

Perhaps only the most romantic among us would suggest that the restless spirit of Hazel Bannatyne, whose corpse was flushed into that very sea like a piece of garbage in the year of our Lord 1979, had stirred up the waters in anger to dash and mutilate the one who got away. Yet when Shaw's body, yanked and pummelled by a drag net, lacerated by rock and gnawed by marine scavengers, was washed ashore ten days after the brine claimed him, not far from the place where Saint Ninian established

Christianity on Scottish soil a millennium and a half ago, and only a dozen miles as the gull flies from where Hazel's body was actually deposited into Kirkcudbright Bay, it would provide her siblings with the knowledge that at least their beloved sister's awful murder had finally been fully avenged.

In the days following their arrests, enough of the Hellfirers would confess to enable the police to construct an accurate picture of the ungodliness that had unfolded beneath a ruined priory near to Biggnarbriggs Hall in Balmakethe Parish in the goodly old Stewartry of Kirkcudbright.

Major Jock Lindsay Balfour-MacWhinnie had revived an extinct Hellfire Club in 1977, and lavishly funded it using the fortune his father had amassed from Apartheid-labour diamond mining. The original club had been founded by Walter the Bastard, the Black Earl, during the mid-eighteenth century. Walter had made like-minded friends in Balmakethe, one of whom had heard rumour that there existed caves beneath Linn Priory – the perfect place in which they could conduct their affairs. So Walter and his comrades had located and dug through the seal, and then created a hidden door using a false gravestone. Hellfire Clubs typically exalted the ancient deities, and the Black Earl wanted to worship the original horned god of fertility who had been honoured in Sabbats since days of yore.

The Major had long been fascinated by the Black Earl. When he was a boy, he had befriended a strange old man who lived in a cottage in the forest, at a shadowy dell of black bryony near to where the burn water ran dark. The old man had been quite taken with the Major, and had confided in him this near-extinct legend of the Hellfirers using lost catacombs for their ceremonies and amusements. Years later, the Major would find a similar account in the library at Biggnarbriggs Hall, and also one of the legend that the Black Earl and his brethren had murdered the eighth baron Greatorix after he stumbled across them at ritual. The Major had removed these references from the Greatorix family annals as he didn't want the stories to be widely known.

The Major's Hellfire Club was at first small in scale, but over the years more initiates moved to the area. Most he had met through Freemasonry circles (the others were required to become Freemasons) where a brother had first confided in him the existence of a plexus of chapters who kept the traditions of the Hellfire Clubs alive. When he bought Maidenhead House, the Major was unable to possess the priory and therefore the catacombs, so he resolved to deny people access through his property. He interpreted the clue on the false gravestone and prised it open. Later he enlisted Chas Shaw – one of his earliest lieutenants – to replace the hinges and put a new mechanism on it, and to undertake certain improvements inside the catacombs.

The Major designed the symbol for his brotherhood, which honoured the horned deity Baphomet and evoked the Masonic roots and influences of the eighteenth-century members. In the same spirit he collected antique setting mauls contemporaneous with the Black Earl, which if required would be wielded as weapons, in homage to the original brethren.

The Major met some of his other recruits in the army, such as one-legged Tam, who was allowed to squat in a cabin on his land. The Major was untouchable in certain establishment circles because as a junior officer he had been hand-picked by MI5 as a kind of political commissar to oppose Marxism and seditious elements in the country, culminating in his role in the affair at Heathrow Airport in 1974.

The Hellfirers would meet to conduct esoteric rites and Bacchanals. The chef at the Green Man Inn was brethren, a culinary genius who would whip up the most extraordinarily exotic dishes in the kitchen at Maidenhead House and have them despatched to the caves for consumption. The parties also involved heavy drinking and orgies with prostitutes who were brought up from England; they were blindfolded even before they were conveyed into the county so that the locale remained secret.

Sacrifice was central to the ceremonies, although usually an animal was sufficient. However, every few years the Major demanded a human oblation for Lammas or some other feast day as in ancient times. Mostly they were untraceable illegal immigrants picked up in some city or other, so as not to draw attention to the area. However, in 1979 the Major could not resist the allure of Hazel Bannatyne, who he had become obsessed with (in the same way as he'd become fixated on a young holidaymaker a couple of years before). He had to go back to duty in Ulster, so he had Chas Shaw snatch her on the prescribed date and keep her prisoner until he returned. He had invented a pretext to justify a trip to the Stewartry before Hazel was to be the first given up to the Styx, but as it happened he didn't need to use it, as events in Northern Ireland providentially placed him back in the vicinity.

The Major became similarly obsessed with Lauren McDowall. Chas groomed her, compelling her to keep their affair secret. He showered her with gifts and took her for drives in the green saloon, which was kept at the derelict petrol station. As soon as Lauren was snatched, that vehicle was swapped with the black Mercedes, which belonged to a chapter of Hellfirers across the border. Lauren's abduction was to take place on the precise date of 25 July, in order that the seven-day ceremonial preparations for Lammas could begin. She had left her home earlier than instructed – she was supposed to meet Chas at ten o'clock at the priory, after Brian and Donald were well out of the way. By the time Chas met her she'd been drinking, and he then dosed her with Rohypnol. Chas kept her ready until the chapter convened after midnight. One of the brotherhood laid a false scent trail from the priory by dragging some of Lauren's clothing, that way diverting the police's attention from the locus. He had parked at the lot by the forest road and when he got to his car he just drove off with the girl's clothes (he headed home and incinerated them, then came back to join the others at the priory), hence breaking the trail and making it appear that she'd been picked up or abducted by a motorist. Lauren died that first night before any mischief could be done to her. In her drug-addled state she had been terrified by the Major, who had undergone his 'transformation' into union with the spirit of the Black Earl, a piece of melodrama which his minions all seemed quite taken in by. Apparently Lauren had backed away in fear, toppled into the so-called Styx and was washed away.

Maxwell Blythman, a loyal member since 1980, had been condemned to death for one error too many: losing his setting maul when attempting to dispose of Leo in Scoulag Woods. A day after that incident, Maxwell had been ordered to leave the locale until the heat died down, which allowed the brethren to convene a conclave and decide his fate. On the day of his return he had popped into the Green Man. As his second drink was being served he was invited into the back shop for a 'chat'. There he was seized, dragged outside, stuffed into the boot of the Merc and whisked away to a secluded farm. Leo would conclude that evidently the hooded figure he had seen in the woods that day had not been Maxwell, but a different Hellfirer. Maxwell was forced to write a suicide note stating that he alone had kidnapped and killed Lauren McDowall, and then dumped her body at sea. Maxwell's car had been driven to a remote spot on the Solway coast with the note left in it, and a little dinghy set adrift.

It had been Maxwell's idea to leave the bouquet with the fabricated message on the Mini's windscreen, although it was actually planted by Chas. The Major wanted to put the frighteners on 'Rachael' by revealing to her that her cover was blown (the Major boasted to have 'sensed' her true identity, another supernatural claim by him which his subordinates readily accepted). Maxwell used a fragment of an unsent letter written by Cynthia to a lover because he thought it might be amusing to potentially land his unfaithful wife in hot water.

On the night Maxwell was to be disposed of, Jimmy Handley had been caught snooping near to the entrance to the catacombs as the Hellfirers undertook the final circuit of their torchlight procession. Chas had crept up behind him and struck him a blow with his setting maul that had proved fatal. Chas then went inside and heard Leo and Fordyce in the passageway. The Major had signalled to his minions to slow-march through the woods, while Chas, Lyle and himself lay in wait for the duo to emerge.

As Leo had suspected, Gilbert Doyle had been deliberately frightened to death. After his final stay at Biggnarbriggs Hall, the Major and Chas had followed him to London and broken into his house. The Major had staged one of his transformations, which must have seemed convincing enough to Gilbert in the dead of night. The reason they wanted Gilbert dead was that prior to leaving for London he had stopped off at the Cauldron for his usual contemplative smoke and encountered Chas and Lauren *in flagrante delicto*. Gilbert was scandalised and drove over to the Major demanding that he sack Chas, saying that if he didn't he would personally march to the House of Lords and tell Baron Greatorix what he had witnessed. The Major appeased him, promising that Chas would have his bags packed by the end of the week. The Major then summoned Chas and fulminated because he had sampled the girl before him; he was only supposed to have charmed her enough to enable her abduction. Chas was placed on ferryman duties – the least glamorous job – indefinitely, and when the Major calmed down, the pair plotted to kill Gilbert.

The Major claimed to have detected Leo's powers of second sight and that he had identified him as a future adversary when he spied him at

Gilbert's wake. He became concerned about Leo's snooping around and had him watched and followed, such as when he and Elaine had driven to Drymen and Glasgow. After Leo was heard investigating the Major's alibi in the Rose and Crown by a Hellfirer present in the bar, the Major decided that he was to be disposed of, preferably at night; hence Maxwell's failed attempt at murder. The chapter knew that Leo was given to nocturnal sleuthing because he had been seen by Chas returning to Biggnarbriggs Hall across the great lawns after the badger baiting. Tam McEwan couldn't keep up on the night he observed him trailing Brian to his tryst with Cynthia, otherwise he would have clubbed him to death. It was Lyle who had watched Leo and Elaine making love at the Wood of Larg. He knew Leo was armed with a pistol or he would have disposed of them both. Leo and Elaine were run off the Raiders' Road because Chas had alerted the Merc driver that they were heading his way.

As for the pagan clues – the fairy tree, the gillygog and the crucified fox – these had indeed been planted to blur the lines of investigation, to make the police think that a group similar to Talorc's druidic cult was around, or make them suspect local hippie cranks. The desecration of the Stations of the Cross on Scoulag Hill last autumn had been committed merely out of spite; the Major had ordered Chas to do it, to annoy Donald Kennedy.

And so did the Hellfirers reveal the depravity in which they had participated. The confessions were delivered through gritted teeth or in desperate attempts to shift blame or obtain mercy, and Diane Dalton had to strain hard to maintain a professional demeanour during the interviews, lest her face betray the repulsion she felt for these men.

Day Sixteen

L EO awoke. He was lying on one of the sofas in the drawing room at Biggnarbriggs Hall. Light winked through a gap in the deep red brocade curtains and someone had draped a tartan blanket over him. His right hand was horribly swollen and his head ached. The grandfather clock informed him it was twenty-five to eleven. He sat up and recollected the latter events of the previous night. Elaine had been upset after making her statement to DCI Dalton because of the news that Chas had escaped. She had conveyed them to the hall in the Mini and gone upstairs to waken Evelyn. The plan was that Elaine would drive them all to the Royal Infirmary in Dumfries to be with Fordyce, but Leo must have dozed off through exhaustion.

Evelyn entered the room and smiled at him. 'We're just back from the hospital. Fordyce is going to be fine,' she said, sitting down beside him.

'Thank God!' croaked Leo.

'Elaine has gone upstairs to rest. When we came down last night you had conked out here and we could barely rouse you, so we decided it best to let you sleep.'

'Evelyn, I must apologise for dragging your brother into danger. Especially as I had vowed to myself to shelter you both from the fallout from my investigations.'

'There's nothing to apologise for, Leo. Fordyce went to the priory with you of his own volition.' Evelyn gazed into space. 'It's going to take time to come to terms with everything that's happened. Poor Lauren and poor Jimmy! And to think that people we trusted were involved in such . . . *beastliness*.'

Leo placed a comforting hand on Evelyn's arm. She then rose and said, 'Forgive me, Leo, but now I must get some sleep.'

*   *   *

Leo went to his bedroom and telephoned his mother, Stephanie and Rocco to inform them that he was safe lest they switch on the news and become worried. He struggled to shower properly, what with his latest injuries.

He dressed, went to the kitchen, ate a morsel of cheese, then strolled out of the rear door holding a glass of fruit juice. He was gratified to see Unity and Brian standing by their cottage, holding hands tenderly as they watched their children at play in the glorious sunshine.

Brian noticed Leo and approached him. 'Evelyn's told me to drive you to the health centre in Kirkcudbright, to get your heid seen to.'

However, while in the kitchen, Leo had hatched a theory he urgently wanted to explore. 'Thank you, Brian, but first would you please furnish me with a fishing float and weight,' he requested.

Leo walked round the hall, past the entrance where a constable stood sentry, and, for the last time that summer, headed across the meadows. A sweet scent was rising from the warm turf. At the priory, officers wearing white forensic garb were scurrying around. Leo noticed two stretchers bearing covered corpses being lifted out of the entrance to the catacombs and instinctively made the Sign of the Cross. He saw DCI Dalton and greeted her.

'Hello, Mr Moran. My being pleased to see you is curtailed somewhat by the fact that you held out on me regarding your girlfriend's real identity.'

Dalton noticed that Leo was gazing at the stretchers, and informed him that police frogmen had earlier found the bodies of Lauren and the Major swirling in a little cave next to the main cavern, the water trying to push them further onwards through a narrow aperture. She also told him that an item of jewellery thought to have belonged to Hazel Bannatyne had been discovered in an alcove. She said that her remains, and the remains of the other women sacrificed down the years, would have eventually been washed downstream, and that the frogmen suspected the water flowed underground as far as the sea.

'Did you happen to view the Major's body?' asked Leo.

'Yes.'

'Was there anything unusual about his face?'

'No. It was a little bloated and cut, but that was to be expected, what with him churning around in that cave all night.'

Elaine's theory about the Major's transformation had apparently been right, and the torrent must have washed off some prosthesis, like the stuff Fordyce had put on during the hide-and-seek game. But from time to time during the years that passed following these events, the whim would take Leo that what he had witnessed was indeed some terrible metamorphosis of the Major's body and soul, undone upon the old fiend's expiry.

'I wonder, Chief Inspector, would you be so good as to help me with an experiment?'

Leo walked towards Carlin's Burn, avoiding a bevy of media vehicles that had descended on the forest road. He noticed Jimmy Handley's old Audi 100 still parked askew and forlorn on the verge, and felt a wave of sadness. He arrived at an elbow of the pretty brook and waited. He had instructed Dalton to give him twenty minutes before she launched the weighted fishing float into the water in the catacombs. After a while, he saw the small red and yellow plastic item bob cheerfully down the stream.

'Leo Moran, you're a genius,' he said as he waded in to retrieve the float.

He returned to the priory and brandished the thing at Dalton with a triumphant flourish. The copper couldn't help but bequeath an uncharacteristic smile.

'I remembered today my discovery that the word *carlin*, which is the name of a burn not far from here, is an old Lowland Scots term for a witch or a hag,' explained Leo. 'Last night, when I was incarcerated with Maxwell, he told me that the nuns who once inhabited this priory had sealed off the catacombs due to witchcraft committed down there by some hag. The Hellfirers and your officers have speculated that the stream continues underground to the sea. They are incorrect; there is no extensive underground water system hereabouts. There is just a distributary of Scoulag Burn that briefly – and so innocuously as to be uncharted by man – dips beneath the surface for a mile or so from the Cauldron. It flows through the catacombs, then emerges to the southwest of Biggnarbriggs village as Carlin's Burn. People must have forgotten that where Carlin's Burn rose was merely the distributary issuing through the sandstone; they would have come to think it was the source of an entirely different watercourse. It was evidently once known that this was the same stream, hence its name. Therefore, the body of a victim would flow down Carlin's Burn, which joins the Water of Tarb, which then joins the River Dee near to its confluence with the Solway Firth. Probably the corpse would be much decomposed by the time it got through the aperture your frogmen discovered, and hence much less likely to be recognised as human remains as it flowed by.'

Leo shook hands with Dalton and bid her adieu. He decided to walk back to the hall via the Nain Community. As he approached, he exchanged greetings with the minister from the village kirk, who was strolling down the driveway. He found Father Larranzar and Donald Kennedy seated at the table in the shade of the ash tree. They were delighted to see him.

'Reverend Thomson has just left,' said Donald. 'He told us there was apparently some drama at the priory last night, but he doesn't know any details.'

Leo sat down and related recent events to his hosts, who listened with shock and horror. They prayed together, then Donald went to fetch some lime cordial while Larranzar laid his hands on Leo's wounded head and made a blessing.

Donald returned and poured the cordial as the friar quoted from St Paul: '"Our struggle is not against flesh and blood, but against the rulers, against the authorities, against the powers of this world's darkness, and against the spiritual forces of evil in the heavenly realms." What you uncovered last night, Leo, was the sharp end: the priestly class engaged with a visceral manifestation of evil. But on a more banal, everyday level, Western civilisation has become narcissistic and self-indulgent to a degree that portends its demise.'

'What will you do now, Father, after everything that's happened at the priory?'

'Exactly the same as we've always done within those ancient walls of Christian worship. That which our Lord commanded: turn humble bread and wine into His blessed Body and Blood, then eat and drink of it. And know this: there is no malediction in the universe that can defy the power of that sacrament. Now, if you'll excuse me, I'm going to telephone Reverend Thomson and tell him about poor Lauren; he'll want to be with her mother. Then I need to visit Cynthia Blythman.'

'Really?'

'Of course. The woman has just lost her husband.'

'I didn't realise you were close,' said Leo. The little priest was silent. 'You're not going to tell me that Cynthia is a troubled soul, are you, Father?'

'I'm not going to tell you anything that betrays a confidence, Leo. But, in general terms, I would say that even people with apparently indomitable exteriors possess hidden depths and vulnerabilities. I shall visit Cynthia, and then return to chapel to pray in the presence of the Blessed Sacrament for everyone affected by these sordid episodes.'

'Even the Major?' joked Leo darkly.

'Especially the Major.'

'You're not serious!'

'I expect he requires it more than his victims. Yet in the end, God will overcome even this disaster, and call everyone's true self to Him.'

Leo found Elaine resting on a steamer chair on the terrace of Biggnarbriggs Hall, a parasol defending her against the broiling sun. She was wearing a summer dress with a vibrant floral print which Leo had previously seen Evelyn wearing, and her loose, recently washed hair was drying in the heat. Leo sat upon the balustrade and hoped that his face wasn't too ugly with fatigue in the unforgiving rays.

'How are you feeling, Leo?'

'I'm all right, my sweet. Brian's going to convey me to the health centre in Kirkcudbright, to get me checked over. How are you?'

'I'm feeling a bit anxious, after almost causing the death of poor Fordyce.'

'You weren't to blame. You didn't realise he was connected to the Major by that rope.'

'I've been asking myself if I truly didn't know, or if my anger had somehow blinded me to the rope. When I first saw the Major last night I was seized by this terrible desire for vengeance. It was beyond rage.'

'Elaine, when you leapt into that maelstrom it was simply the bravest act I have ever witnessed. And I think it's time we both forgave ourselves for past failures. We are the good guys, after all.'

'Let's go for a walk, Leo, in the woods. It will be cooler there.'

And so, beneath the towering wych elms of Scoulag Woods, she broke the heart of Leomaris Moran. She told him that with her sister's murder being solved she felt a profound sense of release, and that the scales had fallen from her eyes. She knew what she needed now: to leave Scotland forever.

No, no, no, no, no, no, no – this cannot be so! To me you are the most beautiful creature ever to have walked God's green earth. Something good and pure and true, succour from life's banality and horror. In the Greatorixes' drawing room that first evening we connected even before we had exchanged a word. Even at that moment I loved you. We were meant for each other. Together we can overcome any obstacle – omonia vincit amor. This cannot be so!

'I'm going to live with my brother and his family in Melbourne.'

'Oh, great, nice and near then,' said Leo mordantly, his agony manifest physically, as though he had been punched in the solar plexus. 'In the name of God, Elaine, we could be *happy* together – I have money, I can provide for you.'

'*Provide* for me?'

'Provide for *us*, provide for *us*. I had it all planned out: we could live together, in Sannox House, once we had been . . . married.' Leo felt embarrassed at this admission and almost blushed when he recalled how he had already envisaged the big day: she in a simple frock, he in new duds tailored by old Arnstein's adroit cousin, set off by a magnificent buttonhole (provided by Evelyn; she would also furnish the flowers for the church). His mother and Stephanie beaming, Fordyce as best man, Father Larranzar conducting the ceremony. There would be ribbons on the waxed Humber – Frederick Norvell would chauffeur them to a posh hotel on Great Western Road that would do them proud with the nosh-up, then a honeymoon in the Italian lakes or the Greek islands. He couldn't hold back. 'What we have together doesn't happen every day, and now you're talking about heading off to the bloody Antipodes to mutilate your vowels. Please don't go – we only met a short while ago, but it feels so *right*. And I thought you felt it too.'

'I do feel it.'

'Are you sure? Are you sure you didn't just take up with me because you knew my powers could help you trace your sister's killers?'

'Leo, how could you say such a thing?'

'I'm sorry. You know I didn't mean it.'

They walked on in silence for a while.

'Look, Leo, why don't you come with me?'

She asked this more in hope than in expectation, but her heart still sank upon his inevitable response.

'Out of the question.'

'Why?'

'My mother.'

'Bring her with you.'

'It wouldn't be fair to ask her to move at her stage in life. And anyway there's my work, the tasks that my second sight require of me . . . it must unfold *here*, I can't explain why. It's my duty, my vocation. I simply must remain in Scotland.'

'And I simply must go,' said Elaine gently as she paused to look Leo in the eye. 'I must be with my brother now, with the blood family I have left.'

'And so the irresistible force meets the immovable object.'

'Which one am I?'

'I've always found you to be the former.'

But in truth Leo was in no mood for levity.

'You've given me something so precious, Leo: hope.'

'If you mean hope that you will see Hazel in the face again, then you shall, as surely as day follows night.'

And with that he kissed her cheek, and she watched him walk across the great lawns, away from her.

The drive to Kirkcudbright passed in a blur. Leo sat in silence, his mind in stasis, his heart feeling as though it had been torn from his ribcage. The sunshine which had bathed these southern fields in glory for weeks on end now seemed to mock him. At one point, Brian floored the accelerator pedal of his Audi Quattro to surge past a chugging tractor, and Leo considered the burgeoning arable tracts to which the machine tended. Soon their bounty would fill the silos, and the days would begin to feel shorter. Suddenly he dreaded winter's darkness. He grimaced with foreboding for the loneliness and unrequited longing that lay ahead. His thoughts descended into a dismal little vortex. Past experience of unconverted love told him that as the weeks gave way to months the pain would ease and his life would return to its familiar drab, solitary routine. But it would be that bit harder to adapt in the wake of his recent bliss.

Whatever faint colours his future life offered would be that degree thinner, the lack of loving human contact would feel that bit more grinding, the prospect of deliverance yet more unyielding. At least booze would provide him with some respite, cauterise the wound for a while. He pined for it, body and soul.

They rolled over a bonny stone bridge that spanned the sparkling River Dee and swept into Kirkcudbright, the capital of the Stewartry, the Artists' Town, a place Leo usually found delightful but which today was dead to him.

'I appreciate the lift, Brian, but once you drop me off, just return to the hall. I'll take a taxi back later.'

'You sure? I don't mind waiting.'

'Yes. I need some time to myself.'

He would later only vaguely recollect the hour or so he spent at the health centre. An X-ray found that his metacarpal was not fractured, and he declined the offer of a sling and a compression bandage. He was checked for concussion, the cut to his head was cleaned and properly dressed, and he was given a prescription for painkillers. He then wandered the quiet backstreets in a daze, eventually finding himself in one which boasted an old steepled tolbooth, a handsome turreted sheriff court, a police station with a quaint circular sign atop a blue pole, and some beguiling galleries and craft shops. The pretty terraced houses were decorated in various lovely pastel shades. Most notably, as far as Leo was concerned, there was a hotel with a public bar. He knew that across the street from it, down an alley, was tucked the lovely little Catholic Church of St Andrew and St Cuthbert.

Leo sighed and considered the beauty of Biggnarbriggs Hall and the stately lands that cradled it, and the joy that he had felt there while simultaneously misery abounded, wrought by the madness of men. He had briefly enjoined the heavenly realities here foreshadowed, but it had been a chimera. It had been founded on a love that would have proven obsessive and implosive; it would have clawed away all the other light, and Leo worried that he was incapable of any other mode of romantic relationship.

However, it occurred to him that although there cannot be a day without a night, neither, logically speaking, can there be a night without a day. Brother Francesco, his former *consigliere*, used to tell him that 'To live is to suffer. To develop, you must enter the belly of the whale. The wounds are where the light gets in.' And whatever heartache he was undergoing would be but modest when compared to that which poor Anthea McDowall was currently enduring, doubtless now informed by DCI Dalton of the discovery of her daughter's body in a swirling abysm, a loss so appalling that no measure of expectedness could blunt its barb.

And then an idea came from leftfield as Leo stood in the quiet, shaded street. An unforeseen alternative. The idea was: I dare you to abide. I dare you to refuse the secondary, consolatory gratification that is self-pity, that is booze. To allow yourself even at this relatively late stage in your life the opportunity to grow as a person by having the courage to choose the more difficult path even though no one apart from God Almighty will know you have taken it.

So Leo Moran meditated upon these things for a while, and saw things more clearly. And he thought about the girl who had perished in a fire all those sad years ago because he hadn't acted on her behalf. But he didn't feel guilt any more, just sorrow for a tragic thing that had unfolded in his life's narrative.

And so it was that he raised his head and strode towards the scalloped arch, towards the small red flame that flickers in the shadow and never goes out.

For, it occurred to him, in the end, there is only love.

Acknowledgements

Thanks to everyone at Polygon, especially my editor Alison Rae who did a heroic job on what was a demanding script. To Martin Greig and Neil White at BackPage Press whose excellent Debut podcasts helped to promote the Leo Moran series, and to Martin for dropping everything to provide feedback on an earlier version of this novel. Thanks also to Marion at Laurieston Hall for kindly showing me around that wonderful community, and to my friends Des Mulvey and David Toner for certain details in the text.